To Remember What You've Read,
Write Your Initials in a Square.

FINN FANCY NECROMANCY

FINN FANCY NECROMANCY

RANDY HENDERSON

A TOM DOHERTY ASSOCIATES BOOK
NEW YORK

FINN FANCY NECROMANCY

Copyright © 2015 by Randall Scott Henderson

A Tor Book
Published by Tom Doherty Associates, LLC
175 Fifth Avenue
New York, NY 10010

www.tor-forge.com

Tor® is a registered trademark of Tom Doherty Associates, LLC.

The Library of Congress Cataloging-in-Publication Data
is available upon request.

ISBN 978-0-7653-7808-8 (hardcover)
ISBN 978-1-4668-5913-5 (e-book)

Tor books may be purchased for educational, business, or promotional use. For information on bulk purchases, please contact the Macmillan Corporate and Premium Sales Department at 1-800-221-7945, extension 5442, or write to specialmarkets@macmillan.com.

First Edition: February 2015

Printed in the United States of America

0 9 8 7 6 5 4 3 2 1

This book is dedicated to my family,
for all the good things.

ACKNOWLEDGMENTS

As this is my first novel, it's tempting to acknowledge every person who's ever had an impact on my life, from the doctor who delivered me unto my mother with a slap on my butt, to the bookseller who delivered this book into your hand (perhaps with a slap to the butt, no judgment here).

However, the Published Author Handbook is very clear on Acknowledgment etiquette—"butt-slapping doctor" is not thanked until at least book twelve, for example. Booksellers and librarians, however, are optional as early as book two (historically established as the point where the author realizes how important they are, and feels really bad for not mentioning them in the first book).

Yet even focusing only on the people important specifically to this book, I find I have more than a few to name. First, my family:

My parents; Elaine, Frank, and Mary Henderson—of all the ways you might have messed me up, thankfully I ended up with Generalized Writers Disorder, and you provided love and support through the years of rejections and really horrible prose. Thank you.

My chosen family; Shelly, Lucas, and Kylie—as we all grew together, you formed the core of my life and helped me find the heart in my writing. Thank you for all the love, patience, and laughter. And gnomes.

My brother, David Henderson, you're always there when I need an ear or a kick in the butt, but thankfully never a kick in the ear. Thank you. And to my extended family, in particular Scott Henderson and Nina Wolsk-Henderson, and Grandmas Janette and

Eleanor, who always expressed encouragement and enthusiasm for my writing, thank you.

Thank you also to my writer and *Finn Fancy* feedbackers: Clarion West class of 2009 (particularly Emily Skaftun and Julia Sidorova for *Finn* feedback), Leslie Howle and Neile Graham, you helped me grow by leaps (sad, awkward leaps that often pulled a groin muscle, but leaps). To Kitsap Writers Group, in particular Larry Keeton for killing Aggie, John Pelkey for saving Mattie, and Anya Monroe, Eryn Carpenter, Gary Snodgrass, Emily Moore, and Rebecca Hudson for feedback; thanks to Cascade Writers and Karen Junker for providing me the opportunity to connect with both my editor and my agent; to Tina Connolly and Keffy Rm Kehrli for reality checks; to Christy Varonfakis Johnson for sanity boosts and crazy suggestions; to Benjamin VanWinkle for continued friendship and geekcm; Tad Kershner for writerly lunches; and last but certainly not least, to Horrific Miscue Seattle, the best circle of writer friends on the planet (as rated by independent poll). If I missed anyone, apologies.

At Tor, thank you first and foremost to my editor, Beth Meacham, whose faith in *Finn Fancy* is the reason why this novel is in the hands of readers; to Amy Saxon, for making things happen when they needed to happen; to word wrangler Wade Newbern for his style and nerd cred; and to everyone else who worked to make this book a reality and as successful as possible. Thank you.

Thank you to my agent, Cameron McClure, for taking a chance on me; and to the team at DMLA.

And finally, to you, who read this book, thank you for giving reality to my dream and life to my words.

FINN FANCY NECROMANCY

I'm Not the Man I Used to Be

It took all my self-control not to push my Fey warden to move faster along the glowing path toward freedom. We were like a couple of floating melted gummy bears made of unicorn snot and dreams, gliding lazily through the fractal rainbow landscape of the Other Realm. Twenty-five years, that's how long the Arcana Ruling Council had exiled my spirit to the Other Realm without true physical sensation, without access to other people, to real music or any of the things that make our world so awesome. Exiled from my body and my life since 1986 for a crime I didn't commit. But my sentence was over at last.

When I get back, I projected at the warden, *I'm never touching magic again, even if my family begs. Just going to find my girlfriend and live like a mundane.*

The warden didn't respond. I was really just talking to myself anyway, nervous that the Fey would somehow yank away my freedom at the last minute.

We reached a raised platform of violet light where a second blobby warden and exile floated nearby, faced away from us. Though we were all in the bodies of unshaped Fey, I could sense the spiritual resonance of the other exile as being human, and male.

My warden raised a handlike glob, and the air in front of me rippled.

A portal opened up, an oval window to my world, good ole Earth version mine. Beyond shimmered a beach, the Washington State variety with the freezing gray Pacific Ocean lapping a shoreline of pebbles and driftwood, all kissed orange by the setting sun. Just seeing those shapes and colors without having to manifest them from my own memory was enough to bring tears to my eyes. Actually, it caused butterflies to leak from the jewel-like lights that floated in the blob that served as my head, but the point is, it was damn good to see Earth again.

I can't say, however, it was so good to see myself standing there on the beach.

I was fifteen years old when they exiled me from my body. And most of my time in the Other Realm had been spent reliving memories of my youth for the entertainment and nourishment of the Fey.

So despite all the mental growth I achieved by reliving and reflecting on my past and all, my physical self-image was pretty well stuck at fifteen. But the dude who stood waiting on the other side of the portal was old. Not Emperor Palpatine old, I mean, I still had all my hair. Too much hair in fact: the wind blew it around my head in a ridiculous black mane. And the changeling who'd been granted use of my body kept me in good enough shape that he probably wasn't even embarrassed to wear those tight jeans and even tighter black T-shirt, though I would not be continuing the David Hasselhoff look once I retook possession. But I looked, like, forty years old. I looked nearly my father's age, or at least his age at the time I was exiled. I'd sort of known that would happen: the changeling might be immortal, but that didn't stop my body from aging normally while he possessed it.

Still, it was a total mind blower.

A man in a black suit strolled into sight of the portal. His braided mustache identified him as an enforcer, a representative of the Arcana Ruling Council and police of all things magical in our world, come to monitor the transfer. He probably had a "we'll be watching you, punk" speech ready for me as well.

The changeling flipped back his Joey Ramone hairdo, and raised his hand—my hand—to signal readiness for the transfer.

And as a bonus for ordering a body transfer today, I'd receive one memory transfer absolutely free. Twenty-five years of selected life history and real-world memories from the changeling—where "I" lived, where I worked, who I'd talked to, what had happened on TV the last twenty-five years—all part of the arrangement so that I wasn't clueless, jobless, homeless, and presumed dead by the mundane authorities when I returned home.

I hoped he hadn't watched *Star Trek IV*. It was just coming out when I got exiled, and I really wanted to experience it myself (yes, despite *Star Trek III*).

And music! Oh dear gods, I hoped this guy had listened to decent music.

Wait. Did I cancel my Columbia record and tape club membership before exile, or did I owe them like ten thousand dollars for a whole stack of unwanted tapes at this point?

Well, I'd know soon enough. The sun melted beneath the horizon and twilight began, a time for transitions. I felt the transfer begin.

On the beach, the enforcer kicked the changeling in the gut and flung something glittering at the portal. The transfer cut off.

What the—?

The flung object disintegrated against the barrier between worlds, and a screech cut through my mind like a rabid cat's claws being scratched across a chalkboard. Roiling clouds of gibbering ink gathered above our heads.

My warden grabbed me in a gummy bear hug. *Betrayers!* The word echoed through my mind. He dragged me back from the portal, but I struggled against him, willed myself forward.

No! I projected back. *I didn't do this! Damn it, let me go you slimy—!*

Beyond the portal, the enforcer pulled out a wand and pointed it at the changeling—at my body! Purple lightning danced from the end of the twisted black stick like a neon snake having seizures, and my feybody heart lurched as I watched the arc strike my real body. Except that, somehow, the changeling deflected the lightning back at the enforcer, flinging the man back.

The dark hair and black suit of the enforcer rippled for a second as he flew into the surf, and I caught a glimpse of blond hair, beard, and black robes beneath. A glamour! Someone had disguised themselves as an enforcer.

The portal began to shrink.

The screeching clouds above me fell silent.

Then a house-size blob of deep black nothingness plummeted down like a screaming meteor of oh-crap-this-can't-be-good.

There was no point in arguing with my wardens now. I reached out to my body, not with my will but through the natural resonance between body and spirit, using skills learned during years of necromancy training with Grandfather. The connection was immediate. I traveled free of the Fey body and through the shrinking portal. As I hit the barrier I felt a cold behind me, the kind of cold that freezes lungs and makes yetis shiver. And then I fell to my hands and knees on the pebble beach.

Sharp points bit into my palms and shins, chilly water splashed over my hands and wrists. The smell of salt air and rotting sea plants blasted into my awareness. I looked up to see the portal flickering. Beyond, the plummeting blackness shredded the warden, like a statue of multicolored sand blasted by high wind. The portal winked out.

"That can't be good," I muttered. A bit of drool fell into the frothy brine between my hands.

Oh wow. I was back in my body. A real body. I was alive! And I was home! Wherever home was. The body transfer worked, but I hadn't received the changeling's memories. I had no clue where I was, other than a beach.

Had the other exile made it out? I looked in the direction he'd stood in the Other Realm, but rocky bluffs rose from the spot. If he had escaped, he was probably miles from here given the funky way distance worked between our world and the Other Realm. And I couldn't sense the changeling. He'd most likely returned through the portal only to be destroyed, which just left me and—

The attacker!

I rose, and wavered a bit as I readjusted to having a physical body. I looked around, but I stood alone on the beach. The attacker must have fled.

Crap. It was nice to not have a foot flying at my face and all, but somewhere out there I had an enemy with the juice to launch an attack into the Other Realm. That was most definitely not awesome.

Why would anyone that powerful want to attack me at all? Then again, who had cared enough to frame me for dark necromancy in the first place, twenty-five years ago? Safest not to stick around enjoying the biting cold sensation of wind and water on my skin, just in case.

Skin. I had skin! And it ached in the cold! How awesome was that?

Okay. Focus.

I took a few tentative steps, finding my balance and control as I pushed the floating mane of black hair out of my face. A clear path cut up between two driftwood stumps and through a bank of beach grass to my right, still visible in the surreal glow of twilight. I willed myself to be at the top of the hill. When nothing happened, I remembered that the stuff of reality no longer responded to (just) my will. So I stumbled up the path the old-fashioned human way, one step at a time.

I was grateful in that moment for the restrictions that had been placed upon the changeling by the Pax Arcana. Not so much the ones against using Fey magic, or interacting with my real life friends and family, or even the one against sex, although by the gods if anyone was going to have sex for the first time in my body it was going to be me! No, in that moment I was grateful for the magical boundaries protecting my mind and memories from the changeling's, and the rules requiring that the changeling keep my body in excellent physical health. From the ache that spread through my head and muscles, I doubted I would be walking and thinking at all otherwise, not after that botched transfer. I might not even be alive.

Too bad that hadn't protected the changeling.

I crested the hills, and ahead a mobile home squatted in a wide gravel lot surrounded by evergreen trees. I both hoped and dreaded that this was my home—hoped, because if not then I had no clue where to go next; and dreaded because, well, it looked like a pretty crappy place to live, oceanfront or not. As I moved closer I spotted a two-seater sports car parked behind it.

I knocked on the trailer and tried the door. It opened, and warm air washed over me, smelling of cotton candy and the faint vanilla tang of magic. No glamoured assassins or teenage mutant fairy attack squad burst out of the trailer and jumped me, so that was good at least.

"Hello?" I called, and entered.

The dead woman lying facedown on the floor really clashed with the Liberace decorating aesthetic.

Perhaps I should have been more shocked by the body, but I wasn't. Maybe because I still felt numb from the events of the transfer. Maybe because I'd been raised around death, helping prepare and destroy the bodies of the dead in my family's necrotorium.

Or maybe I really was just stunned by the gaudy awfulness of the changeling's tastes. It was like Rainbow Brite had been given a BeDazzler, a flock of shedding peacocks, and a credit card and told to go crazy.

"Well, this sucks," I said to the dead woman, meaning her death, not the decor.

The body didn't respond, which was a relief actually. Talking to the dead was one of my arcane gifts, but something I hoped never to do again, not least because it drained my own life away to do so.

I rolled the body over and felt the unpleasant tingle of residual dark magic, like spiders made of ice crawling across my hand. Her head flopped over, and she stared with an expression of frozen horror at the ceiling. A blood-soaked strip of linen covered in silver runes spilled from her mouth, revealing the space where her tongue should have been. Necromancy. Dark necromancy.

"No. Damn it, no!"

Felicity. Our family's au pair before my exile. She might appear human, but she was a feyblood creature, a witch to be exact, though Mother had insisted she was a good witch. She looked older than I remembered, wrinkled as though she'd spent too much time in the sun, but it was her.

What the hell was she doing here?

The last time I'd seen Felicity, she pointed at me from an ARC witness stand and declared that I'd attacked her with dark necromancy. The day before that, I had found her unconscious and bloodied body on my bedroom floor. And the night before that, we were laughing over a game of Trivial Pursuit with my sister and brothers, making up ridiculous answers to the questions.

I'd been made to relive those memories a thousand times in the Other Realm, all the confusion and hurt, the sense of betrayal and anger. But I'd had little choice except to deal with those feelings or go mad. So I turned my anger instead to the Fey who fed off of me, and convinced myself that Felicity had actually done me a favor, granted me a reprieve from the life of sacrifice and necromancy mapped out for me since the day my Talker gift manifested.

I might not have forgiven Felicity, but I wasn't obsessively plotting revenge schemes either. And even if I had been, she was supposed to be hidden away somewhere in the ARC equivalent of witness protection. At most, I'd hoped she would confess the truth someday, and clear my name.

Instead, someone had now killed her, in "my" home, with dark necromancy. Most likely the same someone who attacked my transfer. Had he brought her here by force, or drawn her here with some promise of revenge or reconciliation with me? Either way, she was the perfect choice for a frame job given our history. But why? Why try to kill me *and* frame me? It made no sense.

The bloody rune cloth meant her spirit was warded, so a Talker like me couldn't get Felicity to speak again. And real enforcers might arrive at any minute, tipped off by my attacker or the release of magic. I didn't have time to hang around playing Inspector Gadget.

I considered hiding the body, but there was nothing I could think to do that would keep the enforcers from finding Felicity with magic. And with my luck I'd be caught carrying her into the woods.

I looked from Felicity to the stove. Just one option I could think of; but first things first.

I riffled through the place and found "my" wallet and keys. Nothing in the trailer was really my stuff, not the stuff I left at my family home when I went into exile, and I didn't find anything that seemed like a Scooby clue to explain who was really behind Felicity's death. I went outside and made sure the car started, and was an automatic. I'd never learned stick.

Then I returned inside and grabbed a frying pan, lighter, paper towels, and cooking oil, and moved back to Felicity's body.

Don't worry. Despite what you may have heard, real necromancers don't consume the flesh of the dead. In fact, most of us are vegetarians. That just sort of happens when you can sense life energy lingering in the flesh of anything that once had an active nervous system.

I hesitated, looking down at Felicity. I'd helped to destroy bodies before, but always with respect, following the proper rituals.

"Sorry, Felicity," I whispered. "May your spirit find peace, may your energy bring light to the darkness." The words were rote, but I felt a flurry of emotions as I said them: regret, sadness, and yeah, maybe a bit of satisfaction that this feyblood witch had paid in the end for what she did to me. That last bit made me uncomfortable, kind of like bad gas. But the self-examination could come later. Now was time for the running.

I dropped the frying pan on the floor, dumped cooking oil over Felicity and the paper towels, and lit the roll on fire after several fumbling attempts. Then I turned on the gas stove without igniting it, and ran outside.

A sorry excuse for a cremation, and cooking oil wouldn't burn up a body, but when the propane blew it would be good-bye crime scene, hello unfortunate cooking accident. With luck, the body would take time to put back together and identify, and with the mundy fire department and police involved it would complicate the enforcers' own investigation.

I dropped myself into the car, a Miata so the label read, and sped off along the gravel road.

Time to get someplace safe, and figure out who the hell still had it in for me. And that meant my family—possibly in both cases.

Our House

I have to say, I was a bit disappointed the car didn't fly like in *Back to the Future*. It didn't even run on fusion or anything cool as far as I could tell. After twenty-five years, you'd think there'd be more changes than making the cars really small.

At least I found driving easy. My body still felt a bit awkward to control and balance, but for some reason controlling the car, something external to me, came more naturally.

I was three minutes down the winding wooded road when a flash and boom caused me to look in the rearview. An orange glow lined the treetops. At least the tree line stood a ways back from the trailer and everything looked well rained upon, so Smokey the Bear would have no reason to chastise me, I hoped.

I soon found my way to Highway 101 North around the Olympic National Rainforest, and finally to Port Townsend, my hometown. The clock in the car said 9:27 P.M. as I passed the first outlying houses and shops.

Unfamiliar streetlights and strip malls had replaced what once was a wooded approach to the small seaside town. But I had no fear that I would find my family home replaced by a record store or 7-Eleven. Port Townsend protected its funky old houses, and our family would never sell that house anyway. Beneath it lay our necrotorium. The work my family performed there—properly disposing of dead arcana and feyblood creatures saturated with magic—had resulted in the land being contaminated with whatever magic managed to escape our capture.

I heard that someone once built a Dunkin' Donuts down near

New Orleans, and the round donuts became mini portals to a shadowy corner of the Other Realm. The only way to close the portals and stop the invasion of gremlins had been for a group of enforcers to eat all of the donuts, followed by a pot of mushy lentils. Lentils, by the way, are a quick and dirty cure for ingested magics should you ever need one. In fact, there are few foods less magical than lentils.

Anyway, it turned out the land under the Dunkin' Donuts had been a necrotorium in the long ago, and the records were lost during one of the Fey-Arcana wars. Point being, graveyards and old Indian burial grounds have nothing on necrotorium sites for lingering mojo.

So it was with relief but little surprise that I found my family home standing much as I remembered it, its peaked towers and gabled roof visible over the madrona trees that screened the property from the road.

I spotted movement in a car parked across the street and a little ways past our house. A pale face framed by an equally pale bowl cut leaned forward, watching. No beard. So not the guy who attacked me at the transfer. But there was something familiar about him—

I turned off our street before passing him, and hoped he took no special notice of me.

Memory clicked, and I knew who he reminded me of. Felicity. Which made him one of the Króls, the Germanic clan of feyblood witches that Felicity came from—or escaped from, by her account—when she moved to America. I'd feared they might seek revenge on me for my supposed past crimes against their kin, but I'd expected to have enforcer protection from them when I returned. Unfortunately, until I figured out who'd just killed Felicity, enforcers were the last people I wanted to see. Going to the arcana authorities last time about Felicity's assault had resulted in my exile. I didn't trust her death would lead to better results.

Were the Króls behind the attack on my transfer? Possibly. And equally possible they'd killed Felicity for leaving their clan at the same time they sought revenge against me for hurting her. Witch clans had their own twisted sense of justice that more resembled something from a bad mafia movie than anything sane or logical.

I took the back streets through town and drove around for several minutes to make certain I wasn't followed. The residential streets were imaginatively named. There was "A" street, followed by "B" street, followed by "C" street. You'd think Big Bird had been the founding mayor.

The town had changed quite a bit since I'd left. Before my exile, a clash had begun between wealthy retirees versus the resident hippies, laborers, and artists, a clash that ran like an undercurrent through everything in the town. Clearly, that clash had continued during my absence, evident in the large golf course, cookie cutter mansions, and a lot of new franchise stores and restaurants versus the funky old houses and artsy Ma and Pop storefronts. I wondered how the culture clash had affected the more one-sided tensions of the arcana community living hidden among the mundies.

I glanced in the rearview. Nobody followed me, and I hadn't begun to burst into boils or flames or any other subtle symptoms of a deadly curse. I circled back and parked a couple blocks from our house in the lot of a local hardware store, then snuck through backyards, empty lots, and grassy alleyways to the garden gate behind our home.

I paused, one hand on the cold black iron. I'd hoped to deal with my family—their expectations, and my feelings of being abandoned in exile—on my own terms and on my own time. I looked in the direction of the street where the Król witch waited. For all that I was free from exile, I still didn't have much freedom of choice it seemed. I needed help.

I sighed and passed through the gate.

Mother's garden filled most of the backyard. After her death, it took on a mind of its own—or rather, its mind was a bit more vocal than other gardens due to the high concentration of magic on the property. Now, its once carefully tended beds had become a mysterious jungle surrounded by a tangled and thorny wall. If I didn't know better, I'd think a Cthulhu cult had moved in and were trying to breed tomatoes and roses together to create a plant of ultimate chaos, destruction, and evil red yumminess.

I skirted the edge of the garden, and approached the back door. As I neared the house, a red glow lit up the darkness to my left and caused me to jump. Then I registered the sickly sweet scent of a clove cigarette, and my eyes caught up with my nose. A woman stood in the shadows, smoking.

"Hello?" I said, prepared to run for my life at the first itch of a curse.

The woman stepped forward into the light from a nearby window, and smiled. She had short-cut black hair, thick black glasses, and a nose ring. She looked familiar, and yet not. There was something of Mother in her face, and something of—

"Sammy?" I asked, surprised.

"Hello, brother. Sneaking in the back way? You do realize Father can't ground you anymore, right?"

"Sammy!" I threw my arms around her. She stiffened for a second, then hugged me back. We stepped apart, and I said, "You still live here?"

"Hell no! I'm here for your welcome home party."

"Party?" I glanced up at the house. "So the whole family's here?"

"Well, not the uncles and all, but our happy little nuclear disaster family, yeah. The enforcers were supposed to tell you, but I guess they forgot after giving you their lecture, huh?" She dropped her clove and ground it out.

"Anyone else here?" I glanced toward the street, where the pale man watched the house. "Anyone from the local council, maybe?"

Sammy snorted. "As if our family weren't bad enough."

That might be truer than she knew. One of the many things I realized during my long exile was that someone in my family likely helped in framing me. Our home is pretty well warded against outside magical influence or unwanted guests, yet Felicity had been attacked all those years ago in our home, in my bedroom, and with necromancy. But now that I stood here, about to face my family, I found the idea hard to accept. We were hardly the Brady Bunch, but dark necromancers? Murderers?

"All right, let's get this over with," Sammy said and turned toward the house. She paused, and turned back. "Look, a lot has changed since you . . . left, Finn."

"No doy," I replied.

"No *doy*? Oh man, I haven't heard that in years. Glad to see you're still a dork." She looked away. "I actually missed you." She sounded surprised.

"I missed you too, sis."

"Yeah, well, you got to enjoy exile from this stupid world. Me, I had to deal with our family."

"I see you're still a people person."

"And you're still a smart ass."

"Hey now," I said. "My humor is a legitimate coping mechanism. My therapist said so."

"Uh-huh. Worst money Father ever spent, sending you to an empath."

"Worse than sending you?"

"Touché. Come on, dear brother, the sooner we get this reunion over with, the sooner I can leave."

We climbed the creaky steps to the back porch, and Sammy led the way inside to the mud room. The tingle of the house's wards buzzed over me like a waterfall of love bees as we crossed the threshold. I glanced back out into the night before closing the door. Whoever or whatever was after me, I felt a little safer now.

A little.

I turned to find my mother's ghost smiling at me and Sammy. The cascade of straight black hair that had been her pride in life shifted behind her like a cape in a nonexistent breeze, and the glowing tan skin inherited from Grandma Ramirez shone now like brown garnet in a jeweler's case.

"How was school, kids?" Mother asked. Her voice had a distant quality, as though channeled via drive-thru speaker.

"Holy crap," I whispered. Mother's ghost? This shouldn't be possible.

"*Mira,* interesting fact," Mother said, a phrase that I'd heard constantly growing up. "The Catholics have an entire vault full of petrified poopies they think might have belonged to Jesus, and they don't know what to do with it all. There's been a fierce war going on for centuries as to whether the holy crap is actually holy, or entirely unholy. On the one hand, it came from the body of their messiah. On the other hand, it is the waste rejected by his body. You would be surprised how many major conflicts in history were really the result of those two factions secretly fighting for power and—"

Sammy sneezed, the kind of sneeze that registers on weather maps, knocking me back a step with her elbow.

"Are you feeling well, sweetie?" Mother asked.

"I'm fine, Mom," Sammy said. "We have homework to do."

"Oh. Yes. Of course, sorry dear. Go get yourself a snack, and then right to your homework."

"Yes, Mother." Sammy waited until Mother's ghost drifted off, then looked at me. "You okay?"

"Yeah. No. I don't know. How can Mother be here? We diffused her energy properly."

"Apparently it has something to do with the garden," Sammy said. "She put a lot of her energy into it. And she's just a ghost, obviously."

Ghosts were not spirits, or "souls," but just copies usually impressed on the world by a traumatic death.

"Still—"

"Hey, you're asking the absolute wrong person, remember?"

"Oh. Right. Sorry." Sammy could channel magical energy, but she was highly allergic to it. That had made her a bit of an outsider growing up, and grumpy whenever the topic of magic came up. More grumpy, that is. "I didn't realize how much I missed Mom's crazy stories."

"Yeah. It was nice, at first. But, you know, she's pretty much stuck where she was when this echo was created. I've heard the same stories repeated my entire life."

Stuck where she was at, no memories of the decades since. I was little better off than a ghost.

"Sorry," I said. "I can imagine it's been hard for you especially, seeing Mom all the time, but it not really being Mom?"

"Sometimes. But not as hard as when Father forgets who I am."

"Father? What's wrong with—"

A young teen girl burst through the swinging door from the hallway into the mud room, and stopped short when she saw us. She looked amazingly like a fifteen-year-old Sammy. "Auntie Sam!"

"Hi, Mattie," Sammy said.

"I'm so glad you came!" Mattie said. "Oh my gods, Uncle Finn? It's so cool to finally meet you!"

Mattie threw her arms around me and gave me a hug that would have put a pro wrestler to shame, then bounced back and said, "Dad's really excited to see you. He's in the dining room. I have to run, I'm helping downstairs. Love you!" Mattie ran through a door on the left that led down to the basement.

I blinked, then said, "Is she hopped up on Pixy Stix or something?"

"No. That's just Mattie."

"Wait. *Uncle* Finn?"

"Oh, yeah, Mort spawned offspring. You're an uncle. Congrats!"

For some reason, this hit me harder than seeing myself and Sammy aged, or even finding a dead body on my return. All of that had felt a bit surreal yet almost normal after what I'd been through before. But seeing Mattie, a girl barely younger than Mort or I had been when I was exiled, and discovering she was Mort's daughter? My brain started to feel like, well, any one of the computers Captain Kirk caused to self-destruct by arguing with it—reality did not compute. I really wasn't the age my brain kept insisting I was. I couldn't just pick up my life where I'd left off, with everyone a little older. I'd missed a lot, lost a lot, in being gone for twenty-five years, things more important than movies and music. Adult things.

I might have been a parent by now.

I might have had a wife by now.

Or at least had sex.

I thought of Heather, the girl I fell in love with the year before exile, the kind of deep, true, certain love that made me feel like I could do anything. Anything except, of course, tell her how I felt.

"Hey," I said. "You know whatever happened to Heather?"

"Heather Flowers?"

"Yeah."

"Ask Mattie," Sammy said. "Miss Brown's her teacher."

"Who's Miss Brown?"

"Heather."

"Wait. What? I—Oh! Oh." Heather had married. Of course.

"Yeah." Sammy shrugged. "She's divorced now though."

"Oh?"

"And she had a kid when she was, like, nineteen. And stop saying 'oh.'"

"O . . . kay," I said.

"You can always stalk her online, see what's what."

"On what line? You mean call her?"

Sammy stared at me as though I'd just asked what music was. "Oh my motherboard," she said. "You really don't know, do you? And you didn't even know about Mattie. Weren't you supposed to get a bunch of memories from that Fey jerkling?"

I realized my mistake too late. As much as I wanted to trust Sammy, I couldn't know for sure who to trust, not yet. The last thing I wanted my enemies to know was how much I *didn't* know.

"Yeah, of course! I was totally kidding."

Sammy shook her head, her eyes narrowed. "Nice try, but I can tell something's up. Come on, out with it."

"It's nothing. I just—something didn't go right in the transfer is all. I didn't get all the changeling's memories."

"Shit. That sucks," Sammy said. "Or maybe not. At least you get to experience stuff yourself, rather than second hand. Hell, I envy you. To hear Nirvana for the first time? Or Sleater-Kinney? But look." She glanced up the hall, toward the dining room entrance, and stepped closer to me. "Don't let on to Mort or the others that anything went wrong with the transfer."

"Why not?"

"Mort's been running things here, but you know everyone kind of expected that you'd take control, being the Talker and all. And Grandfather definitely wanted you in charge. Or at least, he put all that stuff in his will about wanting a Talker to take over. Mort definitely hasn't forgotten that."

I shrugged. "Grandfather also wanted someone with children to take over, to continue the line. He didn't know I'd be exiled for twenty-five years."

"Maybe. But you're still the only Talker left in the family, and that trumps kids according to Grandfather's whacked-out logic."

"Yeah, well, I loved Grandfather but I never asked to be a Talker, or to run things." I flinched a bit as I said so, half expecting Grandfather's spirit to appear, slap his thigh, and give me an angry lecture about duty and responsibility. I loved Grandfather and owed him a lot, not just because the knowledge he'd given me saved my sanity in the Other Realm and my life during the attack, but also because I'd felt his spirit watching over me during my exile. I hated the thought of disappointing him. But I also hoped he would understand why.

"Besides," I added, "most of the biz is just spirit dissipation and collecting the magic anyway. Mort and Pete can do that just fine, especially with Father's help. And Mort's the oldest. That's good enough as far as I'm concerned."

"Maybe," Sammy said. "But Mort treats—gods, this is why I avoid these gatherings. I've been here ten minutes and I'm already talking shit behind Mort's back."

"Look, Sammy, I know you're just trying to help. But to be honest, I have zero desire to pay the price of Talking, or to spend my life around the dead. I'm taking this chance to officially leave the family biz, make a fresh start." Hopefully with Heather.

"Seriously? Doing what? Your necromancy gifts'll give you about as many career options as a degree in women's history. Believe me, I know."

"I was thinking maybe I'd make video games, like the Commodore ones we used to play together. I wouldn't be around grief and death all the time, or people bickering over magic. Nobody would have reason to try to kill or exile me. And best of all, making games won't suck the life out of me. I could kick even your butt at writing BASIC before I left, and I had some cool ideas—"

"BASIC?" Sammy shook her head. "Oh, man. You— Wow. You've got a lot to catch up on. Just, please, be careful while you do. Mort'll be looking for any excuse to stay in control, and you shouldn't decide to let him until you get to know him again is all."

"Fair enough," I said. "Shall we go see him, then?"

We walked down the hall, and through the kitchen. The lingering smells of garlic, vinegar, and baked cheesy goodness made my mouth water, reminding me that I hadn't eaten in, oh, about twenty-five years. An arched doorway led to the dining room. A table long enough for eight seats to a side filled the center of the room, covered in a red cloth and a row of mismatched dishes containing veggies, breads and cheeses, and various bumpy brown entrées, all lit by two electric chandeliers.

I noted with some disappointment a complete lack of pizza.

Two men stood beside the table, talking with their backs to us. I easily recognized my younger brother Peter even from behind. Petey had always been a big guy—not fat, or all muscles, just big, like Bigfoot is big, and when he turned in profile I saw that he still had a round baby face. That face fit him more than the size did, since he'd always had a kind of childlike simplicity to him.

I didn't recognize the second dude until he turned to the side. Mort had grown to look a lot like Father, who looked a lot like

Leonard Nimoy. And he appeared to have changed in more ways than just growing older. When I left, he'd been into Michael Jackson and breakdancing, calling himself Turbo Morto. Now, he dressed like Dracula's attorney in a black suit with red shirt. And the Vandyke beard made him look like evil Spock, but with a receding hairline and a diamond in his left (non-pointy) ear.

Mort took a big bite of a brownie, then offered it to Petey. "Man, that's damn good. Sure you don't want some?"

"I can't eat chocolate," Pete said, and pushed it away with a leather-gloved hand. "You know that. I put the list of stuff I can't eat on the fridge. Again."

"Ooooh, right. Sorry." Mort grinned, and took another bite, then spotted Sammy and me. "Hey! If it ain't Finn Fancy Necromancy Pants, in the flesh."

"Finn?" Pete said, and turned. "Finn!" He rushed at me and grabbed me in a bear hug.

"Hey, brother!" I gasped. He released me. Everyone adjusted to form a small circle, and I struggled not to sneeze from Mort's cloud of musky aftershave.

"Wait," Pete said, a very earnest expression settling across his face. "I have to say something quick. *I* took your Pac-Man watch."

"What?"

"I took your Pac-Man watch. I wanted to tell you before, and then you got sent away, and I felt real bad, and I told myself I would tell you as soon as I saw you so that I wouldn't not tell you before you go away again."

I laughed, and slapped him on the shoulder. "I sure missed you, dude. It's totally okay."

If any other family member had said "before you go away again" after the evening I'd had, my spidey senses might have tingled. But Pete wasn't the type to be plotting against me. That would require him to say one thing and mean another, and Pete could barely manage a single train of thought chugging along in his one-track mind. Add another train to that track, and it would be a disaster.

"Wait right here, I'll get it so I don't forget," Pete said.

"No, wait, that's—"

Pete rushed off without hearing my words. I sighed, and looked at Mort as he stuffed the last of the brownie in his mouth.

"No chocolate, the gloves—" I frowned. "Petey doesn't still think he's a waerwolf, does he?"

Mort gave the "whatcha gonna do" shrug, and grinned.

Pete got bit by a dog shortly after Mother's death, and insisted it was a waerwolf. He took Mother's death pretty hard, and seemed excited at the thought of being a waerwolf. We just didn't have the heart to tell him he wasn't, not right away. On the next full moon, he went out to our tree fort and tied his ankle to the trunk with rope so he wouldn't hurt anybody. Mort used a garden claw to scrape fake claw marks in the trunk as Pete slept, and cut up Petey's pajamas. Pete woke convinced he'd transformed during the night.

Soon though, he began threatening to bite or scratch us at every turn. I tried at that point to tell him he wasn't a waerwolf. He told me not to be jealous. I told him not to be an idiot. He waited until I left, then peed on my new KangaROOS gym shoes.

That's when Mort told me his idea of offering Pete a potion to stop the transformation—not a cure, of course, but something that must be drunk every full moon. I admit, I joined in on the prank. It took quite a bit of experimentation to come up with the perfect mixture. I won't reveal the full contents, but will say that the tangy creaminess of the mayonnaise and sharp bite of the orange juice was nicely contrasted by the pyrotechnic sweetness of the coke and pop rocks.

"Nobody's told him the truth, still?" I asked.

Sammy shrugged. "I tried to tell him once, but he kind of freaked out on me." She glared at Mort. "I think Mort still gets some thrill out of toying with him. But Pete seems happy, living here close to Mother and Father, so I just let it be."

"Still," I said.

I could believe that Pete wouldn't want to leave home, but there was no reason for Mort to still be tricking him. It was just cruel at this point.

That, and Sammy's warnings, only made it easier for me to believe what I'd struggled to accept: Mort was surely the one who'd helped frame me twenty-five years ago. Who else could it have been? Mother and Grandfather were dead, Sammy wanted nothing to do with magic or the family business, Petey was incapable of such plotting, and Father, well, he had nothing to gain from it. That left Mort.

Yet I didn't want to believe it still. Mort and I were brothers, we'd had some good times together growing up. He'd pulled quite a few pranks on me out of jealousy or sheer mischief, and the joke on Pete was beyond excessive at this point, but attacking Felicity and framing me for dark necromancy was a whole other level. It wasn't like I'd ever caught him torturing the neighbor's dog. Spray painting, yes. Torturing, no.

Maybe some feyblood had mind-tricked him into it, or some trickster god or other Fey Elder Spirit. Maybe even Felicity?

But even if that were true, why then had he not told the ARC and gotten me released from exile?

"Earth to Finn," Mort said. "You look like your brain's still in the Other Realm."

I shook my head. "Sorry. Still adjusting."

Pete arrived, breathing heavy, and held out my old Pac-Man watch. I laughed, and strapped it on. "Thanks, bro."

"I'm really glad you're home, Finn," he said.

"Yeah," Mort said. "Welcome back to the world. If there's anything you need, you just let me know. I imagine you'll probably want to live at your place, but anytime you want to crash here you're welcome. We kept your old room just like you left it."

"Because Father threw a fit when you tried to pack it up," Sammy muttered.

"Point is, *mi casa es su casa,* brother," Mort continued.

Sammy arched one eyebrow. "Don't you mean *su casa es mi casa,* now that he's back?"

Mort shot Sammy an annoyed look. "I'm just trying to make my brother feel welcome."

"Oh, yeah," Sammy said. "You're drowning him in unconditional love right here. I'm surprised he can even breathe."

Petey looked between Sammy and Mort, shrinking in on himself a bit.

"It's okay, guys," I said. "Really, I'm just glad to be back."

"That's all I'm trying to say," Mort said. "It's nice to have the whole family back together."

"Yeah," I said. Nice, in much the same way the first American Thanksgiving was nice. "Hey, speaking of family, congrats on being a father. That totally surprised me. I mean, no offense, but, dude, who would marry you? And when do I meet her?"

Mort crossed his arms. "I didn't marry Mattie's mother. And she left shortly after Mattie was born. I'd rather not discuss it."

"Left? Her own child? Why?"

"Reasons. Good ones. And I said I'd rather not discuss it."

"Oh. I, uh, sorry." Something told me Mort didn't want to discuss it further. "So . . . where is Father?" It wasn't an easy question for me to ask. The last time I'd asked it was the day of my trial by the local Arcana Ruling Council, and Mort told me that Father was so heartbroken at the thought of losing me that he couldn't be there.

"Father?" Pete asked. Mort and Sammy exchanged quick glances, but Petey just grinned. "Father's downstairs," he said.

Sammy sneezed an explosive sneeze.

And then a real explosion shook the house.

Mad World

The explosion rattled the dishes and caused a bit of plaster dust to fall from the ceiling. Another attack? I grabbed Sammy and shoved her under the nearby arched doorway for protection, then pressed my back against the door frame.

Mort brushed a bit of plaster dust off of his suit jacket and scowled as he replaced the covers on some of the dishes on the table. Petey stared up at the ceiling and grinned with his tongue stuck out as though the falling plaster were snow.

"What's going on?" I asked.

"Father," Sammy replied, and wouldn't meet my eyes.

"Come on," Mort said, and waved for me to follow him. "Let's go see how bad it is this time."

I followed Mort back down the hallway and through the basement door. The stairs creaked, and a cloud of dust swirled beneath the yellow bulb at the bottom of the stairwell. I heard coughing as we descended.

"Father? Mattie? You all right?" Mort called out.

"Okeemonkey," Father's deep voice came from below, more tremulous than I remembered.

"We're fine," Mattie added. "The doves exploded is all."

I glanced at Mort, but he didn't appear to find the statement at all odd. I took a deep breath and continued to follow him down into the basement.

Thick wooden beams were spaced out to support the ceiling, and a wall with frosted glass windows separated the basement into two halves. Through the frosted windows, light shimmered off the stainless-steel tables used for preparing bodies, and the equipment used to drain and pump fluids, the same as might be found in any mortuary. But the area we now entered held our necrotorium: ritual tables surrounded by protective circles embedded in the floor, the collection altars to gather and store magic from the dead, and cabinets and shelves lining the walls. Beneath the concrete floor, warded and insulated, sat hidden our personal cache of mana—magic in its captured and preserved form.

Under the fading smoke, the basement smelled of earth mixed with bleach.

Everything stood much as I remembered it, though I noticed that many of the older and more valuable family artifacts were missing, including several of the protection amulets from the open cabinet to my left. I snagged the family's hex protection amulet as we passed and slipped it on. If the Króls managed to throw a curse at me outside the house's wards, I'd have some protection at least.

Mort led me to the right, to the recessed space where Father practiced his thaumaturgy—creating objects that used or worked by magic. Except it no longer held the ordered workshop I remembered. It held Frankenstein's lab.

Gizmos flickered with lightning; gadgets buzzed with plasma; doohickeys covered with dials and levers and meters hummed and pinged. There was no bolt-necked monster, thankfully, but a table held several probes pointing down at two scorch marks that I assumed were all that remained of the exploded doves.

On the far side of the table stood Mattie and my father, both wearing wide grins beneath goggles and hair that danced in static haloes.

I felt a sharp pang in my chest at the sight of my father. Every one of the past twenty-five years showed in his wrinkled face, his shrunken and slimmed frame. But his smile and twinkling eyes still looked young.

"Ah Finn, good, there you are. I have something for you. It's just over there in the platypus."

I looked to where he pointed. An Easy-Bake oven covered in

painted runes emitted a blacklight glow. "Platypus?" I asked, feeling a growing chill, like a winter shadow made of dread.

"What?" Father said, and jumped as though he'd forgotten I was there.

"You said platypus. I don't see a platypus."

"Of course not. The platypuses were all made into pudding years ago. Who let you into my lab?" He turned to Mattie. "Who let the monkey into my lab?"

The dread exploded into full realization: My father was mad.

"He's not a monkey," Mort said in an impatient tone. "He's your son Finn. What's going on here? Mattie, I told you no more explosions."

Mattie lifted the goggles to the top of her head. "Papa G made Finn a welcome home gift. He said it's really important."

Mort rolled his eyes. "You should know better. He always says it's important."

"Important," Father agreed, nodding sagely. "From the Latin *importantus,* to import ants." He looked down at Mattie. "Why do you suppose the Romans imported ants? I'm sure your grandmother would know. Where is she?"

"Enough," Mort said. "Father, clean this mess up before morning. We don't want to scare off any customers."

"Our customers are dead," Father said. "They're past being scared."

"I meant the— Oh, never mind. Mattie, make sure he cleans this up." Mort turned to me. "Do you see what I've had to deal with since you left?"

"I didn't leave, damn it, I was exiled."

But I did see. And I felt the bottom drop out of the cereal box of my heart. Despite all my worries that he'd abandoned me, I realized how much I'd counted on my father being there now to help me figure out what was going on, to help me stop it. To help me make sense of everything, including my exile, and my feelings about it. Instead, I found myself wishing I could help *him.*

I moved closer to Mort and whispered, "How long has he been like this?"

"Crazy?" He didn't bother to whisper. "Since you left. Sorry, since you were exiled. Actually, it started a little before, when you were arrested. That's really why he didn't come to your trial."

The accusation wasn't even subtle. It was my fault Father was crazy. Except, if Mort was the one who got me sent into exile, then this, too, was really Mort's fault. And convenient, too, if all of this was about Mort running the family business.

"Where's my tree?" Father said, and his voice sounded close to tears.

"In your room, Papa G," Mattie said. "We'll go there soon."

"Tree?" I asked her.

"A bonsai. He's been trying to find the right shape for years."

"The right shape for what?"

Mattie shrugged. "He won't say. I think he just enjoys working on it."

"You still need to clean up this mess," Mort said.

"We will," Mattie replied without any of the sullenness or rebellion I would have expected in her voice. "Uncle Finn, don't forget your gift." She nodded to the Easy-Bake oven.

I opened the plastic oven, and on a mini–cake pan inside I found a silver ring. The ring was too small to fit over my fingers and didn't appear to have any gaps to resize it.

"What is it?" I asked.

"Not for the blood, but for the heart," Father said.

"What?"

"Scribble scroble, nib to noble."

"Ignore him," Mort said. "He rambles like this all the time, and it never makes any sense far as I can tell. Come on. Let's get some food before it goes bad."

I grabbed Mort's arm. "Hey. Have you taken him to a mind healer? Have you tried to find out what's wrong with him?"

Mort shook me off. "I know what's wrong with him. You know the signs as well as I do. Something bad got into his head."

Mort was right, that would explain Father's behavior. Being possessed against your will could scramble the brains a bit, especially if the spirit was of something that had never been human. But I shook my head. "Father's not a necromancer. He wouldn't have been summoning anything. And we have all kinds of protections against possession or attack from the outside."

"Yeah, well, maybe he was distracted by his son being arrested, and did something dangerous to prove your innocence. Doesn't matter now, does it? I took him to a healer, and they couldn't help him."

Footsteps sounded on the stairs, and Sammy appeared. "Enforcers are here."

Ah, crap.

Mort went pale. "What?" He looked around as though afraid he'd left a pile of drugs or guns lying about.

Sammy arched an eyebrow, and said without taking her eyes off of him, "They asked for Finn."

Double crap.

Know Your Rights

Enforcers. Their arrival meant nothing good, even assuming they really were enforcers and not more assassins in disguise. I felt a simultaneous urge to flee and to vomit at the thought of being dragged back into exile and Fey custody.

I turned in a circle, picturing every exit from the house. But even if I managed to escape the enforcers, which was unlikely, I had nowhere to go and would be vulnerable to another attack. Home remained the safest place for me—even if my older brother seemed to be plotting against me, and my father, the one person I'd counted on for help, was exploding doves and spouting gibberish.

"Finn?" Sammy asked.

I swallowed down my panic. It seemed I had little choice but to face the enforcers.

"Coming," I said, and followed after Sammy.

She glanced back as we climbed the stairs. "I don't know what's going on, Finn, but things have changed since you left. Don't let the enforcers bully you. They can't force you to do or say anything without good cause, not anymore."

I'd believe that when I wasn't exiled again. But the sharp certainty in her tone did calm my racing pulse a bit. "Thanks, sis. How do you know so much about what enforcers can and can't do? Raising trouble while I was gone?"

"Actually, yeah, sort of." We exited the stairs into the hall. "I started a support network for mundy women who were dumped or widowed by magicals. You know, some arcana or unicorn or whatever comes along and blows up their mundy reality, then just as they're learning to deal with the magical world they lose their one real connection with it all. And the ARC likes to send enforcers around, wanting to violate their minds, wipe their memories—" She fell silent, having worked herself up into an unusually emotional state.

"I think that's awesome," I said as we passed through the kitchen. "What you're doing, I mean, not what they have to deal with. I'd never really thought about it before, but—"

"Big surprise," Sammy said. Then she sighed, and put her hand on my arm. "Sorry. I know you aren't like the assholes I'm always dealing with. Hell, you're my brother, I barely even think of you as an arcana, or a man for that matter."

"Gee, thanks," I said.

"Any time." We stopped at the double doors to the entry hall. "Ready?" Sammy asked.

"No. But I don't have any choice."

"You'll be fine. If they start acting up, I'll read them the riot act."

I smiled. "Thanks, sis."

I opened the doors. Two enforcers waited for me in the front entry hall, one an older black man who looked like Louis Gossett Jr.'s angrier brother, and the other a young woman who reminded me of Jo from *The Facts of Life*. At the time of my exile, enforcers wore enchanted *Miami Vice*–looking outfits—their way of blending into the mundy world and, I suspect, of looking cool at the Arcana Ruling Council's expense. Now they both wore black suits and ties like the "enforcer" at my transfer, reminding me of 1960's federal agents.

One thing that hadn't changed, however, was the standard-issue enforcer mustache, a long horseshoe Fu Manchu affair with silver-traced beads braided into the dangling ends. The beads meant something, though I didn't know what—rank, or powers, or maybe enforcer merit badges for being honest, brave, helping bad old witches cross the street into oncoming traffic, and beating the crap out of any arcana or feyblood that broke the Pax or ARC laws.

The female enforcer didn't actually have a mustache. She had two thin braids instead, one in front of each ear, with the beads dangling near her jawline. Too bad. I would have loved to see how she pulled off a mustache.

With the enforcers stood a tall weathered-looking dude wearing a biker jacket, his receding silver-blond hair pulled back in a ponytail. He sported the mustache of an enforcer, but free of any beads. Biker dude's eyes locked onto me as I stepped fully into the room, as did those of the enforcers.

"Phinaeus Gramaraye?" Enforcer guy asked.

"Yes." I braced for a tackle.

"My name is Reggie, and this is Jo." He nodded to the female enforcer. "We're here on ARC business. Is there somewhere we can talk privately?"

"Huh?" I responded cleverly. I'd expected the enforcers to throw me on the ground, slap binding cuffs on me, and drag me away, regardless of what Sammy had said.

Jo—I wondered if she'd picked that name—gave an impatient sigh. "We understand something unusual happened during your transfer from exile, and we'd like to ask you about it."

"Oh, uh, sure, in here." I waved them back into the dining room. I followed them in and closed the double doors behind us, leaving Sammy in the entry hall. When I turned back around, biker dude grabbed me by the throat and shoved me up against the doors, lifting me up to the balls of my feet.

"What the hell's going on?" he asked in a voice so gravelly it gave my ears road rash. "And don't lie to me, fool. I can read lies."

"Zeke, stop," Enforcer Reggie said, his tone making clear the command was more form than substance. "I told you we've got new rules now."

"Yeah," Zeke said without taking his eyes off of my face, which no doubt turned interesting colors as I gasped for air. "I heard. But I ain't an enforcer no more, am I?"

Sammy pounded on the door. "Hey! Finn, you okay in there?"

"Reggie," Jo said. "I know he was your partner and all—"

"Zeke," Reggie said. "You still gotta respect the rules, or I'll get busted for it. Please put the bad necro down."

Zeke grunted, and stepped back, letting me drop back to my heels. Sammy opened the door, but I waved her back. I wasn't sure what was going on, but I didn't want her involved. She frowned, and closed the door again.

I rubbed my throat. "I'm not a dark necromancer," I said and coughed.

Jo glanced at Reggie, her eyebrows raised. "I didn't detect a lie."

"You read his file, rook," Reggie said and smiled at me. "The evidence was overwhelming. Sometimes, the truth gets hidden behind the words. He says he's not a dark necromancer, but maybe that's because he thinks he's a holy warrior using evil to fight evil, or he's a savior releasing their spirits, or thinks he really changed in exile."

"I didn't attack anyone, period," I said. "I was framed."

"Interesting," Reggie said. "And I'd love to figure out just what you think that means in your funny little world, but we're not here to discuss your past crimes or hold a retrial, Mr. Gramaraye. So why don't you tell us what happened tonight?"

"You mean with the transfer?"

"Yes."

"Somebody attacked us," I said. "Somebody glamoured to look like an enforcer. I managed to get through the portal before it closed. I came here hoping to figure out what's going on and what to do next." All true. I just left out the part about finding a dead body in my trailer.

Zeke's eyes narrowed. "Do you know the person who attacked the transfer?"

"No."

Reggie crossed his arms. "Did you in any way help to coordinate or have knowledge of the attack before it happened?"

"What? No! That's crazy! Why would I attack myself?"

"The spell targeted the Fey but had no effect on human spirits. You were in no real danger."

"You're sure?" I asked, confused. Had I just been in the wrong place at the wrong time?

No. Felicity's death wasn't a coincidence. She'd been killed, silenced with necromancy, and left in my home for the enforcers to find, probably with my resonance somehow planted on her. But then why attack the Fey at all?

"We're certain," Reggie said. "Another arcana being transferred from exile was struck but unharmed."

"Unharmed my ass, that attack hurt like hell!" Zeke said. "And I barely made it through my portal." He jabbed a finger at me. "After I survived twenty-five years getting mind-humped by a bunch of Fey, you came along and messed up my homecoming, fool. I didn't get no memories, I don't know nothing about the fool job he left me, and I'm on the hook for my warden and changeling gettin' toasted. I wanna know what's going on!"

"Look," I said, my palms as sweaty as a three-hundred-pound jogger in Florida now. "I honestly don't know what's going on, why the attack happened, or who the attacker is. I hope you catch whoever it is, I really do."

The enforcers exchanged looks. Jo gave the slightest nod, and Reggie sighed. "He's telling the truth, Zeke."

"Maybe," Zeke said, and squinted at me. "So what happened to this mystery attacker?"

"He was gone by the time I had control of my body."

"Anyone else there?" Reggie asked. "Other arcana?"

"No." Truth, technically. Arcana were human magic users. Felicity was not an arcana.

Reggie's eyes narrowed. "Any feybloods?"

Crap. Feybloods were the nonhuman magicals in our world, created centuries ago when Fey spirits crossed to our world and blended with people, animals, even plants. They included everything from unicorns to elementals to waer creatures. They also included witches, like Felicity's clan.

But Felicity had been dead when I found her in my trailer, her spirit moved on. So technically, she still wasn't there either. At least, that's the thought I held firmly in my head as I said, "Not another living soul, I swear, unless you count the wildlife."

"I see," Reggie said. "Any idea why someone would attack the Fey during your transfer?"

"No."

"Any guesses?" Jo asked, her polite tone now strained.

"Because the Fey suck? I don't know. I thought maybe the Króls were seeking revenge on me, but you said the attack wouldn't have harmed me, so now I don't know."

"Revenge?" Zeke snorted. "Thought you said you didn't do nothing, you're all innocent."

"I am," I said, feeling my own anger rising. "And you guys sent me into exile anyway. So as far as the Króls and everyone else are concerned, I'm guilty, right?"

The enforcers exchanged glances again.

"He appears to believe what he's saying," Reggie said as if I weren't standing right there. "Maybe we shouldn't focus on the Fey attack. There's the matter of his—"

"Seriously?" Zeke said. "You can't tell this fool's hiding something? Give me five minutes with him, and—"

The doors behind me opened, and a tall gentleman let himself into the room. From his outfit, I wondered if he'd just left the men's club—in the 1960s. Gray suit pants, a double-breasted navy sports jacket with gold buttons, a red handkerchief and tie. His conservative haircut was slicked back and waxy looking. It took me a second to recognize him, helped by the fact that his manner and appearance reminded me of Grandfather.

"Jimmy?" Jimmy Grayson was a necromancer two years older than me, and a Talker. Jimmy's mother died in some kind of accident when he was a child, and he'd never known his father. He got fostered out to a family with no Talker to train him, so Grandfather tutored Jimmy alongside me for several years. He'd idolized Grandfather, and we'd been friendly, but not friends. He was too quiet and withdrawn. And he completely lacked a sense of humor. "Nice outfit, Jimmy Jam."

"I'm addressed as Magus Grayson now," he replied. Still no sense of humor, it seemed. "Hello, Finn. I trust these enforcers have been treating you properly?"

I glanced sidelong at Zeke. "Uh, yeah, totally."

"Good. Enforcers," Grayson said, nodding to them. "And Mister Wodenson. I understand there's some concern that Finn here's involved in a crime? Surely that's a mistake. He's only just returned."

Reggie stepped forward, and bowed his head briefly to Grayson. "Magus," he said, and glanced behind him. "Zeke, why don't you wait in the car. Jo can keep you company. And please close the doors behind you."

Zeke looked between me and Grayson, then huffed from the room. He glared at me, unblinking, as Jo closed the doors behind them.

Reggie waited until the doors closed, and said, "Magus, there was an attack on the Other Realm during the transfer. And the enforcer assigned to monitor the transfer is missing."

"So I've heard. And don't you think perhaps you should go out to the transfer site and investigate before harassing Mr. Gramaraye here?"

"We did."

"Really?" Grayson sounded dubious. "And?"

"And we found no sign of anyone but Gramaraye and his changeling." He glanced at me. "If someone else was responsible for the attack, they erased their presence completely. Or somehow masked their resonance to Gramaraye's here. At least, as far as we could determine—the investigation has been complicated by mundy involvement."

"Mundies?" Grayson frowned. "Why would they be involved?"

"Because somebody set fire to Gramaraye's little feyhole." Reggie looked at me. "Which was going to be our next topic of discussion."

Crap. No mention of Felicity, at least, and he hadn't asked me about her before, even when I mentioned the Króls. That much had gone right, at least.

Grayson turned his frown on me for a second, though his eyes focused elsewhere. "Was the fire magical in origin?" he asked finally.

"No, it looks like a propane explosion," Reggie replied. "But obviously—"

"In other words," Grayson said, "you have no legal justification to further harass my friend here?"

Reggie's jaw twitched. "Not *yet,*" he said.

"Well then," Grayson said. "Why don't we go out to the site and take a second look? I'll arrange to have some of our people in the FBI step in, give you cover as consultants or whatever you need. Then we can find what you missed, and prove Finn's innocence rather than interrogating him in his home, hmm?"

Oh crap. "Jimmy—I mean, Magus Grayson—it's fine. I completely understand why they questioned me. I mean, it's not like they're throwing me in a cell for the night. Uh, you're not, right?"

Reggie arched an eyebrow at me.

Grayson moved to stand beside me. "Finn, you and your family have been through enough already. I will not have you spend your first hours of freedom under suspicion and the constant threat of arrest. It borders on persecution."

Reggie crossed his arms. "Persecution would be letting Zeke beat the truth out of your friend here. Mr. Gramaraye is our only suspect, after all, and the only one we can verify as present during the attack."

"Wait," I said. "*Are* you arresting me?"

"No," Reggie said. "However, I'm giving this investigation seventy-two hours. If we don't have the answers we need by then, we'll take the necessary steps to get them."

"And what does that mean?" Grayson asked.

Reggie shrugged. "Most likely, we'll go in after the changeling's memories."

I touched my forehead. "But I thought that couldn't be done? That they were walled off by Fey magic and arcana magic both?"

Grayson narrowed his eyes. "It can be done, but it will most likely cause damage to your mind, and probably destroy your own memories."

"Maybe," Reggie said. "Maybe not."

I took a step back from both of them. "But I didn't do anything!"

"You're hiding something, I'd bet on it," Reggie said. "And we're talking about an attack into the Other Realm. You do realize what's at stake here?"

"Yeah," I said. "My freedom. Again."

"More than that. The destruction of two changelings and Fey wardens? And a missing ARC enforcer? Wars have started for less."

"War?" Grayson asked. "You really think it might come to that?"

"Do you want to find out?" Reggie responded. "Under the Pax, we have six days to resolve any breach of border security before the Fey are given jurisdiction in our world, and things get messy fast." He looked at me. "Until and unless I find solid evidence pointing to your guilt, I'm giving you three of those days to enjoy while we continue our investigation and deal with the mundies, which is frankly more generous than I'd like to be."

I could see Grayson's frustration clearly on his face. But in the end, there was only so much he could do. Enforcers were part of the Arcana Ruling Council but not under the direct control of the magi due to the ARC's checks and balances. Just one of the many fun and exciting facts of the arcana world I'd learned during my summers at arcana school.

Grayson met Reggie's stare for a second, then said, "Very well. I'm sorry, Finn. He's right. It seems you must remain a suspect. But we shall get this whole mess cleared up as quickly as possible. Nobody is going to go tromping through your head." He looked in the direction Zeke had gone. "In the meantime, I expect Mr. Gramaraye to be treated with the respect due an arcana, and a Talker, is that clear?"

"Of course," Reggie said. "But if I were you, Gramaraye, I'd avoid any necromancy until this is all cleared up. If someone really is out to get you, don't give them any help."

"At this point, I'd be happy to never touch magic again," I replied.

"Right," Reggie said. "Well, if you suddenly remember something new about the attack, or the trailer fire, or anything else I might need to know, contact me."

He produced a business card and handed it to me. I wiped the sweat from my hand before taking it.

Reggie moved to the doors, and paused. "Oh, and one more thing. I'm afraid I have to impound your car. You know, as part of the investigation." He turned and walked out.

"Finn, be careful," Grayson said after the doors closed. "I shall do what I can to protect you, and find out who's behind all of this. But while I do, you may still be in danger, and not just from the enforcers."

"I know."

Grayson's brow furrowed. "If you know something, or are involved in any way, I hope you'll tell me. We all want to resolve this as quickly as possible, and if anyone can or would help you, it's me."

"There's nothing. Really." At least Grayson couldn't detect lies like enforcers.

"Very well."

I walked him to the front door, and looked out into the night as Grayson stepped onto the porch. If nothing else, maybe the enforcers had scared off the Król lurker. Grayson turned back.

"If you do discover anything, or leave the house, please check in with me," he said. "I can only protect and help you if you trust me, and keep me informed."

"Okay. Thanks, Jimmy," I said, protocol be damned, and held out my hand. He may have a stick up his butt, but Grayson had stood up for me, given me the support I'd hoped to find from my family. In fact, it had felt a bit like Grandfather was still alive, fighting to protect me the way he'd always fought to protect our family's safety and reputation. "Grandfather would be proud of you, and grateful you're helping me."

A smile twitched up the corner of Grayson's mouth, and he took my hand. "He was a great man. And good to me. I'm just glad I have this chance to repay him even a little bit. Get some rest, Finn."

I closed the door behind him and leaned my back against it, my legs a bit shaky, my whole body jangly with nervous energy. I had Zeke, the Króls, and possibly another enemy all gunning for me, and Felicity's body just waiting to be identified. And I had three days at most to figure everything out, or they were going to make scrambled eggs of my mind.

Yeah, I'd sleep like a baby tonight.

I Feel for You

My family surrounded me a heartbeat after the front door closed.

"So?" Sammy asked. "What was that about?"

"About the problem in the transfer," I replied, still distracted by the confrontation.

"Problem?" Mort asked.

Crap. "Nothing major," I said. "Some problems in the Other Realm I guess. Look," I rubbed at my eyes, "I really appreciate the welcome home party, but it's been a crazy evening. Is it okay if I just crash in my room and we can all catch up over breakfast?"

Mort shrugged. "I still have work to do anyway."

"I'll pass," Sammy said. "But we'll hang soon."

"Breakfast is my favorite!" Pete said.

I exchanged quick hugs with Sammy and Pete, and said good night to Mort.

"Mattie," he said, "why don't you show Finn up to his room."

As if I was a guest, or could forget the way to my own bedroom.

"Sure!" Mattie turned to me. "We should grab you fresh blankets though. I don't even want to know how long yours have been in there."

"Sounds good."

Mattie led the way down the hall. "Wow, this is so weird," she said. "I've heard all about you, so I kind of feel like I know you, but it's like, I wasn't even born when you went into exile, you know?"

"Uh-huh," I said.

I followed Mattie to the laundry room, then back to the main stairs and up to my room. On the way I learned an interesting fact—teenage girls can talk without taking a single breath. I didn't remember this from my own youth, but then neither Heather nor Sammy had been the talkative type, and I'd never felt comfortable enough around other girls to actually test their talking limits.

Bits of Mattie's continuous monologue were interesting, glimmers of the world I'd returned to, but there was quite a bit in there about some girl at school who kept copying Mattie's style, and her friend who was allowed to drive already, and other apparently world-ending facts mixed with words and phrases that I could only guess at their meaning.

One thing I did learn, however, was that Mattie was lonely. She hid it well. But maybe this was one of the advantages I had over other adults in her life—I remembered very clearly what it was like to be a young teenage necromancer, having relived all of those awful, awkward, emotional moments of my life for twenty-five years. And though Mattie was a girl, and her world, personality, and experiences all very different from mine, I still recognized something of myself in her.

She didn't even have the benefit of having my mother and father as parents—at least, not as they used to be. She'd had only Mort. From her stories, I could tell Morty gave her whatever she needed, except for time and attention. And the occasional visit with Aunt Sammy couldn't make up for that.

The door to my bedroom had a license plate with my name on it. Mattie opened it and preceded me inside. "Should be just like you left it," she said.

Well, not exactly as I left it, I hoped. I could do without Felicity's bleeding and unconscious body on the floor. But other than that, the room was indeed as I'd left it. Posters and music magazine cutouts covered the walls, and familiar faces greeted me—The Smiths, The Cure, Talking Heads, Prince; Buckaroo Banzai, *The Terminator,* *Indiana Jones,* and *The Goonies.*

A bed, a bookshelf, and a small desk were the only furniture. My worn and creased paperbacks lined the shelves like old friends waiting for my return. My Commodore 64 called to me from the desk, and lined up beside it stood my notebooks full of dungeon maps, character stats, and game ideas.

In fact, the room was so much the same that I felt a second of panic. Was I still in the Other Realm? Was everything I'd experienced tonight just illusion, the cruel joke of some bored Fey lord or lady manipulating my memories like their own personal playground?

I focused on the differences: the plain blue blanket Mattie swept over the bed in place of my threadbare *Star Wars* comforter; the complete lack of ants in my ant farm; Mattie herself. I'd never seen her before. I'd relived every memory of my life enough to be certain of that, and the Fey only played with the stuff of real memories.

I flipped the power switch on the Commodore and turned on the monitor. After a few seconds, the blue screen cast the room in a comforting, familiar glow.

```
**** COMMODORE 64 BASIC X2 ****
64K RAM SYSTEM  38911 BASIC BYTES FREE
READY.
```

Ah, what a beautiful sight. My fingers itched to begin typing on those plastic brown keys.

"I'm so glad you're back," Mattie said. "Uncle Pete's always telling stories about how much fun you were."

"Yeah, well, I'm not sure how long I'll be here," I said. The last thing I wanted to do was lie to Mattie and set her up for disappointment three days later.

"You're not *leaving* leaving, are you?" Mattie asked. "You just got here. And we haven't even had a chance to talk or anything, not really. Ooo, and I was hoping to see what Papa G's present was for!"

I'd forgotten about the ring. I touched its outline in the little coin pocket of my jeans. One more mystery to solve.

"I'm not sure what I'm doing yet," I said. "But I won't be going anywhere for at least a couple days, I promise."

"You'd better—oh, sorry, hang on." She pulled a black rectangle the size of a thick playing card out of her pocket and touched it. Light bathed her face.

"What's that?" I asked.

"Just my phone. Didn't your changeling know about cell phones?"

"Uh, yeah, I just hadn't seen one myself yet."

"Oh, well," she turned so I could see the phone. It had a small video screen on it.

"So it's a, uh, video phone?"

"Well, I use it mostly for texting, but sometimes I play games or watch videos, so yeah, I guess. Oh, I've so got to show you this 'She Wants Revenge' video. The music's so eighties, like that one group . . . Bauhaus? And the girl in the video could totally be a feyblood. You'll love it!"

"That tiny thing, it does all of that?" I felt a sinking feeling in my stomach.

"Oh yeah, that, and e-mail, and plays music and stuff. The camera's pretty weaksauce, though."

I could see why Sammy laughed at me. I glanced between my Commodore and Mattie's phone. I couldn't even imagine the code it would take to make that thing work. It was like a supercomputer in the palm of her hand.

"How about a nice game of global thermonuclear war?" I muttered.

"What?"

"Sorry. Nothing. I just—I could really use some time alone now."

"Oh, of course. I should go check on Papa G anyway." She moved to the door. "Good night, Uncle Finn. Welcome home." She left.

I stared at the closed door. What now?

Three days. Three days to figure out who was after me or it was exile with a side of brain scramble.

The first step was to give my enemy a name. Things were always easier to deal with when they had a name. Enemy, I name thee . . . Romulans? The Gamalons?

Legion of Doom. Yeah, that worked.

So, I needed to figure out who the Legion were and stop them from ruining my life. But what could I do that the enforcers and the Arcana Ruling Council, with all their power and ability, could not?

Well, I could launch my own investigation into what really happened twenty-five years ago. The ARC might consider that a closed case, but I knew better, and the enforcers didn't know about Felicity's death, at least not yet. Surely the two attacks were related.

But where to start?

Mort. I could dig a little deeper into what my brother was up to. He was my only potential lead at this point. Well, other than the Króls, but I wasn't eager to chase after a clan of vengeful witches if I had another option.

Three days.

The room felt suddenly too small, the walls pressing in. I opened the window, took a deep breath of the cool night air, and finally turned to look at the floor. A throw rug covered the spot where Felicity had laid, no bloodstains to be seen. But I could still see her unconscious body, my memory filling in a ghostly image of it.

"Who attacked you?" I whispered. "And why frame me for it?"

She wouldn't answer. I could try Talking to her until I felt as if my head would explode like in *Scanners*. But I knew from experience there was no Talking to a warded spirit.

Tears burned at the back of my eyes. I paced the small space of my room for a minute, trying to shake the growing fury, and finally plopped down at my desk. Maybe a quick game of Wizball would make me feel better, help me feel a little of the joy of homecoming. But I found myself rearranging my books and notebooks in order of size, as my mind fixed on Mattie's tiny little phone computer. A computer that fit in her hand. Amazing. And for some reason, it was the straw that humped the camel's dam.

"WHY?" I shouted. I leaped back up and paced rapidly, my thoughts scratching at me like an angry cat demanding attention.

Twenty-five years, gone. My father, my family, my life, so many changes. Raw emotion boiled up inside me. All of the anger I'd pushed down, told myself wouldn't help anything, it all erupted back up into my chest now. Twenty-five years. I'd convinced myself it was a good thing, dreaming of a life with Heather, a life free from the magic that had become a curse, and of the ARC who'd thrown me into exile to be fed on by the Fey. Free, and in control of my own life.

Except now I was back, and I realized how much I'd lost. I realized how much my Other Realm dreams were lies I told to keep myself sane. My obligations and choices were the same as they ever were, but I would have to struggle even harder to make my place anywhere, to find happiness anywhere. Assuming I wasn't mind-humped and sent back into exile in three days, of course.

If my room weren't so small, I might have danced the *Footloose* anger dance, punching at the air, literally flipping out. I settled for beating the crap out of my pillow until the muscles in my arms burned.

A knock on my door.

I stood panting for a second, feeling hot, and sweaty, and a tiny bit better. Another knock.

"Yes?" I called, my voice thick. I rubbed my face and eyes dry.

"It's me, Pete."

I took a deep breath and exhaled slowly before saying, "Come in."

Pete entered the room, making it feel considerably smaller.

"Hey," he said. "I was thinking, maybe you could sleep in my room tonight? Then we could talk and stuff."

I glanced back down at the floor where Felicity had lain, then at the bed I hadn't slept in for twenty-five years.

"That might be nice, actually." In fact, if someone wanted to try to attack me again, or place Felicity's body on my floor again tonight, it might not hurt to be someplace they wouldn't expect. If I were careful about it, not even Mort would know I'd changed rooms.

Petey's round face broke into a grin. I grabbed the blue blanket, and a pair of my old pajamas out of the dresser. There, waiting in the drawer where I'd left it, sat my persona ring. A simple-looking silver ring with a small black stone, it might have been mistaken for a mood ring. But every arcana over twelve had one. They were the official ID of the arcana world, containing information about my identity, my arcana gifts, my ranking in the arcana hierarchy. And the color marked me as a necromancer, my dominant gift, though my family had at least a touch of the wizardry, sorcery, and thaumaturgy gifts as well. The only one of the five branches of human magic our family hadn't manifested at some point was alchemy.

I closed the drawer without taking the ring, and followed Pete outside.

I dashed through the cool night air between the main house and the mother-in-law cottage, searching the dark for any signs of danger. The dark was signless.

Looking up in case of falling death meteors or swooping terrors, I did see that a cable still ran from outside my bedroom window and disappeared over the hedge bordering this side of our yard. Many video games, cassettes, notes, candies and other oddities had been sent back and forth along that cable between my window and the window of Next Door Dawn's room. Or at least, her room when we were teenagers.

Dawn was a mundy, and Grandfather didn't allow mundies in our house except on business. The rope system was just one of the many small ways I got around that. By the time of my exile, I probably spent more time with Dawn each day than anyone except Heather and my siblings. She was like my second sister. I wondered where she lived now, what her life was like. It didn't feel quite like a homecoming without seeing her.

I began to ask Pete about her, but stopped. It felt like even a whisper would carry loudly in the night air. And if the news of Dawn was bad, I wasn't sure I wanted to hear it, not tonight.

Pete bounced with excitement as we entered his tiny home.

The cottage used to be Mother's escape from us children. She didn't call it that, of course. She called it her office, and it used to be mostly filled with gardening supplies. But she'd also had a chair and reading lamp, a futon, and a small still in the bathroom for making her home brew. Now it looked like a proper apartment with all the standard furnishings, and a simple kitchenette. What really marked the space as Pete's were the Rubik's cubes and similar puzzle games piled on his dresser and shelves. That, and the walls were covered nearly floor to ceiling in paint by number paintings, most featuring wolves. He'd always had a gift for space and numbers that itself bordered on magical.

Pete hung his head and shuffled from foot to foot in that golly-gawrsh way he had, and said, "Do you like it?"

"I think it's awesome, dude. You've gotten really good at the paintings."

Pete beamed at me and said, "I'll make us some hot cider."

I changed in the tiny bathroom—the Speed Racer pajama bottoms had that softness that comes only from long wear, but they were a bit snug and short now that I'd fully grown. I considered just sleeping in my boxers, but I wanted to be a bit more clothed if someone attacked during the night, and I'd never been able to sleep well wearing jeans.

As I changed, I also noticed that I'd become extremely hairy. Before exile, I wished for enough facial hair to grow even a Prince mustache. Now I had enough hair on my back alone for a small beard. Not cool.

Once changed, I set myself up on the sofa. Pete served up the hot cider and crawled into his bed.

"Finn?" Pete said. "What was it like? In the Other Realm?"

"Lonely," I said, hoping he'd let it lie at that.

"But what were the Fey like?"

"I didn't exactly hang out and play games with them, Petey," I said, irritation creeping into my tone. "I was just food to them. They came, they got what they wanted, and they left."

Pete's face fell, and I felt like a jerk. Of course he still thought of the Fey as some wondrous fairy beings. And why shouldn't he? They had, after all, begun as just that, manifested from the dreams and fears and imaginings of all those ancient shamans, oracles, and wise women whose vision quests and spirit journeys took their minds into the Other Realm. And many people still idealized the Fey, spoke of them like they hadn't changed or committed terrible acts.

But in fact they had long since become sentient individuals with their own petty drives and needs, dividing up by their nature into Demesnes and warring against humans when not fighting among themselves. I had wished a thousand times in the Other Realm that I could go back in time and prevent the bastards from ever being created. And I understood Grandfather's dislike of the Fey and feybloods now, though before my exile I had just chalked it up to him being prejudiced from the last Fey-Arcana war.

I certainly didn't feel like maintaining the lie of Fey wonder and shininess. But I felt even less like letting my own anger hurt Pete.

"Well, actually, there was this one Fey, Blobby McPheron, or at least that's what I called him 'cause he kept telling me to not worry, that happiness was a state of mind and my mind was everything I had. He was cool for a Fey, would thank me, and tell me jokes or stories in return for the memories he viewed." Blobby had helped me stay sane those first few years. But he'd been an exception, not the rule. "I really missed you though, dude. I'm glad to be home."

"Me too. So, did you see the Silver Halls? Or the Forest of Shadows?"

"No," I sighed. "I was in the wilds with the shapeless Fey, in neutral territory, not one of the Shaped Demesnes."

"Oh. So, what did you do?"

I shifted on the couch, pulled the blanket up around myself. "I relived memories."

"Good memories?"

"All of my memories. The good ones, the bad ones, the stupid boring ones. The Fey would come to experience and feed off of the energy and emotion manifested through the memories."

Petey frowned. "Did it hurt?"

"No. I didn't feel a thing, except what I remembered, or dreamed."

"That doesn't sound so bad. I like remembering. Sometimes I

like to just lie on the grass and remember stuff. Especially about you, and Mother, and Grandma Ramirez, and Grandfather Gramaraye, and all the people I can't see anymore."

"Well, I certainly remembered you, dude." And Grandfather, since I would often feel his presence in the Other Realm. Perhaps it was just my imagination since I never felt the presence of my other family members, alive or deceased, but I preferred to think it was real, that his spirit had been able to breach the wall between Realms thanks to some spiritual aftereffect of all my Talker training with him and the resonance that had built between us.

Pete sipped loudly at his cider. "Did you remember the time we climbed up on that billboard with Dawn and ate a whole box of Ding Dongs?"

I smiled. "Yeah, I remembered that."

"And the time I dumped Walter Ryan in the trash bin because he called Dawn the N word?"

"Yes, Petey. I—"

"And the time Grandfather told Mort to do your chores all summer, and Mort made me do them instead, and Grandfather gave him a pimple potion the first day of school as punishment?"

"Pete, I remembered everything."

"And the time I got stuck crawling through the attic and we found Mother's journal hidden up there?"

I sat up, cider sloshing hot onto my hand. "The time we did what?"

"We found Mother's journal in the attic and you had to pull me out, and I got splinters on my belly?"

I cleaned my hand, and frowned. "No. I don't remember that. Are you sure I was there?"

"Yeah. Remember, Mother had drawn Kimba? Do you remember Dawn's dog? Mother was all worried because Kimba was a Doberman pinscher, and they were supposed to be mean, but Kimba was really nice."

"Yes, I remember Kimba." But not the journal, or Pete getting stuck in the attic. "Where's the journal now?"

"I think Grandfather burned it after Mother died, 'cause it was private."

I thought the Fey had summoned every last memory of mine, repeatedly, but I didn't remember anything about Mother's journal.

Had something gone wrong during the transfer, even more wrong than just not getting the changeling's memories? Had I lost some of my own memories somehow? Memory was a very tricky thing, especially when you had two beings using the same brain.

But wouldn't I remember remembering it in the Other Realm, even if I didn't remember it actually happening, or . . . something? So did that mean the memory was somehow blocked or destroyed before my exile?

The only memories that should have been officially blocked were related to my necromancy training and use—the ARC didn't want the Fey to learn any more about our magic than could be helped. But those blocks had all dissolved naturally once my spirit reentered my body. I knew, because I could remember every boring necromancy lecture from Grandfather.

"I'm sorry," Petey said. "Maybe I shouldn't talk about Mother, or Grandfather. I know you were their favorite, you all being Talkers and everything."

"Favorite?" I heard Mort's influence there. "Petey, Mother loved us all the same. And Grandfather—I'm not sure he even liked me some days." Grandfather gave me more attention and focus than Mort, Pete, or Sammy, it was true, and I loved him. But Grandfather's brand of favoritism had been less a prize and more like catching the Eye of Sauron at times. I'd tried everything to earn his respect, and still wasn't sure I ever did. "Enough about me, it's your turn. How have you been? What have you been up to while I was away?"

Petey shrugged. "Nothing special or anything. Well, I did go to Waerfolk Anonymous for a while."

"Really?" It made me uneasy thinking of Pete being around so many feybloods. It would be just like them to infect him with their waer curse for real, and claim it was an accident.

"Yeah, but the leader, he said I graduated and shouldn't come to their meetings anymore, because it made the others feel bad, not being as good at controlling their animal spirit as me."

"Of course he did. Well . . . congratulations." I took a sip of cider, and let the steam and smell of cinnamon apple yumminess waft over my face as I hid my smile, and my relief.

"Thanks," Pete said.

"And you've been helping Mort with the business?"

"Yeah. I still do all the lifting, and driving, but Mort also made me the head of security after this one time when a troll family tore up the viewing room."

I winced. "That must have been scary."

"Yeah."

There was a long silence while Pete sat hunched over the pillow in his lap like a bear embracing its cub, then he said in a quiet voice, "If I ask you something, promise not to laugh?"

"Of course."

"Promise? Because Mort would just laugh."

"I promise, Petey."

"Okay. Will you help me find a girlfriend?"

I laughed. "I'm sorry. I just—a girlfriend? What makes you think I can get you a girlfriend? I've never had one myself, not really. Besides, I just got back from exile. I don't know anyone."

He looked up with his wide, puppy eyes. "Yeah, but you're my brother," he said, as if that explained everything.

And I guess it did, in a way. As much as I might have teased Petey growing up, I'd also been the one to protect him from the worst of Mort's pranks, to let Petey play games with me and my friends, and the one he came to when he had problems. I'd always been his big brother—even though he was the one who protected me when it came to bullies—and clearly exile hadn't changed that.

After all the things about my life and the world that I'd found changed in the last few hours, all the things I'd realized were lost to me during my exile, Pete's trust in me as his big brother was comforting, and I found myself wiping tears from my cheeks.

I cleared my throat. "Are there any girls you like?"

"No," Pete said, then looked down. "Well, yes, but they're mundy girls, you know? And besides, there's my monthly visitor."

I sighed. "Pete, I thought I told you not to call it that."

"It's what Mort calls it."

"Well, I'm telling you not to, okay?"

"Okay. Trolling for vampires?"

"What? No! For cheese's sake, you need to stop listening to Mort. Call it, I don't know, your wolf time."

"Okay. Well, how am I supposed to date anyone with my wolf time?"

I had to be careful here. I couldn't just tell him he wasn't a waerwolf. After so long, he might think I was trying to trick him like Mort, and I wanted him to trust me. Especially if I only had three days to spend with him, I didn't want to spend them with him mad at me. I'd tell him, but later. Maybe I'd mail him a letter just before exile. That was best all around.

"Well," I said, "you have the potions. So you don't have to worry about transforming, right?"

"But what if I scratch or bite her?" Pete said.

I resisted the urge to ask him what exactly he thought dating involved. Then I realized I had an easy solution.

"Actually, I think I might know how to cure you, all the way and forever."

"Oh." He didn't sound excited.

"What's wrong?"

His voice went soft. "Well, if I stop being a waerwolf, there won't be anything special about me."

"What?" I sat up. "Pete, that's not true."

"Yes it is. I'm not a Talker like you, or smart like Mort and Sammy, I'm just . . . me."

"Oh man, Pete, you're totally awesome, dude! Are you kidding me?"

"Really?"

"Heck yeah! You protect us, you make us smile when we're feeling bad, you're one heck of a painter and, well, I wish I had a heart half as big and good as yours."

Pete frowned down at his chest for a second, then looked up and smiled. "Thanks, Finn."

"No problemo, brother. So, what do you say, get rid of the wolf time?"

"Maybe," Pete said, though he still didn't sound excited at the idea. "But I still have to find a girl who'd like me."

"Well, that shouldn't be hard," I said, and hoped I wasn't lying.

A knock sounded at the door, and I almost fell off the couch.

Oh crap. Had the enforcers returned?

"Pete?" a woman's voice called from outside.

"Oh!" Pete said, looking at me. "I forgot to tell her you were coming home tonight."

"Who?"

"Dawn," Pete said. "She comes over sometimes at night, to talk. She usually brings dessert." He licked his lips and glanced longingly at the door.

Dawn. I looked around the room. Memory welled up as sudden and sharp as if summoned by the Fey.

Dawn closed the door to the mother-in-law cottage and turned on the boom box radio that sat on a shelf between empty flowerpots. Tina Turner's "What's Love Got to Do With It" filled the room.

"Uh," I said. "Um." I was smooth like that at age fourteen.

"It's just a dare," Dawn said, pushing her glasses up. She'd put multicolored bands all along the side frames that matched the ones in her cornrows. "You don't have to get all weird about it."

"Mort dared you to make out with anyone in the circle," I said. "I think he wanted you to pick him."

"Yeah, well, your brother's stupid. And if he says 'Chaka Dawn, let me rock you, let me rock you, Chaka Dawn' one more time, I'll beat him stupider. So, you going to kiss me or what?"

"Really?" I glanced to the door and back to Dawn. "I thought, uh, you just wanted to pretend to kiss or whatever." I glanced down at her body. I couldn't help it, my eyes just did what they wanted sometimes.

She grabbed my hand and placed it on her "Frankie Says Relax" T-shirt—over her breast. Holy hand grenade. My hand was on her breast!

"See," she said. "They're just boobs, not magic or anything. You don't have to get all stupid around them." Her words came out fast, even for her, and her hand on my wrist trembled lightly.

She stepped in close to me, looked into my eyes. I could feel the heat of her this close, could smell coconut, and bubblegum, could hear my own heartbeat.

I kissed her.

Her lips were soft. I expected them to be soft, but not soft like this, warm and melting. Her tongue touched mine, and I tried to match its movements, to follow its rhythm as it moved in and out, a feeling like hunger rising with each thrust.

I found myself shaking now, trembling as if my muscles were exhausted.

Dawn pulled away, and I reluctantly opened my eyes to find hers staring into me. Waiting. Wary.

"Uh," I said.

She stepped back, and punched me in the arm. "Don't go all stupid on me. It was just a kiss. It's not like you're my boyfriend now or anything."

She turned and rushed out of the shed, leaving me flushed and confused.

Another knock on Pete's door broke the memory trance. I blinked. Was such vivid memory an aftereffect of exile?

Dawn's familiar voice called out, "Pete, are you awake?" She had the kind of voice you'd expect on a twelve-year-old girl if she'd been smoking for half those years—soft and sweet sounding, but with a scratchy edge.

"Yes," Pete said. "Just a minute." He looked at me, and whispered, "You want me to tell her to go home?" He didn't sound too happy at the thought.

"No! Let her in." I definitely wanted to see her, to catch up with her.

And an idea occurred to me: Perhaps it wouldn't be so hard to find Pete a date after all. Or at least a practice date.

Pete grinned, bounced out of his bed, pulled on his gloves, and unlocked the door. Dawn walked in.

The woman who stood in the doorway looked wildly different from the Dawn of my memories. The glasses were gone, replaced by a silver piercing on her left eyebrow. The cornrows had become a wavy lavender afro. And she'd gone from scrawny to Mother Goddess curves. She carried two plates with slices of what looked like berry pie.

"Hey, Petey, I brought—" She stopped when she spotted me. "Finn? Is that you?"

I smiled. "Hey, Dawn."

"Holy son of Godzilla! Long time no see. You look good. I heard you were living way off the grid down south or something, but Jesus man, why the hell didn't you ever just drop me a line? That was really shitty of you, you know?"

Ah, shoot. Of course Dawn didn't know I'd been in exile. As far as she knew, I'd simply left without saying good-bye. And she'd never had a lot of friends besides me and Pete and Sammy. Being new in town was part of that at first, and the fact that she was one of only two black kids in all of Port Townsend probably didn't make it any easier to fit in. Mostly, though, she was just weird. Like the way she said whatever random crazy thought popped into her head.

Man, I'd missed that, especially in the perpetual sameness of the Other Realm.

But I could only imagine how my disappearance must have seemed to her.

"Uh, yeah, I'm really sorry about that, Dawn. You know, I was having some real problems, and I needed to get away, time to deal and, you know . . . find myself." I winced. Lame.

"Hey, you're talking to the queen of self-exploration, my friend," Dawn said. "Not masturbation, though I'm pretty well the queen of that too, but I meant, you know, trying to figure all that head and heart crap out." She crossed her arms. "So how'd it go?"

"Uh. I . . . good?"

"You don't sound so sure there. I'd be happy to help you explore yourself some more—again, I'm talking head and heart here. Mostly. Although this place brings back some memories, huh? Well dangity, I don't want to interrupt a family reunion or whatever—"

"No, no, it's fine, really, come in."

"Naw, I think I'll just go. You've kind of thrown me, to be honest, appearing out of the blue and all, and I need to process some things. But here, you two can have these. I've got plenty more at home."

"Really, you don't have to go," I said.

Dawn set the plates on Pete's end table. "But I want to go, and these days, I pretty much do what I want."

"Well then, do you want to go to dinner in town tomorrow? With Pete and me?"

Dawn stopped, and stared at me in silence. Just as it began to feel really uncomfortable, she said, "I don't know. Are you going to wear those adorable pajamas?"

I looked down and blushed. Great.

"Probably not."

"Well, that's a shame. But still sounds delovely and delicious. Let's say the Belmont, six o'clock? See you there." And she left.

I blinked at the closed door for a second, and then shook my head. "Well, she hasn't changed much."

"Uh-huh." Pete looked down at the two pieces of pie. "Which one do you want?" he asked, as though afraid of my answer. One of the pieces was nearly twice the size of the other.

"I'll take the small one, dude. You need your pie."

Later, as I drifted off to Pete's snores, I made a decision. I couldn't control what my enemies did, even if I could prove my innocence in time to save myself. If the past was any lesson, I was pretty screwed, in fact. That didn't mean I wouldn't try to save myself, just that success was a long shot.

So I would make the best of whatever time I did have. That's what I could control. As much as possible, I would spend the next three days enjoying my family and friends.

And hopefully lots of pizza.

Hot for Teacher

That night, my dreams were vivid memories, another delightful side effect of the long exile and mind transfer. But as I dreamt, I felt like I searched for something, that I tried to reach across time to my younger self and find an answer to a question. Or maybe I was searching for the right question . . .

A car drove by as I walked Heather home from school. Foreigner's "I Want to Know What Love Is" blasted out the window.

We walked past block after block of homes that seemed to be in competition for the Most Likely to Be Owned by a Fairy-Tale Witch award, houses with towers or cathedral windows, weather-worn or with stylistic paint jobs, or that hunkered down in yards filled with overgrown gardens and gnarled trees that looked like they could come to life at any second.

I thought about trying to kiss Heather the entire walk. Fifteen years old, and I still hadn't had a girlfriend, not really. But Heather was the one.

Dennis Holmes zipped by on his ten speed. "Dorks in love!" he shouted as he passed us. Dennis was a total douche. I mean, yeah, Heather looked like she could be Pat Benatar's dorkier sister—the home-cut short hair, the glasses, the rockingest plaid and neon outfits layaway could buy at Sears. But I didn't care. And dudes like Dennis didn't know her, so they didn't get it.

"Are you going out with Dawn?" Heather asked.

"What? No! Why?"

"I just—you guys are always hanging out. And I thought she liked you."

"No. We're just friends. Neighbors. Why?"

"Nothing. I just—no reason." We reached the path leading up to her family's mobile home. "I guess I'll see you Monday." She looked down at her backpack.

"Definitely."

She didn't leave. After a second, she said, "Do you want to kiss me?"

Blood rushed from my brain faster than the Flash on speed.

"Uh," I said.

No! Don't talk! Don't mess this up!

I stepped closer to her, putting one hand on her arm, then changed my mind and put it on her cheek. I closed my eyes, leaned in, and—

"Heather!"

I jumped, and so did Heather. Her father stood on the path, anger squatting on his face like an ugly toad. That face was aged beyond its years, lined and gaunt, the salt and pepper stubble less Miami Vice and more Miami bum, and his eyes were red, bloodshot I was sure, but it added nicely to the angry vibe.

"Heather, get home, now."

"Yes, Dad," Heather said in a voice that thrummed with barely checked anger. She looked at me. "Sorry, Finn. Bye."

She rushed past her father, up the trail.

"You, stay away from my daughter," he said, echoing the advice my parents had given me, to stay away from the Flowers family.

Perhaps it was because the blood hadn't all returned to my brain yet, or maybe it was actual bravery, but I didn't just apologize and walk away. "Mr. Flowers, I don't mean any disrespect. But I would like to—"

"I know what you want, Gramaraye. And I won't have my daughter mixed up in your family's business."

I frowned. "Necromancy?"

He shook his head. "You don't know nothin'. Just go home, boy, and don't come around here, or my family, again."

I walked away, my thoughts spinning. How could I get Heather alone tomorrow?

And what was wrong with my family's business?

I woke the next morning after a long series of ever-more chaotic dreams, grasping at the blanket and looking wildly around me. My hands shook as I set the blanket aside, and I anchored myself in the primary-colored details of Pete's cottage room. Pete turned over with a snort. This was real. This wasn't just another memory manipulated by the Fey. I really was home. I let out a slow breath of relief as I uncurled, untangled, and pushed off the sofa like a badly assembled Transformer robot.

The clock read 6:31 A.M., but I didn't feel the urge to go back to sleep. Had the changeling trained my body to rise early? Gods, I hoped not.

I stretched. A lot. My body might be all athletic and manly now, but sleeping on a sofa didn't used to make my back and neck ache like I'd been used for wrestling practice by André the Giant. If this was what getting older meant, it sucked.

For my day's coming adventures, I chose to wear a long-sleeved camouflage shirt I found in Pete's closet. I figured if the Legion attacked again and I had to flee or hide for some reason, the camo couldn't hurt. I also looked for clippers in Pete's bathroom but didn't find any, so I just tied my black waves of rock-star awesomeness back in a loose tail.

Then I roused Pete and went to join what I anticipated would be a fun-filled episode of Awkward Family Breakfast, especially once I started asking Mort what he knew about Felicity's attack, and why he hadn't done more to clear my name.

I found Mort and Mattie already eating breakfast burritos in the dining room. Pete rushed off to the kitchen to get his own.

"Good morning," I said. "I—"

The doorbell rang.

Mort glanced at his watch—Grandfather's old watch. "We don't have any appointments this early."

"It's Heather," Mattie said. "She called this morning. She's dropping off some potions and giving me a ride to school." She grinned up at me. "I think she wanted to say hello to Uncle Finn."

Mort looked in the direction of the entry and stood up with an uncomfortable expression. "Well, I have chores to run anyway. I'll leave you all to visit."

He wiped his mouth and tossed the napkin on the table, then hurried from the room by the kitchen exit, ignoring me as I said, "Wait, I wanted to talk—"

Mattie rolled her eyes.

"What was that about?" I asked. Then Heather entered the dining room from the main entry.

Heather Flowers—Heather Brown, I corrected myself—had changed like everyone else I'd known. She was leaner now, the muscles of her neck and arms clearly visible as she carried a small cooler into the room. But the changes went beyond just aging. She'd always been serious, driven, when I knew her. But now resignation and weariness appeared etched into her features, and seemed to hang around her in a harsh and bitter cloud like cheap perfume.

Heather set the cooler on the table. "Well, if it isn't the mysterious Finn Gramaraye." She looked me up and down, a frown flitting across her features before she smiled.

Crap. I glanced down at the camo shirt, and resisted the urge to touch my bound puffball of hair. Perfect. I'd wanted this moment to be as embarrassing as humanly possible.

"Hey, Heather. How are you?"

"Living the high life, what else? So . . . I guess I should say welcome home, GI Joe. What are your plans now that you're back?"

My plans?

When I'd imagined this moment in the Other Realm, I'd been better dressed and groomed and had a perfect response that went something like: *What are my plans? I've spent the last twenty-five years reliving my dreams, and my dreams of you were among the brightest, the ones that led me sanely through exile like guiding stars. So I thought we'd work now on making your dreams come true, together.*

But reality made that, like so many of my Other Realm dreams, seem hopeless and naïve. "I, uh, don't know yet. I have to get settled in, figure out my options."

"Understandable," she said.

Long, awkward silence.

"I'll go grab my bag," Mattie said. She stood and rushed from the room.

"Well," Heather said, and slid into Mattie's emptied chair. "I heard a rumor that you had some trouble getting home."

"Rumor?"

"My son, Orion, he's apprenticed to an ARC magus."

"Oh." Her son. And apprenticed, which made him at least eighteen, older than Heather had been when I last saw her. Awesome. "Yeah. There was an . . . incident."

Heather glanced in the direction Mattie had gone, then leaned in closer. "You know, if you need help, or someone to talk to, I won't go blabbing to those ARC bastards."

I smiled. She hadn't changed. "Thanks. So still not a fan of the ARC, then?"

Heather exhaled through her nose. "No, you could definitely say not."

"I see you're still doing alchemy though. So you found a way to get free of them, like you always talked about?"

"Yeah." She looked down. "You could say that."

"Is—are you okay?"

"Yeah. Sorry. I just have a lot on my mind." She took a deep breath and straightened her shoulders. "You're sweet, to worry about me when you have so much going on. I meant what I said. If you—"

Mattie swept back into the room. "Ready. You want me to just wait out in the car?"

"Sure," Heather said. "I'll be right out."

"Okay. See you, Uncle Finn. Happy first day back."

"Thanks." I stood as Mattie left. "I'll walk you to the door."

"All right." Heather led me out to the entry hall in silence.

As she opened the door, I said, "So look, I set up a kind of practice date for Pete, and I'm going along to help him out. I was just wondering if, you know, if you're not busy or whatever, maybe you'd want to meet me there?"

Heather blinked. "Oh." She looked at me a second, and I saw her eyes glance up to my hair, and down to my clothes again. "I would really like that. But just to be clear, I really think maybe it's best if we keep things on a friend level. Is that okay?"

Heat blushed up the back of my neck and burned my ears.

"Yeah, totally, whatever," I said. "You know, I was just thinking like friends, you know, like we could catch up or whatever like you said, but yeah, I understand."

"Of course. Where and when?"

"The Belmont, tonight at six. I could pick you up."

"No, that's fine. There's a chance I might be late, or have to reschedule. It's best if I just meet you there."

"Okay. Great. See you tonight. Or not. It's totally cool either way."

"Right." Heather stepped outside into the dawn light. "I'm glad you're home safe, Finn."

"You too." I winced. *You too?* Really?

Heather smiled and walked to her car.

Well, that hadn't exactly gone as planned. Still, how many times had I watched her walk away, regretting I hadn't asked her out? At least this was some kind of progress. Twenty-five years late, but better late than never.

Pete appeared beside me, and glanced from me to the car. "I like Heather," he said.

"Me too. I mean, she seems to be good for Mattie."

"Yeah. But I'm glad it didn't work out between her and Morty."

A sick feeling washed over me. "Work out? Are you saying Heather dated Mort?"

As if on cue, Mort's car idled up from the side of the house along the gravel driveway.

"Uh-huh," Pete said, "but just the one time."

"Just once?" The sick feeling lessened. Slightly.

"Yep. And I wouldn't have even known about it, except she stayed the night. She makes good waffles."

The sick feeling exploded into white-hot anger.

Welcome to the Jungle

My car had been confiscated, but the family hearse still squatted in the driveway. I ran through the house, grabbed the keys from their spot on the kitchen wall, and dashed out to the car. By the time Mort had turned right onto the street, I had the engine running and the transmission in drive, grateful the old beast still ran.

I looked for Król lurkers as I nosed out into the street but didn't spot any. Maybe it wasn't the best idea in the world to go outside the house's protections, but I had the protective amulet, and I'd have to face my enemies eventually. Right then, I wanted nothing more than to confront one possible enemy in particular.

I sped up the street after Mort like the Dukes of Hazzard on a bender, the old hearse bouncing over the cracked and aged pavement and swerving a bit as I got used to the controls again. I only slowed when I spotted Mort's car ahead, turning left.

Mort wound through the lumpy bumpy streets of Port Townsend's neighborhoods and through the gates into Fort Worden State Park. My spidey sense started to tingle. The old seaside military base turned state park had been built on land riddled with a network of tunnels, some through the earth, some through the fabric of reality, the result of the last Fey-Arcana war when the folk of the Other Realm tried to establish a beachhead in our world.

I waited in the shade of a giant madrona tree as Mort drove past the row of old military housing that were now vacation rentals, and turned onto the road to the upper park grounds. I counted to three, then followed. A local family of waer-deer grazed on the open grass of the parade field. They glanced up as I drove past, their ears and tails twitching, but they didn't bound off.

Mort's car sat empty near the entrance to one of the hiking paths. I pulled past a barracks house and parked, then continued to follow on foot. I knew the path, like I knew all the paths in the park from countless hours of youthful play and exploration. It arched up over a thickly wooded hill and then meandered down to the coastline. At its peak sat a row of concrete bunkers with circular bowls that might have been mistaken for small amphitheaters but were actually foundations that once supported cannons able to fire thousand-pound artillery at any enemy ship that tried to invade the Pacific Northwest.

And on a little-used side path sat another ring that also looked like a shallow amphitheater, though this one was made of natural stone and had runes carved around its entire perimeter. Unlike the canons, which had never been fired at an enemy ship, the stone circle saw heavy use in the last Fey-Arcana war. Its exact nature and use were shrouded in mystery, however, and whatever deadly weapon once sat at its heart had long been secreted off to some ARC warehouse.

But the protective circle remained. And while not a toadstool ring, it had become a handy spot for summoning local feybloods for meetings since it also had the effect of diverting mundies away from it, sending them along one of the side paths through the forest. I wasn't a mundy, however, and so when the path branched and I felt the compulsion like a tingle between my eyes guiding me toward the left branch, I took the right branch instead.

I left the path before reaching the stone circle, and crept through the woods, reminded of the many games of tag and capture the flag played with my brothers, and Sammy, and our friends. Except this was no game.

The air was cool in the shade of the forest, and everything smelled of damp earth. Morning dew quickly soaked through my pants legs where they brushed ferns and lichen-strewn branches. I reached a spot on the hillside above the circle, and moved from tree to tree downhill until I had a clear view of what happened below.

Mort stood in the circle facing a dozen gnomes.

The gnomes each stood about two feet high, and looked much like the garden statues modeled after them. But these gnomes had clearly come prepared for trouble, or perhaps they meant to cause it. Their red pointy hats were pulled down low to shade their eyes, and they wore no shirts under their green and brown vests, revealing corded muscles covered in tattoos of vines, flowers, butterflies, and the occasional flaming skull. Instead of shovels or wheelbarrows they wielded sickles that glinted in the afternoon light.

Gnome families ruled the black market of the magical world. Stolen goods of a magical nature always seemed to find their way into gnome hands—usually because the gnomes were the ones who stole them. If you needed an illegal magical artifact, or a legal one that was too expensive to get legally, you could put a note under any gnome statue and an offer of payment, and if the gnomes accepted the deal you'd soon enough have the object in hand, no questions asked.

You don't want to know what happens if you put that same note under a plastic flamingo.

The gnomes normally delivered right to your doorstep. Obviously, however, Mort didn't want anyone to know about his little deal. The one gnome with a blue hat stepped forward from the group to face Mort, and tucked his sickle into his wide leather belt.

"Gramaraye," he said in his munchkin voice.

"Priapus," Mort responded. "Respect to the Giardani family."

"Respect us by payin' what you owe, necromancer," Priapus said.

"Pay," the other gnomes chanted in the creepy way that gnomes do.

Mort reached into the bag at his feet and pulled out a mana vessel and set it aside. Then he pulled out a polished wooden box. He opened the lid, showing the contents to Priapus.

"Ten Toths of mana, and a full set of spirit stones, as agreed.

Set these into a protection circle, and they'll help contain even an Elder Spirit."

Priapus nodded and held up what looked like a bit of carved bone that glittered with silver tracing.

Son of a bitch! Mort was trading our family's heirlooms for illegal artifacts.

Something made me look to my right, but I saw nothing except dust motes and flies dancing in the slanted pillars of light between the trees. And then a sasquatch burst out of the tree line and charged across the path at Mort and the gnomes.

Oh, crap. A sasquatch mercenary, it had to be. The creatures didn't show themselves unless paid or forced to.

The natural magic that camouflaged the sasquatch in the forest didn't work in the open, at least not against an arcana. A mundy would probably see a bear, or perhaps a hairy Grizzly Adams–looking fur trapper type. But I could feel the itch of magic between my eyes, and the giant, loping shape of the sasquatch became clearly visible. It was a male—I could tell by the extra fur that hung like a loincloth. He looked pretty much just like that grainy Bigfoot footage from the 1970's, except the nose was a lot bigger, the eyes small and beady . . . and he wore a pair of giant combat boots.

Nobody in the circle reacted. The sasquatch charged with its natural predatory speed and silence at Mort's back, and the gnomes, short as they were, appeared unable to see the sasquatch over the top of the concrete bowl.

I opened my mouth to shout a warning and hesitated. Not out of fear, but because the little voice in my head actually questioned whether I *should* help Morty. He'd betrayed me with Heather. He was betraying the family with his illegal trading, and that made it easier to believe he'd helped frame me twenty-five years ago. And damn it, what did he expect would happen when dealing with fraking feybloods?

But all that didn't matter, really. I couldn't just stand by and watch him be hurt. After all, if the sasquatch killed him, I couldn't beat him to death.

"Mort!" I shouted, and began running down the hill. "Look out!"

Mort turned, frowning, and spotted the sasquatch loping toward him. He yelped, and then scrambled at his jacket pocket and stumbled backward.

"Ambush!" Priapus shouted. "Retreat!" The gnomes formed up into a line and ran for the far edge of the circle.

I nearly twisted my ankle on the uneven ground, plowing with reckless speed through ferns and over mossy logs and bumpy roots. Hitting the level path was a shock to my entire body, but I managed to keep from falling and continued lumbering forward.

That's when a female sasquatch leaped out from behind a boulder to cut off the gnomes. Her fur was the color of redwood. A curtain of hair swung loose from where it covered her breast, like furry fringe on a halter top, and unlike her partner, her feet were bare, and big enough to make a clown feel inadequate. With one swipe of her hand, three gnomes went flying through the air. With the other, she snatched up Priapus.

The stream of fleeing gnomes split in a move as coordinated and practiced as a marching band. Priapus shouted something in squeaky Gnomish, and with a "Crack!" the stone beneath the sasquatch fractured. Vines grew up around her feet, her ankles, and kept growing.

At the same time, Mort threw a bottle at the male sasquatch—I named him Harry. What can I say, it's hard to be original when you're tripping your way through a suicidal charge to save your brother. The bottle struck Harry in the face and exploded in a yellowy liquid splash.

The sasquatch screamed and wiped at his face with the frantic motions of someone fending off bees.

I hit the edge of the circle, and this time I did stumble and fall down onto stone strewn with pebbles and pine needles. Pain burned through my palms and elbows, and pounded through my knees and shoulder as I scraped and rolled my way to a stop on the damp ground between Mort and the sasquatch.

At which point I wondered what the hell I was doing.

"Mort, run!" I scrambled to get my feet under me. My hands slipped in oily mud. Castor oil, probably mixed with marigold root, milkweed sap, and sea salt, one of the "potions" arcana kids learn when playing alchemist without the actual alchemy. Excellent natural defense if, say, a family of gnomes decides to turn on you, but little more than an irritant to sasquatches.

My advice, it turned out, was unnecessary. Mort was already running. The female sasquatch—Harriett—grabbed him by the back of his jacket, however, and swung him around to knock down a line of gnomes who had turned to attack her. The gnomes went tumbling, tiny skulls cracking against the concrete. Harriett tossed Priapus aside, and the vines stopped winding up her legs.

I scrambled toward Mort, but a hand the size of a medium pizza wrapped over the top of my head and jerked me to a neck-wrenching stop. Harry twisted me around to face him as I beat at his unyielding arm, then he grabbed me by the neck and lifted me off the ground. I began to choke, and I tore at his thick and matted fur, trying to get at the flesh beneath, but it was like digging through steel wool. Harry didn't even flinch. I heard Mort screaming in pain behind me, but it sounded distant, as though coming down a tunnel, and the edge of my vision started going hazy.

The sasquatch sniffed, and his brow furrowed. He drew me close and snuffled my head, surrounding me with his musky cedar scent, then growled in an annoyed tone and laid me gently down on the ground. As I coughed and sucked in gulps of air, the sasquatch stepped over me. I turned to follow his movement as he stomped across the mana vessel and bag of spirit stones toward Mort. Harriett held Mort dangling by one ankle, and with her free hand tore the last of the vines from her legs. The gnomes had disappeared.

I began a painfully slow crawl toward them, freezing whenever I thought Harriett might notice. Not that I had any idea what I was going to do when I reached them. The only effective attack I knew of was to tickle a sasquatch's feet, which at most would render them helpless with laughter. But to do that, I needed to get them off their feet. That didn't seem likely. Not only could they pretty much tie me up like a pretzel if they chose, but those big feet made for an awfully stable base. And Harry's feet were protected anyway.

"Is yonman target?" Harry asked.

"Yes," Harriett replied. "And meself has the badbright mage-stick." She showed the bone artifact Priapus had been trading with Mort. She dropped it, and Harry crushed it beneath his giant boot.

Harriett nodded at me. "Why no skullcrush yonman?"

I froze.

Harry looked back at me. "Himself be the one bigwarned not to hurt."

I stared and wanted to say, "Watchoo talkin' about, sasquatch!"

Someone had told them not to hurt me? What the hell did that mean? Was it possible the Legion of Doom actually didn't want me hurt? Yeah, it was possible: neither the attack on the Fey nor framing me for Felicity's death would have led to my death, at least as far as I knew. Or perhaps someone else had sent the sasquatches. Either way, it surely didn't mean anything good.

"Allthis giving meself bad rumblings," Harry said. "The gnome-brights rabbitted away."

"Gnomebrights not going tongue-wagging to the magemen for shine of getting holed theyself," Harriett said. "Youself be shiver-shaking baby-heart." She lowered Mort to the ground, still holding on to his ankle, and raised her foot to crush his head.

I'd crossed a quarter of the space, but I was still too far away to do anything. "Wait!" I shouted.

"Wait!" Harry said at the same time, surprising me. "Meself no baby heart. Rightsay, allthis not feel right."

Harriett lowered her foot to the ground, and lifted Mort back up, shaking him at Harry. "Boss say—"

"Meself not liking boss, sister-mine."

"Youself not liking nothings. Youself tiny poopy foot."

Harry roared, a sound of frustration that echoed off the hillside.

"Meself not . . . poopy foot! Meself not baby heart! *Boss* not good-entrue. We leave him, quickrun to mother's cave 'til badbright stormings done."

"No!" There was an edge of panic to Harriett's voice, and she clutched Mort's leg against her chest like a doll. "Meself needs the boss's brightjuice! Youself heartswore—"

A sharp retort echoed from the hillside, and Harry was knocked off his booted feet as if hit in the head by the invisible fist of a giant. He howled in a sound of raw anger and pain.

A battle cry filled the air, and then Zeke leaped into the concrete circle. I tried not to stare. The giant Norseman was dressed *Miami Vice*-style in an old enforcer uniform—white jacket and pants, and pastel blue T-shirt—and he'd shaved his white-blond hair into a Mohawk, Mr. T–style. He held one of those telescoping batons in one hand, and a Dirty Harry–looking silver revolver in the other. He must have followed me to the fort, hoping to catch me alone or breaking the law. At that moment, I didn't mind.

Harriett roared a challenge and tossed Mort aside.

"Grab your brother and get down to the lower bunker," Zeke said, then fired his gun at Harriett. She flung her arm up over her face and a puff of dust burst from a spot on her forearm. She fell back a step, then screamed and charged Zeke, while Harry pushed himself to his feet and shook his head.

"Go, you fool!" Zeke shouted, then fired again. Harriett twitched to the side but didn't stop her charge. She swiped at Zeke. He raised his own arm, and her clawed hand rebounded off the white sleeve of his jacket with a flash of blue light. He stumbled back, almost falling.

I sprinted over to Mort, who lay moaning on the ground. "Come on," I said, hooking a hand under his armpit and hauling him up. He staggered to his feet, and cried out in pain.

"I think my back is broken!" he said. Another gunshot rang out.

"Don't be an idiot," I replied. "You wouldn't be able to move if it was broken. Now come on!"

Together we stumbled away from Zeke and the two sasquatches.

Harry was up now and charged Zeke from the side. Zeke fired his gun at the female again, hitting her in the stomach and causing her to double over. Then he spun low. His baton caught Harry behind the knee, sweeping the creature's enormous booted foot out from under him and sending him flying onto his back once more.

Then Mort and I passed over the rise and headed downhill in a stumbling run. Mort leaned heavily on me, and with his limping it felt like we ran a three-legged race. Again I was grateful that the changeling had kept my body in good shape, and that we were running downhill. We rounded a bend, and the vista opened up beneath us. The Salish Sea gray and choppy, framed by cliffs to the left and the lighthouse to the right. And directly below, between us and the beach, stood the three-floor concrete structure of Kenzie Battery.

Kenzie Battery was a young boy's fantasy fort. The lower level was a series of open chambers connected by a labyrinth of winding, lightless tunnels barely wide enough for a person to fit through, the ultimate playground for games of tag or hide and seek. The second level was a series of steel-lined concrete rooms that had once held ammunition and supplies, and so had great rusting metal doors, and dumb-waiter-like alcoves and shafts meant to pass supplies to the upper level. At either end sat a concrete circle, perfect opposing bases for games of capture the flag. The upper level was open to the sky, a wide concrete slab, with paths that ran through the beach grass behind it down to the rocky shoreline.

Two more gunshots behind us, then the sound of heavy boots pounding down the dirt trail.

"Run!" Zeke shouted.

Near Kenzie, a family speed-walked away from the concrete structure, a father, mother, and a little girl. They must have heard the gunshots. The father spotted us, swept the little girl up in his arms and they began running in the direction of the parking lot.

Great. The last thing we needed was park rangers getting involved.

Well, actually, the last thing I needed was to be fleeing sasquatch mercenaries to begin with, but life is what happens when you're making other plans and all that. Thankfully, this early on a chill March morning, there did not appear to be anyone else exploring the battery at least.

A flicker to my left, in the trees. Damn. The sasquatches were flanking us.

"Watch ou—" I managed to shout before a ton of hairy unhappiness flew out of the trees and bowled me and Mort over. A giant hand shoved me aside, and Harriett advanced on Mort. A series of blue flashes at the edge of my vision told me that Zeke battled the other sasquatch nearby.

I leaped on Harriett's back, and tried to put a chokehold on her past the cushion of hair and thick muscle. But she just ignored me and raised a meaty hand to swipe at Mort.

I scrambled up higher on her back and fumbled at her face until I found her nose and dug my fingers in.

She roared in pain, and grabbed my wrists. She whipped me around her like a bullfighter swirling a cloak and tossed me to the side of the trail gently enough that no bones broke, though I'd have a nasty bruise. I flicked thick mucus off my fingers.

"Stay out," Harriett grunted at me, then turned back to Mort.

Zeke plowed into her side. A blue flash, and she lifted up off her big feet and flew into a nearby tree. Zeke hauled Mort up and looked at me. A bloody gash across his forehead painted the left side of his face red. "Move!" he shouted, and shoved Mort at me.

We all raced the rest of the way to the concrete bunker. We reached the sandy ground at its base, and passed beneath the arch of the concrete trilithon that stood before it.

Zeke stopped and turned, facing behind us. "Into the tunnels, hurry!"

Of course! The tunnels were too narrow for the sasquatches.

Mort and I limped into the cool shadow of the nearest concrete room, and headed for a narrow gap that led into the tunnel maze. I let Mort enter first. The tunnels were barely wide enough to enter without turning sideways. Mort let the walls support him as he slid along into the darkness. We were just inside the tunnel when the shaft of dim gray daylight behind us was blocked. I turned to find Zeke's enormous frame blocking the entrance. Then he shouted in pain, and grabbed my arm with one hand and the concrete wall with the other as his legs rose up behind him.

I grabbed his arm. "Shit! Hang on!"

I was no match for a sasquatch's strength. Zeke's fingers slipped free of their hold on the concrete wall, and I was dragged along with him back toward the concrete room.

I had only one chance. It made me queasy even thinking about it, but there was no time for internal debates over ethics or risks, or even what I really wanted.

I let Zeke go, and pulled his hand free from my arm.

"Gramaraye!" he shouted. "I'm gonna get you, fool!" Harriett pulled him free of the tunnel.

I charged the sasquatch as she turned away, and jumped on her back again. Except this time, I didn't claw for her nostrils.

I clawed for her soul.

I learned that I was a Talker when I was twelve years old.

My best friend, John, and I returned from a bike ride to the little corner mart where we had spent two dollars snuck from John's mother's purse. The little store had recently added an awesome new arcade game, Sinistar, and every spare quarter we could beg, borrow, or steal was eaten by that electronic beast.

"I hunger, coward!" John called from behind as we pedaled single file up the side of the road. "You want to stop and get some plums out of the corner yard?"

"Sure!" I shouted back.

"Sweet! Beware, plums, I live!" John gave Sinistar's mwah-ha-ha laugh.

"More like beware, you die," I called back. "I keep telling you, you need to go for a free man on the first level."

"*Whatever,*" *he replied.* "*So have you talked to that girl who moved in next door yet?*"

"*Her name's Dawn. She's weird.*"

"*Weird how? Because she's black?*"

"*What? No! Just weird. Come on, let's cross the street.*"

I rode across the two-lane road. John didn't follow right away, but took the opportunity to jump a driveway. He gave a whoop, then swerved out to follow me.

The pickup truck smashed into him full speed.

John and his bike went spinning off to the side of the road in a tangled mess. The truck skidded to a stop, then peeled out and drove off.

I jumped off my bike and let it fall as I ran across the road to John. "*Oh crap! Oh crap! John! Are you okay? Oh crap!*"

John was not okay. He shook in convulsing, rhythmic spasms of his entire body, and blood streamed from the corner of his mouth.

"*Oh fuck. Oh no. John, don't die. Don't die.*" *I fell to my knees by his side. I touched his head, his chest, gently, as though afraid I might injure them further, but I wasn't sure what to do. I'd helped my father prepare a hundred dead bodies, doing patch-and-polish work to hide the injuries and incisions for the viewings. But I'd never had to fix someone still alive.*

The convulsions grew softer, less frequent, like a fading heartbeat. Then John made one last gasp, as though he were a fish needing water, and lay still.

"*John, don't do this, man. Johnny!*" *I laid my head on his chest but couldn't hear a heartbeat. I lifted his head and put it in my lap to make him more comfortable. He just stared up at me, his mouth and eyes fixed wide open. I closed my eyes and began to rock back and forth.* "*John, come back, come back. I'm sorry. We shouldn't have crossed the road there. I'm sorry. Come back.*"

I felt a disorienting sensation, like when a carnival ride suddenly drops and it feels like you're leaving some part of you behind.

"*Dude,*" *John said,* "*did you see that jump?*"

I opened my eyes. "*John?*"

"*Yeah?*" *he said. Except he didn't talk. His eyes remained unfo-*

cused, his mouth remained fixed open, unmoving, and the voice sounded distant.

I recognized what was happening. I'd seen my mother do it before. I was talking to the dead. I was Talking to the dead.

John was dead.

Yet the fact that I could still talk to him made it less awful somehow. "Are you . . . are you okay?" I asked.

"Dude, you didn't beat me that bad. You know if it was Tutankhamen I would have totally kicked your butt."

"No, I mean, do you feel okay? Does it hurt at all?"

"Oh yeah, right, it hurts so bad. You got the high score, I think I'll go home and cry now. So, have you spoken to your new neighbor yet?"

I realized he was in a kind of shock, unwilling to recognize that he was dead. And I didn't have the heart to tell him. I waited with John until the cops and the ambulance arrived, talking about things we had done together, about plans we had made and never fulfilled, about dreams we'd shared that would never come true. And then they took John's body away.

As I was led away from his body, I felt a pull, like a rubber band being stretched, and then it snapped.

I vomited. And then I passed out.

I remained in a fevered sleep for nearly a week during which my mother nursed me with soup and potions and tears. I finally woke at home, starving and thirsty, and stumbled into the bathroom to find that I'd grown hair where none had been before. And my clothes had shrunk; they were all a little short on my now-skeletal frame.

In one week I'd grown months older.

Grandfather explained the facts of unlife to me. How Talking used my own life energy and aged me—the longer I Talked, the more it would age me, which is why Grandfather rarely used his ability, and when he did it was only to ask an important and specific question. I'd been lucky that John's own life energy was still dissipating from his body when I Talked to him and had partly fueled the Talking session; otherwise, I might have aged years rather than months and died from the physical shock.

I swore to never Talk again.

Grandfather made me learn to control my "gift" anyway.

Harriett growled as I landed on her back.

I wasn't going to let Zeke die, not like Mother died. Not like John and Felicity died. Not after he'd risked his life for us. Not when I could do something about it.

I called up the magic that glowed at the locus of my being, reached out for Harriett's spirit, and summoned her.

Harriett's growl turned into a yelp of shock and pain. She dropped Zeke and fell to her knees, her hands clutched just below her heart. I held on to her back, and to the summoning.

Magic and life energy both drained from me in a slow but steady stream.

Attempting to summon a spirit still tied to a living brain was a bit like trying to start a car that was already running, or to talk on a walkie-talkie to someone you're standing toe to toe with. It was pointless, and the screeching feedback was a bitch. I'd been prepared for the feedback. Harriett was not. She rocked her head in a violent figure eight, like Stevie Wonder singing punk rock, and screamed like a girl who'd just watched her cabbage patch doll and My Little Pony come to life and kill each other—a sound of shocked surprise filled with horror and fear and pain.

Strong hands grabbed me, pulled me off the sasquatch, and dropped me to my feet. I broke off the summoning as Zeke shoved me toward the tunnel and said, "Move!"

I let Zeke's shoves guide me into the narrow tunnel. Weariness washed over me like I'd just taken a three-day math test on a treadmill during a nonstop church sermon. I'd already lost twenty-five years in exile; I didn't want to think about how much more of my life I'd just lost.

We made our way back into the pitch black of the maze, feeling our way along the cold concrete walls, stumbling over the flat bits of driftwood laid on the floor to keep our feet above pools of collected rainwater. It smelled of wet stone and old urine, and the sound of our heavy breathing was broken only by the occasional crinkle of beer cans or clank of bottles knocked aside by our feet.

We were safe for the moment, but what now? We couldn't just wait around for the sasquatches to leave. They might simply out-wait us, or bring in smaller partners who could reach us.

A light flared in the tunnel behind me. I turned to find Zeke's baton glowing with a blue-white fire, like a small lightsaber. I imagined him saying, "I'm Zeke Skywalker. I've come to rescue you."

Instead, he grabbed me by the front of my shirt and slammed me up against the side of the tunnel. "If I die here, Gramaraye, I'm gonna kill you."

A sasquatch roar echoed through the tunnels.

Sledgehammer

Zeke looked between me and Mort in the harsh white glow of his baton, as the sasquatch's roars bounced around the concrete tunnels. "What the hell is going on here?" he demanded.

Mort muttered, "I sure as hell could use some morphine," and leaned against a tunnel wall.

"I don't know," I answered honestly. "But wouldn't it be better to talk about it back at my house?"

"Gee," Zeke said. "Let's see—go back to your center of power surrounded by a family of witnesses and hope you won't bullshit me; or we could chat here, with nobody to whine about rules, and an angry pair of sasquatches waiting to eat you if don't make me happy. Tough choice, tough choice. I think I'll go with door number stop asking questions and tell me what the hell you know right now, Chuck. How's that sound?"

Anger flared up in me, the kind of righteous, fed-up anger that comes when you find out your tyrannical algebra teacher doesn't know how to do the math without looking in his teacher's edition. I shoved at Zeke's chest with both hands, and he fell back half a step.

"Listen here, Svenny Crocket!" I said. "I got sent into exile for a crime I didn't commit, I've got someone—multiple someones, probably—trying to kill or frame me again, I've got more family problems than a white trash *Brady Bunch,* and you're going to come around and bully me like *I'm* the problem here? I just saved your ass when I could have left you to become Wookie food! So back the hell off!"

Zeke considered me for a second with raised eyebrows, then

grunted. "Yeah, you did help me. And so far, you haven't lied, least not as I can detect. So I'll give you one 'get out of an ass kicking free' card. But that still doesn't make us even for getting me nearly killed in the Other Realm, and screwing up my memory transfer. I want answers, Gramaraye, starting with who attacked you in the Other Realm and why."

"Yeah, well, when you get those answers, let me know," I said. "I'd love to hear them."

"I'm sure that statement was true, but it doesn't really deny that you know the answers yourself, now, does it? You can't expect me to believe you're all innocent here. Obviously your family is into some shady dealings." He glanced at Mort, then back at me. "And don't think I didn't see what happened with the sasquatches."

I frowned. "What? That they tried to kill us?"

"No, they tried to take your brother. You, they were careful not to harm. Now, why do you think that might be, huh?"

Damn. He'd noticed. "I don't know," I said. "And I'm getting pretty tired of saying that. The only reason I'm even here is because I followed my brother." I turned to Mort. "How could you trade away our family heirlooms? And to feybloods! And what were you trading *for*?"

"Don't play all righteous with me," Mort said sharply, then winced, and leaned back. In a more controlled, even tone, he said, "You're the one who got exiled for trying to gain power."

"What?" I felt as though Mort had just punched me in the gut. "You think I actually attacked Felicity, that I really practiced dark necromancy?"

"If you didn't, why were you exiled, huh?"

"I can't believe you! You're the one who's obsessed with running the business. You're the only one I can think of that benefited from me being exiled. How do I know *you* didn't attack Felicity? And how the hell could you sleep with Heather? You knew—"

Zeke thrust his baton between us. "Odin's balls! Enough with the family drama already! You two are like a damn soap opera. I want more answers and less whining." He pointed the baton at Mort. "What *were* you doing trading with gnomes?"

Mort glared up at Zeke. "You're not a real enforcer. Hell, you were exiled. I don't have to answer your questions."

Zeke conked Mort on the head with the baton, not hard enough to cause any bleeding or sleepy time, but damn, that must have hurt anyway.

"OW!" Mort shouted, confirming the hurtiness.

"Listen up, fool," Zeke said. "If you don't answer my questions, you're gonna *wish* there was a real enforcer here to protect you. Now, what were you trading for?"

Mort looked from the baton to me, then he sighed, and closed his eyes. "It was a Talker charm."

"Seriously?" I said. "And you accused *me* of dark necromancy?" A Talker charm would allow any necromancer to speak to the dead like a Talker, but the life energy it required could be drained from any living being, not just the person using it. Funny thing, people who used Talker charms rarely seemed willing to give up their own life to make it work. And the rituals to create a Talker charm in the first place—I shuddered. It was a very rare artifact, and for good reason.

Mort's face turned red. "It's not like I made the thing. It was already made. If I didn't use it, someone else would, and at least I'm a licensed necromancer."

"But why?" I said. "Why do it at all?"

Mort laughed. "You really are clueless, aren't you? About me, about Father, about everything."

"Gods," Zeke said. "This ain't family therapy time. Just tell me why someone would send a sasquatch team after you. Who'd you piss off with enough power or mana to pull that off?"

"Nobody," Mort said. "At least, not that I know of."

"Well, who'd the gnomes steal the charm from?"

"Some goth rocker who just thought it was a cool bit of art. Nobody who would've sent sasquatches."

I shook my head. "They destroyed the charm anyway, on purpose. I don't think they were trying to get it back."

"Right. Okay," Zeke said. He rubbed at his forehead with his free hand. "I hate when things don't make sense. I'm feeling the need to beat the truth out of some fool. That's always so much easier." He paced for a second, then said to me, "We're gettin' off track here. What I really wanna know is who the hell attacked us in the Other Realm and why? I'd say it was somebody who wanted you sent right back into exile." He looked at Mort, his eyes narrowing.

"No," I said. "Even if Mort wanted to stop me coming back, he doesn't have that kind of power, or the ability to buy it."

"Gee, thanks," Mort said.

"I'm defending you, you idiot," I said. Mort really didn't have the power to attack the Other Realm. But he might be involved with those who did. Whether he was or wasn't, I wanted him alive to question him myself, and not have Zeke beat him to death looking for a confession.

Zeke gave a grunt that could have been acceptance, or possibly the result of a bad lunch, and resumed pacing.

"Okay. Reggie used to always say, start at the beginning. You keep saying you were framed twenty-five years ago. Let's say that's true. Were you sleeping with the girl who accused you?"

"What? No!"

Zeke snorted. "I figured. So forget angry lover. Had you recently come into possession of wealth, or a valuable artifact of any kind, that someone would want?"

"No."

"Then the question is why you, and why then?"

"That's two questions," Mort said. "And the answer to why Finn is obvious. He's a Talker. What else could it be? There's nothing else all that special about him."

"Hey!" I said.

"What?" he said in a mocking tone. "I'm defending you, you idiot."

I shook my head. "Doesn't matter anyway. Nobody asked me to do any Talking, not that I remember."

Zeke began stroking his long mustache. "Maybe they wanted to *keep* you from Talking to someone." He glanced at Mort. "Or to keep anyone in your family from Talking to someone. If that same enemy sent the 'squatches, it would explain why they wanted the Talker charm destroyed."

"But then why not just kill me?" I asked. "Why go through all the trouble to frame me and attack the Fey? And the sasquatches sure seemed ready to kill Mort."

"Maybe they didn't want you dead, maybe they even need you alive for some reason. So they just want you safely out of the way."

"Wow, there's a first," Mort said. "Someone thinks Finn deserves special treatment."

"Fine," I said, not taking Mort's bait. "So, now what? We figure out who they *didn't* want me Talking to?"

"That could be anyone who ever died," Mort said.

Zeke tapped my head with the baton, causing a starburst of pain. As I rubbed at the spot, he said, "Try to remember anything significant that happened in the days and weeks before you were exiled. Any deaths, any strange visitors or clients, anything at all that was suspicious or struck you as odd or frightening."

I shook my head. "I don't remember anything like that. Believe me, I've tried remembering anything that could help me figure out what happened and why, and nothing stands out. I was living a totally normal life one day, and being charged with dark necromancy the next." I remembered the conversation from the previous night with Petey. "Although, there may be some memories I've lost, or that are blocked, I don't know. Maybe they have something to do with all this."

Zeke's eyes took on a distant haze, and he tugged a few times at his mustache in an irritated manner. Finally he said, "I might know someone who can help you remember what's important." He didn't sound too excited about it.

"I'm not letting the ARC scramble my brains to dig out memories, not until they make me."

Zeke's gaze refocused on me. "I didn't say nothing about no ARC, fool. I know a girl who's familiar with mind healing. Trust me, she wouldn't scramble an egg if she thought it'd hurt the mother hen's feelings."

"Maybe," I said. "I'll talk to her." It wasn't like I had a lot of better options.

"Oh goodie. But first, we got to get outta here." Zeke grabbed a couple of beer bottles from the ground, and handed them to Mort. "Fill these up." He looked at me. "And you, go find a couple more and do the same."

Mort frowned. "You can't dip them in the puddle yourself?"

"I don't need water. I need piss. Your piss." He snatched up another bottle, and walked a couple of feet down the tunnel, his body blocking most of the light from his baton. There was a zip, then a distinctive tinkle.

Mort looked at me in the gray light. "Is he serious?"

"I think so." I shrugged. "He must have a plan." I walked down the tunnel away from both Mort and Zeke, found a couple more bottles, and filled them as requested.

Mort and I rejoined Zeke, and I offered him my bottles.

"Not thirsty," he said. "Just hold on to them."

Zeke closed his eyes, and black lines snaked up from behind and around his neck, tying into a complex mandala that covered his throat from his chin down to his collarbone, a flowery shape made of interwoven runes and pictographs. The black of the lines wasn't the dull carbon gray of ink but looked more like thin cracks in reality through which I could see the night sky of an alien world.

Wizards were a bit like the replicators on *Star Trek*: they could transform the raw potential of magical energy into almost any physical outcome, assuming they could discover the right words and thoughts and images to materialize their goal. In olden times, wizards would lock such a manifestation into an artifact—a wand, a staff, an amulet or ring—which could perform a single function. Then wizards discovered they could make themselves into the Swiss army knives of artifacts by using tattoos.

Such tattoos were now the main tools of wizardry. And they were totally awesome.

I admit, I'd always been envious of wizards. I think all children dream of doing magic of one kind or another, but as an arcana I had the bonus of knowing it was more than mere daydreaming, it was truly possible. And wizardry was the branch of magic that most embodied the awesome potential and power of magic that a person might dream of. It was even possible I had enough of the wizardry gift to perform such magic. But I'd never know. As a necromancer, ARC law forbade me even a single tattoo.

There'd been necromancers in the past who gained wizard tattoos and, craving power, would horde the magic from the dead for themselves. Even worse were the ones who weren't satisfied to wait for a dead arcana or feyblood to come their way, but went out and deadified folks themselves just to take their magic. Add to that the possibility that a Talker might force secrets of power from the dead, and a necrowiz was a dangerous wiz if ever a wiz there was. So lucky me, I got to play with the dead but not throw fireballs or anything cool like that.

And yet people wonder why necromancers so often lurk in the corner at arcana parties, looking sullen and bitter.

I didn't recognize the mandala forming on Zeke's throat, though I did recognize some of the runes and pictographs, and worked out that the Potential had something to do with transformation. I'd seen quite a number of tattoos on dead wizards, and I knew the five standards that enforcers received for superhuman speed and strength, camouflage, armored skin, and controlling their mass. This tattoo was none of those.

I wondered if Zeke had lost his enforcer tattoos during exile. Probably. I didn't imagine it was something he would want to talk about either way.

Zeke began to utter a series of sounds, shaping and projecting the Potential into an Expression. He motioned for Mort and me to hold up our bottles, and he tapped each one lightly with the baton, causing them to clink in rhythm to his chant. The bottles in my hand continued to vibrate. The mandala on Zeke's throat pulsed with rainbow light, and that light poured out of his mouth and into the bottles.

The mandala unraveled and snaked back under Zeke's shirt. He wavered for a second, like he'd taken one vodka shot too many, and then shook his head.

"Okay," he said, and cleared his throat. "Pour the bottles over yourself." He began to do just that, yellow liquid running down over his silver-blond mohawk, dripping from his dangling mustache, trailing over the pristine white of his jacket and pants.

"Uh, no," Mort said. "No way."

"What will it do?" I asked.

"It will make you invisible, least as far as scent is concerned."

Made sense. The sasquatches hunted by smell. And using our own pee would key the magic to our personal scent. I sniffed tentatively at the beer bottle and smelled nothing. Even the stale urine and musty scent of the tunnels vanished, canceled out. I paused, then took a deep breath, squeezed my eyes closed, and poured the first bottle over my head.

When I was done emptying both bottles, I shook the excess out of my hair and carefully wiped my face before opening my eyes or unclenching my lips.

"Not that this spell isn't handy in the current circumstances," I said, "but I'm just curious. Why take up valuable tattoo space with something like this?"

Zeke shrugged. "Enforcer spells, they make you strong and all that, but sometimes you need a weapon."

I nodded to the baton. "Enforcers get enchanted weapons."

"Yeah, sure, but what if you're captured or disarmed? And guns, they can run out of bullets. So I thought, what could I use as a weapon, what kind of ammunition could I make anywhere?"

"Piss?" I said.

"Piss," he agreed.

Mort finished covering himself, and tossed his bottles aside. "Gross magical deodorant isn't much of a weapon."

Zeke grinned. "Making the pee mask our scent ain't the only thing I can do with that spell. Let's just say, when a doc asks me if it burns when I pee, I tell them, not unless I want it to."

This unfortunately caused an image to appear in my head of Zeke pissing a stream of flames, laughing wildly as he swung his . . . weapon around like a flamethrower, engulfing hordes of oncoming enemies.

Zeke clapped his hands. "Enough with the jibba jabba, let's move."

We followed the tunnels away from where we'd entered. Mort had stiffened up during our break, and leaned heavily on me now, groaning and moaning with every move.

We reached the back exit, two opposing sets of stairs that led up and out to either end of the structure. Zeke muttered a command and quenched the baton's glow.

"Which way?" I whispered.

Zeke listened for a second, and whispered back, "The wind's blowing from our left. The sasquatch would be downwind, to the right of both stairs so it can catch our scent. I'll go first, but keep an eye behind you in case it decides to come down the other stairs." Zeke led the way up the left stairs, and I followed with Mort as quietly as possible, glancing over my shoulder every couple of steps.

We emerged on the upper level of the structure. As Zeke had predicted, Harriett stood hunched over on the far side of the stairs, nose thrust forward sniffing the air. The fight or flight jolt surged through me, but we continued to move cautiously, quietly around to the side of the structure, and down a path carved into the sandy soil of the hillside. The ocean wind blasted us as we followed another path away from the beach, up and around to the front of the structure.

A man dressed in the brown uniform of a park ranger faced Harry. Zeke held up his hand, and we stopped, moving close to the edge of the structure and peeking around the corner. I wondered why we didn't just sneak by while the sasquatch was occupied, but then I understood. If the ranger spotted us and said hello, or worse, called us over, and the sasquatch couldn't smell us, it would give us away.

I relaxed my eyes, sort of like trying to make a Viewmaster 3-D image come into proper focus, and caught a glimpse of the sasquatch's glamour. He looked like one of the hair metal rockers from Poison, with a mighty mane that covered his face and draped down over his shoulders; but rather than the glam leopard-print spandex and scarves, he wore a real fur jacket, and wool leggings with furry leg warmers above his combat boots.

"I don't see any filming equipment," the park ranger said.

"We just rehearse," Harry replied.

"Well, no more fireworks in a state park, understand? And if you're going to film a rock video or whatever that might disturb the other guests, you should drop by the office and make sure it's okay first, yeah?"

"Yes," the sasquatch said. "Rock on."

"Yeah, okay. Enjoy the rest of your visit." The park ranger walked away, speaking into his walkie-talkie as he left.

Zeke motioned for us to stay put, and we waited until Harry walked back under the eaves of the structure. Then we hurried at an angle away from Kenzie Battery, and along the narrow path that led into the park. The sasquatch ignored us.

It looked like we'd narrowly escaped a hairy situation.

Who Can It Be Now?

We drove back to the house and I helped Mort to limp inside. Not even nine in the morning and already I wanted to crawl into bed and start the day over.

Mort dropped onto the couch. I glanced at Zeke's blood-encrusted face and pointed up the hall. "Bathroom's down on the left if you want to clean up."

Pete walked in and jerked to a stop, his wide eyes going from me to Mort to Zeke. I could hear the leather creak as his gloved hands balled into fists.

"Did you do that to Mort?" he asked Zeke. His voice was soft as ever, but it trembled slightly, and there was an edge to it that made me very glad it wasn't aimed at me.

"Nope," Zeke said. "He did that to himself." He moved toward the hallway, but Pete stepped in front of him.

"Petey," I said. "It's okay. Zeke helped save Mort."

Pete frowned, but stepped out of Zeke's way and looked at Mort. "Protection is my job. I am the head of security, and that's my job. Why didn't you take me with you?"

Mort shifted and grunted. "I didn't *know* I was going to get beat up, Petey, or I wouldn't have gone."

And Mort didn't want Pete or anyone else knowing he was selling off the family's heirlooms to secure his own position running the business. I glared at Mort, but he avoided my eyes, looking instead like a petulant, pouting child staring off into space.

"Everything's okay, Pete," I said. "Can you call a healer to look him over, make sure nothing's broken except his brain?"

"Ha-ha," Mort muttered, eyes closed. "I think I need a potion."

"You aren't dying," I said. Healing potions were extremely expensive and difficult to make, and largely worked by accelerating the body's natural healing process. I'd learned from Pete that we'd managed to stockpile five of them over the years thanks to Heather being a family friend and all, but still, they were best saved for a painy day. "You can wait for a healer. Pete can even hold your hand while you wait, if you'd like."

"Why?" Pete asked. "Where are you going?"

"To get some answers."

Petey crossed his arms, and his face scrunched into a determined scowl. "Then I'm going with you."

"It's not going to be dangerous," I said, though I had no way to be sure after the morning I'd had. I just didn't want him involved if there was another attack. Bad enough the whole world seemed determined to ruin my life, I wasn't going to drag my family into it, any more than they already were into it, anyway.

"I still want to go," Pete said.

Morty sighed. "No, really, I don't need that healer. Don't worry about me."

"Sorry, Petey," I said, "but you just can't go."

He growled, though it sounded more like an angry dachshund than a wolf. "I'll bite you," he said.

"I'm calling the healer myself," Mort muttered, and pulled out his mobile phone.

"No, Pete," I said. "You wouldn't bite anyone. And anyway, it isn't up to me. I don't think Zeke would bring you."

"Sure I will," Zeke said, returning at the absolute wrong time. "He looks like he'd be more help in a fight than you or your diva brother there." I looked at Mort, who was talking into the phone as though he were a dying soldier on the battlefield telling his comrades . . . *cough* . . . to go on . . . *cough* . . . without him. "Besides," Zeke added, "we're not going anywhere dangerous."

Pete beamed. I sighed. What the heck, at least I'd get to spend more time with the brother I actually liked.

"Fine. Whatever. Let me clean up and we can go."

Mort's phone buzzed, and he touched the screen. "Hello? What?" He sighed and held out the phone. "Finn, it's for you."

"Who? The healer?"

"No. It's James Grayson. It looks like he called earlier too."

Crap. He wouldn't be happy I'd left the house. That thought shot a spike of irritation through me. Who was Jimmy to act like my babysitter? I took the phone. "James! What a pleasure!"

"Finn, where have you been? I thought I asked you to inform me if you left the house." His irritated frown could actually be heard through the phone. "I can't protect you from being arrested or worse if I don't know where you're at or what you're doing."

"Well, after I saw your snappy outfit, I realized I needed to go shopping. I mean, imagine my embarrassment that half-shirts didn't make the big comeback I thought—"

"Finn! This isn't a joke! I've put my own position on the line to protect you. And you've got less than three days before the enforcers start mining your brain for information. Maybe you could try to take your own life as seriously as I do?"

I sighed. "Sorry, Grayson. You're right. I just went to help Morty with some chores, and then—" I glanced at Zeke. "I, uh, ran into Zeke. You know, the other guy who—"

"I know who Ezekiel is, Finn, better than you. He's dangerous. Did he threaten you, or—"

"No. Not at all. Actually, he helped me."

"Helped how, exactly?"

I hesitated and glanced at Morty. Best if Grayson didn't know about Mort's activities, or what happened at Fort Worden. Grayson might be helping me out, but I suspected that had mostly to do with how his association to our family might taint his reputation should I be found guilty of another crime. So while he wouldn't allow me to be falsely accused of any crime, he would almost certainly turn Mort and me both in for any real crime to avoid being named an accomplice after the fact.

"Well," I said. "Zeke, uh, thinks he can help me recover some memories that might give us answers."

"Finn, don't be foolish! That's exactly what the enforcers want, remember? Obviously, they sent him to trick you—"

"I don't think so. We're not going after the changeling's memories."

"Once they have a seer in your head, how do you know what they'll do?"

I glanced back at Zeke. He stared at me intently, like a dog watching someone about to step into his yard. If the enforcers had sent Zeke, then the incident at Fort Worden gave them enough reason to have me arrested and do whatever they wanted. But no enforcers were kicking in my door.

"I think I can trust him," I said. At least, trust him not to turn me in if he thought he could get more answers his way.

"Don't. You need to stay safe, and stay clear of any trouble. And Zeke is trouble."

"I can handle—"

"Listen! Things aren't going well with the investigation, Finn. Someone was in your home when it burned, a woman, we don't know who yet. There's no trace of the man you say attacked the transfer. And the Department of Feyblood Management says the Króls were never allowed entrance to this country. Location spells all say the nearest Król clan member is in Amsterdam."

"But I saw—"

"Someone with blond hair? In passing? At night? Finn—"

"I know what I saw! And I know that I'm innocent. And I'm going to prove it."

"Finn, don't—"

I pressed the red End button on the phone and tossed it on the couch beside Mort.

"Come on," I said to Zeke. "Let's go get some answers."

We grabbed leftover breakfast burritos for the road, and piled into Zeke's all-black Trans Am. The car looked a lot like KITT from

Knight Rider. Pete took the backseat but had to lay across it sideways since even a snake would complain about the legroom.

We rode in awkward silence for well over an hour. I realized where Zeke was driving us just shortly before we arrived. The Hole.

Its official name was Haven House, but everyone called it The Hole. A mixture of hospice, halfway house, and sanatorium for feybloods, waer, and some arcana, it housed those who were not able to care for themselves, or were a danger to themselves or others. They were not criminals, or if they had committed a crime they'd served their sentence already. They were just people and beings whose magical nature made them too dangerous to let wander the streets homeless, or go without whatever special care they required.

The Hole was where my father might be right now if he didn't have family to care for him.

I'd never been to the Hole, but I'd always imagined it was something like the mental hospital in *One Flew Over the Cuckoo's Nest,* add fairies and monsters.

"Wait," I said. "You don't plan to use electroshock or something to make me remember, do you?"

"Actually, that's not a bad idea," Zeke said. "But I'll call that plan B."

"And Plan A?" The edge of panic suddenly pressed against my chest. "Oh gods, you're not going to let some feyblood at my memories, are you?" This was too much like going back to the Other Realm. I found my hand on the door handle, and consciously put it back in my lap.

"Just relax, fool. I don't like feybloods no more than you."

"So, this friend of yours, she works as a healer here?"

"No," Zeke said in a tone that made clear the topic was closed.

"Are we going to a hospital?" Petey asked. "Do they have one of those food bars where you can pick your dessert? I love hospital pudding."

"You love any pudding," I said, trying hard to believe I could trust Zeke. "And who could blame you?"

"Not chocolate," he said.

"Nope, not even chocolate could blame you."

"No, I meant I can't eat— Oh. I get it." Pete rubbed his head. "I have to get used to your jokes again. Not even Sammy jokes like that anymore."

"Well," I said. "I guess that's one good thing about exile, life didn't beat—"

Zeke hit the dashboard. "There's nothing good about being exiled! Nothing!"

I didn't argue. What could I say? He was right.

Zeke squeezed the steering wheel like he wanted to make a balloon animal out of it, and stared ahead.

The entrance to the Haven House grounds was blocked by a black iron gate with a guardhouse. The guard recognized Zeke, and opened the gates. We passed through onto a property that was part garden, part shrubbery zoo. Pete oohed and ahhed on the drive up to the building.

The Hole itself stood on a grassy hillside, a large, blocky gray structure, four stories high in the center, with a three-story wing on each end. The windows all had bars on them.

We parked and entered the depressingly bland lobby. Zeke signed in at the reception desk. An orderly wearing a white padded jacket and gloves guided us to a stairwell that was caged in with a wire-grated security door at the bottom. Zeke stepped in front of the orderly and stopped the man with a hand to his chest.

"She's still upstairs?"

The orderly arched an eyebrow, looked down at Zeke's hand, and back up into his face. "Yes."

Zeke stepped in closer, and looked down at the shorter man with a glare like Laser-Guided Screw-You-Vision. "She was supposed to be moved down here and given a proper room 'til I can take her outta this stinkhole."

The orderly sighed. "Mr. Wodenson, your request was considered, but the doctors decided that for the comfort and safety of all, we couldn't bend the rules to—"

"I suggest them fool doctors reconsider their decision, for the comfort and safety of their own asses, or I'll bend more than their rules."

"Sir, you do realize where you are, right? We have guests whose stare can turn you to stone, or make you their willing slave. So glare at me if you want, but it isn't likely to change the rules."

"Maybe," Zeke said, and leaned in until his nose was practically touching the orderly's. "But your guests are all locked up, aren't they? Me, I can go anywhere. Even, say, your home, while you're sleeping?"

The orderly swallowed. "Fine. Whatever. I'll pass on your request. But you know, she is free to leave with you if you don't want her here. Your paperwork was approved."

Zeke jerked back. "Did you tell her that?"

"No, I just—"

"Good." His tone held clear relief. Then he sucked in a deep breath, and his glare returned. "Because I'll take her when I'm good and ready, fool, and not before. And in the meantime, I expect you to do what I asked, got it?"

"I'll do my best, of course."

Zeke grunted, and stepped out of the orderly's way. "Stop with the dilly dally then and let's go."

We filed into the stairwell. As we climbed, something howled from one of the floors above us, a cry that sounded half wolf and half Lucille Ball on helium.

"What's that?" Pete asked in a worried tone.

"Chupacabra," the orderly said. "We've had a flood of feybloods addicted to some new mana drug. They're all safely locked away on the high-security floor though. Where you're going, the residents are much better behaved. Least, as long as you follow the rules. And here we are."

We faced another security door. A large warning sign read:

CAUTION! SOME RESIDENTS MAY BE DANGEROUS. PLEASE
WEAR THE APPROPRIATE PROTECTIVE GEAR, AMULETS, OR
ARMOR AS REQUIRED FOR EACH RESIDENT.

And below that, a shiny whiteboard with a list written in marker:

> Not allowed: weapons, mana, meat, music players, knives
> or scissors, silver, iron, Diet Coke, lentils, or monkeys.

The orderly unlocked the door and led us down a hallway lined with rooms, their numbered and windowed doors all closed. Each door had a smaller whiteboard on it with additional items listed, and faces peered out through a couple of the windows, human faces more or less. One man whose mane of white hair had been shaven at the front had a single small nub of white horn showing, and an ugly scar across his left cheek—no virgin female visitors allowed. A woman blinked at me, her pupils going slitted briefly before returning to round pinholes—no flutes, lutes, or newts for her. Another woman watched me intently from above the mask covering her mouth—no riddles or books permitted.

I couldn't help but feel like maybe these feybloods should be in a zoo, not a facility like this, sharing space with arcanas. Mother wouldn't be happy at such thoughts, not after all the times she'd scolded us kids for telling feyblood jokes—heck, she'd hired a feyblood au pair for her children—but she hadn't been mindsucked by the Fey for most of her life.

We reached our destination, and the orderly knocked on the door. The whiteboard read: *No nuts, especially peanut brittle.*

"Violet?" the orderly called. "You have visitors. Your brother and two of his friends."

"Brother?" I said.

Zeke glared at me in response.

"Let them in," a girl's voice called from the room.

The orderly looked in through the window, nodded, and unlocked it. "Knock when you're ready to leave. I'll be right outside here. Oh, and keep an eye on your stuff. She has a way of, uh, squirreling things away." He opened the door and waved us through.

Zeke went first, glaring at the orderly as he passed, and Petey and I followed.

The room was larger than I'd expected, but it was still a small space to spend all of your time in. A bed, desk, and bookshelf filled the corners, all made of metal, and the shelves appeared to have metal covers that could be lowered over them and locked into place. A small television sat in one upper corner of the room, turned off and protected behind a metal wire cage. And a door led to what must be a private toilet.

Paintings of trees covered every surface of the room and furniture.

On the far side of the room stood a woman I might have described as a plump Valkyrie, except she looked less a warrior and more "Fragile: Handle with Care." It was the sadness in her eyes when she glanced over at us, maybe, or the way she stood a bit hunched in on herself.

Babies of most species emanate an energy field that creates a strong and immediate sense of protectiveness in observers. Zeke's sister gave off a similar vibe that made me want to help her somehow, even though I didn't know what was wrong.

She wore a plain gray sweatshirt and pants, and bunny slippers, as well as a paint-stained apron and gloves. She painted the wall, dipping her brush onto a pallet and then jabbing at the surface in front of her.

Zeke waited while the door closed and locked behind us, then took a single step toward his sister. "Are you okay, Vee?" His voice sounded gentle, caring. My brain had a hard time reconciling the voice to the man, like watching a badly dubbed kung fu movie when a big tough guy talks in a wimpy voice.

Vee continued to ignore him, stabbing at the wall with her paintbrush.

"Sis, I'm sorry. I told them to move you to a better room."

Vee waved the brush at Zeke, but still didn't look at him. "Sarah is angry. You told us you would take us home." Her voice had the same sad vulnerable feel as the rest of her.

"I know. But I just got back, and the place that the fool changeling had me living—I need a couple days is all, Vee, I promise. But right now, I need your help."

Vee glanced down next to her for a second, then said, "Sarah says she doesn't think we should help you until you help us."

I exchanged surprised glances with Petey, then concentrated on the area where Vee was looking. I didn't see any spiritual energy there, no signs of ghosts. Either there was something hiding behind an excellent glamour that I couldn't feel, or Vee had an imaginary friend.

"Damn it, Vee," Zeke said. "How could you say that after all I've done for you already?"

"I didn't say it. Sarah said it, because that way she'll know you're real. Our doctor told us it is very important to know what's real and what isn't. We've been tricked before." She rubbed at the back of her left hand.

"Vee, please," Zeke said, and his tone held a mixture of frustration and sadness. "Enough with the Sarah stuff. I'm not one of your fool doctors. Why can't you just talk to me? Remember how we used to talk to each other before?"

Vee shook her head. "How do I know you're not one of Sarah's dreams?"

Zeke's hands clenched into fists at his side, and he took a deep breath, then released both slowly. "Okay. Tell Sarah I'll get us all someplace with a nice big tree in the yard, maybe even a walnut tree, and I'll build her a tree house. How does that sound?"

"It sounds like one of Sarah's dreams."

Zeke blew out his mustache and rolled his head, stretching his neck so that it made several loud pops. "Okay." He glanced at Petey and me, and frowned, then took a step closer to his sister. "Remember when Father took us onto the ship where he worked, and showed us the factory and the giant freezer inside? And we got to eat in the cafeteria with the other fishers and you ate so much pudding that you threw up? Sarah wouldn't know that, right, because she wasn't there."

Vee looked at Zeke now and said, "No. It was just you, and me, and Papa." Her eyes filled with tears. "I miss Papa."

"I miss him too, little dragon."

Vee's mouth twitched up into a smile. "Little dragon. I remember when you would call me that."

"Because you were so strong. And I need my strong little sister now. I need your help."

Vee glanced at me and Pete. "You want me to read one of them, find something?"

Zeke patted my shoulder. "This one."

"Too bad," Vee said. "Sarah thinks the big one's cute."

Pete's boyish face glowed red.

That energy field I mentioned that babies give off? Well, besides protectiveness, it also creates blind adoration in most adults. Side effects include the desire to rub one's face on them, a numbing effect on the speech center of the brain, a compulsion to capture and view images of them, and an irrational spawning yearn without thought to the consequences or burdens of offspring. Interestingly, women's breasts emanate an energy that has almost exactly the same side effects on potential mates.

I don't know if Vee was actually giving off that energy field. But I felt pretty sure Petey was experiencing all those side effects right about then.

Zeke glanced back at Pete. "Don't get any ideas, loverboy," he whispered through clenched teeth.

"Hello," I said. "My name's Finn. This is my brother Pete."

Zeke turned his glare on me but didn't say anything. Vee set down her brush and pallet on the floor and stepped closer. "Hello Finn and his brother Pete." She held out her gloved hand, and as I shook it I realized she wasn't gloved to protect her from paint, but rather to protect us from her scratches. The same reason Pete wore his gloves.

She was a waer.

I jerked back, even as Pete held out his hand, a shy smile on his face. Oh gods. Poor Petey. Here was a girl who shared the same condition that he supposedly had, who'd called him cute, who was even as tall as him—and she was crazy and the sister of an ex-enforcer with anger issues. And she was a feyblood. Maybe not by birth, but a feyblood nonetheless.

Vee saw Pete's gloved hand and jerked back much as I had.

"What form?" she whispered.

"Wolf," Petey said, confusion in his voice.

"Sarah doesn't like wolves," she said. "And I don't trust other waers."

Well if that wasn't the pot calling the kettle Fey. I put a hand on Pete's arm. "My brother's a good guy. He wouldn't hurt a fly."

Vee shook her head. "No. No, this is no good."

Zeke pushed Petey back, toward the door. "It's okay, Vee, I'm getting him out of here."

"No!" I said. The thought of being locked in a room alone with a feyblood mind reader was just too close to exile. It made me shiver. "No. Pete stays."

"I'm sorry," Pete said to Vee over Zeke's shoulder, as if he'd actually done something wrong, but she wouldn't look at him. His hurt puppy expression made my heart ache. Damn it.

"It'll be okay, Petey," I said. "Zeke, if Pete leaves, I leave."

Zeke said, "Fine. Vee? I promise I won't let nothing happen."

"That's what I'm worried about," she said in a sad tone. "I just—" She rubbed at her hand. "I don't want you to go away again."

"Neither do I, sis, I promise. I won't lose control."

She turned away and said, "Okay. As long as he stays over there."

"Good," Zeke said. "Now, please, can you read this guy?"

Vee nodded and moved to the desk. She sat down on one side and motioned to the other chair.

I'd come here hoping for answers. But I'd spent twenty-five years reliving memories at the whim of others, and facing the reality of losing touch with my body once again, of anyone making me live in my memories—

I found myself shivering, and a wave of nausea rose from my stomach to my chest.

"Is this really safe?" I asked. "I mean, the enforcers, they wanted to go after the changeling's memories, and they said it might damage me."

"Yeah, that probably would," Vee replied. "But changeling blocks are part Fey magic, and really strong. You just want me to find your own memories, right?"

"Yes." I tried to move to the desk but couldn't bring myself to. It felt like I was in a dream already, the kind where your legs won't move. Tears actually welled up in my eyes. At least in the Other Realm I'd felt Grandfather's spirit keeping watch over me, protecting me. Here, in my own body, I felt more alone and vulnerable, even with Pete in the room.

"What's the hold up?" Zeke said. "You lie to me about the memories, fool?"

"No. I . . . I just think maybe this was a mistake, maybe there's a better way. You have enforcer contacts, maybe—"

"You're afraid," Vee said. "Sarah can smell it. But it's okay."

Zeke stepped up to my side. "Whatever or whoever you're afraid of, be more afraid of me if you made me bring you here for nothing."

I gave him a sharp look. "How would *you* like to have someone digging through your memories just like the Fey?"

Zeke looked surprised, and stepped back. Had he really not thought about what he was asking me to do? Maybe not. Maybe the fact that Vee was his sister made this seem perfectly safe and natural to him.

"I understand," Vee said in a soft voice. "I don't always know what's real or what is Sarah's dreams. But this is different. You'll always be aware of your body," she said. "You can wake whenever you want. You'll have control."

Control. I looked into her glacier-blue eyes for several heartbeats. There was sadness there, and empathy, I could feel it. And she was no Fey come to take from me; rather, I had come to her seeking to gain something.

I had a choice. I had control. As if that word were magic, a huge portion of my tension and nausea evaporated.

I sat down across from her. She smiled and said, "Lay your head down on the desk, get comfortable, like you're going to take a nap."

I crossed my arms on my desk.

My Pac-Man watch was missing. "Hey—"

"Oh, sorry," Vee said, and lifted the watch from her lap. "Sara took it. She does that sometimes. I'll keep an eye on her, I promise. Now lay down your head."

I strapped my watch back on.

Oh gods. I was about to let a crazy pickpocketing feyblood into my head.

But the alternative was letting enforcers and the Fey mind rape me instead.

I took note of the time, so that if any went missing I'd know it. 10:20 A.M., though it felt like it should be afternoon already.

I sighed, then did as Vee asked. The weight of my head stilled the trembling in my arms. After a second, Vee rested her hands on my head. I flinched but didn't pull away. I could tell she'd removed the gloves.

"What is it you seek?" she asked in a formal tone. "What is it you need me to find?"

"He was exiled, like me," Zeke responded. "He says someone framed him. We need to find out who."

"That sounds like enforcer work," Vee said. "I wouldn't know where to begin."

"I need to remember something about my Talker skill," I said, trying to calm my breathing. "We think it might explain why someone wants me exiled. And I think some of my memories were . . . lost during the transfer from exile. Or maybe before."

"That, I can help with," Vee said, her tone more confident. "Okay, we'll be jumping around a bit, because each memory is really like a mix and match of bits of other memories, and—well, you'll see. But the more memories we visit, the more I'll be able to find the holes and fill them in."

"Will it take long?" I asked, not sure how well I'd hold up once it began.

"It should go quickly, though it might not feel like it to you, since you'll be in dream-time. I'll need a starting point. Take deep breaths, relax, and try to remember the last time your Talker skill was used or discussed before your exile."

I closed my eyes and breathed deep. Vee was not going to feed off me, I reminded myself. I was doing this myself, for myself. My heartbeat slowed, my nausea lessened, my breathing grew slow and steady. I let my mind travel back to the day twenty-five years before, when I found Felicity's body in my bedroom.

I felt a tingling where Vee's hands touched my head, and my physical senses took on a distant quality, as though I observed them happening to someone else. But at least I was aware of them.

A roar echoed in the distance, and Zeke said in a tone that vibrated with tension, "Stay with it, Vee, I'll be right back."

And then memory swallowed me.

Wishing (If I Had a Photograph of You)

I woke with a start to R2-D2 chirping and whistling on my *Star Wars* alarm clock, the sunlight already streaming in through my bedroom window.

Ah crap! How long had it been going off? I glanced at the clock. Five minutes to eight. I might still make it.

My fifteen-year-old body was rather unhappy about being up before eleven, especially after a late night of coding "Zorrko," my latest text adventure about an arcana in Old California. But my entire *TV Guide* strategy for Saturday mornings relied on getting to the television by eight, and went something like this:

I would claim the right to watch *Voyagers!, Ewoks,* and *Droids.* At which point Petey would throw a fit about wanting to watch the *Muppet Babies* and *New Zoo Review.* And Sammy would back him up, knowing I would give in to Pete, and he would be easier for her to then goad into watching *The Smurfs* (as she was obsessed with Smurfette).

At which point I would say fine, but afterward I get to watch *Dungeons & Dragons, Land of the Lost,* and *Spider-Man and His Amazing Friends,* absolutely no buts, takebacks, or requests to play ColecoVision. Once negotiations were complete, I could go back to bed for two hours.

I sprang from bed, made a dash for the door—and tripped over a body on the floor.

A pile of dirty clothes cushioned my fall. I flipped over, scrambling back from the body in surprise. The zippers from a pair of parachute pants dug painfully into my palms.

"What the—"

The body was our au pair, wearing her white sleeping robe, with her hands crossed over her stomach and her blond curls fanned out around her head, free from their normal braid. And there was a red stain on her stomach, over the locus point where magical energy lived. For a second, I thought her dead. But then her chest rose, and fell.

"Felicity?"

She didn't respond. I rushed to her side, shook her shoulder gently. "Felicity! Wake up! What happened?"

She didn't stir.

"Father!" I shouted. "Father, help!"

I'd learned CPR after Johnny's death. But Felicity wasn't dead, didn't need her heart or breathing restarted. She needed a healer.

"Father!" I took her hand. Her fingernails were always dirty from working in the garden. "It'll be okay," I said, tears welling in my eyes. "Hang on."

Felicity, who had been with us for two years, since Mother's death, was a feyblood witch from Austria earning her residency status through the ARC. She was twenty years old. She often smelled like Irish Spring. Mort believed he was going to sleep with her. Petey loved her dinosaur-shaped pancakes. Sammy resented her at first for taking Mother's place in any way, to the point where she'd even made a voodoo doll of Felicity, but even Sammy had finally begun to warm up to her.

I found it embarrassing when she washed my underwear.

My door opened. Father looked down at me and Felicity and blinked. "Finn, what did you do?" he asked. He sounded confused. Maybe he was in shock. First Mother's death, now Felicity, dying.

"I don't know what happened! Can you help her?"

"You didn't try to Talk to her, did you?"

"No," I said. "She's not dead."

"Good. You get dressed," he said, and walked away. "I'll call the ARC."

"What about Felicity?" I asked, but Father didn't answer. I

hoped it was just that he was out of hearing, and not because he thought I'd really hurt Felicity.

I looked down at Felicity and said the only thing that came to mind. "I'll find whoever did this to you, and make them pay. I promise."

⬛

"There," Vee's voice settled over my awareness like misty rain. "A connection."

⬛

"I promise," I whispered to my mother, who lay in her casket with eyes closed. "I'll make you proud."

I did my best to ignore the people entering the room in ones and twos behind me, taking seats in the rows of benches. Family friends, neighbors, local arcana, and my uncles, aunts, and cousins, I could feel all of their eyes on the back of my head.

My mind fixed on the small details of Mother's face, the professional observations. Father had done an amazing job with the restoration. I couldn't imagine how difficult that had been for him to work on Mother's face, but the results spoke of his love. ARC Laws said she could not be dissipated by her family, that her magic had to be collected by an impartial other party, but Father had fought for the right to at least prepare her body for the viewing. "Nobody knows her face like I do," he said.

I was glad for it. She didn't look like the photo beside the casket, a frozen moment—she looked healthy, full of life, with that slight smile at one corner of her mouth that said she was about to share an amusing fact. I didn't want to see her as a lifeless shell. And I didn't want to remember her as she was at the end, struggling against cancer that infected a body made vulnerable by the drain of Talking, laying there an impossibly thin caricature of herself.

"I should have spent more time with you," I whispered. "I'm sorry." She was asleep so often near the end, and with the tubes, and the way she looked—tears flowed freely down my cheeks. "I'm sorry." I was so stupid. It didn't matter how difficult it was for me. I would never get another chance to talk to her. To tell her how much I loved her. To hear her say she loved me.

I felt a familiar tugging at the locus of my being.

A hand clenched on my shoulder. "I know that look," Father said, his voice rough with emotion. "You can't Talk to her, son."

"Why not?" I whispered without looking at him. "It's my choice, isn't it? It's my life energy. How is saying good-bye to Mother going to harm anyone?"

He squeezed my shoulder again. "I know. I know it hurts, Finn. You think I want to let some stranger dissipate her? You think—" His voice broke. He continued after a second, "You think I don't want to talk to her again, just one more time, even if it's through you? But that is exactly why the law is not stupid. Don't forget about your great-grandmother—" His voice broke again, and he squeezed my shoulder so hard it hurt.

My great-grandmother had died of grief, or more specifically from Talking without stop to her dead husband until her life energy was used up, and she joined him.

"I only want to say good-bye," I whispered.

A brief moment of disorientation—the haze of grief—and my father suddenly stood at my other shoulder. I turned to give him a hug.

"Thank you, son," he said as the hug ended. "Why don't you go and sit until the ceremony begins. I want a few last minutes with your mother."

I nodded and walked up the aisle, past the gathered relatives and family friends. I didn't meet their eyes but continued out to the entry area where I could be alone for a minute.

More pictures of Mother had been arranged on boards to either side of the double doors. I moved past them, away from them, to the hall where people had hung their coats, where I could wipe at the tears that burned my eyes without being watched by everyone.

"You like *Star Trek*, right?"

I turned, startled as much by the question as the voice. Dawn stood there. It was the first time I'd seen her in a dress, and with bows in her cornrows.

"What?" I asked.

"I saw this one movie where the pointy-eared dude—Spork?"

"Spock."

"Right, Spock, he died. But they put him in this missile thing and shot him onto this planet that was, like, a paradise."

"The Genesis planet," I said automatically.

"Yeah. And someone told me in the new movie, the planet brings him back to life. Anyway, what I'm trying to say is, it's messed up seeing your mom in a casket. I know, because I did too. But maybe just think of it like one of those missile things, and really she's just being shot off to paradise, where she'll be reborn."

"Actually, the Genesis planet became a hell and fell apart. And Spock was reborn because he transferred his consciousness into Doctor McCoy." I couldn't tell her, of course, that doing that might actually be possible if it wasn't entirely forbidden. Or that the reason my mother got cancer in the first place was because she'd weakened her body and spiritual barriers by Talking to spirits who, as far as I could tell, weren't in any paradise.

"Oh. Shit," Dawn said. "I suck at this, I guess. Well, here." She went to her jean jacket and reached into the pocket. She pulled out a Walkman. I'd been asking for a Walkman since the previous summer, but Father said we didn't have the money, and Mother—

I turned away.

"I picked strawberries all last summer to get the money for this," Dawn said. "This year I'm going to get a ColecoVision. If you want, you can come with me. To pick strawberries I mean, not to get the Coleco. Though you could do that too. Here." She handed me the headphones, tapping my arm with them to get my attention. "Put them on."

I did as she instructed. Her tone and manner made me feel that I didn't have a choice.

"I listened to this after my nana died," she said, and pushed a button on the Walkman. A few seconds later, the music started. The sound quality was amazing, like my father's good stereo.

A man began singing in a deep voice filled with sadness and longing. Leonard Cohen, singing "Hallelujah." The lyrics didn't speak to my feelings, not really, but the feel of the song, the emotion of it, hit me hard. I didn't believe in any particular god— knowing the truth behind the mundy myths made that a little difficult—and I didn't get the sense that the singer did either, but when he sang the word "Hallelujah," I burst into fresh tears.

I turned away from Dawn, embarrassed to be crying in front of her. She put a hand on my arm.

The music, and Dawn's touch, felt like they possessed some kind of magic—not one of the five known branches of magic but a power that reached deep within me and tore down the dams holding back my grief. I wanted to talk then, to let my thoughts and feelings come pouring out, but I swallowed the words. Dawn was a mundy, and so much of what I felt and thought was tied in one way or another to our family's magic, and to the Talker gift I shared with my mother. I couldn't share the truth about magic with Dawn, no matter how much, in that moment, I wanted to.

I had some idea then of why Grandfather always said I would never be truly happy with a mundy partner, that when the time came, I should marry an arcana girl.

"Almost there," Vee said. "I just need to fill in the edges—"

"How much more of this are you going to make me relive?"

"Just enough," she said. "What?" Her tone suddenly held worry, fear.

"What what?" I asked, but then I realized Vee wasn't speaking to me.

"Grab a partner," my biology teacher said.

Grab a partner. Words not quite as bad as "pick teams" for a thirteen-year-old geek like me but still less fun than, say, a physical exam.

Then Heather Flowers stood next to me. "Wanna be partners?" she asked.

"Uh," I replied. Despite my worries about being the last person in the room without a partner, I wasn't sure how to respond. Time slowed down to a bionic crawl as I felt the eyes of my classmates on me.

I knew who Heather was, of course. Her family were arcana, alchemists, though Mother forbade any of us kids from going to their home, and the Flowers family rarely showed up to local arcana gatherings. They were among the black sheep of the local magical community.

But that wasn't why I hesitated. What really made me hesitate was the fact that being a lab partner with Heather Flowers was dangerous. Not in the social reputation sense, though that possibility squatted in the back of my mind like one of the dead clammy frogs waiting for our dissection. No, what made her a risky partner, the reason I felt pretty sure she was talking to me and not one of her fellow brains in the class, was that she tended to make things go boom—in her chemistry class, in photography class, even in home ec. Plenty of students had made cakes implode, but how did you make a cake *ex*plode?

Alchemy gone wrong, I felt pretty certain.

"Have you been, like, sniffing the formaldehyde?" Heather asked.

"What?"

"Well, you're just staring at me like you're totally stoned or something."

"Oh, uh, sorry." I glanced around. Everyone else had partnered up. Awesome. "Sure, we can be partners."

"Bitchin'," she said.

The whole Valley Girl thing had been cool for, like, a week the previous year. Heather had never exactly been on the leading edge of cool. But like me, I guess she hoped to start fresh as a freshman, to put the nerd label from elementary and middle school behind her.

For me, that meant a spiked haircut with a rat tail, a new

wardrobe from the thrift stores that looked like Adam Ant's cast-offs, and plans to make the creepiness of my family's "mortuary" business work for me rather than against me. I was sure to make new friends any day, and not just the ones in my programming class.

Heather's attempt at reinvention had been even less successful. She did cut her hair short over the summer, Pat Benatar short, and started wearing this cool shirt that buttoned diagonally across the front in a flap like the new Starfleet uniforms. She also stopped wearing her glasses except when reading. But that just meant she walked around squinting all the time. The only groups she joined were still academic groups. And she wore that one same "cool" shirt every other day for weeks.

And then there was that whole tendency to make things go boom.

"Seriously, hello?" she said. "Do I have a booger showing or something?"

"Sorry," I said and blinked. "I just have a lot on my mind."

"Uh-huh. Come on, let's go dissect Kermit."

I followed her to the nearest lab station where a frog waited in a shallow pan, and the sharp smell of the formaldehyde made my nose burn.

"Uh, do you want to cut the frog or take notes first?" I asked.

"Actually," she whispered and glanced around us, then leaned in a bit closer. "I wanted to see you make the frog jump."

"What?"

"You can do that, can't you? Animate it, make it, like, a zombie frog?"

Now I glanced around to make sure nobody could hear us. "Are you serious? Even if I could do that level of nec—of stuff, you know we're not supposed to do . . . stuff without permission, not until we're ARC licensed. We shouldn't even be talking about it."

"I know, but—" She looked out the windows at the gray clouds a second, then said, "You know about my parents, right? Of course you do. I know the other arcana, they talk about us."

I shrugged, feeling very uncomfortable. "Yeah, I mean, it's not like my family sits around gossiping about you or anything, but I heard maybe your parents were . . . doing stuff they shouldn't be?" Like dealing potions illegally to the feybloods, and maybe even being potion addicts, though if that were true I didn't understand why the ARC hadn't done something about it. I knew that the Flowers were the poorest arcana family in Port Townsend, so they couldn't be making much money selling potions if it was true.

"Yeah. Well, I'm not going to end up like them, okay? But you know how the ARC is, they stick their noses in when they shouldn't, and totally ignore it when people are doing stupid crap if it helps whatever bogus secret plans they have. If I try to just leave, to get a good mundy job, they might screw it up for me just so I *have* to do alchemy for them."

I frowned. "Really? I don't think the ARC would—"

"How would you know?" Her harsh whisper took on an edge as cutting as a Ginsu lightsaber. "You live up in your nice little house with your nice little family sucking magic out of dead people and giving it to the ARC, of course they wouldn't give you any problems. But how nice do you think they would be if you stopped doing what they wanted, stopped giving them all that magic? Even if it was making your life hell, even if—"

She choked to a stop, her face going red. I glanced around, and realized several students were watching us. I gave a nervous smile, and a couple of the students gave me a "Dude, glad I'm not you" look before pretending to go back to their work.

"I'm sorry," I said once the masking buzz of other conversation finally began again. "I guess I didn't really think about it."

And it was weird to hear my family being held up as a desirable one. I mean, my parents didn't beat me or anything, but they were also constantly making me work and study necromancy, and putting all kinds of restrictions on what I could do or who I could hang out with and—but I guess, as Little Einstein would say, it's all relatives.

"Yeah, well, forget what I said," Heather snapped. "I'm not

asking you to apologize for the ARC. I just want to know if you'll make the stupid frog jump."

"Why? How would that help?"

"I need something to pay off the ARC with, a new alchemical formula that's really worth something. I think I've even found someone who'll help me, if I can make the right potion for him."

"And the frog?"

"The mundies use formaldehyde to preserve dead flesh, but I think I can use it as a base for a formula to actually reanimate dead flesh. If you animate the frog, I can sneak some samples of it, break down the alchemistry of it."

"Uh," I said. "Don't get mad, but you sort of have this reputation for making things blow up, and I don't want a Michael Jackson Pepsi incident here, end up running through the halls with my hair on fire or something." A valid concern, since I had enough Dippity-Do for a half-dozen candles holding up my spikes. "Besides, I really can't animate the frog. It's forbidden, part of the dark necromantic arts. It's like . . . turning lead to gold for alchemists."

"I won't catch you on fire, I promise," Heather said, a promise I wondered if she'd given before; a promise, I thought, one should not have to make at all in a high school biology class. "And I don't care about the ARC's stupid laws. Alchemists are forbidden to turn lead to gold because the gold always ends up radioactive. But the only reason necromancers can't make zombies is because the ARC says so, because the ARC doesn't want anyone having more power than them."

"I don't know about that. . . ."

"Come on, what are they going to do, exile us? You think my . . . accidents in those other classes are the only times I screwed up? No. And do you see any enforcers dragging me off?"

"I guess not," I said. "But really, I can't do it. I don't know how." And I had no desire to be grounded for life even if I could.

"Fine. Whatever. Let's just do the stupid assignment then. I'm sure you know how to cut up a dead body better than me, so you cut, I'll write." She picked up the worksheet and held it close to her face, squinting at the instructions.

We did the assignment in a cloud of awkward silence and chemical stench, exchanging only enough words to identify the various organs and other body parts, to make slides for the microscope and agree on the results.

As we worked, I got to really study her, up close. She wasn't shy, or afraid to talk or assert herself like I'd thought, at least not when it came to getting the class work done. I caught her squinting at me a couple of times, studying my face as I worked on the frog. So I looked at her when she squinted and focused on writing out the results. She really was pretty cute, actually. And I felt bad that I hadn't made more of an effort to be friends.

After class, we entered the stream of students in the hall and headed in opposite directions, but I stopped and hurried back after her instead.

"Hey, Heather, wait a second."

She flinched and turned to face me. "What?"

We stepped close to the wall, out of the flow of students.

"Look," I said. "I was thinking, maybe you'd want to come over to my house and hang out sometime?"

"What?" She sounded as surprised as I was at the question.

"Uh, well, we have a whole library of books on necromancy and stuff, I just thought maybe you could learn something to help you. And, well, we could play games, or you could hang out with my sister, if, you know, you didn't want to go home or whatever."

She squinted at me a second, frowning, perhaps trying to figure out if I was serious. Was she blushing?

"Okay," she said. "I mean, yes, that would be really cool. I—"

Then something weird happened in her chest area. There was a light snapping sound, and a twitch, and suddenly it looked like her small breasts had shifted to either side of her chest, impossibly far apart. It took me a second to realize what had happened, and then only thanks to the fact that I had a sister. Heather must wear a padded bra, and it had snapped apart in the front.

Her light blush turned into a full red glow, and she turned and ran up the hall, one arm held across her chest.

"Finn! Wake!" Vee's voice cut through the desire to rest, and I rushed up toward white, fluorescent light.

I emerged from the world of memory to the bleachy antiseptic smell of Vee's room, and to my arm and hand tingling from the pressure of my forehead. My watch blurred into focus. 10:27 A.M. Only seven minutes—

My head jerked up at the sound of the door crashing in.

Vee screamed, and I blinked as my brain attempted to make sense of what my eyeballs were shouting at it.

The door to the room leaned open and dented, the door frame splintered, and from outside came shouting and growling and howls of pain.

And just inside the door, Elvis threw a karate kick at Petey.

Burning Down the House

"Pete!" I shouted, as though he needed my warning.

Petey doubled over as Elvis's foot made contact with his gut.

"Ha!" Elvis said, and ran a hand through his glossy black pompadour. "You ain't nothing but a hound dog, son!"

He wasn't the real Elvis, of course. As should be no surprise, the real Elvis was an arcana. He hoped to forge the perfect musical weapon against the Fey, who enjoy human music the way a slug enjoys a salt-covered hammer. But the Fey managed to infect him, turning him into a waercreature. Although the resulting change in his metabolism led to tragic consequences for his waistline and his life, even worse is that those infected by the Elvis waerform turn into pale imitations of him when the conditions are right—for some, if they hear an Elvis song; for others, when they enter the dark energy vortex of the Las Vegas area; or, in some extreme cases, if they smell peanut butter and banana.

I jerked to my feet, sending my chair tumbling back, and rushed to my brother's aid. Vee was a step ahead of me, several steps actually, and shouted as she swung her chair at Elvis's head.

"Ki-YAH!" Elvis shouted, and punched through the chair, breaking it to pieces. "You'll have to do better than that, pretty momma."

Pete howled like a wolf, and charged shoulder first into the waerElvis, lifting the portly man from the ground and sending him flying back out into the hallway.

Vee followed Pete, wielding a chair leg like a club and making a weird chirping, chittering noise.

"Wait!" I shouted to the empty doorway as I chased after her. Unsurprisingly, the doorway didn't respond.

The hallway was a chaos of noise and motion and bodies.

The orderly who'd shown us to the room lay just outside the door like a welcome mat, eyes closed. Vee knelt beside him, slapping him—I assumed to wake him and not as some kind of payback.

A number of other bodies lay on the floor around the doorway: a leprechaun, a satyr, a reptilian dog with quills I assumed was a chupacabra—the mana-drug addicts. The Legion must have released them somehow. Perhaps the Legion had even addicted them to begin with.

I had a sudden memory of Harriett, the female sasquatch, saying she needed juice.

To my right, Zeke fought a small troll. By small I mean it only stood as tall as Zeke, even though every part of it was four times as thick, and hard as stone.

But Zeke wasn't just fighting. He'd gone berserk. Literal, old-school berserker. He shrugged off punches from the powerful gray creature, and responded with two-handed blows of his baton that sounded like a hammer clunking into concrete. The troll barked in pain and fell back step by lumbering step. Zeke laughed maniacally, spittle flying into the air, and shouted a string of words that sounded mostly like gibberish.

To my left, Petey battled Elvis, and a kappa—a feyblood with yellowish skin, beaklike nose, a humpback that was hard like a shell, and an indentation on its head that held water. The creature's indent was covered with an upside-down plastic bowl secured with an ace bandage.

Pete landed a punch that floored Elvis, but at the same time the kappa threw itself backward at Pete in a kind of wrestler move, hitting him with its hard shell. Pete tripped backward over the fallen satyr and tumbled to the floor. The kappa advanced, its mouth snapping.

I grabbed the unconscious leprechaun, and with a running

start I heaved him at the kappa's head. Yeah, I'd probably have some really bad luck coming my way. But that was a problem for another day.

The kappa hissed as the tiny red-headed man crashed into it, knocking off its bowl. The distraction gave Pete time to scramble back to his feet.

I knelt beside Vee, and began patting the orderly down.

"What are you doing?" Vee asked, the edge of panic in her voice.

"This guy's got to have a tranquilizer gun or sleep powder or something for situations like—aha!" I found a wand. I pulled it out and turned it round in my hand. Thankfully, there were instructions.

> **DIRECTIONS: point at target and say "Dormio."**
> **CAUTION: make sure thick end of wand is toward you.**
> **Don't use on persons driving or operating heavy machinery,**
> **or standing on a ledge or other precipice. Don't—**

Blah blah bah. I pointed the wand at the kappa, and shouted "Dormio!"

My hand tingled at the discharge of magical energy. The kappa jerked as if slapped, slumped down to its knees, and then leaned back against the wall, its eyes closed. It began to snore.

I turned to zap the troll, but as I did Zeke brought his baton down on the creature's head in an overhead swing, and the troll crashed to the ground.

Zeke turned toward us, panting, and I raised the wand again, realizing I might have to use it on him. His eyes were wild and showed no sign that he recognized us as he took a step toward me, raising his baton. Then he wavered, the baton fell from his hand, and he slumped to the ground.

I looked at the wand, and to Zeke. "I didn't—"

"It's what happens after he berserks," Vee said, rushing to his side. "He needs rest, and food, or he's going to get really sick."

"Let's get out of here," I said. "Pete, lend me a hand with Zeke?"

As I stood, light flared at the end of the hall. The exit door swung shut, and through the narrowing opening I saw the blond and bearded enforcer—pretend enforcer—who'd attacked my transfer, as he turned away and headed down the stairs. But not before leaving us a present. A tiny lizard no bigger than a mouse scampered toward Zeke and Vee, its body wreathed in orange flames. Behind it, fire spread from its burning trail, skittering across the top of the tile floor and seeking more flammable sustenance.

Vee scooped up Zeke's baton as I pointed the wand at the salamander. "Dormio!"

Nothing happened. As I'd feared. It was difficult enough binding a wizard spell to a wand, they rarely had more than one charge.

Pete reached Zeke and Vee. He grabbed Zeke under his shoulders and dragged him back, away from the salamander.

Striking the creature would only cause whatever struck it to burst into fire. What sort of lunatic had let a salamander out of containment? How did the people here deal with it?

I looked down at the orderly. The gloves. Like Zeke's uniform, they were probably enchanted to protect the wearer. I yanked and pulled at them, and managed to get one off, then the other. I pulled them on as I ran at the salamander.

"Finn!" Pete cried out as I sprinted past him.

I reached the salamander. It hissed at me, and tried to jump past me, at Zeke.

I slapped my hands together, catching it in mid-air. Already I could feel the heat burning through the gloves, rapidly growing too hot to handle.

I turned, ran, and tossed the salamander into the kappa's exposed water indentation.

Steam exploded outward, filling the hallway like fog. A fire alarm sounded, and sprinklers burst into action, raining water down on us. When the fog had cleared, I could see the salamander crawling weakly out of the kappa's indent, its fires quenched. It flopped glossy red to the ground, hopefully unconscious. And the kappa would be fine. It might have a bit of a burn on its skull, but the worst losing its water would do is paralyze it, and already the sprinkler system replenished its supply.

I stood panting for a second, looking at the carnage and chaos in the hallway and feeling a wash of relief at surviving. And a bit of pride as well.

In this moment of victory, I'd like to thank Mom for teaching me about elemental feybloods, Dad for telling me to always wear protection, and Zork for teaching me to solve a problem by combining two objects found in the environment.

Zeke moaned, snapping me out of my moment of self-congratulation.

"Okay," I said. "Let's get out of here before the enforcers show up."

Vee looked down at the troll, tears streaming down her face. "Is it dead, do you think?"

"I think it's for the Hole wardens to figure out. We need to go."

"You don't understand. This is what happened last time. He went berserk and killed the waer who bit me. I don't want him to go into exile again." She grabbed my arm. "Please, don't let them send him into exile again!"

The troll twitched, and Vee burst into tears of obvious relief. Pete and I hefted Zeke to his feet, and half dragged him down the stairs, Vee following close behind.

Orderlies blocked the bottom of the stairs but let us through. Vee had to sign release papers, and we roused Zeke enough to do the same. The staff seemed a little dubious about releasing Vee into Zeke's care given his state, but thankfully they had more pressing issues to deal with, and, I got the impression, were happy enough to have one less person to care for.

We all squeezed into the TransAm, with Zeke and Vee in the back, and Pete drove for Port Townsend, the engine roaring and the tires squealing like in a movie. "KITT, turbocharge!" I said. Nothing happened. Oh well, worth a try.

I looked back at Vee. "You okay?"

"Sarah hates cars," she said. "But . . . I'm okay. Thanks."

"Finn?" Pete said. "Are we going to get in trouble for beating up all those feybloods?"

"No, of course not," I said. "It was self-defense."

Unless the Legion meant for us to get in trouble. Did they know why I'd come here? Were they worried about the memories? Or had this in fact just been another attempt to frame me for something, and maybe kill off some of my support at the same time? Either way, if they somehow made it look like we were responsible for releasing the feybloods as well as attacking them, it would stir up even more trouble for me. And it wouldn't help smooth relations with the Fey either.

I'd certainly be enjoying another visit from the enforcers soon. But there was nothing to be done about it now, and no reason to worry Petey.

Zeke began acting more himself by the time we got to the house, able to walk on his own and even talk a bit (mostly to complain about the way Pete drove his precious car), though I could tell he wouldn't be in shape for fighting any more monsters without at least a good night's sleep and a heaping bowl o' Wheaties.

We all hurried inside, and I sighed as the tingle of the house's wards washed over me. I imagine for some folks it is a particular smell, or maybe a set of family photos in the entryway, that gives walking into their parents' home that unique comforting feel (or in some cases, I suppose, a discomforting feel). For me, it was the tingle of the wards that always told me I was truly home. That, and Mother's greeting.

"Oh! Hello," Mother's ghost said as she floated into the entryway, her black hair trailing her like a cape. "New friends? Are these the kids from Arkansas?"

That was a code our family used to ask if someone was an arcana.

"Yes, Mother. Excuse us, we need to do our homework."

Heather swept down the stairs that faced the front door and smiled when she spotted me. "There you are! It's a half-day at the school today, so I brought Mattie home, and I thought maybe we could—" Her eyebrows rose as Zeke and Vee stepped up beside me. "Oh. You've got company."

"Yeah, they're, uh, friends. This is Zeke, and his sister, Vee. They're staying here for a bit," I said.

Zeke and Vee looked equally surprised and unhappy at the thought. Petey, on the other hand, smiled like I'd just announced a second Christmas.

"I don't think—" Zeke said.

"I really couldn't—" Vee said.

"See?" I said, as Heather descended the remaining stairs. "It's practically like they're family already. Everyone wants to argue."

Zeke glowered at me. "We ain't family."

"Fair enough," I said. "But someone seems determined to make my life suck. And like it or not, Zeke, it seems you and your sister are now on their radar. I just figured you'd feel better having your sister close by in a warded home while you help me stop the bastards. Unless you have a better plan?"

Zeke scowled at me for a second, but finally shook his head.

"Right," I said. "So, Zeke can take Pete's old room, and Vee can have Sammy's."

"Well," Heather said, stepping close to me. "Gone twenty-five years, and still taking charge."

"Um—did you see Mort?"

Gods. Really, Finn? Idiot.

"Yes. He's taking a nap."

"Oh, good." That would give me time to think of how to get the truth from him. I looked at Vee. I felt a twinge of nausea again at the thought of letting Vee probe my memories, but nothing like before. "I know you've been through a lot already today, but would you be willing to finish what we started?"

Vee shrunk in on herself. "Sarah wants a nap. Maybe tomorrow."

Zeke put a hand on her arm. "I could sleep for a week myself, sis. But it's important, and this fool only has a couple days to figure things out."

She sighed. "Fine. But you owe me."

"What's all this?" Heather asked.

"Nothing," I said. "Vee's just helping me remember something."

Heather frowned, and put a hand on my arm. "I don't know if that's such a good idea, Finn. I mean, memory magic is touchy stuff as it is. No offense," she said to Vee, then squeezed my arm. "Your body's been through a lot of magical stress, and you've had a Fey lurking around in there for a while. Surely there's another way. I know Magus Grayson is working hard—"

I put my hand over hers, and gave a gentle squeeze. "Thanks, but I'm not going to put my life in the hands of the ARC again. You totally get that, right?"

"Yes, it's just, you've been gone so long. I hate to see anything happen to you, is all. It's . . . nice having you back."

"Believe me, I like being back," I said. "But Vee's already raised some memories with no harm I can see so far—"

"Blocked memories?" Heather asked. "Did you remember anything new?"

"No, not yet. But—"

"There you go, then. I'm sure she's great at pulling up normal memories, but digging past memory blocks, that's dangerous. I know there are potions that help with memory. If you give me just a little time—"

"That won't help," Vee said in a quiet voice.

"What?" Heather asked.

"Memory potions," Vee said. "They make it easier to remember things. But they can't find specific memories, or get past blocks. Potions can't replace a complex skill. No offense."

Heather's eyes narrowed.

I turned so that I was between her and Vee. "Look, I understand you're worried about me, and I appreciate it, but I have to do this."

Heather looked like she wanted to argue further, but then her shoulders slumped, and she sighed. "Okay. I'll be here with healing potions if you need them." She looked past me to the others.

"You all look like you've been through hell. I'll go make some lunch while you're risking Finn's brain. It's the least I can do."

"Yes, please!" Pete said.

"Thank you, Heather," I said. "Really. I'm glad you're here." I gave her hand a final squeeze, then said, "Follow me, guys." I led Zeke, Vee, and Pete back down the left hallway to the family library.

The midday sun shone through stained-glass windows depicting unicorns dancing in a forest, painting the library with mottled pastels. A table with chairs of carved dark wood and red cushions sat at one end, and at the opposite end rested a chaise longue, and a wide marble pedestal on which sat a plain leather-bound tome. The walls were lined with books on black oak bookshelves, except the far wall, which held a fireplace and, above it, a silver-coated sword that once served as our family's protection against angry customers. And in the room's center, two deep lounge chairs with sides like forward-swept wings flanked a short end table with a Tiffany lamp.

I'd spent more hours than I cared to remember in this room, learning arcana history and necromancy on top of my regular schoolwork.

Pete went to his favorite shelf, filled with illustrated bestiaries. Vee plopped down in one of the lounge chairs. She motioned to the other one, and I joined her. Zeke took a final glance out into the hall, then closed and locked the door and leaned against it, arms crossed and eyes drooping.

Vee closed her eyes. "Just give me a minute. I'll try to reform the map in my head so we don't have to start from the beginning again." She sat still as a statue for a minute, strands of pale hair falling over her face. Then her eyes opened, she leaned forward, and said, "Relax, close your eyes." I did, and felt her hands on my head. "Sink back into the chair, feel yourself melting into its cushions, falling down into sleep, down into dream, down into memory . . ."

I tried to study the tome of necromantic rituals laid out on the library's large table as Grandfather sat reading his own book across from me, but my brain refused to focus. I stole glances at Mort and Petey to my left, and Jimmy Grayson to my right, but they were staring intently at their own books.

I looked back down, and tried to distract myself by making up my own School House Rock songs in my head, arcana-style.

> *I'm just a wiz, yes I'm only a wiz, and I'm bored with all the family biz.*
> *Elbow room, elbow room, not often there's a coffin with elbow room.*
> *Necromancy Nancy, what's your fancy? Summoning spirits and dressing up dead people.*

That didn't help.

"Grandfather?"

Grandfather looked up from his book. He was a thin man, his gray hair always meticulously combed and parted, and on most days the lines on his face vigorously defended it against any smiles that attempted to invade its stoic position. He was the kind of man who always dressed for dinner, even if the family was having pizza.

But he also frequently shared secret and forbidden nuggets of arcana knowledge, or the kind of joke equally secret and forbidden under Mother's rules. He'd given us boys pellet guns with silver pellets for Christmas (for shooting garden fairies, he'd said with a wink). And apparently he'd actually asked Mother's permission to take Mort to a nymph over by Lake Quinault on Mort's fifteenth birthday.

The trick with Grandfather was knowing when he was in a serious mood, or a joking mood. Get it wrong, and it usually meant extra chores or a long lecture.

"You have a question?" he asked. "It had best be about necromancy. This is study time."

Clearly, a serious mood day.

"It is," I said. "But not from the book. I had a dream last night that I was a bird, and it made me wonder—if a necromancer can animate dead birds, and if a person's spirit, their memories, can be transferred into the Other Realm, can't I maybe, you know, transfer myself into a bird someday?"

Mort, Pete, and Jimmy all stopped pretending to study, and looked at Grandfather to hear the answer.

Grandfather closed his book. "I'm glad that you're creative and explore new ideas. So many of the young arcana these days, they seem content to just sit around with their television and Atari machines and grade school magics. But you must be careful. You—"

"Of course, I'd be careful," I said. "I wouldn't ever—"

"Respect!" Grandfather said, slapping the arm of his chair.

I sank back in my chair. "Sorry, Grandfather."

"Hrm. As I was saying, you must be careful. Trying something like transferring yourself into a bird, or any other body in this world, you would need to keep your own spirit from dissipating or worse, and that would require, well, more magic than you could access now that the Other Realm is walled off. This is why our lessons are so important. There are many things you might do with your power, Finn, that would destroy you in the end." He leaned forward and patted my shoulder in a stiff, awkward manner. "And I for one would be very sad if you were destroyed."

"Yes, Grandfather, but—" I stopped myself. I didn't want him to feel I was arguing with him.

"But? Go ahead, ask."

"But the Fey were able to inhabit animals as well as people. Isn't that how the feybloods were created? The waer, and the monster races?"

"Some of them, yes. And don't let your mother hear you call them monsters; you know how women get about such things. But we're not Fey, Finn. We are arcana. And be glad of it. We're their creators, their betters. We gave life and shape to them in the ancient days when we spirit quested into their realm, or rather the Fey took on shape and life by feeding on our memories, on our dreams and fears as we passed through their realm. It is this fact that allows our spirits to inhabit their realm and bodies still."

"But haven't they evolved?" I asked. "They have entire kingdoms now in the Other Realm."

Grandfather snorted. "The Fey have no true form, no true self like us, Finn. They're nothing but a manifestation of our carelessness, a constant reminder of our folly. And they are just waiting for their chance to start another war, never doubt it."

"But . . . what about Uncle Ichabod?" Petey said. "He married a dryad. Auntie Sylvia seems nice, and really smart too."

Grandfather frowned at Petey, who sank back in the chair, shrinking in on himself. "Clearly, I shouldn't be speaking of such things around you, not at your age, anyway. But yes, there are some reasons to envy the Fey. Their immortality, for one. If not for that advantage—" He glowered off into space for a second, then shook his head. "Get back to your studies now."

I slumped back into the chair and sighed. "Yes, Grandfather." Mort and Petey echoed me. Jimmy remained silent.

"Is something wrong with studying?" Grandfather asked. "I could have you clean out the furnace if you prefer?"

"No!" we all said and looked down at our tomes.

"Actually, Mortimer, Paeteri, why don't you go fetch lunch. I'd like to talk to Finn and James alone for a bit."

"Yes, Grandfather," Mort said, and shot me a glance full of resentment, then stood and moved to the door. "Come on, Petey. They're going to share secret Talker stuff."

"There," Vee thought. "That was the final piece of the puzzle. I have mapped the holes, now I just need to find my way through."

"Can you tell who made them?" I asked.

"No. It was skillfully done, though. It is a bit like the walls around the changeling's memories, though weaker, and it was done separately, just days earlier, I think. I found—there. Got it. Now let's see what was hidden."

I stood with my father looking down at Mother's body, as family and friends who had gathered for the viewing shifted and coughed and whispered at our backs. Father squeezed my shoulder. "I know. I know it hurts, Finn. You think I want to let some stranger dissipate her? You think—" His voice broke. He continued after a second, "You think I don't want to talk to her again, just one more time, even if it's through you? But that is exactly why the law is not stupid. Don't forget about your great-grandmother—" His voice broke again, and he squeezed my shoulder so hard it hurt.

"I only want to say good-bye," I said.

"There," Vee's voice whispered.

Grandfather stepped up to my right, and Father shifted over to my other side.

"Someday," Grandfather said, and looked at me with eyes rimmed red. "When you're ready, and if you truly need it, you will be able to speak to your mother again. I made sure of it."

I frowned, and looked up at him. "But her spirit will be warded." Necromancer spirits were always warded, to protect the secrets of their family's craft and to protect the secrets of every spirit they'd ever Talked to.

"I'll let you in on a little secret," Grandfather said, leaning in closer and whispering softly. "There are ways to Talk to a spirit that's been warded, if someone of your close family blood did the warding. Ways I will teach you someday."

Father shook his head. "We must let her spirit rest, Finn. She earned it."

Grandfather shot Father a scowl.

I knew what secret Grandfather spoke of. The Anubis spirits.

A flash, as though my mind jumped to hyperspace, and then—

"Finn!" Petey called ahead of me in the crawlspace that ran around the attic.

"Pete, shhhh!" I whispered. "Someone might hear you below." I nearly sneezed from the dust.

"I'm stuck!" Petey said.

I rolled my eyes as I rounded the corner and saw Pete ahead. He was wedged between wooden beams in the narrow, triangular space where the slope of the roof met the unfinished floor. "That's it, Petey. No more third helpings of Boo Berry from now on."

"That's not fair! The hole is a triangle, and I'm . . . Pete shaped. I just don't—hey, there's something here."

"What?" I asked as I reached him.

"A book. I . . . I've got it. Pull me out."

I grabbed his feet, backed up a bit on my knees and elbows, and pulled.

"Ow!" Pete said. "My belly!"

"Exactly," I said.

Pete slid free, and sat up, dislodging some insulation. He had a leather-bound journal in his hand.

"What is it?" I asked.

He opened it up, flipped through the pages. "I don't know. Here." He handed it to me, panting, and began examining his stomach, plucking at splinters.

I took the journal and flipped through it. It was filled with tiny, neat writing, and hand-drawn images.

"That looks like Kimba," Pete said, glancing at the pages.

The picture did look a bit like Kimba. But as I read the writing beneath it, I learned it was actually an Anubis. Not the Anubis of legend, but one of many Anubis spirits the legend was probably based upon, ancient Fey spirits who crossed into our world long ago and remain disembodied, surviving by feeding off the magic and life energy of the deceased.

According to the writing, a ward against Talking was really a binding of sorts on an Anubis spirit, not on the actual spirit of the deceased, forcing the Anubis to block all attempts of the deceased's spirit from returning to our world even if summoned.

Still, while there was no way to summon a warded spirit, the journal said this didn't prevent a necromancer from visiting a warded spirit on the other side of death's veil, if a bargain could be reached with the Anubis warding that spirit. But, it warned, such a bargain was likely to carry a heavy price for the necromancer.

I flipped more through the journal and realized what it was. "Pete, this is Mom's diary. I don't think she'd want us looking at it. Put it back, quick, right where you found it."

Another flash and jump—

I rushed to Felicity's body, spread out on my bedroom floor.

"Father!" I took Felicity's hand. Her fingernails were always dirty from working in the garden. "It'll be okay," I said, tears welling in my eyes. "Hang on."

My door opened. Father looked down at me and Felicity, and blinked. Something red speckled the edge of Father's sleeve. Not faded red, not dark brown, but red as the blood on Felicity's robe.

"Finn, what did you do?" Father asked. He sounded confused.

"I want to wake!"

I rushed up into warm light, to the smell of old books, and the velvety feel of the chair's fabric. I blinked and looked around the room, half expecting to see my grandfather still there. But he wasn't. He was dead. I was no longer a boy.

And my father had attacked Felicity.

Where Is My Mind?

I sprang to my feet, and rushed toward the door. Zeke pushed off the wall like a drunk and put a hand against my chest.

"Woah there, Speedy Gonzales. What did you remember?" He sounded almost too exhausted to speak, but his hand remained solid as a wall.

Petey stepped up beside me. "Don't push my brother around."

Zeke's eyebrows rose. "Or what, Paunch? You'll give me fleas?"

I put a hand on Pete's shoulder. "It's okay." I glanced back at Vee. Did she see my memories, or only the shape of them? Had she been able to read my thoughts even when I wasn't talking to her? She just sat rubbing her eyes and pinching the bridge of her nose.

"Don't look at my sister," Zeke said. "It's a simple question. What did you remember?"

"I'm not sure yet. I need to check on something, process it a bit."

Zeke's eyes narrowed for a second. "Fine. Just don't leave the house without me."

"Wouldn't dream of it," I said, and moved past him. I opened the door. Heather jumped, raising one hand as if to knock.

"Oh! Hello," she said. "I was just coming to let you know lunch is ready."

"Thanks. Is Father in the dining room?"

"No. Mattie took a dish to him in his room."

"Okay. I need to talk to him before eating." I slid past her.

"Sure," she said. "Should I have Petey show these nice folks their rooms if they're staying?"

I turned back. "Actually, if you could take Vee? She's not comfortable around, uh, waerwolves."

"It's okay," Vee said. "Pete seems . . . safe."

Zeke's gaze snapped to Petey, and back to Vee, and he frowned. "Why don't someone just tell us where the rooms are, and I'll take my sister there."

Heather sighed. "I'll show you both up, it's no trouble at all. You said Pete and Sammy's old rooms?"

I nodded, and Heather led Zeke and Vee back up the hall.

Pete watched Vee leave. I patted him on the arm. "I can tell you like her, bro, but I don't think it would work out."

Now Pete looked as though I'd canceled Christmas.

"Why not?"

"Well, her brother wouldn't let it work, for one. And she's—" I was going to say a waer, but that would only appeal to Pete. He thought himself immune to the danger of infection, and he couldn't care less that she had a Fey spirit infecting her. "I think she may be a little crazy, Pete. I'll find you a girlfriend who's right for you. Trust me."

"Okay." Pete didn't look or sound convinced at all. A lost puppy peering in through an orphanage window during a rainstorm couldn't have been sadder, and my own heart lurched in response.

"Hey," I said. "Tell you what. If you want to help out Vee, maybe you should call Sammy and have her come over? I'm sure Vee could use someone to talk to besides her brother. A woman." It didn't seem like she and Heather were meshing. And Sammy's experience helping women adjust to new lives might be especially helpful.

A look of purpose replaced Pete's sad expression. "That's a good idea. I'll call Sammy."

He scuffled off toward the kitchen. I started down the hall on the opposite side of the stairs, back toward the master bedroom, but had a better idea. I diverted to the basement and grabbed an amulet first, then resumed course for my father's room.

The master bedroom was the only bedroom on the main floor. Bookshelves lined the walls, still mostly filled with the romance novels and literary classics my mother had loved. In one corner sat the small love seat where, as a child, I'd sometimes curled up in Mother's arms while she lay there and read a book in the evenings. It appeared smaller than I remembered, the colors faded.

Father sat at his small desk by the window looking out on the garden. I remembered the desk covered in pieces of polished driftwood and shells and bits of brass and copper, the materials from which he created the little art pieces he sold in the souvenir shops on Water Street. Or used to sell, I suppose. Now the desk held only a half-eaten bowl of pasta, and a small tree in a ceramic planter. Father inspected the tree branch by branch, a pair of pruners in his right hand, and he appeared oblivious to my arrival.

Mattie sat at Mother's old desk, eating pasta and typing away on what I realized was a connected Apple computer and monitor that together were no thicker than a magazine. I stared at it for a second, reliving the same sense of lost time and opportunity that seeing her mobile phone had given me. Then Mattie looked up and smiled. "Uncle Finn! How's it going?"

"I've had better days," I said, watching Father from the corner of my eye. He still showed no obvious reaction to my arrival.

"Oh, I'm sorry," Mattie said. "Hey, I downloaded a Commodore emulator on my laptop. Wanna see?"

Even though I only understood half of what she'd just said, I understood Commodore and could tell she was trying to connect with me.

"I can't right now, but definitely later, I promise," I said.

"Sure, okay. No problem."

She sounded her normal bubbly self, yet I got the feeling she heard that promise a lot.

"Really, Mattie, it sounds fun. Tell you what. I have some stuff to do, but when I'm done, I'll find you and we can compare computers. I'll show you how awesome Wizball is, and you can show me all the cool stuff I've missed. But first, I need a few minutes alone with Father."

"Sure. I need to vacuum anyway." She folded her Apple computer closed and left.

I shut the door behind her, then moved to stand beside Father, on his left, away from the pruning shears.

"Father?"

"Hello, Finn, yellow Finn, hope you know how to swim." He didn't look at me as he spoke.

"Father, what happened with Felicity? Why was I framed?"

Might as well get right to the point. I already knew from my recovered memories that Father was involved somehow in Felicity's assault. And I felt certain he'd been possessed when it happened, that something had made him do it. That explained his madness, and why he would have done something so terrible to begin with. And that explained the how of it as well, since he couldn't have performed necromancy, dark or otherwise, on his own. But I needed to be sure.

Father looked up at me, and nodded sideways at the tree. "Branches and brains," he said. "Make you do funny things." He returned to studying the branches.

"Father, concentrate! Try to make sense. This is important. What possessed you? Who keeps trying to frame me? Why did Felicity blame me? Did she do it on purpose, or did somebody make her do it? Please, help me understand."

Father prodded at a branch with the pruner, and waved me away with the other hand. "The blame for frame falls mostly in the rain. Go dig dirt, it's what monkeys doo doo."

I didn't immediately dismiss his words as gibberish, hoping that maybe a real answer hid among them, that enough of my father remained to try to reach me through the madness. Father had a touch of prophecy, and that gift was always made stronger by madness for some reason, which led to the unfortunate fact that the more important a prophet's words, the less likely they were to be heeded. "Are you saying—is there a clue of some kind buried in the yard outside? Or someplace else, in the dirt?"

Father laughed. "Monkey did it in the parlor with the banana lickity-split. Dance little monkey!" He danced the shears across the desktop and hummed tunelessly.

I paced away from him. Tears burned my eyes. There were no clues in his words, just gibberish after all. The truth behind everything that had happened to me was within reach, and yet still unreachable.

But I still couldn't believe that my father was beyond help, beyond helping me. I'd seen him stare down trolls who demanded all the magic from their deceased, seen him spend hours patiently piecing together a delicate artifact, felt his strength and quiet wisdom throughout my life before exile.

I paced back to him, and knelt at his side. I squeezed his arm. "Father, please. I need your help. I need you. I know you can do this, you can fight this madness and speak to me clearly. What happened with Felicity?"

Father frowned, and the whole left side of his face twitched. He shook his head, as though arguing with someone, and pounded his fist on the table. "No! I . . . I have to make the snakes dance right. Go ask your mother. She knows everything about every ring around she knowsy." He shuddered, and closed his eyes for a second, then went back to inspecting the branches.

I sat a minute and watched him, watched his bleary eyes scanning the branches, his left cheek still twitching every second or so in a barely perceptible tic. Finally I stood and rubbed his back with one hand. "I love you, Father. And I forgive you. I know you didn't want to hurt Felicity, or me. I promise you, I'm going to make this all right somehow."

A tear fell from Father's nose onto the nearest tree branch, but otherwise there was no sign he understood me.

I crossed the room to a painting that hung between two bookcases. Created hundreds of years before my birth, the painting showed a desk of wood that looked black except for the deep red-brown highlights, its surface covered by a book, ink, quill, and

several objects of silver and bronze and bone, artifacts of the necromantic arts. Painted above the desk hung a round mirror of
polished bronze framed in what looked like pale wood, but I
knew it to be shaped bone.

I touched the painting and felt a chill seep from it into my
hand. I called up a portion of the magic at my core, and shaped it
to my intent. "*Facere realis,*" I said. The magic drained from me,
through my hand to the painting, and the glamour lifted. I stared
into a real bronze mirror now, which reflected my face back at me.
"I am of the family blood and have a right to that which you protect," I said. My face in the mirror wavered, and then said back,
"Proceed then, child of Gramaraye."

I reached into the painting, now become a portal, and grabbed
the book. If I'd not been of Gramaraye blood, the portal would
have closed, neatly cutting off my arm and adding my hand to the
objects in the painting. But I was able to pull the book free without incident.

I knew right away this wasn't the family ledger I remembered.
The leather binding was new, not blackened from age, the pages
white and crisp, not yellow and filled with the records of all those for
whom my family had performed necromantic rites over the past few
centuries. And the entries in this book started soon after my exile. I
reached back in, searched the desk drawers for the old ledger, patting
around the edges of the space out of sight just to be sure. No luck.

"Damn it!"

I turned to ask Father where the old ledger was but realized
that would be pointless. He wouldn't answer. And I could guess
anyway—destroyed, to hide exactly what I wanted to know.

I did find a copy of Grandfather's will, and glanced at it before
putting it and the new ledger back. Grandfather had set up rules
for inheriting the family business—first, that the person be of
Mother's lineage, thus bypassing Father even though he'd taken
the Gramaraye name. And that it go to a Talker, and if no Talker
was of age and able to run the business, then to the oldest Gramaraye that had a child to carry on the family line.

Which conjured up a terrible thought—did Mort have a child just to secure his right to run the business?

I looked up, in the direction of Mort's room.

Father wasn't really the killer, he was the weapon. He was as much a victim as I was. And how perfect an opportunity for Mort, to get rid of Father and me with the same single act of betrayal and murder and have the business all to himself, to be in charge the way he always wanted.

Yet I'd seen Mort in all his inept glory and thought I'd made some progress in understanding him. I still saw him more as the boy I grew up with than whatever man he'd become. I just couldn't believe that Mort, my big brother, would have willingly participated in harming Felicity and Father, even if he nurtured some kind of obsessive grudge against me.

Still, I wasn't willing to risk anyone else's life on that brotherly feeling. I would need to confront Morty and get some answers from him once and for all.

I restored the glamour on the painting, and crossed back to Father. He rocked in small, fast bobs now as he studied the tree, and he began to hum the tune to the Doors' "Light My Fire."

"It's okay, Father," I said. "Here, I want you to wear this. It'll keep you safe. Do not take it off." I showed him the amulet I'd grabbed, a protection against possession, and hung it around his neck. I kissed the top of his head, tucked the amulet beneath his shirt, then left and closed the door.

I stood in the hall facing the door, collecting my thoughts.

If I told the others about Father, it could destroy what life he had left. Mort might insist on sending him to the Hole. Pete would be devastated. Sammy, I had no idea how she'd react. And if the ARC found out—I didn't know what they'd do. But I certainly wasn't going to throw my father to the enforcers on maybes and half-crimes. If he'd been possessed, then he wasn't at fault for the crime. And he didn't make Felicity testify against me.

But if the Legion possessed Father before, even through the house wards, I had to assume they could again. The last thing I wanted was to wake up in the morning with Vee's body on my floor, or someone else hurt.

Father did have the amulet now. And if someone possessed him again, it would most likely be while we slept like last time, when the Legion needed some kind of sneaky work done and no necromancers were awake to banish the possessing spirit. Besides, I'd already slept one night at home without incident, and it'd been twenty-five years since the last possession. Whatever trick they used to get past the house wards before, maybe they couldn't do it now.

Either way, it looked like I'd be crashing in Father's room until this was over. If he did become possessed, I didn't want him harming anyone but me, not if I was keeping silent about the danger.

Well, I had to tell Zeke the truth, at least. I couldn't put his sister in danger without telling him. And I'd need his help to confront Mort.

"Uncle Finn?"

I jumped, and turned to face Mattie.

"Uh, hey. Yes?"

Mattie looked down and tapped at the carpet with her toe. "I know you and my dad don't get along the best—"

"No, Mattie, that's not true—"

"It's cool. My dad doesn't get along with a lot of people. But . . . he's not a bad person. He's just worried all the time about the business and stuff, you know?"

"I know."

"And Sammy, she tells me stories about when you guys were younger, how you used to play around, and play jokes on each other and stuff. That you and my dad were like a team, at least until you had to do all the Talker training."

"Yeah. We definitely had some good times." Lots of them dangerous and stupid, but good.

"So, well—maybe you can try to be his friend again, and help him have a little bit of fun? I just—I worry about him. I don't want him to be so unhappy all the time, you know?"

I sighed. "Yeah. Okay, Mattie. I'll try."

Mattie smiled. "Thanks, Uncle Finn." She put on a pair of headphones and went bouncing back up the hall, humming.

Talk about bad timing.

I left to go find Zeke, and accuse my brother of framing me.

Bésame

I headed back to the dining room and found Heather and Pete sitting at one end of the table, eating pasta. Heather also had a bottle of wine out, and it looked like she'd drunk at least half of it. Zeke stood spooning pasta into two shallow bowls. He looked ready to fall asleep on the spot, wobbling a bit as he stood there.

The smell of butter and garlic made my stomach growl, reminding me I hadn't eaten since breakfast. Heather stood and moved beside me. She put a hand on my chest and asked quietly, "You okay? Need to talk?"

"No. Thank you. Maybe later, but not right now." I looked past her. "Pete? I don't suppose you know what happened to the old family ledger, the one in Father's room?"

"Someone burned it," he said around a mouthful of pasta. "Same night as . . . you know, the bad stuff happened. At least that's what Mort said." He went back to eating.

Right. Pretty much what I'd guessed. "Actually, Heather, maybe you could help me research something? You were always better at the research than me."

"Of course," she said. "Whatever you need." Her cheeks flushed red.

Music began playing from her pocket. She pulled out a mobile phone, and frowned at it. "I . . . I need to take this. Excuse me?"

"That's fine. I need to talk to Mort about something first anyway." I moved to stand beside Zeke as Heather rushed from the room. "Where's Vee?"

"Upstairs resting," he said. "She's pretty drained." He paused and looked at me. "I hope it was worth it."

"It was," I said. My mouth watered as I eyed the pasta, but lunch would have to wait. "I'll walk up with you, and we can talk about it."

"And don't worry," Pete said as he scooped seconds of pasta. "I'm saving room for dinner with Dawn."

Oh. Crap. I'd completely forgotten about the "date" I'd set up. What had I been thinking?

"Dinner?" Zeke asked. "You taking your brother on some kind of date?"

Petey blushed. "It's just a practice date. Right, Finn?"

"Totally," I said.

Zeke turned, scowling. "You can't be serious?"

"We can talk about it upstairs," I said.

Zeke yawned. "Fine. Then let's get walking so you can start talking, fool."

Neither of us spoke until we reached the second-floor landing.

"So," Zeke said. "You're going out on a date while someone's trying to kill you?"

"Yes, I am. Whoever's out to get me, they've already taken twenty-five years of brotherhood away from me and Pete. I'm not going to let them take any more. Besides, my enemies don't seem to want me hurt, right?"

"Yeah, I noticed," Zeke said. "One of the many reasons I don't believe you're all innocence and flowers, Gramaraye, whatever you say. But even if you're officially in hands-off status, that won't do much to keep them from hurting your fool brother or his date."

"Pete's date is a mundy, and we'll be around other mundies most of the time. If the Legion attacked mundies—"

"Legion?"

"It's what I'm calling our enemies. If they attacked mundies, that'd get the ARC's attention in a way I don't think the Legion wants."

"Maybe not. Still seems like a pointless risk."

"Helping my brother isn't pointless."

Zeke headed for the hallway to our left. "Fine, little miss Emma, you go play matchmaker and I'll keep trying to get us clear of this mess."

"Wait, did you just make a Jane Austen reference?"

Zeke paused, then resumed walking. "The only Austen I know is Steve Austin, the six-million-dollar man."

"Uh-huh. Then what did you just say, then?"

"I don't remember."

"I do. My mother used to read Austen's books, and I'm pretty sure—"

"I'm pretty sure you'd better drop it, fool! If Steve Austin ever writes a book—"

"Wait, the character, or the actor?"

"—writes a book about his adventures kickin' ass, and they make it into a movie starring Chuck Norris, then you go right ahead and bring up the name Austen again. Otherwise, why don't you just start over and tell me about the memories you recovered?"

Right. I took a deep breath.

"Twenty-five years ago, something possessed my father and made him attack Felicity," I said in a low voice. "Or made him help her to stage an attack. I'm guessing whoever summoned and controlled the spirit is the same enemy trying to frame me now."

Zeke stopped in front of Vee's door and squinted at me for a second. "All right. So we go to the ARC and let their sorcerers poke around in your father's head now that you know where to start, maybe figure this all out. We can get some enforcers in here to protect everyone, and finally start busting some feyblood heads for answers—"

"No," I said. "You're not telling the ARC about my father."

"Maybe you're not, martyr boy, but why shouldn't I?"

"Because of your sister."

Zeke leaned over me. "Is that a threat, Gramaraye?"

"No. I meant because you understand. You went into exile to protect your sister. It turns out, I went into exile to protect my father. And I'll do so again if I need to. If Vee had been made to commit a crime without her control, and you served your exile in her place, would you want the ARC to then turn around and exile Vee anyway?"

Zeke leaned back, and glanced at the door to Vee's room. "No. But if you're right, if your father was made to commit the crime, the ARC will see that too and be lenient. Besides, when the ARC learns they exiled you for twenty-five years and you really were innocent, they're going to owe you big-time."

"Right. And the reason they would owe me big-time is they screwed up. So why should I trust they won't screw up again and send my father into exile? And even if they don't exile him, he'll be thrown into the Hole. Would you take that risk with Vee?"

Zeke exhaled heavily through his nose and pursed his lips, causing his long mustache to dance. "Fine. We do it your way for now. I'm too tired to deal with the ARC anyway. But if they come to us, I'm not lying about what I know."

"Thank you. And one more thing." I glanced down the hall, to Mort's room. "I need you to come listen as I ask Mort a question, tell me if he's lying or not."

Zeke's stomach growled. He frowned. "I need to eat and sleep before I fall over. How 'bout I save you time, and let's just assume he's lying?"

"The question's kind of too important for that. Please? Would it help if I said you might have to force the answer out of him?"

"You really know how to woo me. Fine. One fool question. Then I'm off to bed."

"Deal."

"Hang on, then." He went into Vee's room and came back out a minute later empty handed. "Let's go."

I knocked on Mort's door. Twice.

"Yeah," he finally responded in a groggy voice.

"It's Finn. I need to ask you a quick question. It's pretty important."

"Fine. Come in."

I led Zeke into Mort's bedroom. It looked much like I assume Darth Vader's bedroom would look. The bed, entertainment center, dresser, end tables, curtain rods, all were matching black and chrome. The thick curtains were closed against the weak Pacific Northwest sunlight, but a television the size of a view screen played a baseball game. What a waste. I could only imagine how awesome something like *Battlestar Galactica* would look on a screen like that.

Mort had his head propped up on black pillows. As we came in, he pushed himself into a sitting position.

"Hey, guys," he said in an oddly cheery tone. "You wanna watch the game?"

"No," I said. "Uh, how're you feeling?"

"Good. Good. The healer gave me a little something that made all the pain go away, like little bubbles, pop pop pop." He chuckled, and his attention wandered back to the television. "I, hey, thanks again for helping out. No hard feelings, right? I mean you—ooo, look how fast he can run."

No hard feelings? For nearly getting us killed by sasquatches, or for something worse?

"Mort, can you focus for a second? I need to ask you a question."

Mort looked at me, or rather his eyes looked in my direction. They actually focused on me a second later. "Sure. What's up?"

I glanced at Zeke, and cleared my throat. I didn't want to completely alienate my brother, especially after Mattie's plea. But I needed to clearly determine if Mort was guilty or not, and I didn't have time for subtlety. "Mort, did you have anything to do, accidental or not, with the attack on Felicity, or making it look like I attacked her?"

"What? No! Of course not. Like I told you, I really believed what the ARC said, that you'd hurt Felicity. But, you know, I'm really sorry about doubting you, man."

Zeke's eyes narrowed. "He told the truth about having nothing to do with the attack on Felicity or framing you. But the rest—"

Mort blushed. "Fine. So I'm not sorry for doubting you. But that's not a crime."

"Right," I said. "Great. Sorry for bugging you."

"But—" Zeke began.

"That's good," I said emphatically, and motioned to the door.

Zeke grunted. "Whatever. I need some sleep anyway."

"Thanks for checking on me," Mort said as Zeke stepped through the door. "It was a pleasure."

"Uh-huh," I said, and I started to close his door but stopped. Damn it. Mattie's plea poked at me again. And this was not how I wanted to relive this moment for the rest of my life in exile, or leave things with Mort anyway. I leaned back into his room. "Look, I know things have been a little . . . rough since I've been back. But when everything settles down, maybe you and me, we can go do something together? Something fun, like in the old days?"

"I don't know," Mort said, staring bleary eyed at the television again. "We'll see."

"Right. Okay. Later." I closed his door.

Zeke waited by the door to his room, between Mort's and Vee's. "Real winner, your brother," he said.

"I don't think Mort's involved in what's going on with us. But it probably wouldn't hurt to keep an eye on him anyway."

"Well, at least we agree on that," Zeke said. "So before I grab a little Odinsleep, is there anything else you want to tell me? Like what it is you need Heather's help researching?"

"Oh, right. Well, I think whatever's going on, it has something to do with the fact that I can still Talk to a spirit that's been warded, but only if my family did the warding. That's the other bit of memory they tried to hide. So that should make it a lot easier to figure out who exactly my enemies don't want me Talking to."

"And then we go Talk to that spirit anyway. Good. I like it. Go do your research and let me know what you find. Tomorrow. Right now, I—"

"Need your sleep. Yeah, I got it."

Zeke blew out his mustache at me, then went into his room.

I headed back downstairs just in time to find Heather clearing the last of the food from the table. "You ready to do that research?" she asked.

I eyed the remains of the pasta and sighed. "Yeah, let's do it."

Heather followed my gaze and said, "Here. Eat up first. You need your energy."

Heather downed another glass of wine as I shoveled pasta and vegetables from the bowl to my stomach with only the briefest stop in my mouth, and then we walked to the family library.

I closed the library doors behind us, and when I turned back around, Heather stood close enough that I smelled the apple scent of her shampoo. She locked the library doors, and put her other hand on my chest. She looked into my eyes for a second, and something like uncertainty or sadness flashed through hers. Then she straightened her shoulders.

"Don't be nervous," she said, and I could smell the wine on her breath. "I don't bite, much. Unless you beg for it."

She leaned in for a kiss. I jerked back, and hit the library doors.

"Uh, I don't think this is a good idea. What if someone comes—"

"Everyone's busy, and nobody comes in libraries anymore. Though I'm hoping we can change that." She leaned in again. I put my hands between us.

"Wait, I just—this is kind of sudden. I mean, it's not like I haven't thought about it—I mean, you know, not that I pictured you . . . doing stuff, but—there's just so much going on, and I don't know—" How to do it, I thought. Actually, my brain didn't know. My body knew exactly what it wanted, and a wild gang of hormones did their best to stuff my brain into a sack and beat it into submission.

Heather pouted. "You know, for someone who's been without companionship for twenty-five years, I thought I'd be fighting you off, not the other way around."

"It's not like I don't want . . . not like I don't like you or anything, but—"

"The only buts I like when it comes to sex are the ones I can grab. Let's not ruin this with a bunch of thinking, Finn. I want you, you want me, there's absolutely no reason we shouldn't have a little harmless fun. Are you being shy because you're a virgin?"

"What? I'm not—that is, what makes you—"

"I think we both know better. You couldn't even bring yourself to kiss me before you got sent away. But you don't need to be nervous." She pressed against me. "I'll enjoy every minute of it, and so will you, I promise." She sounded like she was trying to convince herself as much as me, but then she moved in again for a kiss, and I had nowhere to go but for it.

Her kiss was different from Dawn's truth-or-dare kiss, which I'd replayed in my head (voluntarily and involuntarily) thousands of times. Where Dawn's kiss all those years ago had been warm and melting, Heather's felt more like the suggestion of a true kiss, her lips hesitant, her tongue in retreat from mine.

The kiss ended, and I leaned back, opening my eyes.

"Well," she asked. "Worth the wait?"

"Definitely," I said. What else was I going to say? That it felt somehow . . . lacking? Yeah, that would pretty much end any chance I had of rebuilding our friendship, let alone taking it further. Still, while it didn't feel like I'd kissed my sister or anything, there was certainly no Hallelujah choir singing in the background either.

Maybe it was just me. Maybe I wasn't in the right frame of mind. It wasn't like we'd had a fun-filled day together and were at some basement party or something. And there was the fact that she'd slept with Mort. And that she had a grown son. And that—

"Are you sure everything's okay?" Heather asked. "You look like you're somewhere far away."

"No. Sorry. I mean, yes, I was just thinking about us, and about the kiss. It really was great."

"Wow. Thanks, Tony Tiger. It's an honor to be an important part of your nutritious breakfast."

"No, that's not what I meant. I meant—"

"Oh, so now you think I'm imagining things?"

How had things gone so bad so quickly? "No, really, I—"

"You do. You think I'm cuckoo for Cocoa Puffs." She glared at me for a second, and then the corner of her mouth quirked up.

The knot of anxiety lifted from my chest. Mostly. "Hey, you do know I think you're magically delicious, right?"

"Uh-huh. Prove it." She kissed me again. This time, with more passion. Or maybe it was determination.

She pulled me away from the door, still kissing me, and we kiss-stumbled our way to the nearest hardback chair. She plopped me down onto the chair and straddled me, wriggling down on my lap with a smile that belonged on a cat in an aviary. Then she pulled my head to one side and lunged for my throat. I jumped, but she held me pinned down. Her teeth didn't break skin, just bit playfully at the side of my neck, and then it was warm lips and hot breath on my throat, my jaw, my earlobe. That last caused waves of heat to pulse through me, and I began to thrust rhythmically against her. She made a soft encouraging moan in my ear. She grabbed my hand and slid it along the low opening of her shirt, under her bra. Her nipple pressed hard against my fingertip, and her lips brushed my ear as she whispered, "Do you want to kiss them?"

"Yes," I said, feeling awkward and weird to be saying it out loud. But with her body pressed against mine, her breath hot on my ear, and a similar heat now warming my lap, yes, I most definitely did.

"Mmmm. Say yes, Miss Brown," she said.

And for some reason, hearing her name was like a slap. And not the good kind. It jolted me out of the pleasant, sultry bubble in which we existed and back into a reality where she wasn't Heather Flowers, the girl I'd loved, but Heather the grown and experienced woman. I felt like I'd been floating in a kind of dream, an extension of moments with the Heather of my memories and, oddly, with Dawn. Another side effect of my exile maybe?

My hands moved over to her arms.

"Heather—"

"Miss Brown."

"I think we should stop."

"No." She nipped at my earlobe. "I think that's a terrible idea."

"No, really." I lifted her up and away as best I could, but that only budged her an inch or two. "I'm sorry," I said. "It's not you, it's me. I need more time to recover from exile, and to clear my head I think."

"Why?" she said, and her hand rested on my crotch. "It doesn't feel like you need more time. And I can take care of your head." She wriggled in close again, and kissed the corner of my mouth as her hand squeezed the most sensitive part of my body, pumping good feelings all through me. She whispered, "I can give you a memory you won't mind reliving. And I can teach you how to make a woman very happy." She kissed me then, a long, deep kiss, and when our lips parted she whispered hot into my ear, "Do you want me to teach you?"

My hands slid off of her arms, to her waist. I could feel her mouth spread into a grin, pressed against the side of my face.

"Yes," I exhaled.

"Yes, what?"

"Yes, Miss Brown."

She Blinded Me with Science

I lay sprawled across the chaise longue, dozing, with pleasant feelings still shivering along my legs to the tips of my toes. Heather left to use the restroom with a promise to be right back.

My smile stretched so wide I felt the pull and pressure of it.

Right there, right then, the anger and fear and frustration of the past day were weak and distant creatures, in no danger of killing this pleasant feeling. For the first time since, well, before my exile, I felt truly relaxed, truly at peace. I glanced at my watch. Just after 2 P.M. My first day of freedom was more than half over, and we'd spent more than an hour playing around in the library, making zero progress on proving my innocence—I grinned. If anything, Heather had made me significantly less innocent. And I felt only the faintest concern about the enforcers' deadline. If I was going back into exile to relive memories, this was certainly a better way to spend my time than fighting feybloods or accusing my family members of crimes.

And another thing—I finally felt at home in my body. I hadn't realized until now, but since my return I'd been uncomfortable in my own body. It wasn't the body I remembered. But over the past couple of hours, I'd been made acutely aware of every inch of skin, and controlled and flexed and stretched muscles that I normally wouldn't even think about.

I got up and dressed, retracing the trail of clothes between the wooden chair and the chaise longue, with a stop at the table to set the silver candlestick holders upright. I actually blushed a bit there. It would certainly be a long time before I let anyone see my memories now.

I moved to the doors. Heather was taking a long time. Maybe I should grab us both something to drink. That seemed like the right thing to do.

I heard Heather speaking beyond the doors in a low tone. "Well now I'll never know, will I? I have to go."

I stepped back from the door just as she opened it.

"Everything okay?" I asked.

Her hand touched the outline of her mobile phone in her pants pocket. "What? Of course, why?"

"I thought I heard you on the phone. You sounded upset."

"Oh. An argument with Orion. Money stuff." She closed the door. "In some ways, you're lucky. You haven't really had to deal with all the crap of adult life yet."

"Yeah. Lucky." I moved to her side, ran my hand down her arm, took her hand. "So, does this mean, you know, that we're dating?"

She lifted my hand, looked at it, then pulled me over to the chaise and sat down, pulled me down next to her.

"Is that what you want?" she asked. "To date me?"

"Yes. I thought about it a lot in exile."

She leaned against me, laid her head on my shoulder. "That's the problem, Finn. You're a former exile. And you're obviously in some kind of trouble now. But I've already got problems I'm dealing with. And a son to think about." She straightened, and held my hand to her chest, so that I felt her heartbeat. "I want to say yes, Finn. It would be nice for it to be us, together against the world again. But before I make any decision, I really need to understand what's going on. I just can't take any risks right now. And I need to know if you're going to be here a week from now, still wanting to date me."

"I know. I get that." I sighed. Finn and Heather against the world. A promise I'd made to her many times. "Okay. I'll tell you everything. But it is only for you to know. I'm not sure yet who I can trust."

"I promise," Heather said.

I told her, about the attack on the Other Realm, the sasquatches at Fort Worden and the feybloods at the Hole, about the memory of my mother's journal. For some reason, I just couldn't bring myself to tell her about Felicity's body though. Or about my father.

I was protecting her. That's what I told myself at least.

"Wow," she said when I was done. "And that's all you know?"

"Yeah."

She looked at me a few seconds, and tears filled the corners of her eyes. She looked away as they ran down her face. "Okay."

"So, what do you think? About us, I mean?"

Heather took a deep breath, expanding her chest beneath our entwined hands, and wiped the tears from her face with her shoulder. She let my hand slide down into my lap. "I think maybe you have enough to focus on without worrying about me."

"But—"

She held up her hand. "If you're still here in four days, and . . . and if you still want to ask me out, I'll say yes. How's that?"

"Right," I said. "Of course. No, you're right."

Heather stood, and crossed to the waist-high marble pedestal with the large tome on it. "So, someone wants you back in exile, and doesn't want you speaking with a warded spirit?"

"Yes." I stood and joined her.

"And I assume whatever you wanted help to research is related?"

She opened the tome, revealing blank pages.

Research. Right. I sighed.

"I need a list of every being my family warded against Talking."

Heather arched an eyebrow at me. "That's going to be a long list. Do you have any other criteria, maybe something that would help narrow the search a bit?"

"Well, I guess we can forget anyone who was cremated, or unmade." Throw a ward on a spirit and then destroy the body, and I'd have to practically kill myself just to connect to the spirit, let alone Talk to them. There wouldn't be much need to exile me.

"Still has a body. Got it. Anything else?"

I considered. "Try anyone warded between nineteen eighty-five and eighty-six." It made sense that the warding took place close to my exile. My Talking gift had been fully active for several years before my exile, so why wait until that particular Saturday to frame me, unless I hadn't been a threat before that?

"Well, that should be a short enough list." Heather closed her eyes. After a minute, she opened her eyes and frowned. "A really short list." She lifted her hands, and the words '*Non Respondet*' appeared in black ink on the page. "It seems any records of your family's activities from that period have been expunged."

Surprise, surprise. "Who could do that?"

"A head librarian, probably. Or someone in the ARC with the right access."

I paced across the library for a minute. I knew the Legion had serious mojo, but actual positions in the ARC as well? Gods, I hoped not. With luck, they just had an evil head librarian on their team. My situation was rapidly shifting from pretty screwed to totally hosed as it was, I didn't need the ARC as my enemy too. "Okay, if we can't find the records in the library, could they be anywhere else?"

"I don't know, I'm sorry."

"Frak! The ledger and the library, they were my best shots."

"Then maybe you should do something else for a bit? Maybe spend some time with your family. I find the answer often comes when you're *not* looking for it. Meanwhile," she pulled out her mobile phone, looked at the screen. "I've got some errands to run. But I'll see you at dinner."

I sighed. "All right. Thank you. And . . . thank you."

Heather smiled a sad smile. "Of course. Happy to help."

I left the library and made my way to Father's room. He sat on the love seat watching a gardening show on television. Mattie sat at Mother's desk, typing away on her computer.

"Hi, Mattie," I said. "Sorry that took so long."

Mattie grinned up at me. "No worries. Did you and Heather, uh, find what you wanted?"

I blushed. Did Mattie know? Maybe she just thought we'd made out. "Actually, no. It seems the records were erased in the library."

She tapped her Apple computer. "You should Google it."

"Google it?"

"Yeah. Here." Mattie caused the computer's screen to go white, with the word Google prominently displayed. Between the word and the primary colors, I assumed it was some kind of children's game. "What are you looking for?" she asked.

I glanced over at Father. I didn't feel comfortable discussing it in front of him. What if the Legion still had access to him somehow? They could learn what he knew.

"Why don't we go up to my room. I was going to show you my Commodore anyway."

"Cool, okay."

Mattie closed her computer and said, "Papa, just ring if you need anything."

Father looked at me. "Ring around the heartsie, you'll see."

"Okay, Father. Love you." I followed Mattie out. "Thank you for taking such good care of him," I said as we headed for my room.

"Of course," Mattie said. "He's lots of fun."

"Really?"

"Oh yeah. He tells me stories sometimes, and we play games, or work on his inventions."

"But wouldn't you rather be hanging out with your friends?"

Mattie shrugged. "I hang out when I want to. Most of the time, though, there's not much going on. They just sit around playing video games, or talking about boys, or want to go smoke and drink in the woods, and I'd rather just do my own thing, you know?"

We reached my room. As I opened my door, Sammy stepped out of Vee's room into the hallway and turned back to give Vee a hug. Sammy now wore skin-tight red jeans and a black shirt with silver wings printed on the back.

I'd forgotten Pete had called her. Vee waved at me, then shut her door.

"So," Sammy said, turning to face me. "It seems you've been busy."

"Yeah, it's been aces."

"Aces. Right. What are you two up to?"

"Nothing," Mattie said quickly. "We were going to check out his computer."

"Uh-huh." Sammy crossed her arms. "I know that look, Mattie. And don't think I didn't notice you trying to hide your laptop from me. What's up?"

I shrugged. "She was going to help me search the Google for information I need."

"Search the Google, eh?" She eyed Mattie. "I thought we talked about this. I showed you the Infomancer layer so you could help research cures for Father, and that was to be it."

"Infomancer layer?" I asked.

"But this is Uncle Finn," Mattie said. "It's still helping family."

"And still dangerous," Sammy said. "If anyone's going to do this, it should be me. Come on." She shooed us into my room.

I turned on my Commodore 64 and the monitor, letting it warm up. Not to search the Google, of course, but to play Wizball with Mattie as promised. In fact, I promised myself I would find time each day to do something fun with her. Especially if I only had three days to do so. Mattie set her flat little Macintosh on my desk and opened it, and the screen lit up right away. Sammy moved to sit in the folding chair.

"Wait," I said, and hit Play on my boom box. Prince's "I Would Die 4 U" started playing. "First, I think we need to teach Mattie how to dance!" I launched into my Ed Grimley dance, knees bent, one hand flopping around in front of my forehead.

Sammy glared at me. "No."

"Ah, come on," I said, and pulled my pants up over my belly button. "She's going to think you don't know how to have fun."

"It's not happening."

"Should I tell Mattie about your Stormer obsession? Or how about the famous She-Ra incident?"

"Sure, if you want me to show her pictures of your perm."

"Go ahead," I said. "People have been rooting around in my memories for years, you think that scares me now? So, Mattie, Sammy had this She-Ra costume from Halloween, and—"

"Okay! Fine. I'll join your stupid dance party."

Sammy knocked her fists against each other sideways, then again behind her in a half-hearted manner.

"Feet too, Stormer," I said. "You're a loner, a rebel. Own it."

Sammy exhaled sharply through her nose, then launched into her full Pee-wee Herman big shoe dance.

"Bitchin!" I said. "Mattie, your turn."

Mattie shook her head. "I don't dance. I look like a spaz."

"Oh, come on," I said. "Do you really think you could look any worse than me?"

"Just do it, Mattie," Sammy said. "He won't stop until you do."

"Fine," Mattie said. She stood up and started dancing, weaving her hands around each other.

We danced and soon were laughing, and when the song ended, Mattie gave me and Sammy a big hug. "You guys are the best."

"That's true," I said, breathing heavy.

A smile twitched at the corner of Sammy's mouth, but she just said, "I feel exhausted," and plopped down in the chair. "So, what are we looking for?"

I sat on the edge of my bed where I could still see her screen.

"Family records. I need a list of anyone our family warded against Talking in the year before I was exiled."

"Okay." Sammy typed a string of words and symbols into the little box beneath the Google logo.

"So," I said. "Since I didn't get the changeling crash course on modern computers, maybe you can fill me in here? Is this Google thing like a private arcana bulletin board or something?"

Sammy hit Enter. The screen filled with a list of paragraphs, each starting with underlined blue words. "I'm not here to teach, just search," Sammy said as she scrolled down through the paragraphs. She clicked on one, and the screen went black, with a blinking white cursor. "But lo, your sad questions have filled my heart with pity for you. Mattie, while I do this, why don't you explain to uncle Finn all about the Internet and World Wide Web."

"What about them?" Mattie asked.

"Everything," Sammy said. "Like he was five years old. Which shouldn't be too hard, the way he's acting."

I bit back a sarcastic remark. Computers were the one area Sammy and I had always clashed. She excelled at programming, and made it clear she felt it was unfair I should be good with computers *and* a Talker. Looking back, I should have helped her more when she needed it, and recognized it more when she exceeded me, which was more often than I'd wanted to admit. Now she was light-years ahead of me, and the least I could do was let her enjoy her moment of gloating.

So Mattie explained the World Wide Web to me like I was a child. I'd learned all about Arpanet and bulletin boards before my exile. I was even hoping to get a modem and QuantumLink for Christmas. But the interweb sounded cool. Almost William Gibson cool. I'd read *Neuromancer* a half-dozen times that last year before exile, in between watching *Bladerunner, Tron,* and *WarGames* over and over on VHS.

But the awesomeness of the Web made me oddly sad.

I remembered when Pac-Man came out on the Commodore, and suddenly my parents wanted to use my computer. This felt much the same. Something that once had made me feel special for knowing about it and understanding it had become as popular and common as watching television. Worse, suddenly I was on the outside. I could hear in Mattie's voice a hint of the same patient and somewhat pitying tone I would use when trying to explain technology to Grandfather.

"Okay, I get it," I said. "Cyberspace. The matrix, more or less."

"Yeah, sort of," Mattie said. "Except, most of the boys you meet online are no Keanu, that's for sure. And, you know, there's no squiddies, just trolls."

"Squiddies? Wait, trolls are using computers now?"

"Some, but that's—never mind," Mattie said.

Sammy hit Enter again, and the black screen became pure white, this time without any logos or buttons, just a blank page. She turned to face us. "We should see results in a second, if there's any to see," she said.

"Could mundies search our family's records using that Google thing?" I asked.

"No. I mean, they could search, but they wouldn't find anything related to magic. The ARC has sorcerers who mess with the info on the Web, hiding things, putting up a bunch of fake stuff, so the mundies don't figure out the truth about magic or feybloods."

"Okay . . . so then what are the results we're waiting for?"

"I hacked the Infomancer layer. Whenever they delete or change something on the mundy Web, it leaves an imprint in the ether. It's a bit like necromancy, actually. I was able to put all that stuff Grandfather taught us to use after all. I created a kind of summoning program that goes in and searches the ether for resonances left when specific data was deleted, and sort of calls it back. So whatever they deleted, I should still be able to find it."

"Wouldn't they have just wiped the ether or whatever too?"

"Maybe. But I doubt it. It would be like wiping a hard drive just to—here we go."

A list of names began appearing line by line on the screen. Some I recognized just from hearing their names from other arcana. Some I recognized because they'd made names for themselves in the mundy world, like Orson Welles. Each name had asterisks next to them, from one to five.

"What do the asterisks mean?"

"How close they match what you were looking for."

And then I saw it. The name of a woman who'd visited our home when she lived in Port Townsend, an arcana that even then

I'd felt held some great secret wisdom. A woman with five asterisks next to her name.

Archmagus Katherine Verona, Hero of the Realm, ender of the last Fey-Arcana war, and once owner of the finest yarn shop in Port Townsend.

Weariness crashed down on me. My brain felt unable to process what it meant that Katherine Verona and my being exiled were somehow connected. And Zeke was likely comatose at this point anyway. It would be a couple of hours at least before I could risk waking him without him reflexively snapping my neck. I glanced at my watch. Still over three hours until I was supposed to meet Dawn, and hopefully Heather, for dinner.

Sammy nodded at the screen. "So, what does this mean?"

I rubbed my eyes. "It means I need a nap."

And if whatever trouble I was in touched on the Archmagus, it also probably meant I was bantha poodoo. But I'd worry about that later. If there was one thing I felt pretty certain hadn't changed since my exile, it was that naps made everything better—at least for as long as it took to nap.

Hungry Like the Wolf

"Magus Verona, huh?" Zeke mumbled from his bed.

"Yeah." I leaned against the door to his room. I still felt a bit tired even after my two hours of sleep, but Zeke *looked* terrible. Pale evening sunlight leaked between his bedroom curtains, making his Mohawk and mustache look limp and pale, and turning the shadows under his eyes into deep violet bruises.

Zeke grunted, blinking sleepy eyes at me. "What the hell does the Hero of the Realm have to do with you?"

"I don't know, exactly," I said. "I know she and Mother were friends, and I remember her coming over a couple of times to talk with Grandfather."

"Then you're luckier than most," Zeke said, and propped himself up on one elbow, looking a bit more alert now. "Hell, I'd practically give my left nut to have talked to her. Did she ever say anything about, you know, the big secret?"

"You mean what weapon she used to end the war?"

Zeke rolled his eyes. "No. I mean whether she soaked her hands in Palmolive to get them so smooth. Yes! Of course I mean the weapon, fool!"

"No."

"Of course not. Well, do you know why she went all hermitlike?"

"No. I didn't really talk with her. She always seemed so . . . sad."

"Yeah. Well, she saved lots of lives by ending the war when she did. I don't know why she'd be sad."

I shrugged. "Maybe it had nothing to do with winning the war. She did lose her daughter in the fighting, you know."

Zeke scowled. "Maybe, but I don't buy it. There were the fey-blood registration drives, and the Pax negotiations, and all the rest after the war, and she didn't want nothin' to do with none of it. Hell, if I lost my daughter to the damned Fey, and I had the kind of power she did, I wouldn't have stopped until I'd blasted the bastards back into formlessness, and made sure we had free access to the raw magic again. I wouldn't have hid away from the world, from my duties."

"Well, she wasn't you."

"Obviously. So, you think someone's trying to keep you from talking to her now? Why?"

"I don't know. Maybe they thought I could get the big secret out of her for some reason? But if she wouldn't share it with anyone before she died I don't see why anyone would think she'd share it with me afterward."

"Maybe it ain't *the* secret, but just a secret. I'll bet plenty of fool rebels and Feyist groups and the like tried to get the secret out of her so they could do something nasty to the Fey or feybloods. Maybe they didn't want their identities or plans getting out after she died."

Zeke's words stirred up the memory of an overheard conversation between my grandfather and Verona.

"Just tell me the way of it," Grandfather said.

"No," Verona replied. "You don't want this burden, Gavriel, no matter how much you or your friends think your cause is worth it, or how you justify the cost to yourself. Trust me."

"Your daughter volunteered, Katherine. She went willingly to—"

"Don't! Don't talk about my Bea. And don't ask me for help again, Gavriel."

Had Grandfather been a Feyist rebel of some kind, hoping to strike at the Fey despite the Pax? I found the thought ridiculous. Grandfather had been all about following the rules, about arcana tradition. More likely he had been working on behalf of the ARC to try to get the information, assuming the weapon was even the topic of their discussion. But that didn't mean that some other group hadn't also tried to get her secrets from her, like Zeke said.

"You know what, it doesn't matter," I replied. "If I really can Talk to a warded spirit, I can just ask her."

"You're right, it don't matter, fool," Zeke said and laid his head back on the pillow. " 'Cause no way you're Talking to her, ward or not."

"What? Why not?"

"Are you kidding? She's the Hero of the Realm. Her body's locked up in an ARC Sanctum someplace, under layers of security. It'd be suicide to try and get at her on the sly. So, unless you can get us in all official-like, as a necromancer . . . ?"

Damn. "No, you're right, not into an ARC Sanctum, not without an invitation. I'm not sure I could even find out where she's being kept. Could you? Use some of your enforcer connections or whatever, maybe get us in?"

"Well, I got friends who might tell us where she is, but no way they'd help us get in. Good news, though, is I got a different lead, one that ain't a big ole impossibility sandwich with suicide sauce. Friend in the ARC who monitors black market activity has a lead on a spike of witchcraft supplies being sold in the area. If your Króls really are here and hiding somewhere, we might be able to track them down after all."

I shook my head. "I think *that* would be suicide. Felicity, she didn't talk much about her family, but I always got the impression they were bad news and she'd more escaped than left them. And far as they know, I'm the guy who attacked their kin, remember?"

Zeke grinned and cracked his knuckles above his head. "Now see, everything you're saying is just making me like my idea even more. Interrogating hostile witches is just the sorta thing to make me feel better right about now. Well, that and more sleep. Besides, they're still prime suspect numero one in my book. If they thought this Felicity chick betrayed them, and your family helped her do it, they might've decided to pay you both back. Maybe your father wasn't even possessed; maybe he was witchy hoo-dooed."

Everything he said made sense, but for some reason I still felt resistant to going after the Króls, and I didn't think it was just the fear of being turned into a big pile of cursed flesh. But I didn't have any better ideas. I'd been so focused on avoiding and protecting against the Króls, I hadn't considered an attack.

And remembering the tortured look in Felicity's eyes when she spoke of her family, I decided maybe it wouldn't be so terrible to let Zeke use his subtle "baton to the head" questioning method after all.

"Fine. But will you still see if you can find Verona's location? Call it a Plan B, just in case the Króls don't work out."

Zeke closed his eyes. "I call it Plan B Stupid, but you're right, I suppose. Might be good to know for sure just how impossible it is so, you know, you'll shut up about it and let me get back to sleep."

"Awesome. I have to get ready for my brother's date anyway."

"You do that, fool." Zeke cracked one eye open to glare at me. "And tell your fool brother to stay away from Vee. I don't like the way he keeps looking at her."

"Let me guess—like a fool?"

Zeke opened the other eye to glare at me fully. I quickly closed his door and left him to his sleep.

Pete drove us down to the waterfront to meet Dawn, even though it was a lovely evening for a stroll. Harder to ambush a moving car than a couple of guys walking. As the passenger, I found myself craning my neck to take in the sights like a tourist.

The town's many grand Victorian buildings spoke to the dreams of its early builders, that this was going to be one of the biggest port cities in Washington. Unfortunately, the Great Depression, a lack of railroad connections, and a nasty infestation of gremlins killed that dream. But when most mundies abandoned the town, the area's rich and important magical history made it an ideal home for arcana.

Then a paper mill got built outside of town, bringing bad smells, coastal debris, and a lot of jobs. And a bunch of mundies rediscovered the charm of Port Townsend and started to move or retire here, "fixing up" the area around the time I was born. I hoped Water Street, at least, remained untouched by the "renewal." All of the changes made me feel unsettled, like maybe I'd returned to the wrong world.

I distracted myself by checking my hair in the rearview. Mattie had kindly cut off the rocker locks, and with a bit of Mort's hair gel it was close to my old short and spiky do. A vast improvement.

Petey readjusted the rearview. "I can't see. It's not safe."

"Sorry."

"You said you would give me some tips," Pete said. "On dating and girls and stuff?"

"Oh. Right. Well, let's see. First of all, compliment your date. And ask her about herself and act interested in what she says even if it's boring."

"I don't want to date someone boring," Pete said.

"Good point. But you don't want to be rude either, so maybe just pretend, and then not date her again if you don't want to?"

"Oh. Okay. What else?"

"Um . . ." My knowledge on dating, I realized, was not extensive. I began to dig through lessons I'd gleaned from the movies. "Well, if you get an anonymous love letter and think it's from the girl of your dreams, it's really from the girl next door. Don't let your computer fall in love with the girl you like. If you have the choice between suicide or dating a cute French girl, date the girl. Don't give a geek your underwear. And, uh, if your girlfriend likes to take long salt baths, she's probably a mermaid?"

Oh gods. Thankfully, I stopped myself before warning him about the dangers of having sex with bisexual New Wave models while aliens waited on the roof to suck out his endorphins. I mean, I might have sounded like a real idiot then.

"I'm not sure I'll remember all that," Pete said. "Can you tell me again when we get to the restaurant so I can write it down?"

"Why don't we just see how the date goes?"

"Okay. Oh, and Finn, Dawn is mad that you didn't call her or anything while you were gone. I told her the story like I was supposed to, but I don't think she's happy with you anyway."

Bat's breath. I really should have thought about a better cover story before now. Funny how constantly fighting for your life can get in the way of such things.

The best lies have some element of truth to them. The story told to mundies about me was that Felicity committed suicide, and her death coming so soon after my mother and grandfather's deaths really messed me up so I had to get away for a while, especially away from the family's mortuary business.

But that story wasn't going to be good enough for Dawn. She was right to be angry. We'd been close, and then I just went and disappeared on her without any warning or word. From her perspective, I'd avoided her for twenty-five years. Short of exile to another world, what could justify that?

A coma maybe?

"Okay. Pete, I'm going to tell Dawn that . . . I had amnesia. And I need you to say it's true if she asks you."

Pete frowned. "I don't like lying."

"I know. But Dawn is a mundy, Pete, and this is part of my cover story. If I could tell her the truth, you know I would."

Pete drove in silence for a minute, turning onto Water Street, the main tourist drag that ran along Port Townsend's waterfront.

"Okay," he said at last. "But I don't like it."

"Me either, bro. Me either."

We parked a couple blocks away and walked to the Belmont. It felt good but strange to be walking along Water Street again, past the windows displaying local arts and crafts, funky clothing, antiques, and books. Many of the shops and restaurants were familiar, my favorite being Elevated Ice Cream, where the entire family had often gone for treats. But the place where I used to buy toys and comics was now an art gallery with glass and wood sculptures. Lame.

The Belmont Restaurant and Hotel stood unchanged as a fine representative of old Port Townsend, a building of exposed timber and mossy brick. Dawn waited for us in front wearing a striped dress. Small white ribbons like butterflies danced in her lavender afro. "You're here!" she said. "And it's barely six. Count me surprised."

"You thought we'd be late?" I asked.

"I thought you'd ditch. Now come here and give me some love."

Dawn pulled me into a hug. She smelled like exotic candy. As we stepped apart, she squeezed my arm. "Damn, Phinaeus, you've been working out." I felt myself blush. Dawn just smiled and opened the door to the restaurant, waving us in. "Ready to woo me, boys?"

I couldn't help but notice Waterfront Pizza just a couple doors down. I gave it a sad, longing look, then entered the Belmont.

The Belmont lobby was small, with a couple of lounge chairs, a rack of tourist brochures, and sepia pictures of the restaurant in its early days. The smell of something cooking in oil and garlic made my mouth water so much I had to swallow before speaking.

"So, Dawn," I said as we stood there, waiting to be seated. "What have you been up to?"

"About a seven, I'd say," Dawn said.

"She plays music," Pete said. "She's really good too."

"My biggest fan," Dawn said, giving Pete a side hug. "I play gigs around town some weekends. I also volunteer at the animal shelter, and do tarot readings during the day at the Phoenix or wherever. But that's all just to support my exciting hobby of being a waitress."

"That's awesome," I said. "The music I mean, not—anyway, uh, how's your dad? What does he think about your music now?"

"Wow, you really have been in your own little world, haven't you?" Dawn sounded angry, maybe a little hurt. "My dad died almost fifteen years ago, Finn."

"Oh. Man. I'm sorry, Dawn, I didn't—I'm sorry I wasn't here."

"Yeah, about that—" Dawn said, and then a redheaded woman dressed in black slacks and a vest approached. She looked familiar, but I couldn't place her. Maybe someone I'd gone to school with? "Three for dinner?" she asked. I nodded, and she guided us back through a tunnel-like passage between booths and up a flight of stairs to the main restaurant area, a cozy space of tables with lit candles, original brick walls to either side, and large windows overlooking the water. We sat at a table near the windows, Dawn on one side, me and Pete on the other. An older couple sat outside on the deck, and a husband-wife-child trio sat several tables away in a corner; nobody close enough to worry about being overheard.

"Can I bring you anything to drink?" the waitress asked.

"Goddess, yes," Dawn said. "Bloody Mary, and make it as spicy as Shakira shaking her hips in a jalapeño field, please."

The waitress blinked, then turned to me. "And you, sir?"

"Iced tea," I said and looked at Dawn. "Make it sweet as Debbie Gibson sharing Pixy Stix with an Ewok."

"Well played," Dawn said. "If we were twelve. Your powers are weak, old man."

I shrugged. "You can't win, Dawn. If you strike me down, I shall become more eloquent than you can possibly imagine."

"Maybe I should strike you down, then, so you don't bore me during the dinner conversation."

"Ouch."

The waitress appeared unamused. She turned to Pete. "Did you want anything, sir?"

Pete looked between me and Dawn. "Um, can I have a vanilla milkshake, and make it as vanilla as vanilla ice cream in a vanilla envelope?"

I exchanged smiles with Dawn and slapped Pete lightly on the arm. "Good one, bro."

"Damn," Dawn said. "I wish they really would make vanilla envelopes. Stamps too. I swear I can still taste the horse in whatever glue they use."

Petey beamed proudly.

The waitress had already inched several steps from the table. "I'll be right back with your drinks." She didn't sound excited at the prospect. As she walked away, I realized she hadn't even left us with menus and appeared to be ignoring the attempts of the family in the corner to get her attention. She was either new or just a really lousy waitress.

"So," Dawn said, slamming her elbows on the table and resting her chin on her hands. "I'll start, and you finish. Once upon a time, my best friend disappeared on me, and everyone in his family acted all weird every time I asked about it, saying he had, like, a breakdown and needed to go live with one of his uncles. Now, since this friend of mine had never said much good about his uncles, I found this pretty hard to believe. But what really sucked Donkey Kong was that he didn't even bother to say good-bye, or write, or call, or anything. Then one day he shows up, acting like nothing's changed in over twenty years, with a wonderful explanation that goes like . . . ?"

"I had amnesia."

"Sure. And I'm Dawn's evil twin, pregnant with the child of the power-hungry mayor."

"No, really. I lost all memory of who I was. They said it was a reaction to finding Felicity dead. Then, a few days ago, I remembered my past. It was like waking up. Except now I can't remember anything from the past twenty-five years."

"Come on, seriously? That's the story you're going with?"

"It's the truth."

"Pete?" Dawn asked.

Pete fretted with his cloth napkin and glanced up at me sideways. "Yeah, it's true."

Dawn watched Pete for a second, then smiled at me. "Well, damn. That's rough, man. But I won't have to beat you up for being a jerk, so, you know, that's good. Huh, I guess this means you don't know if you're married, or have a girlfriend, or maybe a boyfriend?"

"I'm pretty sure I don't have any of those," I said.

"I don't know. Twenty-five years, surely Other You dated. For all you know, you have a raging case of herpes right now, and a meth-head of a girlfriend waiting somewhere with your five juvenile delinquent offspring."

"I don't have herpes!" I realized I'd said that rather loud, and I glanced at the dining family. The parents looked away from our table. Great. I couldn't tell if Dawn was testing me, or teasing me, or honestly curious, but there wasn't much I could do about it. I was trapped by my own lie, and would just have to take it.

"How do you know you're not all sexually diseasified?" she asked. "Did you get a medical exam in the last few days?"

"No. I just know, okay?"

"Come to think of it, my friend Dallas said he saw someone who looked just like you turning tricks over in Bremerton for drug money. You're not feeling crack withdrawals or anything, are you?"

"Gods, Dawn, I said I lost my memory, not my brains."

"Okay. Well, amnesia, that's pretty tricky stuff. Best to be sure. So I'm guessing if you think you're still, what, fifteen, sixteen years old—"

"I don't think I'm fifteen, Dawn. I know I'm older now, I just can't remember anything that happened since I was fifteen."

"Still, I'm guessing you're wanting to pretty much pick up where you left off? Well, FYI, Heather is a forty-year-old divorced teacher now. If you're still going to act all stupid over her, it would be like having a crush on Ms. Fabbershaw, our old English teacher. Just sayin'."

The waitress brought our drinks. "Menus?" I asked, grateful for the interruption. The waitress grunted something and left.

"So, uh, Dawn, I just wanted to say thanks for being such a good friend to Petey all these years. And I was hoping maybe you could help him out."

"How's that?" Dawn asked.

"Well, he's asked me to help him find a girlfriend. But with my memory issue and all, I'm not sure I'd be much help. So I was thinking, maybe you could, like, coach him. Help him pick out a good wardrobe, teach him the right way to talk with a girl so she'll like him, maybe how to dance or cook or something?" The montage played in my head. This always worked in the movies—she would help him become the perfect date, and they would have lots of fun and laughs doing so, and then the first time he actually went out with someone she'd realize that he was *her* perfect date. 'Twas a good plan.

So why did it make me unhappy to picture it working?

Pete didn't look too comfortable about it either. He had a good blush going.

Dawn snorted. That, and loud burps, were two of her trademark noises. "You have the wrong lady, and the wrong plan, my friend. It's not like there's a lot of competition in the nice single guy department 'round these parts. Pete'll find the right girl just being himself. I wouldn't want to screw that up the way I've screwed up my own love life. Besides, I'm more interested in *your* dating plans."

"What? Dating plans? Why?"

"Look, Finn. Here's the thing. I know we need to get to know each other again, and we've both changed and all, but I don't want to play the stupid game we did before, like some fricking teenage romantic comedy. So let's just get to the part where you realize I'm some kind of wonderful and ask me out already."

"What?" Pete and I said together.

Dawn took a long, long drink of her Bloody Mary, and burped into her napkin.

"Okay," she said. "Here goes. I know you like me. Or at least you did. And I'm way more awesome now than I was then. Well, okay, I'm a mess in a lot of ways, but mostly in fun ways, or ways that shouldn't change how you feel. I'm not saying let's just jump into bed or anything here. I'm just saying you should ask me out. For reals. Now."

"Wow. Dawn, I—"

"Hey, guys," Heather said as she approached the table. "Sorry I'm late. I wasn't sure I could make it."

Dawn stared at Heather a second, then looked up at the ceiling. "Are you frickin' kidding me?"

Love Plus One

Heather looked between me and Dawn. "Is everything okay?"

She looked amazing, wearing an asymmetrical black dress that exposed a left leg covered in lacy stocking. Her hair was up in some kind of fancy bun with jeweled pins that matched her jeweled black glasses, reflecting candlelight from the tables and the gold evening light coming in through the restaurant's windows.

I could feel Dawn's eyes on me, and hoped the heat radiating from my neck and ears didn't compete with the evening sunlight. "Everything's fine," I said.

"Dawn just—" Pete began.

I felt the swift passage of Dawn's foot on the way to Pete's shin. He jumped, and she said, "Finn, is there anything you wanted to say?"

I looked between Dawn and Heather. "Uh, I don't know. I think I need to, ah, think about what you said."

Dawn gave me a sad look. Heather took the empty chair, and said, "You're sure I'm not interrupting?"

"It's fine," Dawn said. "Finn probably won't remember anything tomorrow anyway. He has amnesia."

"*Had* amnesia," I said.

"Amnesia?" Heather raised her eyebrows. "Really? You mean you weren't shipwrecked on a deserted island? Or maybe abducted by aliens?"

"I know, right?" Dawn said.

I gave Heather a tight smile, and said while barely moving my lips, "Not helping."

"So, Heather." Dawn played with her butter knife on the table. "How's your kid? Seems like a while since I've heard talk of him being arrested for anything."

Heather's eyes narrowed at Dawn, then she smiled at me. "Orion's twenty now, and he's doing well. He just needed to find his purpose in the world, something bigger than himself and his immediate wants. That's a struggle Dawn can probably relate to, right, Dawn?"

"Oh," I said, hoping to steer the conversation onto a less rocky path. "What does he—"

"Wow, twenty," Dawn said over me. "It must be weird to have a kid who's the same age you were when you had him, huh? But I guess the nice thing about having them young is you can still have a life after they move out, right?"

"Actually—" Heather began.

"You know, Finn," Dawn continued, "you'd have been amazed to see Heather back in the day. She really came out of her shell after high school. I don't think I played a single gig where I didn't see her dancing with some new guy—"

"That's right," Heather said. "I forgot you were going to be a musician."

"I am a musician."

Petey nodded. "She's really good."

"Of course," Heather said. "Sorry. I meant like a musician who makes money. Didn't you run off with that boyfriend of yours to do the homeless thing for a while? What was his name?"

"Phoenix. And we weren't homeless." Dawn looked at me. "We were exploring the world, you know? We worked our way from small town to small town, and I'd play music and he'd do his art. It was a better education than any college could've given me, that's for sure."

"Wow," I said. "That sounds great. I always wanted to—"

"He made things out of garbage, right?" Heather asked. "I always thought that was brave of you, supporting him all those years while he tried to make that art thing work. Whatever happened to him?"

Dawn looked at Heather in silence a minute, then said, "He left because he didn't want to deal with my father's on-again, off-again cancer, or how it affected me. He certainly didn't want to help with the medical bills."

Heather winced. "Shit. I'm sorry."

"Don't worry about it. Having Petey to talk with every night really helped me get through," she said, and patted him on the arm. "That, and my music of course." She looked at me. "I'm in a pretty good place now. Content. Even happy most days. Lonely sometimes, but happy. Now if you'll excuse me." She stood up. "I just realized I have to get ready for a gig tonight."

"Really," Heather said. "You don't need to leave—"

"I know I don't. I'm choosing to leave. Petey, didn't you say you'd drive me home?"

"I did?" Petey asked, then caught Dawn's gaze and said, "I mean, yes, I did." He looked mournfully at the milkshake as he stood.

Dawn nodded at Heather. "Lovely to see you."

"You too," Heather said, and put a hand over mine on the table.

"Later, neighbor," Dawn said to me. "Come on, Petey."

She walked off, and Pete looked at me. "Uh, do you need me to come back later or something?"

"No, I can walk."

"Or I can drive him home," Heather said.

Pete looked between Heather and Dawn, and I could see the unhappiness roiling across his face. Then he followed after Dawn.

"Well," Heather said. "I take it setting up Pete and Dawn didn't go so well?"

"Uh, no, not exactly. What's up with you two? Did she bully you in high school after I left or something?"

"No. We just have our . . . differences. A lot of folks in town have their differences with me, in fact. I'm sorry if it ruined your dinner. May I?" she asked, pointing at an untouched glass of ice water. I nodded. "So, amnesia, huh?" She took a sip.

"Give me a break. You know it's not easy hiding things from mundies sometimes, especially the ones close to you."

"That's true." Heather sighed. "I guess that's why so few arcanas end up dating mundies. I have something for you, by the way." She dug in her bag and pulled out my old Walkman. "You did just lend it to me, after all."

A grin stretched my face as I took the Walkman and popped it open. Inside was the tape I'd made for Heather, under the excuse that her parents only listened to Country-Western and she needed an education in good music.

But of course, that wasn't the real reason for the tape. Creating a mixed tape to reveal your love to a girl (or a boy, I'm sure) is a ritual every bit as complex, delicate, and potentially dangerous as summoning a powerful Elder Spirit. The choice of songs must find that balance between letting her know how you feel and still being able to claim that the tape was just a friendly gesture should she reject that feeling. You can't be too obvious, so no more than one fourth of the songs should have the word "Love" in the title, if any. And it's good to throw in a couple of "plausible deniability" songs that have nothing to do with love, and support your ability to claim "Oh, yeah, I totally just want to be friends too" should the worst happen—yet those songs should still somehow show that you understand her like no other boy ever could.

I remembered every song on the tape, having relived its creation many times. "Broken Wings" was one of my plausible deniability songs. So were "We're Not Gonna Take It" and "When Doves Cry." The other songs, however, were all about the loves. "Time After Time," "Love Cats," "Hello," "Running Up That Hill," "Take On Me," "I Just Called to Say I Love You," You Shook Me All Night Long, "Your Love Is King," and of course "I Melt With You."

"Thanks," I said. "This is awesome. So you enjoyed the tape?"

She laughed. "Yeah. Wow, it's weird, talking about it like nothing's happened since you gave it to me." Her smile faded. "But, you know, a lot has happened. A lot has changed. I've changed."

"I know."

"You really don't. But, in a way, I kind of like that." Heather gazed out at the water as a sailboat floated by. "I like that you look at me as if I'm still that girl who didn't know The Cure from The Clash. That hadn't made the choices I've made, the mistakes. It makes me feel like a good person. And I honestly haven't felt that way in a long time." She looked at me again. "You know, I really was sorry my father interrupted us that last day. I'd been waiting for you to kiss me for weeks."

That made me think of Dawn's words, about not playing the same stupid teenage games this time. And thinking of Dawn caused all kinds of confusing feelings to swirl through my head and chest.

No. I wasn't going to mess this up with too much thinking again. I leaned in to kiss Heather.

She pulled back.

"Shit! I'm sorry," I said. "I know you said we weren't dating, but I thought—sorry." I was suddenly aware that the family in the corner had gone silent. Way to make us the center of attention, Finn.

"No," Heather said. "You didn't do anything wrong. I just— maybe this was all a mistake. We really don't know each other, not anymore. And if you did know me now—I mean, this is crazy. But when I saw you this morning, it made me think about every- thing that's happened, made me remember who I was when you knew me, and—" She looked out the window for a second and wiped at her eyes. "What say we order some food, and you can tell me what the Other Realm was like?"

"Uh, if it's okay, I'd rather not. There's not much to tell anyway, just me reliving memories. I'd rather hear about you. Like how you got out from under the ARC controlling your life?"

My question was more than just curiosity. I hoped that such a life was possible.

"Luck," Heather said, looking down at the glass of water. "I just picked the right customers, people with influence. They keep the ARC off my back. Can we not talk about me though? I just want to forget me for tonight. How about we talk about the good old days, huh?" She looked toward the kitchen. "And where's the waiter?"

"I don't know. I think she's new or something." I bent to finally take a sip of my iced tea. Heather sucked in her breath, and knocked the glass away from me. It splashed across the table.

"What the heck?" I said, scooting back and standing to avoid the tea streaming off the edge of the table.

Heather stood up, looking around the restaurant, and whispered, "There was a witch's brew in it!"

Goose bumps sprang up on my arms. "Are you sure? How could you tell?"

Heather tapped her glasses. "Alchemy specs. I think maybe we should leave."

This was crazy. Who would attack me while mundies were around? I looked over at the family and realized they were sitting, eyes open, but just staring as if in a trance.

"I think maybe hell yes. Let's go."

I led the way down the stairs, then stopped. The narrow passage to the front door was blocked by the waitress and a hulking blond man with a bad bowl cut—the man who'd been lurking in a car outside the house last night. And seeing his features beside the waitress's, I realized who she reminded me of: Felicity. The red hair had thrown me off.

They were Król witches.

I grabbed Heather's arm, swung her around the banister and headed down into the basement level. Heather threw something down behind us, and blue flames spread across the stairs.

"You're going to burn the whole place down!" I said.

"It's witchfire. It only burns blood magic."

"Oh. Clever." If the Król wonder twins up there tried to pass through it, the magic inside them would burn, but nothing else would. I wondered briefly why Heather ran around with a vial of witchfire in her purse, but I had more important matters to worry about at the moment, like escaping crazed Germanic witches.

The Belmont's basement showed evidence of the underbelly of Port Townsend's history, a history of speakeasies, Shanghai tunnels, smuggler's passages, and the feyblood underworld. Brick archways led to dark rooms closed off by glass doors and a partially closed iron gate, and one archway led nowhere, filled in with concrete that bulged out from the wall like a partially exposed boulder. There were a number of small sealed archways as well, no higher than my knee, from the days when gnomes and other feybloods were able to move more freely through the town.

"Here." I pulled my hex protection amulet out from beneath my shirt. "You take this. It'll protect against curses."

"I have my own protection, thanks," Heather said. "Do you have some plan for getting out of here?"

"Maybe." I crossed to the large sealed archway.

"The tunnels?" Heather said. "I'm not sure that's a good idea."

"It's okay. If we run into any of the underworld feybloods, they should respect the Pax. Especially for a necromancer."

"Gramaraye!" The large man's silhouette appeared at the top of the stairs, though he stayed well clear of the blue witchfire. He called down with a thick Arnold Schwarzenegger accent, "Come out now. You have nowhere to run."

"Gee, let me think about it," I called back, and looked at Heather. "See, they don't even know about the tunnels. Come on." I moved toward the concrete-filled doorway.

"I'm sorry," Heather said, and ran to the woman's restroom.

I ran after her. The blue flames were half the size as when they began. Heather closed and locked the door just I reached it. "Heather, come out!" I said in a loud whisper, worried that the Króls would come down and trap us away from the tunnel entrance. "This is crazy."

"Just go," Heather said. "They're after you, not me. They're not going to stick around once you're gone, and I can protect myself."

"I'm not leaving you. Don't make me kick this door in."

"You do, and I'll kick your nuts in. Damn it, Finn, will you just listen to me and go while you still can? I have plenty of potions. I'll be fine, I promise."

She was right. I knew she was right. The Króls wouldn't stick around to fight an armed alchemist if I was gone, not when more mundies could show up any time. But I couldn't do it. I couldn't just leave Heather here and hope the Króls didn't do something stupid and crazy anyway.

The blue glow of the witchfire faded fast now. I didn't have much time.

"Okay. Stay quiet," I said to Heather, then went to the tunnel entrance and placed my hands on the rough concrete. I called up a bit of magic and said, *"Aperire Ostium!"*

The magic poured out of me, and the concrete receded as though dragged back from the doorway, revealing a pitch-black tunnel that led to the right. But instead of entering, I turned and skimmed the wall out of sight of the stairs, back to the men's bathroom. I locked myself in the toilet stall, climbing up to squat on the toilet. After a second's consideration, I carefully lifted the heavy ceramic back off the toilet and held it ready to smash on the first head to peek into the stall.

After a minute, I heard the faint sound of the Króls arguing in German, and the grind of the tunnel entrance closing. Then silence. No sound of the women's bathroom door being smashed in, or of Heather fighting the witches. Finally, I left the stall and peeked out of the bathroom door. Nobody in sight.

I went to the women's bathroom to get Heather, but the door was open.

"Heather?" I called. There was no response. She must have left before me, on her own. The door would be broken open if the Króls had taken her.

I rushed up into the restaurant, still wielding my toilet cover. An Asian waitress was at the top of the stairs, her hair a bit disheveled and a confused look on her face. "What—?" she began.

"Sorry," I said. I set down the ceramic slab, turned, and rushed from the restaurant.

And ran into Grayson, literally.

"Finn! Watch yourself." He tugged his jacket straight, and brushed his slacks as if I'd gotten dirt on them just by bumping into him.

"Jimmy? What are you doing here?"

"I heard you might be here. I was hoping to talk to you."

"You couldn't wait until I got home?"

"You seem to be running around quite a bit of late, despite my warnings and advice, and I have more important things to do than sit around waiting on your convenience."

I glanced behind me, uncomfortable to be just standing there talking.

Grayson raised his eyebrows and looked past me. "Is there some concern?"

"I was just attacked by the Króls again."

"Really?" Grayson pulled a wand out of the inner pocket of his blue dinner jacket and said, "Let's go see these elusive witches of yours."

"I don't think they're still here."

Grayson arched an eyebrow. "I didn't see anyone else leave, Finn. Are you sure?"

"I think they left by the tunnels."

"Ah, of course. Well, if magic was used then a cleanup crew will be here soon enough. Meanwhile, may I offer you a safe ride home?"

"Yes, please."

Grayson drove a big burgundy Cadillac sedan. He leaned forward, peering out into the twilight as he steered the land boat over the bumpy roads toward home.

"Finn," he said. "I've come to recommend, as your friend, that perhaps you should consider confessing to the ARC."

"Confessing?" I said. "Wow. Thanks for the trust, Jimmy Jam."

"Respect!" Grayson slapped the steering wheel, his face gone red. I flinched. Man, he really had taken after Grandfather.

Grayson took a deep breath and cleared his throat. "I am your friend, Finn, whether you believe me or not. I am also a friend to your family. And I am a magus of the ARC. I must consider the greatest good for all here. You have clearly been hiding some fact, some secret, since you returned. I suspect it has something to do with the remains found in the wreckage of your trailer. I don't think either of us wants to see the enforcers rip the truth from you, eh? That wouldn't be good for you, or for your family if you're involved in anything . . . unfortunate."

"There's nothing to rip," I said. "I'm not hiding anything."

Grayson sighed through his nose. "Please, Finn. This could be your last chance. And clearly, being free of the enforcers has not made you any safer. Let me take you in—"

"No."

"I must tell you, you are being selfish, and foolish. I—"

"You *must* tell me that, huh? Well, I think maybe I *must* walk the rest of the way. You can let me out here."

"Finn, don't be—"

"Stop? Please?"

Grayson shook his head but pulled over. We were only a block from home. I climbed out of the car.

"Finn," Grayson called before I closed the door. "I've reached the limits of what I can do to protect you. And of my patience with your disregard for—"

I shut the door and walked away, my shoulders clenched as I waited for Grayson to attack me from behind in an attempt to haul me in. But he drove off into the night, leaving me to the sound of crickets and frogs and the smell of the roadside blackberry vines.

In case the Króls waited out front, I circled around through the darkening night to the back entrance. I jumped at serpentine shadows in the garden, half expecting some Triffid-like plant to emerge and attack. But the flowery vines and bushes were content to just sit and glower at me in their thorny way.

I sighed with relief as I passed through the wards into the mud room. Mother's ghost floated by and simply said, "Wipe your feet," before disappearing. I needed to call Heather. I was worried about her. Not just because of the Króls, but because she seemed to be in some other kind of trouble. At least, it seemed obvious that something was wrong, that she was unhappy. But first, I needed to talk to Zeke, to let him know about the Król attack, but also that Grayson might be siccing the ARC on us at any time.

Zeke's door was closed, but the door to Vee's room stood open. I peeked in to see if Zeke was there.

Sammy's old furniture was gone, but the walls were still covered in a collage of photographs, drawings, greeting cards, posters, and images cut from product packaging, with bare spaces where a pair of wardrobes and bookcases once stood along the walls. The old futon from the mother-in-law cottage sat in the corner where Sammy's bed used to be. Vee sat cross-legged on the floor in the room's center, and Pete lounged in one of the several bean bags that were the only chairs in the room, facing her. Neither showed notice of me. They appeared to be having a serious talk, so I stayed quiet, hoping for a good moment to interrupt.

"That's crazy," Pete said. "I think you're really nice. I don't think you'd hurt anybody."

I could see Vee's blush from across the room.

"You're so sweet. And I don't think Sarah'd hurt anyone either. But you know how out of control it feels when the change happens." I could hear the tears building in her voice. "And I've spent so much of my life in the Hole. I'm not even sure I know how to live in the real world. The rules are so different, and there's so much happening all the time, so much to remember and keep track of and—it scares me."

Pete reached out and took her hand. She flinched slightly but then looked up at Pete, and a smile bloomed across her face as sudden and sweet as the foam appearing on a root beer float. Pete was the one blushing now.

Vee looked down at their joined hands. "It's really nice having someone to talk with, Pete."

"Don't you talk to your brother?"

"Yes. But it's hard with him. I don't think he's really accepted the idea that I'm a waer yet, not in his heart. And the fact that he was exiled because of what happened, lost his position as an enforcer—

I love him, and he tries so hard to take care of me, but he's not easy to talk to. I can't even imagine how he's going to handle it the first time he actually sees me change."

"Don't you use the potion?" Pete asked.

Oh, crap!

"What potion?" Vee asked.

I stepped into the room. "Hey, guys."

Their hands shot apart, back into their own laps.

"Nothing," Pete said.

"What?" I asked.

"Huh?"

"I just said hello. Have you guys seen Zeke? Is he in his room?"

Vee stood up. "He's still sleeping off the berzerking. I really wouldn't disturb him."

"Okay. Hey, Pete, can I talk to you for a minute?"

Pete looked up at Vee, and gave a mournful expression but then sighed and stood up. "Okay. Bye, Vee."

"Good night. I'll see you tomorrow."

Pete smiled. "I can show you my paintings."

"I'd like that." Vee saw us out and closed the door behind us.

I led Pete down the stairs. "Pete, I don't think it's a good idea to mention your potions to Vee."

"Why not?"

"Because . . ." I stopped and looked at Pete. I'd been about to tell him yet another lie, that the potions only worked on wolf-form waers and Vee would be sad about it. But I couldn't.

Pete and Vee liked each other. Despite whatever misgivings I had about her being a feyblood, whatever obstacles they might have, they liked each other. And they did seem to be a pretty good match, even without Pete's supposed waer curse.

And there be the rub.

I'd continued the lie about his waer curse this long because I thought it was what would make Pete happiest. Okay, that wasn't quite true. I'd continued the lie because it was easiest, because I didn't want to risk him being angry at me and trying to deal with that while trying to clear my name and stay alive, not if I had only three days to spend with him.

But if there was one thing I could do to make Pete truly happy, and to fulfill my promise to help him find love, I realized that it was to tell Pete the truth. Hopefully, it wasn't too late already.

"Follow me." I turned around and led Pete back upstairs, to Mort's bedroom. I knocked twice and cracked open the door. For a second, I thought I sensed a stirring of spirit energy.

"Mort? Can we come in?" I said through the crack.

"No," Mort called back.

"It's just me and Pete. We only want to talk."

A sigh. "All right, come in." He sounded slightly less doped up than earlier.

I led Pete inside to Mort's black and chrome fortress of solitude. Mort sat in his bed, propped up in a throne of black pillows and watching some kind of game show on his giant television. I sensed no spirit energies now, and Mort didn't exactly look like he'd been summoning.

"Was there a spirit in here?"

"What?" Mort said, pushing himself up further. "No. Why, you've come to accuse me of something else?"

I sighed. It must have been my imagination, or perhaps Mother's ghost passing through. Now was not the time for investigations anyway.

"No, sorry," I said. "I wanted us to talk with Pete about his curse, and the potions."

Mort looked at me, his expression wary. "What about them?"

"Pete, sit down, buddy," I said. He sat on the edge of the bed, and I paced between him and the entertainment center as I spoke. "Okay. Look, Pete, first off I know you feel that being a waerwolf makes you special. But when you really think about it, everything that's special about you has nothing to do with being a waerwolf. You've always been really good with numbers and directions. You've always been stronger than me and Mort. And Petey, you're the best of us. I wish I had a heart as good and honest as yours. Especially right now."

Pete frowned. "Is this about the cure again, to make me not a waerwolf at all? I think maybe I don't need it anymore, Finn."

"Because Vee is a waer?" I asked. "Because you can't infect her?"

Pete blushed and shrugged but didn't say anything.

"Okay. I understand, Petey, I really do. But think of what it would be like if you weren't a waerwolf. You wouldn't have to wear those gloves all the time. You wouldn't have to drink the potions anymore, or worry about hurting someone if you ever did change and get loose. And Pete, you could eat chocolate. All you wanted. Chocolate cookies. Brownies. Chocolate pudding!"

Pete licked his lips. "I guess." He shook his head. "But then, I could get infected again."

"True, but—" I looked at Mort. "Mort? Don't you want to add something?"

"Like what?"

"Like why you think Petey is awesome without being a waerwolf?"

Mort snorted. "Okay, I know you've been off in fairyland for a while, man, but this is just weird. Since when did you turn into Oprah?"

"Mort, shut up and tell Petey why he's awesome right now, or I'll go tell Zeke you said his mustache is pathetic."

Mort glared at me a second, then said, "You know, you're really killing the nice buzz I had going. Whatever. Pete, you've done a heckuva job as a driver and head of security. If you weren't family, I'd definitely give you a raise." He looked at me. "Happy?"

"Good," I said. "See, Petey, being a waerwolf is not what makes you special, not at all. And I want you to know I love you, man, and I'm very sorry for this. Mort, tell him the truth."

"About what?"

"About his curse."

"I don't know what you're talking about."

"I— Fine." I put a hand on Pete's shoulder. "Pete. I promise, I'm telling you the truth right now. You're not a waerwolf. You never were."

Pete shoved my hand away and stood up, moving away from me to stand near Mort's dresser. "Stop it. This isn't funny. You just don't want me to like Vee. You want all the girls for yourself."

"What? That's not true," I said. "Really, Pete, I—"

"It is so true. You told me Vee couldn't be my girlfriend. And then you asked Dawn out, and then you asked Heather out, and you really hurt Dawn, and—I am so a waerwolf."

"Wow," Mort said, grinning at me. "You've been busy."

"Shut up, Mort. Pete, I know I said dating Vee was a bad idea before, but I changed my mind—"

"The way you changed your mind about Dawn?"

"No! I never wanted to date Dawn, Pete. Or at least—that's not the point. The point is, I want you to be happy. And I can see Vee makes you happy, and I don't want to mess that up with a lie. Remember that first night when you thought you changed? In the tree house? You didn't change, Pete. Mort snuck out there and—"

"Enough!" Pete said, putting his hands to his ears. "I don't want to hear it!"

"Good job, Dr. Phil," Mort said. "I could've told you not to bother. Hey, on your way out, can you ask Mattie to come up? I'm starving."

I didn't bother responding to Mort, and instead put a hand on Pete's elbow. "Pete, come on. You have to hear this. It's the truth. Why does it matter if you're not a waerwolf, really? You're still the guy who saved me and Vee at the Hole. You're still the guy who made me feel truly welcomed home—"

"Geez, thanks," Mort said. "I did put out food."

"And Pete, I love you man. You're my brother, and—"

Pete shoved me, hard. I stumbled back and fell to my butt. My back slammed painfully against the entertainment center.

"No!" Pete said. "Stop saying that! If I'm not a waerwolf, then that means you lied to me, and made me drink those potions, and—I don't want that to be true." Tears streamed down his cheeks. "You're my brother. Everyone else made fun of me, played jokes on stupid Pete, but you didn't, Finn. Tell me you're just trying to be funny. Tell me I'm really a waerwolf."

I took a deep breath. "I'm sorry, Pete. I'm really, really sorry. If I hadn't been exiled, I—"

"NO!" Pete grabbed a cologne bottle off the dresser and threw it in my direction. It flew high, and the television screen shattered in a flash of sparks. I scrambled out of the way of the shrapnel and cologne splatter.

"Fuck!" Mort shouted and began scrambling out of bed. "What the hell, Pete! Do you know how much that thing cost?"

Pete stomped out of the room. It felt like a big hole had just opened up in my heart.

Mort disentangled himself from his blankets, stumbled over to the television, and unplugged it from the wall. "Well, this is just awesome. Good job, Finn. So glad you're home. You just walk in after twenty-five years and think you know what's best for everyone. And look how much better off we are. Father's upset, Pete's upset, I have a broken television, I feel like I've been hit by a truck—"

"That's not my fault," I said. "I wasn't the one trying to buy illegal Talker artifacts."

"I'm trying to secure the future of our business. And I wouldn't have tried to make that deal except I just knew you'd swoop in here with your oh-so-special gift and act like you own the place! I swear, I don't know why Father and Grandfather—"

"Seriously? Dude, I'm not trying to take over anything! I just—"

"Whatever," Mort said, dismissing me with a wave as he crossed back to his bed. "I don't suppose the changeling left you enough money to buy me a new TV?"

"I don't know, but he left me this." I flipped Mort off and followed after Pete.

Zeke stumbled out of his room in tighty-whitey briefs, baton in hand. A maze of glossy pink scars covered his pale skin where his enforcer tattoos had been removed, except for the midnight black mandala around his belly button that was his magic pee spell. He looked up and down the hall with bleary eyes. "What's going on?" he asked, his voice thick from sleep. "I heard fighting, and your fool brother just ran by here looking like someone'd killed his dog."

"It's just a family dispute," I said.

"Hnh. That explains it. Didn't expect that boy to be runnin' from a fight. Anything I should be concerned about here?" He glanced past me, toward Mort's room.

"No. But there's something you should know. The Króls attacked me tonight, at the restaurant. I guess I was wrong about my enemies not wanting to involve mundies."

"I'm shocked," Zeke said in a tone that held no shock whatsoever. "I called about that lead on the witchcraft supplies before hitting the rack, but it was a dead end. So if it really was the Króls who attacked you—"

"It was."

"Then they're damned good at hiding, or really good at hexin' folks who blab about 'em. Maybe both." He made a disgusted sound. "Witch clans. They should all be crushed. They don't respect ARC laws, and they ain't got no honor. Too bad you didn't catch one. I guarantee I'd barely have to bleed him to make him lead us to the rest."

Bleed one to find the others—of course! "I have an idea," I said. "I think I know how to find them. But it's not something I want to attempt while tired, or at night." Or when my emotions were such a mess.

"Fine," Zeke said and headed back into his room. "I could use more sleep anyway. See you in the morning, then, Gramaraye."

"Wait. One more thing. Grayson is pushing for me to turn myself into the ARC. I don't think we can count on his support any longer."

Zeke snorted. "I never did." He shut his door, and I stood a minute in the hallway, trying to decide what I should do next. Probably best to let Pete have some time alone before talking to him again. And I'd need rest to face whatever trials tomorrow would bring. Just thinking of bed caused exhaustion to fall gently upon me like an anvil made of ether. I wanted to lie down and sleep right there in the hall, though I didn't look forward to the dreams I'd have.

But first things first. I tracked down Mattie and got Heather's phone number. I called from the house phone, and after several rings someone picked up.

"Heather?" I asked.

A young man's voice responded, "Who's this?"

"Uh, I was calling for Heather Fl—Brown. Do I have the right number?"

"Is this Finn Gramaraye?"

"Yes."

"Then this is a wrong number for you. You need to stay away from my mother. I don't want her caught up in your problems, understand?"

I heard Heather's voice in the background, "Orion, give me the phone."

"Mother, no. You know why you can't—"

Heather said firmly, "Give it to me."

Orion sighed into the phone, then said, "Leave my mother alone."

I blinked. "Look, I—"

"Hi, Finn," Heather said. "I figured you'd call to check on me, and you don't need to worry. I'm fine. But . . . I think it's best if we don't see each other for a while."

"What? Why?" I said. "If it's because of the attack—"

"No, it has nothing to do with that. I just—I need to figure some stuff out. Good-bye, Finn. And thank you for still caring."

"Wait, I—"

Click and dial tone.

I stared at the receiver for a minute, then hung up. Between

Pete, Dawn, Mort, and Heather, it felt like half the world hated me or wanted nothing to do with me just then. I shuffled back to my father's room to sleep on the love seat, feeling very alone in a house full of people.

Peek-a-Boo

I woke early with a kink in my neck from sleeping on Mother's reading sofa and snuck from the room without waking Father. 6:30 A.M. again. Damn it. I never used to be a morning person. The rules for changelings really should include one against messing with the host's body clock.

I changed into a somewhat snug Thundarr the Barbarian T-shirt from my dresser, and went out to Pete's cottage. I knocked on the door and heard the squeak of Pete getting off his bed, but he didn't answer.

"Pete. Come on, bro. I'm sorry. I know I've lost your trust, and I feel like the biggest jerk in the world. But I swear I'll do whatever it takes to make this up to you. Just give me the chance to start."

Still no response. I wished time would speed up so I could get to the point where Pete didn't hate me anymore.

"Petey, I'm begging here. I know you're mad, and I don't blame you. So hit me, or yell at me or something. But talk to me. Let me explain. We've already lost twenty-five years, I don't want to lose any more time."

I heard the floorboards creak, the sound approaching the door. But then silence again.

Damn it. This really sucked. I waited long enough to be sure he wouldn't change his mind, then marched back inside. I'd taken it for granted that Pete would always bring the happiness and smiles no matter how crappy my own day was, or his. To know I'd helped to make him so unhappy made me feel like I'd just beat a unicorn to death with a Care Bear in front of a small child.

I would make this up to him.

I gathered some equipment from the necrotorium and then met Zeke in my bedroom.

"So what's the plan?" Zeke asked, leaning against the door with his arms crossed. He still looked tired, but not ready to collapse at least.

I pulled the throw rug aside, revealing dark floorboards. "The plan, Sam I Am, is to find the clan if we can."

I proceeded to set up the Kin Finder 2000. At least, that's what I called Father's invention. About the size of a microwave, it looked like half clockwork slot machine, half distillery, and half something that would pop out of Inspector Gadget's hat. Yes, that's one too many halves, but the Kin Finder 2000 looked like it had one too many halves. Still, it worked, and that's all that mattered. In fact, despite Grandfather's disapproval of Mother marrying a thaumaturge, Father's inventions had helped give our family an advantage over some of the other necrotoriums who had larger families, or more money.

I turned the machine to align it to true north according to the compass on its top, then extended the mechanical arm with its thin tube and ring at the end. I slid a topless pen into the ring, and set the end of the tube into the pen. Finally, I set a piece of paper on the floor beneath it all. Zeke eyed the whole thing askance, and stroked his mustache as I worked.

"What's this mess gonna do?" he finally asked.

"This is going to tell us the locations of Felicity's blood kin."

Zeke blew his mustache out, causing the ends to flap. "I already told ya, fool, the ARC couldn't find any Króls near here, and they have the best location spells around."

"Yes, but this thing doesn't use a location spell. It works on the spirit plane, using spiritual harmonics to— Never mind. It will work, don't worry. Assuming, that is, this still holds enough of her resonance to do the job." I held up the lock of Felicity's hair from Sammy's voodoo doll, which had thankfully still been in her bedroom vent where Sammy used to stash her cigarettes and other contraband.

I pulled a different braid of hair out of a wooden box. The control braid. I placed a strand of hair from it into the pot at the device's heart, poured in a bit of the water, and lit the candle underneath. Then we waited.

The water finally boiled. I placed my hand on the small crystal ball at the back of the machine and concentrated, reached out as if to summon the spirit of the person who owned the piece of hair in the pot. The crystal vibrated. I could feel the resonance of the other spirit, like the faintest scent on a breeze, or music so low you could only sense it as a vibration at the edge of hearing. The steam rose from the pot into a copper tube and passed through an arcane series of transformations within the machine, causing gears and wheels to turn, producing an escalating series of *pings* and *clangs* and *sproings*. As the noises neared their crescendo, Zeke leaned forward and watched the device, obviously forgetting his job to appear stoically disinterested.

"Now watch as the spirit world talks to us," I said theatrically.

The arm lowered. It drew a single line out from the center of the page. It rose back up.

Zeke continued to watch for a minute as the machine quieted then finally stopped altogether. He frowned. "That's it? It drew a line!"

"A perfect line."

"A perfectly useless line, fool!"

I smiled. "It's a line that tells us the exact direction and distance to the nearest living relative of the deceased. The sister of the woman whose hair this is happens to be agoraphobic and hasn't left her little cottage since she was a girl, so we always know where she is. And now," I said, lifting up Felicity's lock of hair, "I will do the same thing for Felicity's relatives, and by using this first line as a point of reference, we'll be able to tell exactly which way and how far the other line points to."

"Oh." Zeke leaned back against the door. "I thought it was going to write out an address or something useful like that."

"We're dealing with spiritual energy, not an actual spirit," I said as I rinsed out the pot and put it back with all of Felicity's hair in it. "It's not like we're calling the ghost of an AT&T operator for information. It's more like the way a compass uses magnetism."

The water boiled again. I took a deep breath and reached out for Felicity's spirit. Nothing.

She'd been warded against Talking. But damn it, I wasn't trying to Talk to her. I just needed to pick up her resonance. I closed my eyes, took a deep breath, and placed my free hand on the floor. I spread out my fingers, and let myself sink deep into that place where the rest of the world falls away and there is just my spirit, and the magic, where I could sometimes hear echoes left in the material world like grooves in a record of clichés. You get the idea.

My hand went numb on the floorboards as though plunged in icy water. I felt Felicity then, a faint suggestion of her that brought an image of her face to my mind, and a hint of something else to my heart. Pain. Betrayal. Sadness.

The machine made its noises. I shuddered, and jerked my hand from the floor. I opened my eyes and looked down at my fingers, half expecting to see them blue, dead, but they looked normal.

The arm of the machine lowered and drew a second line, perpendicular to the first.

"So that's it?" Zeke asked. "Ya know where they are?"

I picked up the paper, and set it next to the Thomas Guide, a book of maps divided into confusing grids. "Almost," I said. This was the part where Pete normally helped. He had an uncanny ability to just glance at the two lines and point right to the correct spot in the book. I had to do it the hard way. I used a ruler, started with the line between our house and Miss Shenestiky, figured out the difference in the line length and how much that meant I had to take away from the other line, and, uh—

Shazbat. Indiana Jones I was not. I'd totally be the guy digging in the wrong place for the ark.

Zeke nodded at the paper. "Maybe I should hand that info over to the enforcers," he said.

Crap. Then I'd have to explain that the KF2K only worked with someone who was dead, which would lead to the question of how I knew Felicity was dead, and that was a question I didn't want an enforcer asking me just yet.

"Look, the enforcers already think I tried leading them on a wild goose chase with the Króls. If this information is wrong for some reason, or the Króls get wind that the enforcers are coming and clear out, it's only going to waste everyone's time and probably get me hauled in early. I'd rather check this out ourselves first, see if it's correct."

Zeke pulled on his mustache a second and looked between me and the KF2K, then shrugged. "Fine. Just means we get to question the Króls my way, without all the stupid new rules. I doubt that machine really works anyway."

"Yeah? How's Plan B coming, then?" I tried again to measure out the location on the maps. "Figured out where Magus Verona is yet?"

"As a matter of fact, yeah. She's beneath something called the EMP."

"Isn't that, like, a nuclear weapon of some kind?"

"No. It's a museum over in Seattle. And you can bet they've put enough security on it to kill a dozen wizards. Like I said, only a crazy fool'd try getting at Verona."

"So you're saying you can beat a whole clan of witches but not a security system?"

"I'm sayin' I know how to deal with witches. But who knows what kinda security they got on that crypt? And the ARC might forgive us roughing up a couple illegal witches, but breaking into an ARC Sanctum, that's another matter."

I sighed and gave up trying to figure out the maps. "Well, hopefully we won't need to be crazy fools, then. But if we did, it might not hurt to know exactly how crazy we're talking about."

"Fine. I'll make some more calls. It's your phone bill."

I picked up the maps, and led the way out into the hall. "And I'll see if someone can help me with these."

Mattie stepped out of Mort's room and closed his door. She wore footsie pajamas that made her look like a giant yellow mouse and had a box of Band-Aids in one hand. "Would you believe Petey bit my dad?" she asked as she walked toward Zeke and me.

"What?" I said. "Why?"

"I guess he was like, I want to know if I'm really a waerwolf or not. Chomp!"

I laughed, but Zeke crossed his arms. "What if the fool had been a waer and infected his brother?"

"That's what Dad asked him, I guess. And Uncle Pete said then Dad could drink the potions too."

A smile crept across Zeke's rugged face like waves eroding a sandcastle. "Okay. I could almost like that kid."

Mattie pointed at the Thomas Guide. "What's that?"

"Directions, of a sort," I said. "I need to figure them out, though."

"Oh, the Kin Finder? That's easy. You should try calculus homework if you want hard." She took the guide, and the Kin Finder lines, and flipped through the book. "This is so old school. We so need to figure out how to hook a GPS up to the KF or— Got it." She held out the Thomas Guide and pointed to the map. "There's your spot."

I looked from the map to Zeke. "What say we go visit a family of vengeful witches in lovely downtown Kingston?"

Blasphemous Rumors

I drove across the Hood Canal Bridge, following Zeke's directions to Kingston. Zeke shifted again in the passenger seat, and looked decidedly uncomfortable. He was back in his Magi Vice outfit and looked nearly as white as his jacket.

"You okay?" I asked.

"I hate bridges," he said.

I chose not to ask why, since I felt certain the answer had something to do with me being a fool. I turned on the radio and listened to how music had changed in the past twenty-five years. The first band sounded like a Pixies knockoff, the next two had touches of Grandmaster Flash and New Order. A couple of catchy tunes, though there seemed to be more noise and less melody than I was used to. I might have turned it off, except it obviously annoyed Zeke. I turned it up. He lasted until we passed through the picture-perfect town of Port Gamble, when the singer started scream-whining over a dying drum machine. It was a bit Sigue Sigue Sputnik meets a bandsaw. I imagined it looked impressive on stage though, with Mechagodzilla stomping on robot cats and all. Zeke punched the radio off, his glower daring me to challenge his decision. I shrugged.

Zeke checked the contents of his pockets for the hundredth time. "When we get there, you do what I say. I've dealt with witches before. They may not have the raw power of wizards, but they can be twice as dangerous."

"What's your plan?"

"If we can, we'll sneak in and find their sanctum before

confronting them. A witch is far less dangerous if we can cut off access to their talismans and foci."

"And if we can't?"

"Then stay behind me and be ready for a nasty fight."

"Right." I sighed. It would have been nice to have Pete with us again for extra muscle, though I felt equally glad he hadn't come. The last thing I wanted was to endanger him again.

Kingston was a "blink and you'll miss it" town whose main purpose for existing was its ferry dock, which connected the Olympic Peninsula with "mainland" suburbia north of Seattle. Like Port Townsend, it had grown in the past twenty-five years, with a couple of grocery shopping centers and new housing communities spreading along the main road like ivy climbing a post.

The early-morning sun had just peaked the treetops by the time we neared the location marked on the map, in the heart of Kingston not far from the ferry dock. It looked like the Stepford Wives area of town. I peered up the Króls' street as we passed, and frowned.

"This can't be right." The street led to a cul-de-sac of Easter-colored houses with perfect lawns, flower gardens, and shiny, boxy vehicles in the drives. I'd expected something more like a stone fortress reached by a craggy cliffside road, possibly with horses that whinnied as lightning flashed overhead. Or at least, something that looked more appropriate for a coven of evil witches. I pulled into the next street, parked, and consulted the map. We had the right spot. "Huh."

"Something wrong?" Zeke asked.

"No. I don't know. I just expected something different, I guess."

Zeke glanced around at the houses. "This feels right to me. Easier for witches to lure in fools with a house of bread and cake than a house of bones, yeah?"

Of course. Hansel and Gretel. I should have remembered my lessons. These houses would be a bit tough on the teeth, but they were the color of cupcakes, and probably full of families with their 2.5 plump children.

I resumed driving and parked in the lot of a church several

blocks away. We hiked back along the main road, then cut up into the woods as we neared the Króls' cul-de-sac. No sense in making it too obvious.

Zeke paused and reached inside his jacket as though digging through an inside pocket. The white jacket and pants became brown and green camouflage, blending with the pine trees and ferns around us.

"Nice!" I said. "Jacket by Ralph Lothlórien."

I'd actually seen a real elven cloak once in the Museum of Necromancy, but it was a cloak made from the skins of elves, and not at all what Tolkien had in mind, I think—though I guess it still would have blended nicely into wooded surroundings.

Zeke shot me a glare, then continued marching through the woods. I followed.

We neared the edge of the woods around the cul-de-sac. Zeke pointed to our right and whispered, "I want to circle around. I'm guessing the center house is theirs."

"Why's that?"

"It has gnomes on the lawn."

We circled around the cul-de-sac until Zeke held up a hand, signaling for me to stop. I moved behind a nearby tree and waited, peeking around the edge. Zeke knelt down, pulled back the left sleeve of his jacket, and held up his wrist to reveal a silver Casio calculator watch. He moved his arm around, occasionally tapping at the watch.

Zeke finished whatever he was doing and crept back to my position.

"Alarm talismans," he whispered. "See there, where those two branches split?" He pointed up into the tree canopy.

I squinted and saw something in the crook of the branches, a bundle of sticks perhaps, and what looked like a small animal skull.

"What do we do?"

Zeke plopped his duffel down on the ground and pulled out an animal pelt. He turned away from me. "Get on my back," he whispered over his shoulder.

"What?"

"Don't make me ask again. The pelt will hide us, but it's not wide enough to cover two people walkin' side by side."

"Uh, sure, okay." I hopped up on his back, wrapping my arms around his neck and gripping his torso with my legs. He handed me the duffel to hold, then flipped the pelt over both our heads, and lumbered forward.

Not exactly the most impressive way to charge a den of bad witches, I suppose.

Speaking of bad witches, riding piggyback reminded me of Pete, who'd often given me piggyback rides when we were younger, which reminded me again that Pete wasn't with us, which reminded me *why* he wasn't with us, which made me sad. It also reminded me of the time I gave barefooted Heather a piggyback ride across a field of gravel while walking her home, which reminded me that she wasn't talking to me, which again made me sad. That was a lot of bad whiches indeed, which was too bad because I suspected that piggyback rides came along very rarely in adulthood, and it seemed a real shame to not enjoy them. Even the ones given by grumpy Vikings.

I braced for the animal skulls in the trees to begin shrieking, but none did. We reached the edge of the woods, and Zeke said, "Off."

I slid onto the ground, and Zeke rushed to the side of the nearest house. I copied him, pressing my back against the peach-colored siding.

He stuffed the pelt back into the bag and shook his arm so that his watch settled down near his hand. He tapped on the calculator keys and held the watch near me, then hit a couple more keys and grunted.

"Something wrong?" I asked.

"No."

"What are you doing?"

"I'm calculating how annoying your questions are, but my watch doesn't go that high, fool."

He moved along the back of the house to the sliding glass doors, and I followed. Zeke squatted down low and peeked through the doors. After a few seconds he tapped at his watch again, appeared satisfied with whatever the result was, and pulled a skeleton key from beneath his shirt, hung on a leather cord. This was a true skeleton key, made from the enchanted finger-bone of a skilled thief, a rare artifact that combined necromantic and thaumaturgic magic yet was, for some reason, not very popular with thieves.

Zeke touched the finger bone to the edge of the sliding door, and then pushed gently on the door itself. It slid open.

"Stay very close to me as we pass through the threshold, dig?" he whispered. He crept forward, and I got as close as I could, my hands on his back. I felt the tingle of wards as we passed over the threshold, but again no alarms sounded.

We were in what looked like a family room, with a sofa and lounge chairs, a large television, and plastic musical instruments.

Zeke turned in a slow circle, consulting his watch. I drew the family gun from my jacket pocket, an old revolver loaded with silver bullets.

"Why didn't the alarm go off?" I whispered.

"If I tell you, will you shut up?"

"Maybe," I said.

He continued to look at his watch as he muttered, "I measured our magic level, and created a subtraction field around us to cancel it out so the wards didn't— There. I'm picking up something this way."

He led me to a laundry room, and then to the shelves at the back filled with cleaning supplies. He touched his skeleton key to several spots along the shelves and the wall around them, until a soft *click* sounded, and the shelves swung out from the wall.

"Let's see what the Króls have going on," Zeke whispered. I swung the hidden door fully open, and Zeke led the way into the small room beyond.

The paraphernalia of dark witchcraft filled the room, including engraved skulls, crucibles, animal bones, silver knives, blood drawing equipment, black candles, and cupcake tins.

I noted a complete absence of rock albums and D&D modules, however, which would have come as a sore disappointment to our old mundy neighbor, Missus Bumshaw, who'd repeatedly informed me that such items were the gateways to evil and witchcraft. Instead, a desk sat against the back wall, covered in papers. Above it hung a sheet of paper with big red letters printed on it, some crossed out:

1) ~~Control PTA~~
2) ~~Control church~~
3) Control Town

Beneath the list was a collage of tacked-up news clippings from local papers, a map with lots of circles on it, and photos of people with ziplock bags pinned to them containing hair, nail clippings, bits of cloth, and other items. And mixed in with all of that, a lot of recipes for baked goods.

"Looks like they've been busy," Zeke whispered, then spun around, his baton extending and springing into bright white light in his hand.

I turned and raised the gun, half expecting to see a hex flying at my face. A woman stood in the entrance to the room, her arms crossed. She had square features and thick blond hair and dressed as though her husband was the Republican candidate for president of the United States.

"Who are you, and why are you in my home?" she asked, without any trace of Austrian accent.

"Uh," I said.

"We have a few questions for you," Zeke said.

"Really? I haven't seen an enforcer dressed like that in, well, quite a while. Somehow, I don't think you've come from the ARC. Which makes me wonder how you'd feel if I called them?"

"I'd feel great," Zeke said. "Ask for Enforcer Captain Vickers;

tell him his favorite retiree says I've got a clan of illegal feybloods I wanna introduce him to."

The woman arched an eyebrow. She smiled and took a step into the room. "Very well. What do you want?" Her hand reached out casually to the workbench beside her.

Zeke tapped a nearby jar containing a tentacled something in green liquid. It crashed to the floor. "Oops," he said. "Maybe we should step away from the dark magics and talk someplace less dangerous?"

The woman glared murder at Zeke, but she raised her hands, backed through the door, and continued to walk in deliberate steps backward through the laundry room. Zeke moved in pace with her, and I followed suit. She stepped out into the family room, far enough so we could follow.

Zeke put out his arm, stopping me from leaving the laundry room. "This is defensible," he whispered back at me.

"Is there a problem?" the woman asked.

"Uh, no," I said. "We just really like your laundry room; it's comfy and smells good. What kind of softener do you use?"

"Dryad tears, if you must know," the woman said. "But as long as we're discussing comfort, can I offer you something? Some beer perhaps? Or muffins?"

"I ain't no sucker, to take food from a witch," Zeke said.

"Of course not. But you're guests in my home, and it would've been rude not to offer."

Her home? Facts clicked together in my head. Literally, I hear facts clicking together in my head sometimes. I don't know if it's just my overactive imagination, or some heightened sensitivity to the life energy behind neurons firing, but either way it is a rather annoying and smug sound.

If this was her home, that made her the clan matriarch, though she hardly looked old enough for the role. "You're Aunt Giselle."

"I think if you were my nephew, I'd know it."

"No, I meant— I knew Felicity. You're her aunt Giselle, right?"

"Ah, of course, I see now." She crossed her arms. "You're Phinaeus

Gramaraye. Is this your brother Paeteri, then? I'd heard reports that he was . . . meaty."

"Do we really look like brothers?" I asked, choosing to ignore her choice of words.

Giselle shrugged. "Magic works many changes, not all of them unseen. Who can say what the manner of your conception begat?"

"What's that supposed to mean?"

"Enough distractions," Zeke said. "We know you've made several attacks on the Gramaraye family and tried to get Finn exiled. What's your game?"

"Well, you certainly know a lot," Giselle said. "Unfortunately, none of it is true."

Footsteps and children's voices sounded on the stairs to our right, and a boy and girl appeared. They looked to be about twelve. They were almost too cute for words. But only almost, so the words would probably be "eugenics" and "Village of the Damned."

"The Andersons are bringing their brats over," the boy said to Giselle.

"About time too," the girl said. "I'm starv—"

"Children," Giselle said sharply. "We have guests. I believe you've met?" She nodded in the direction of Zeke and me.

The children froze on the bottom steps for a second, looking at us. Then the girl turned and ran up the stairs.

"Stop!" Zeke shouted, to no effect.

The boy moved to stand beside Giselle and shimmered as he moved, expanded, until the man who attacked me at the restaurant and stalked my house the night of my return stood there glowering at me.

"And now," Giselle said, her eyes fixed on Zeke. "It's time you pay the cost of invading our home." She lifted an object that looked like a dead mouse with a bird skull attached. The veins along her arms and neck went black against her pale skin, and droplets of red appeared on her fingers and lips.

The amulet against my chest grew warm.

I pointed the pistol at Giselle, and Zeke reached into his pants pocket and pulled out a grenade. He yanked the pin free.

"Go ahead!" he said. "Make another move, and I'll toss this back into your little room of fun."

"No!" Giselle said. "Wait!" She lowered the talisman and held up her empty hand instead. The signs of blood magic vanished from her skin. "We can talk."

"Good," Zeke said. "Let's try this again. Why don't you tell us exactly what you've done to attack Finn here?"

"Nothing," Giselle said. "We've never attacked him, I swear."

Zeke gave a surprised grunt. "She ain't lying, not that I can tell."

I waved the revolver at the man. "But your family tried to poison me in the restaurant last night."

"That wasn't poison," the man said, his Austrian accent returned. "We only wanted to talk to you."

"You tried to slip me a witch's brew."

"Ya, just a little something to make you more . . . cooperative, to answer our questions."

"Oh, well, that's okay, then," I said, then remembered that witches were immune to sarcasm. "That is, it wasn't okay at all. What questions?"

Giselle exchanged glances with the man, then said, "We wish to know who was Felicity's lover?"

Felicity had a lover? That was a surprise, but my brain started turning over the possibilities. "I don't understand. Why do you want to know about her lover?"

"Because we think her lover was the same person who attacked her, and forced her into hiding."

Would that mean my father had been Felicity's lover? No, I refused to believe that. He had loved Mother too much, even after her death. But maybe the Króls were right, maybe Felicity's lover was the person who controlled my father. In which case, we were both after the same thing.

"What do you know about this lover of hers?" I asked.

The man beside Giselle said, "He must be someone of influence. He took Felicity away from us, and continued to block our attempts to immigrate here after you were exiled."

"Why did he want Felicity, exactly?" Zeke asked.

I'd never really thought about it before but realized what an important question that was. If the person who brought Felicity to America was the same person who killed her, why go through all that trouble? Why not just use an au pair from closer to home?

"She was beautiful in the eyes of men," Giselle said, the disgust thinly disguised in her tone. "She refused to use her blood gifts, so was not blessed with the markings of our craft."

"That's hard to believe," Zeke said. "You witches tend to eat your own if they don't follow your ways."

"She had . . . other uses," Giselle said. "We require many materials, and she possessed great skill at obtaining them, particularly plants."

The man snorted. "That's all she ever wanted to do, play with her plants."

Giselle smiled at me, an unpleasant smile. "Men desire women who appear beautiful, innocent, pure. They desire to possess such girls as Felicity, to corrupt them, it is in the darkest corner of every man's heart. I understand the one who took her away from us. He was more our kin than Felicity, in some ways. But he must pay nonetheless."

"Do you know anything else about him?"

"Only that her lover was someone in your family," Giselle said. "In your house."

"How do you know it was— Wait. What makes you so sure *I* wasn't her lover, then?" I felt oddly offended.

Giselle laughed. "Because we smelled the virginity on you, at the trial." She cocked her head. "Interesting. You're not a virgin now, though. You've been busy since your return." She sounded disappointed, and I didn't think it was because she'd hoped to be my first. Unicorns and blood witches both loved virgins, and for similar reasons. There was some kind of power in virgin blood. Apparently powerful enough to smell even through a wall of laundry scents.

I wrestled with the possibility that the Króls might be right. Who in our family might have been Felicity's lover?

Petey had been too young, so that wasn't a worry at least.

Sammy? Possible, if unlikely. True, she'd never felt she was part of the family, never liked the family business or much of anything for that matter, and she did resent Felicity for taking Mother's place. But even though I could almost believe her capable of attacking Felicity, I couldn't imagine her pretending to love someone she hated, or hurting someone who was her lover, and I certainly refused to believe she would frame me. Besides, the attack had involved magic, which Sammy was allergic to.

Grandfather—no, just because—*ewww*! And while he'd supported the decision to hire an au pair, he'd also died before Felicity's attack. I supposed it was possible that his was the spirit that possessed Father, but only if summoned by someone else, and even then, why attack Felicity? And who then blocked the Króls' immigration? Who'd been attacking me since my return from exile? Even if Grandfather did manage to somehow exert his will once from beyond the grave for some unknowable reason, he could not have done everything else.

Father? Age difference aside, he'd truly loved Mother. And why would he have himself possessed, attack Felicity, and frame me?

Once again, I was back to Mort. If someone in my family really had been Felicity's lover and attacker, I hoped it *was* Mort. Not because I wanted to believe he was guilty, but just because I wanted even less to believe my father or anyone else in the family was guilty. And I could almost believe it, except for three things: He'd passed Zeke's truth-sensing test, I didn't want it to be true for Mattie's sake, and of course, if he'd slept with Felicity, there's no way he'd have been able to stop himself from bragging about it.

"Don't you have anything else you can tell me, to help me figure out who it is?" I asked. "You've had twenty-five years. What've you done in all that time to find Felicity's real attacker?"

"We did nothing at first," Giselle replied in an icy tone, "though I now regret it. Felicity contacted us after your trial, and told us that she had framed you for some greater purpose, that we were not to take blood vengeance on your family. I thought she had perhaps at last embraced the way of her people. But then she disappeared. For twenty-five years we heard nothing. And then, two nights ago, she sent me a message via the gnomes."

I took a step forward. "You got g-mail from Felicity?"

"We . . . do not call it that anymore, but yes. Felicity told me she was going to apologize to you, and warn you of some danger. She said that—" Giselle's face twisted in disgust. "That guilt had eaten at her heart. She knew I had begun searching for her again, and to . . . research your family. She said that if anything happened to her, that we were not to blame you, and that we should take no action for we would only endanger ourselves."

Zeke grunted. "So you've just been good little witches," he waved back in the direction of the secret room. "It looks to me like you've been busy playing Leave it to Cleaver here."

Giselle shrugged. "We gather our power and influence. Such things will be needed, I think, when we discover what has truly happened to Felicity, and who is responsible."

"The power is not for vengeance, I think," Zeke replied. "You do that for the fun."

"Why, I'm offended," Giselle said, then looked back at me. "We have used all the magic at our disposal to unveil which of your family tasted Felicity's soul, and we've found nothing."

"Then why are you so convinced it was someone in my family?"

"Because the bones say so, and because I feel it."

"Right," I said. "Okay, look. I don't know anything about a lover. But it seems we both want the same thing. So why don't you just agree to leave me alone while I find out who's behind all this, and I'll agree not to bring the ARC down on your heads." Of course, I didn't promise Zeke wouldn't do so.

Footsteps on the stairs again, and the pale girl who'd acted like our waitress the night before burst into the room. "The wards! Something is coming at us, fast!"

"Is this your doing?" Giselle demanded, looking between me and Zeke.

"No," I said.

Any remaining hint of color drained from her face. "Move aside, then! We need access to our magics."

"I don't think so," Zeke replied.

"Damn it—"

Something slammed into the door upstairs, rattling the house, and everyone in the room jumped.

Giselle lifted her talisman like a gun, pointed at Zeke. "Move! Now!"

"Forget it," Zeke said, hefting the grenade. Or at least he started to. The girl on the stairs threw something at him from the side and Zeke froze, frosting over with spiderwebs. At the same time, the man shouted something and flicked a Bic lighter under his hand, and the gun in my hand burned red hot. I dropped it, screaming in startled pain.

Giselle barked a command in Witchese, and a ball of darkness and crackling red energy shot from her talisman at my chest, too fast to dodge.

In the split second before the curse struck, my butt cheeks twitched and felt as though I'd decided to squeeze a burning tortilla between them.

The curse struck me in the chest—and my chest ate it. Well, to be more precise, a glowing image like Pac-Man with a tribal face tattoo appeared on my chest, and ate it.

The energy sat in my chest like heartburn. This wasn't the work of the hex protection amulet. The amulet acted like a shield; it didn't eat stuff, or, for that matter, make my butt cheeks twitch.

"What the—?" I said.

"How'd you—?" Giselle said.

Crash! the upstairs door said. At the same time something

huge and hairy slammed into the glass slider doors to my left and was thrown back with a blinding orange flash. The glass cracked with a sound like Prince squealing over a gunshot, and the orange lines of the ward runes faded.

Giselle howled in frustration, then said, "Upstairs. We'll use the attic."

The Króls retreated up the stairs. Giselle shouted back at me and Zeke, "We won't forget this." And then they were gone.

I was a little preoccupied by the fact that I had just Pac-Manned a curse. I turned to check on Zeke—and burped.

All that dark energy in my chest exploded from my mouth and struck Zeke.

The webbing melted away as if eaten by acid.

Zeke stared at me. "What the—?"

"I know!" I said. "What the—?"

The sliding doors exploded inward, shards of glass showering the family room. A sasquatch stumbled through them wearing clown-sized combat boots. Harry, from Fort Worden, though he looked a bit ridiculous with his hair smoking.

I snatched up the revolver. It had thankfully cooled, though the burns on my hand still made holding it difficult. Harry turned his glare to us, and his beady eyes widened in surprise.

"Youselfs?" he said. "Youself not witchbrights."

"Uh, no," I said. "We're definitely not witches." The stench of burned hair wafted into the laundry room.

"Youself hurt me bigbad at fort," Harry said to Zeke, his voice becoming somewhat growly.

"We'll hurt you a lot more," Zeke said, displaying the grenade.

A crash sounded from upstairs, followed by a roar.

"Youself not the job, you rabbit away now." Harry ran upstairs.

"Sounds like good advice to me," I said.

"Agreed," Zeke agreed. We stepped cautiously out of the laundry room.

A wave of ick rolled over me, causing my skin to prickle into goose bumps and my stomach to gurgle in protest. The amulet grew hot on my chest. More dark witchcraft was being used nearby.

A sasquatch screamed in pain somewhere upstairs.

"Move it, Gramaraye," Zeke said. I crossed to the broken slider doors, and Zeke raised the hand grenade, aiming back into the hidden room.

"Wait!" I said.

I unplugged the television, and yanked out cables from its back. Zeke scowled at me. "Are you crazy?"

I lifted the television from the entertainment center. It wasn't overly heavy, though its size made it really awkward, and my hand still stung from the gun burns. "Okay, bombs away." I shuffled out through the remains of the slider doors as Zeke tossed the grenade.

Zeke joined me on the back lawn and sprinted to the tree line while I lugged the television along behind him.

The grenade exploded. A cloud of smoke rolled out of a new hole in the side of the house.

From upstairs, I heard an inhuman screech that I doubted belonged to either sasquatch, followed by a roar that most certainly did, and what sounded like a sofa, or possibly one of the sasquatches, being thrown against a wall.

Zeke glared at the television as I joined him in the trees.

"My brother's a dick," I said. "But I don't want to go back into exile feeling I owed him anything."

"Theft is a sign of corruption, whatever the reason," Zeke said.

"Hey, they probably paid for this with blood money. And they're here illegally. And possibly dead. So is it really stealing?"

"You're walking a thin line, Gramaraye."

"Actually, I'm walking through the woods with a giant television and my fingers are killing me. Lend a hand?"

Talk Talk

Zeke and I rode in silence most of the way home, each lost in our own thoughts.

Finally, I said, "Well, that didn't go well."

"Coulda gone worse," Zeke muttered.

More silence. I glanced at my watch. Nearly 10 A.M. My three-day window would be half over soon, and all I had to show for it were more questions and enemies than when I started.

"Did you learn anything more about the security around Verona?" I asked.

"No," Zeke replied. "But I did learn a way to learn it. One of the ARC's wardens from the EMP Sanctum recently died."

"So . . . you're going to get a job there as a warden, get inside?"

"No."

"Then—oh." Damn it. "If I can Talk to him, he can tell us all about the security."

"Exactly. And then we'll know how truly screwed we are."

"You know, if my sister dated men, and I didn't like her, I might just try to set you two up. You share such a positive outlook on life."

Zeke snorted. "And maybe if you'd seen half the sick, evil, stupid crap I have, you'd be a little less of an annoying Pollyanna, fool."

I didn't respond. He might be right. Instead, I considered the challenge of Talking to a dead ARC warden.

Wardens were little more than glorified security guards, so there was a good chance he wouldn't be personally warded against Talking, or in a Sanctum like Verona. But his remains would be housed in an official ARC crypt. As licensed necromancers, our family had access rights to the ARC crypts, so that was good. But my name had likely been removed from the access rights during my exile, and I doubted they would be restored without following some complicated official process first.

That left me with one unpleasant option.

Good thing I'd grabbed the television.

I set the television down by my bedroom door, and went into the upstairs bathroom.

I won't describe the contortionist act that followed, but I confirmed a disturbing fact—I had a tattoo on the inside of my butt cheeks. This was disturbing not only for realizing the uncomfortable way (in every sense) that the tattoo got there, but also for the fact that it could only have been done by the changeling. Which was not only forbidden, but the tattoo had not worked like wizard tattoos, at least none that I knew of.

I spritzed my burned hand with spray from the medicine cabinet that was magical only in the relief it brought, then hauled the television down the hall. I tapped on Mort's door with my foot, and leaned the television against the wall to relieve the weight of it.

"Who is it?" Mort said.

"I have something for you," I replied. "A peace offering."

A pause, then, "Come in."

I awkwardly managed to turn the doorknob and pushed the door open, then carried the television into the room as Mort finished tying a robe around himself.

"One replacement television." I set it on the entertainment center, and stretched my aching back. Did I mention that getting older sucked?

"Holy— Is that from your trailer?" Mort asked.

"No, but it's bigger and thinner than your last one, right? So, no hard feelings?"

"Not about the television," Mort said. "Does it have a built-in HD tuner?"

"Uh, I don't know."

"Well, how about—"

"Look," I said. "All I know is it's a huge television, and it's yours. And I'm sorry your last one got broken."

"Wow, that's your way of apologizing?"

I sighed. "Mort, why does this have to be so hard? Look, I get that Grandfather was snobby about the whole Talker thing, and I got a lot of attention because of it. But I swear, I don't want to take over the family business. I'll admit, I'm not exactly thrilled you've been selling off our family heirlooms—"

"Oh, well, sorry for not asking your permission, but you were a little hard to get hold of."

"That's not—"

"If I hadn't sold that stuff there wouldn't be a family business left! Between our uncles, and the necrofams that've started franchising out, taking over the smaller families, and—"

"Okay!" I said. "I just—there's enough crap going on, we don't need to be fighting on top of it, you know? We should be working together, as brothers. Like I said, I really don't want to run the family business, but if you need my help, I'll give it. And, well, it would be nice if I could count on your help to figure out who really attacked Felicity, and who keeps attacking us."

"Ah. So you need my help."

"That's not the only reason I'm talking to you, Mort. I meant what I said about us acting like brothers again. But yeah, I need your help."

Mort smiled. Oh, gods. I knew he'd enjoy this, but I still struggled to hide my annoyance.

"I don't know, Finn," he said and rubbed his stupid little evil Spock beard. "You say you want to help the business, but I'm the public face of our family business now. So if you're in trouble with the ARC again, the less I get involved the better, you know?"

"Uh-huh," I said. "The thing is, Mort, someone's trying to kill me, or at least frame me again, and that means our whole family's in danger. So if you don't help me, there might not be much family left in our family business."

"Oh, okay, so you've endangered us all and now you need me to fix it." He shook his head and sighed, as though at a child who'd spilled Kool-Aid on the carpet. "I'm not going to put our family and the business at risk to fix your problems. Do you know how hard it was to rebuild our reputation after what you—after what happened before?"

I smiled through gritted teeth. "I don't need you to fix it, I just need you to help out."

"Right. But help with what, exactly?" Mort asked.

"I need to get to a body in one of the ARC crypts. I need your necromancer rights of access."

"Meaning they'd have my name on record. What do you plan to do?"

"Just Talk to someone."

"About what?"

"Well, that's the part you don't want to know if an enforcer ever questions you."

"That's what I thought. So you want to perform an unauthorized Talk and gods only know what else with an ARC-protected body, and you want me to put my name all over it. Are you determined to destroy this family? If I got sent into exile, we'd lose the house, the business, everything. Father and Mattie, they'd end up . . ." He shook his head. "The safest thing is to let the ARC sort it all out."

"Are you kidding?" I said. "We reported Felicity's attack to the ARC and I got exiled for twenty-five years! And even with that, the business still suffered, right? And the problem obviously didn't go away. We need to handle this ourselves, and I have less than two days left to do so. So can you help me? Can we do this together as brothers? Please?"

Mort looked at his reflection in the mirror over his dresser for a second, then sighed. "Fine. Okay. I'll help."

I waited for the "but."

"But," Mort said, "you have to use your Talker gift when I ask. And sign papers giving me full control of the family business."

"Fine," I said. "I mean, thank you, Mort. Really."

I left him hooking up his new television, and closed the door behind me. If Mort really was part of the Legion, he played dumb really well. He hadn't asked which ARC crypt, hadn't pressed me on my reasons.

One brother down, one to go. I stopped in front of Vee's door.

Pete's anger at me was understandable. But I'd realized that part of it might actually be fear. Fear of losing Vee when she found out he'd lied to her about being a waerwolf. So to truly make things right with Petey, and hopefully speed up his forgiveness, I needed to be the one who told the truth to Vee and explain how it was all my fault. Hopefully her anger would be aimed at me then. And hopefully Zeke wouldn't punch my face through the back of my head when I upset Vee. That would make eating really difficult. Still, I'd rather go back into exile with Pete happy than not, even if it meant a few broken teeth.

I just wished there was something I could say, some way to handle this, that wouldn't lead to more hurt and anger.

Mother's ghost floated up the hall. "Hello, kiddo," she said in her distant voice. "You look sad. Everything okay?"

"Yes," I said, ready to send her on her way. But then I reconsidered. A talk with Mother, even just an echo of Mother, sounded really good right then. "No. Pete's mad at me. And I have to tell a girl that I lied to her."

"*Mira,* interesting fact," Mother said. "Did you know that in real life, Gipetto was a lonely old thaumaturge?"

"Yes, Mother. You told me. What has that got to do—"

"Gipetto decided he wanted the company of a young mundy maiden in his village. But he'd been lying to her about many things to hide the fact that he was an arcana, and she'd begun to distrust him. So he made her a simple puppet out of wood that could talk, and if made to tell a lie, it's bulbous nose would grow long. He took the puppet to her, demonstrated its use, and had her ask the puppet if Gipetto loved her and if he would care for her always. These were not lies, not that a wooden puppet could tell, and Gipetto was wealthy from selling his inventions, so they were married with her family's eager encouragement. But on those nights when Gipetto was away traveling and selling his wares, the neighbors swear they would hear the young woman telling the puppet to lie, and then tell the truth, over and over and over again. Because, you see, sometimes a girl wants the truth, and sometimes she doesn't, as long as it makes her feel good." Mother laughed and patted my head, or at least she made the motions. "Someday, you'll understand, Finn."

Wow. I'd pretty well forgotten about that story. And now I could see why.

"Uh, thanks, Mother. But how do you tell that girl the truth when it will make her unhappy, but you have no choice?"

Mother shook her head. "Oh, *mi hijo,* look at you. You know better than to play in the snow so long," she said. "You go get out of those wet clothes and I'll make you some cocoa."

She floated off down the hall. I watched after her for a second, my chest aching. She wasn't my mother. She was just an echo of my mother, and this had just reminded me what that difference really meant.

"Finn?" Vee popped her head out of her room, looking up and down the hall. "Oh, I thought maybe you were talking to— Never mind."

"Looking for Pete?"

She blushed. "I haven't seen him all day and, uh, Sarah is really worried."

"Yeah, about that . . . Can we talk in your room for a minute?"

Vee glanced up the hall again. I shook my head. "Zeke's chasing down some info, said he won't be back for a while."

She bit her lower lip, then nodded. We went into her room, and

Vee plopped down cross-legged on a bean bag, her knees sticking far out to the sides, her body hunched over hands clasped in her lap.

I stood for a second, my hands in my pockets, composing my thoughts and dreading how Vee would react.

"Well, here's the thing. Pete's a really good guy. He's the most honest, caring person I know. And trusting, and loyal, and—"

Vee crossed her arms. "And you want me to stay away from him, because I'm crazy, or dangerous, right? Because I was in the Hole, I'm not good enough for your brother?"

"No!"

"Because Sarah says that's what you really think."

"No, just the opposite, I swear." At least now. "I think you guys are perfect for each other. It's just—" I looked down at my hands. "So, the thing is, when Pete was young, Mort played a prank on him. We both did, actually. You see, Pete was having a really hard time dealing with Mother's death. I think he felt, you know, vulnerable, scared. And then this dog bit him, and—"

"He isn't really a waerwolf," Vee said. It wasn't a question. And she didn't sound surprised or upset. If anything, she sounded resigned.

"Uh, yeah, that's kind of where I was going. You knew?"

She nodded.

"Oh. Wait, of course you knew. You were inside my head."

"Actually, no, I didn't get it from you. Sarah told me. He didn't act or smell like a waer, didn't . . . feel like a waer."

"So, you're not mad? Because, well, he really likes you."

"I know." Vee slumped in on herself again, looked down at her hands. "That's why I didn't say anything to him about it. I really enjoyed talking with him, I didn't want to ruin it."

"But that's awesome! I'm sure Pete's worried you wouldn't want to talk to him anymore if you knew."

Vee looked up, and tears marked her cheeks. "I want to, but I don't think I should."

"What? Why not?"

"It's just too dangerous for him. I shouldn't have talked to him at all once I realized the truth. I didn't want to encourage him. Still . . . I didn't want to be alone, either. I was selfish. But we need to stop before he gets real feelings for me."

"Uh, I think it's too late for that."

"Really?" Vee sat up, a look of hope on her face. Then she glanced to her side, listening. "No. You're right," she whispered sullenly, then looked back at me. "It's just not safe. I don't want to hurt him."

"I hope you, and Sarah, will think about it before you say anything to him," I said. "Waerwolf or not, I think maybe Pete and you could be happy together."

Vee frowned at me. "Don't you care that I'm a waer?"

"Not really," I said. Which wasn't exactly true, but this wasn't about me. "I love Pete. I've missed so much of his life. I just want to see him happy, and if I can help make that happen it would make me happy too."

Vee looked back down at her hands. "My brother, he's already sacrificed so much for me. He lost twenty-five years of his life, and now he's dealing with—" She stopped and blushed slightly. I understood. Zeke was dealing with my mess. She cleared her throat. "He's still trying to take care of me. That's another reason I can't take any risks right now. Zeke doesn't need any more problems, especially not mine."

"I know you've both had it rough," I said. "But at some point you're each going to need to start your own lives again, right?"

"Maybe," Vee said. "But what if something goes wrong? What if I changed and attacked Pete? Or even just infected him by accident? I'm not sure Pete would really forgive me if that happened. And Zekiel, he hardly even looks me in the eyes now. But if something went wrong with Pete, and I got sent into exile—" She shook her head. "I like Pete. And so does Sarah. But really, we barely know each other. I think the best thing for everyone is to just keep it that way."

"Well, I hope you'll change your mind. I don't see how your being unhappy and isolated is going to make Zeke happy. Wouldn't seeing you living a normal, happy life make him forget you're a waer more than shutting yourself away from everyone?"

"I don't know." Vee sighed. "We'll think about it."

"Okay. I guess that's all I can ask. Thank you. And, uh, thank you, Sarah."

Vee didn't respond, just looked back down at her hands fretting in her lap.

I left her room, headed downstairs and out to Pete's cottage. I didn't look forward to the conversation, assuming he would talk to me at all. Even the good news that Vee liked him without his being a waerwolf was potentially bad news if it also meant she didn't want to see him anymore.

I wished there was something I could do to make it all work out. But the only sure solution I could think of was to either make Pete a waer—not my first choice—or find a way to make Vee not a waer. That would be ideal. It would be a nice gift to Zeke as well, in return for all the trouble he'd been put through because of the attacks on me. I'd heard rumors of cures, but suspected they were scams or myths. Heather might know—heck, Heather might be able to create a cure if she put her mind and skill to it—but she wasn't taking my calls.

I crossed the side yard to Pete's cottage and raised my hand to knock on the door but heard his voice from inside, too muffled to make out the words.

Then Dawn's voice, near to the door, said in response, "You're sweet. But I'm not getting in a cat fight over Finn. I've got more self-respect than that. And I don't even know if he's worth fighting for anymore, you know?"

Ouch. Not that I wanted Dawn and Heather fighting over me, but it hurt that both of them seemed so unwilling to fight for me. The least of my worries, maybe, but it still bothered me because, really, I couldn't blame them. To the mundy world, I was a loser dropout. To the arcana world I was a dark necromancer who'd only just returned from exile. Even in my own mind, I still had no idea where I fit in anymore, or where I was going now except back to exile. I wasn't sure I'd fight to be with me either.

Pete said something as I stood there pondering, his words still indistinct. Dawn responded, "You have to say that, you're his brother. But if he's too dumb to know what he wants, or appreciate all this, I'm not going to waste my time like I did before."

I heard the crunching of gravel as a car pulled into the main drive. I moved quietly away from the cottage and headed for the front of the house. As I walked, I considered again my feelings for Dawn, which had become no less confusing or uncertain since the night before.

Being honest with myself, I'd seen her differently after our kiss in the cottage all those years ago. She officially went from being my friend to being my friend who was a girl, and I'd occasionally wondered about trying for another kiss. But she'd made it seem like nothing special, so much so that I didn't feel like she wanted to kiss me again. And then I started hanging out with Heather.

If you asked me the first word that came to mind with Dawn, it would be "crazy," but in a way that made me laugh, that made a dull task an adventure. And the second word would be "easy." Not in the slutty kind of way, but because talking with her was easy, and being with her was easy. Or at least it used to be. Maybe part of the reason I'd never really thought of her romantically was because she'd always been, in a way, "my other half"?

I rounded the corner to the front of the house. Mattie and Heather slid a box out of the opened back of Heather's hatchback. I faded back around the corner and watched Heather, taking the opportunity to really look at her without it being awkward.

In those rare moments in the Other Realm when I was allowed to imagine freely, I often imagined a relationship together with Heather. But in my imaginations she was always that girl I'd known, not the woman of hardened edges and sadness that stood a few feet from me now. How much of what I felt for her, or thought

I felt for her, was based on reality? After twenty-five years of living in memory and imagination, I had no idea.

It was possible that, if I hadn't been exiled, we might have dated for a week or two, and it could have been a disaster, just another one of the billions of failed teenage romances. Or we might have been that rare couple who met in high school and went on to get married and live happily ever after.

In a perfect world, I could date Dawn for a week, then date Heather for a week, and see which felt right. But I had the feeling that if I did date one, I'd lose the other, at least as anything more than a friend.

And in that moment, my decision was easy. Trying to think of which one I wanted to be with romantically was just confusing. But in weighing the risk of losing them, one stood out clearly over the other. The realization filled me with guilt over all that had happened in the past day.

I resumed walking, and Heather looked over as my feet crunched across the gravel. She frowned and helped Mattie settle the box by the front stairs, then walked briskly back to her car.

"I'll see you tomorrow, Mattie," she said, and closed the hatchback door. She moved toward the driver's door.

"Heather, wait," I said. I hurried around the front of the car and reached her before she could shut her door.

"Finn—" she began.

"I know. You don't want to talk about us. But I wanted to ask you something else, as an alchemist."

She sighed. "What is it?"

"Do you know of any cure for a waer curse?"

"Other than silver to the head or heart, no," she said. "Nothing legitimate anyway. Why? I thought Pete's curse wasn't real."

"It's not. But a friend is cursed, a girl that Pete likes in fact, and—"

"Is it Dawn?"

"What? No. It's someone you don't know. Why?"

"Just wondered. I'll see what I can find, but I wouldn't hold my breath. If a cure was possible, I'm sure it'd be out there by now."

"Maybe. But then, you've done all sorts of things nobody's ever done before, right?" I smiled.

I meant it as a compliment, and a nod back to her experiments when we were young. But a pained expression flitted across Heather's face. "Yes," she said. "I suppose I have. I need to go. I'm having dinner with Orion, and I don't get to see him very often."

"Wait. I just—I hate to see you unhappy, Heather. I hope you know I'm still your friend. Whatever happens, whatever you did or didn't do, whatever your reasons for pushing me away, I'm here if you need a friend."

Heather laughed through her nose, and shook her head. Then she looked up at me, a sad smile on her face. "You said friend twice in as many sentences. Is there something you're trying to tell me?"

"I—there's a lot going on, you know. I've got a lot to figure out. But like I said, I do want you to be happy, and I do want us to be—"

"Friends. I know." Heather put her hand on mine. "Thank you, Finn. And thank you for offering to help. But you don't even know me, not really. And there's nothing for you to do anyway. I'm not a damsel in distress. I'm perfectly capable of dealing with my own messes. Sometimes life just is what it is, and not even magic can make it better."

She started her car and drove off. I sighed. Real-life relationships were so much harder and confusing than what I'd imagined.

"You okay, Uncle Finn?" Mattie asked.

I joined her by the stairs and peeked inside the open box. It held a few stainless-steel sports bottles that I assumed held potions and what looked like a papier mâché volcano with pictures of various fire elemental creatures painted on its sides.

"What's that?" I asked.

"School project," Mattie said. "Ms. Brown runs an after-school club for us arcana kids."

"The school lets her? How does she keep mundies from joining?"

"She called it a slug identification club. No mundy volunteers for it."

"That's cool. I wish I'd had something like that." It certainly would have been a nice break from Grandfather's strict tutoring. "And the potions?"

"Just some things Dad asked for, for the business. You know, Uncle Finn, Ms. Brown was really distracted today. And she kept just sort of spacing out and smiling when the students were busy. I've never seen her do that."

I sighed. "Thanks, Mattie. That's . . . good to hear, I guess." I lifted up the box. "Come on, let's get this inside."

And then I needed to talk with Dawn.

Mattie stepped into the house. Before I could follow, a sudden heat burned my chest, like being bit by a mosquito made of fire. I dropped the box and slapped my hand to the spot. The hex protection amulet!

The Króls. At least some of them must have survived the sasquatch attack. And they'd gained something personal of mine, something to hex me with across a distance.

Mattie turned at the sound of the box dropping. "Uncle Finn?"

"Stop! Stay inside."

The house wards would protect her. But if the Króls had samples from anyone else outside the house—

Dawn screamed, but it didn't sound like a scream of pain.

Pete!

I ran for the cottage as Dawn shouted for help, her voice sharp with fear.

Blister in the Sun

I reached the cottage just as Pete stumbled out, clutching at his face and groaning through clenched teeth. It looked as though his flesh boiled, bubbles rising and falling all along his skin. One burst, sending out a thin pink mist. Dawn followed him, her green and white dress peppered with fine red dots of Pete's blood.

"Pete! Shit! Dawn, help me get him into the house, fast!" Dawn reached for Pete with the slow movements of someone in shock. I grabbed Pete's arm to guide him, but he screamed in pain and jerked away. He fell to his knees on the lawn, which brought another shout of pain.

"Okay, buddy, let's get to the house. You can do this. Come on." The protection amulet on my chest felt hot enough to blister my own skin now. It was being pushed to its limits, and I doubted it would last much longer.

I couldn't get Pete to his feet, couldn't get him to the protection of the house wards. I needed to bring the protection to him. I ran just inside the door, just past the cool buzz of the protective wards. I yanked off the amulet. "Dawn!" I shouted, and tossed the amulet to her. "Put it on Pete!"

Dawn looked confused, but she hung the chain around Pete's neck. The chain caught on boils as it slid down, and Pete swatted at the air as if being attacked by invisible insects.

The boiling slowed, and then stopped, leaving Pete gasping and covered in oozing, bleeding sores.

"Pete! Come on, into the house!" I called. But Pete just slumped down, moaning and twitching. I clenched my teeth and prepared to make a dash for him. If I were fast enough, hopefully the curse wouldn't damage me too badly.

Vee came running around from the front of the house, holding a metal potion bottle. She pressed the bottle to Pete's writhing lips. "Drink!" she said in a tone that demanded obedience.

Pete did his best to obey. Much of the thick blue liquid spilled from the corners of his mouth or ran off his chin. But when he stopped, he let out a long sigh and stopped twitching.

Tears ran from Vee's eyes as she said, "Let's get him inside. Mattie's calling the healer."

Pete pushed himself to his feet, with Dawn and Vee's help and encouragement, and lumbered into the house.

"I've got him," Vee said as we entered the dining room, leaving Dawn with me. Mattie sprinted into the room, mobile phone in hand and locked the side door behind me and Dawn. "Locking everything down," she said as she dashed off again.

Dawn watched all the commotion with an expression of mixed confusion and fear. "What . . . what the hell just happened?" she asked.

"Let me help get Pete settled and I'll explain." And hopefully I would think of an explanation by then. "Come, sit down." I directed her into a chair. "I'll bring you some water. Everything will be okay, I promise."

I left her as she sat, and hurried around the house, helping Mattie lock doors and windows, making sure the warding spells were all up and humming. I stopped by the bathroom. Vee dug through the medicine cabinet and gave short sobs that sounded like hiccups as Pete rested on the closed toilet lid. He looked awful, his skin a mess of red bumps and open sores. Even after they healed, he might be scarred for life. Fury kindled in my gut at the sight, the desire to hurt the Króls flaring up as sudden and hot as swallowing a mouthful of flaming jalapeño peppers.

And the anger at myself was just as great. I should have handled the Króls differently, taken more precautions, made sure they couldn't hurt us, or at least that they feared the consequences of doing so. But I'd been too focused on getting answers.

"Oh man, Pete. I'm so sorry."

Pete started to shake his head but stopped and winced. "Why sorry?" he said, his voice slurred, groggy sounding. "You didn't do this."

Vee placed a couple of pills in his mouth, then made him sip some water.

"No," I said. "But if I hadn't gone after the Króls, they wouldn't have had reason to hex us."

"Don't be a dumb head," Pete said, then closed his eyes and slumped forward. Vee had to grab him so that he didn't slide off the toilet and carefully propped him up. She held a pair of scissors now and began to carefully cut at Pete's T-shirt. She lifted off the protection amulet, a clear fluid stringing between it and Pete's skin, and dumped it in the sink. It would need to be recharged before it would offer any protection again.

"Finn," Vee said as she worked. "I know you need to deal with your guilt, but Sarah agrees with Pete. You're not responsible for what happened; whoever cast the hex on your family is."

My family. Crap. "Sammy!"

"Is fine. Mattie said her apartment's warded." Vee paused, and after a second, said without looking up, "Was that Dawn, the woman in the dining room?"

"Yes," I said.

"I know you took Pete on a date with her. Are they—should she be back here, taking care of him?"

"No," I said, understanding her real question. "They're just friends. And Dawn's a mundy. In fact, I need to get back to her." I gave a final glance at Pete. "I am sorry," I said to him, even if he couldn't hear me. "I'll make this right, I promise."

I went to the kitchen and fetched a glass of water. It gave me time to think up a story for Dawn.

She looked up from her blood-misted dress as I entered the

dining room, the lights of the chandelier making her lavender afro glisten. "It's strange," she said, her tone subdued. "The only time I've been in your house is when I'm invited to a funeral."

I knocked on the dark wood of the nearest chair. One might think that arcana, knowing the truth of magic, would not be superstitious. But arcana don't assume we know everything about the world any more than scientists do. We just know more about the magical bits than mundies do. So while no wizard has ever proven the effectiveness of knocking on wood, for example, it doesn't hurt to be safe.

"Pete will be fine," I said, both to reassure her and as a ward against ill luck. "I'm sorry you saw that."

Dawn blinked at me, as if waking from a daydream.

"Fuck sorry! Finn, what the hell just happened?"

I set the water in front of Dawn, but she ignored it, waiting for me to answer. I paced beside the table so I wouldn't have to look her in the eyes. "Well, we work with a lot of chemicals, you know, for preserving and disposing of bodies and all. And unfortunately, Pete must have gotten some on his skin, and, uh, something must have caused a reaction. It doesn't happen very often, but it is one of the risks of our business."

Dawn watched me for a second. "Are you lying to me?"

"No," I said, feeling like a jerk. I stopped pacing.

"So throwing that necklace on him, that had something to do with a chemical burn? And why did that woman make him drink something rather than rinsing off his skin?"

"Uh." Crap. "I don't know how it works. It just does . . . pH balance of his sweat or something."

"Okay." Dawn stood up. "Can I see him?"

"Not right now. He's being treated."

"And I'm not in any danger?"

"No."

"Fine. I'll come back in a few hours and talk to him then." It wasn't a question.

Dawn left the room. I escorted her to the side door and held it open as she left. She glanced back at me. "I'm not stupid you know, Finn. I've seen lots of weird shit in the time I've been your neighbor. Strange folks coming and going, strange noises and explosions coming from your basement at all hours. And then there's you, suddenly dropping out of the world and living off the grid for twenty-five years. I don't know if you guys think you're illuminati, or you're terrorists, or what, and until now I haven't really cared too much because whatever else you all are, you were my friends. But Pete, he's like my brother, and this all just got too real for me to ignore. So I'm going to find out the truth, one way or another, you can believe that."

She marched off.

"That could be a problem," Zeke said behind me, causing my heart to leap up into my throat. I spun around.

"Cheeze whiz! Are you trying to kill me?"

"If I was tryin' to kill you, fool, you'd know it. What was that all about?" he nodded in Dawn's direction.

I gave him a quick rundown of events.

Zeke tugged at his mustache as he listened, then said, "Damn it! I knew I should have stuffed a grenade down that smug witch's throat. Vee's okay, yeah?"

"Yeah. I don't think the Króls even know she exists."

"Good. I found the location of the dead EMP warden. Avalon Underhill, in Everett. We can leave soon as I know Vee's safe."

I leaned against the door frame, suddenly exhausted. Thinking about Talking made me feel doubly so. How much more would I have to go through to see the end of all this? I rubbed at my face, and said, "Okay. I'll go let Mort know so he can get ready." If he wouldn't help, I'd need to steal his persona ring somehow.

"I'll check in with Vee." Zeke headed toward the stairs.

"Uh, okay." I didn't mention that Vee was downstairs with Pete. Let them have a few extra minutes before Zeke stormed in playing the protective big brother. I followed him upstairs, and then went to Mort's door.

"Mort? It's Finn. Can I come in?"

"Is it safe?" Mort's voice called.

"Yes."

The door cracked open, and Mort peered past me. "What the hell happened? I heard shouting, screaming."

"Pete's been hexed. But the danger should be over now."

Mort frowned and backed away from the door. I pushed it open. Mort stood there in his satin pajamas, holding a baseball bat in one hand and a clear vial of liquid with an ankh etched into it in the other hand.

"Someone hexed Pete?" he asked.

"Yes. He's hurt, just like I warned you might happen."

"We should call the ARC and get them to hunt down who-ever—"

"We know who did it, Mort. Felicity's clan. And they're not the only threat. If we get the ARC involved, they might only make things worse, remember? But Zeke's found the crypt—it's in Ava-lon Hills. We'll leave as soon as you're dressed and ready."

"I don't know. If there's someone out there throwing hexes—"

"No way they have enough blood magic to cast another one like that, at least not for a while. And the best way to stop these attacks is to find whoever attacked Felicity and framed me, so the Króls throw their hexes at the right person. So come on. This will be fun, an adventure, like when we used to sneak into town to listen to the bands. Remember that?"

Mort leaned the bat against his dresser. "I remember me having to drag you down there, you were always so scared."

"Yeah, well, so don't make me drag you. Unless you're too Scaredy McScaredy Pants?"

"Screw you." Mort started digging through his dresser drawers. "I'll be down in a minute."

"Thanks."

I headed downstairs to check on Pete and make sure Zeke wasn't being a pain.

Someone, or something, pounded on our front door.

I froze at the bottom of the stairs. Thankfully, all of the windows were covered, so whoever it was couldn't see me.

Another knock, then, "It's Grayson, here on official ARC business. Please open up."

Zeke and Mattie appeared, followed by Vee, and we all exchanged glances. Whatever Grayson's reason for being here, it couldn't be good. Even if the local ARC had detected the hex and were here to help, they'd ask all kinds of questions that would risk me and Zeke being detained, possibly even arrested. They surely frowned at vigilante assaults on suburban witches.

"Back door?" I whispered.

Zeke shook his head. "They probably have enforcers at the other exits."

It was a lucky thing we'd locked down the house after the hex attack. That wouldn't stop enforcers from getting in if they wanted to, but hopefully they weren't eager to go all SWAT on us.

The doorbell rang again.

"My room, then," I whispered to Zeke. "I have an idea." A bad idea, but it was better than arrest.

Zeke glanced down the hall, nodded, and we headed up the stairs. Grayson called out, "Let me in, or I'll have to let the enforcers do their work. Please, be reasonable."

I glanced back as we crested the top of the stairs and nodded to Mattie. She nodded back and crossed to the front door.

I motioned Zeke into my room, and continued down the hall to fetch Mort.

"What's going on?" he asked as he tied his shoes.

I made the silence gesture and whispered, "I'll explain in a sec. Come with me."

I led him back to my room, closed the door as quietly as I could, then tiptoed to the window and eased it open. I peeked out to make sure no enforcers were in sight, then tugged on the cable that ran between our house and Dawn's. It felt sturdy. I looked over at Dawn's yard, bright with late-morning sun. The back was a maze with piles of driftwood, bottles, discarded yard ornaments, and other odds and ends I could only assume were meant for future art projects, but the side yard beneath the cable was hidden by the hedge. Hopefully, it was still just grass. I looked at Zeke and motioned to the cable. "What do you think? Father built it, so it will definitely hold our weight."

"I think you're crazy." Zeke paled, an impressive feat for someone whose skin was already on the blue side of white. "I ain't getting on no rope, Gramaraye."

Mort stepped back toward the door. "Maybe we should go talk to Grayson. I for one have nothing to hide."

"You'll be hidin' a black eye if you take another step toward that door, fool," Zeke said without even glancing at Mort. He tugged on the cable. "I'd rather fight our way out than ride this thing."

I shook my head. "If we fight our way out, we'd be putting everyone else in the house at risk. Including Vee."

Zeke tugged at his mustache, and eyed the cable like it was a scorpion trying to sell him a used car.

I heard the low hum of voices coming from the heating duct near my feet. I motioned for silence, then knelt down, putting my head close to the ornate grate covering the duct. Zeke knelt beside me, though he didn't lower his head. Grayson's voice echoed up the duct. They must be standing near the large air intake grate by the stairs. Had Mattie maneuvered them there on purpose?

". . . killed one Król male, and we received an anonymous tip that Finn and Ezekiel were both there. I'm afraid there's little I can do about this, Miss Wodenson. The ARC won't condone this kind of vigilante behavior."

"I'm sure they didn't kill any witch," Vee's voice trembled as it drifted out of the duct. "He doesn't want to go back into exile. There must be some mistake."

"Well, your brother was exiled for exactly this kind of act," Grayson said. "And we know that Finn fought with the Króls at a restaurant in town, and the tip placed him and Zeke at the Króls' home at the time of the murder. If they thought the Króls were threatening you or Finn's family, is it so hard to believe they would take action themselves rather than coming to us?"

Mattie said, "Finn's not a killer, Uncle Jimmy. You know that."

"I certainly hope not. And I wish the Króls were the only reason I'm here. But we've identified Felicity's body. She was killed in Finn's trailer, possibly with dark necromancy. And there's still no trace of the enforcer who was supposed to be at the transfer, or of whoever attacked the Fey."

"I don't understand," Mattie said. "Wasn't Uncle Finn *in* the Other Realm when it was attacked? So you can't blame him for that, right?"

"I do not blame Finn for anything, Mattie. But the ARC isn't so convinced he is innocent. It appears his changeling was in communication with Zeke's. The ARC now thinks perhaps Finn somehow communicated with Zeke in the Other Realm as well, may have coordinated some kind of revenge on the ARC for their exile, or maybe even become agents of the Fey. Finn could have then coordinated with his changeling or loyal feybloods to lure Felicity to his trailer and to attack the transfer for him, or to hire someone who could."

"That's crazy!" Vee said. "Why—"

"I know. I agree. It's crazy. But let's say the ARC is wrong, and someone else did kill Felicity and attacked the transfer. What if that same someone wants to harm Finn and Ezekiel, afraid of what they know? Please, both of you, I will do everything I can to protect them, but they really do need to turn themselves in. They're collecting enemies faster than I can keep track. Where are they?"

"I told you, we don't know," Vee said. "We've been extremely worried."

"We just got hexed like a half hour ago," Mattie said. "Uncle Pete's hurt. And Uncle Finn might be lying somewhere, dying, or—" Her voice broke. She was a good actress.

Zeke and I stood up.

"What do you want to do?" I whispered. "Grayson said he'd help us. If you want to give yourself up, try to clear your name, I'll understand. You wouldn't be in this mess if not for me."

Zeke stared at me, and for a second he held a look in his eyes as though someone told him Santa Claus died by falling from the roof onto his dog. "They really think *I* did all that?" he whispered. "I always assumed, what with all their spells, the ARC never accused no one that wasn't guilty. Even you. But—" He blinked and looked out the window. A determined scowl settled over his face. "You go first, then I'll send your brother after. I'll go last, since I'm heaviest."

"Okay." I grabbed my persona ring and a pair of jeans out of the dresser. I climbed out to sit on the windowsill, and flung one leg of the jeans over the cables, catching it in my free hand. I wrapped the pant legs around my hands a couple of times, getting a solid grip, and looked down.

"Uh, maybe if you pushed m—"

Zeke shoved my back. I managed not to shout as my butt slid free of the windowsill. Maybe I squeaked a bit. A manly squeak. My arms jerked painfully as they suddenly took on my full weight, and I swung to the side and began sliding along the cable, bouncing lightly and swinging side to side as I went.

I quickly realized the first problem with my plan. The hedge that separated our properties had grown in the years since the cable was installed, as had I. While I'd easily cleared the top of the hedge in my youth, I headed now for a groin full of poky branches.

The second problem was that the hedge stood right in the middle between our two houses, where the dip in the cable would reach its lowest point.

I did my best to lift my legs as I neared the hedge. Let's just say I'm very grateful for the sturdiness of denim, as will be any future generations I'm still able to father. Branches slapped and poked me, and I came to a rapid stop in my slide. I started inching backward. Closing my eyes, I let go just on Dawn's side of the leafy barrier. The hedge didn't so much break my fall as break my skin in several places, scraping me as I fell along its edge. But I hit the ground in one piece.

I picked myself up, stumbled away from the hedge, and looked up. Mort sat in my windowsill, gripping another pair of jeans over the ropes as Zeke helped him prepare.

A throat cleared behind me. I spun around, fearing the worst. Dawn stood by the back corner of her house, dressed now in brown pants and a black hoodie, her arms crossed.

"That was impressive," she said.

I raised my hands. "We come in peace," I whispered, and motioned for quiet. And then Mort crashed to the ground behind me. He managed to miss most of the hedge but landed hard and flopped onto his back, breath exploding from his mouth.

I grabbed him as he moaned and helped him move clear of the drop zone.

Dawn arched a single eyebrow, and walked over to join us. "And here I thought maybe you were making some kind of crazy romantic gesture, trying to swing in through my window and all. Obviously, though, this has nothing to do with me. So unless you're prepared to tell me what the hell's going on, you can turn right around and march back home."

"Uh, well, we're sort of in trouble with some people who think we did something bad, and we need to get Everett to prove our innocence."

"Congratulations. You win the vaguest bullshit award. Care to elaborate?"

"I'm . . . not sure I can."

"Uh-huh. Please tell me you're not running from your meth boss or something?"

"My what?"

Zeke hit the ground, the word "Hide!" bursting out with his breath, and he rolled into a crouched position. I grabbed Mort and moved him closer to the hedge, out of view of the upstairs windows. Dawn strolled at a much more casual pace to join us in the shadow of the hedge. Zeke stood up next to me, shuddered, and shook his arms as if to flick water from his hands. "Never again," he muttered, then whispered, "We've gotta move, now. Grayson was coming upstairs to search when I jumped. Do you have a plan for transportation?"

"Uh."

I hadn't really thought out my plan beyond "escape house in super spy style." We couldn't take our own cars unless we were willing to hang around and hope the enforcers left before sniffing us out.

"You can take my car, if you want," Dawn said.

"Really?" I took a step toward her. "That would help so much, I can't even tell you."

"Sure," Dawn replied. "I'll drive, and you can explain everything on the way."

"Not happening," Zeke said.

Dawn just continued to stare at me, expectantly. And I couldn't look her in the eyes and lie one more time.

"Screw it," I said. "Dawn, if you really want the truth, I'll give it to you. But I'm telling you right now, it's not going to be easy for you to hear."

"Sure it will. We'll keep the radio low," Dawn said. "Meet me around front."

A Kind of Magic

Dawn disappeared around the back of her house. We made a dash to the far side of her front porch, using an apple tree for cover. I leaned back against the weathered gray house and dabbed at a couple of scrapes from the hedge.

"Finn, Dawn's a mundy," Mort said.

"Dawn's as good as family," I replied. "And she could've been hurt today if the Króls had used fire or something worse. She deserves the truth."

Zeke grunted. "It's against the laws—"

"Then go back there and rat me out to Grayson," I snapped. "It's the least of the things the ARC will charge me with."

"But this charge would be true, yeah?" Zeke pressed. "The others may not be."

"As if that matters," I said. "You heard the stuff the ARC believes about us."

Zeke looked away, his jaw jumping as he clenched his teeth. Dawn drove up in a wood-paneled green station wagon, and waved us over.

Mort moved close to me and said in a low voice, "You know the ARC will just go in and mess with her memories if you tell her, right?"

"Only if they find out she knows, and they think she's a threat." We hurried to the station wagon and piled in. I took shotgun, next to Dawn.

"So we're headed for Everett?" she asked.

"Yeah." I glanced at my watch. Just after 11 A.M. The ride to

Everett would suck up a good portion of the remaining day, but I had little choice.

"Allrighty. Please keep your head and arms inside the vehicle at all times. Asses, feel free to hang out the window."

I kept glancing in the side-view mirror until we reached the edge of town, but nobody appeared to be following us.

"So," Dawn said. "You were going to tell me the secret to life, the universe, and everything?"

"Actually, something like that," I said. I could feel Zeke's disapproving glare on the back of my neck. I cleared my throat. "The big secret is, magic is real. And I don't just mean in the sense of your tarot readings, or Wiccan spells. There's a whole world out there hidden from you and the rest of the mundanes."

"I see. So I'm a muggle, and you're a wizard, Harry? Is that it?"

I frowned. "No, I said mundane, not . . . muggle? And I'm not a wizard. I'm a necromancer. My whole family is, though we do have some wizardry in our bloodline. Well, except Father. He's a thaumaturge. And he's shown touches of sorcery, seeing hints of the future from time to time."

Dawn gave me a worried look. "Necromancers? Please tell me you don't dress up in robes and do sick things with dead bodies, or drug people all *Serpent and the Rainbow* style?"

"No. We mostly do the same thing as regular morticians, except we can actually manipulate life energy and the body somewhat, we can bind, dissipate, or destroy spirits, and we can extract latent magic from a body. And . . . I can talk to the dead."

"You see dead people. Got it. And this explains your running away all these years, and all the weird shit that happened today, how?"

"Uh, right. Okay, let me back up a bit." I composed my thoughts. "Basically, there are two realities, at least, that we know of. There's our reality, and there's the Other Realm, which you can think of sort of like fairyland, and it's where most raw magical energy comes from. A long time ago, shamans learned to access the Other Realm, to travel there on dream quests and such. And their dreams and memories took shape in the Other Realm, became living spirits, and these spirits began to travel back into our world, hitching rides with the shamans. Some of these early spirits became gods or other beings we call the Elder Spirits. The others joined with people, with creatures, even with plants in our world. They created the magical races such as the waerfolk, unicorns, kelpie, dryads, and all the rest, which we call feybloods."

"Holy shit," Dawn said. "That's amazing."

"I know it's a lot—"

"No, really. I was just telling Tinkerbell this same story the other day while we were flying back from Never Never Land, and she was all, 'Bitch, please stop smoking the crack,' and I was all, 'Yeah, you're right, who'd believe such a load of crap? I mean, fairies can't be real, right?' "

"Dawn—"

"Wait, I'm not done. And then Tink dropped dead right there because I didn't believe in her, and I felt really bad, so I ate an entire carton of chocolate ice cream and had sex with the Old Spice guy *at the same time,* and then I realized, shit, I must be dreaming and fairies *aren't* real, and I woke up hungry, horny, and really pissed off. Okay, all done now. You were saying?"

Mort chuckled in the backseat.

I looked over my shoulder. "Shut up, Mort. It's not like I've ever had to do this before."

Zeke looked out the window. "You shouldn't be telling her at all," he muttered.

"This is awesome," I said, looking back at Dawn. "I'm telling you the truth, and I'm getting crap for it from every side."

"Yeah, well, you seriously can't expect me to believe what you're saying? I'm back to thinking you're a meth cooker at this point. You know that shit rots your brain, right?"

"Tell you what. When we get where we're going, you'll have all the proof you need. But for now, just humor me, okay?"

"Oh, you're plenty amusing without adding my humor," Dawn said. "But go ahead. Talk away."

"Fine. Where was I?" I glanced back at Mort.

"The Fey created the feybloods."

"Right. Well, long story short—"

"Too late," Zeke muttered.

"—the Fey themselves evolved into true, thinking beings, and eventually tried to negotiate as equals with the arcana, to protect the feybloods and set up rules of trade for the magic from their realm, but the arcana dismissed that as negotiating with a dream, or a pet. Even today, there are sects who don't believe the Fey are any more than very lifelike dreams, without real feelings or desires of their own. These conflicts have led to several Fey-Arcana wars."

Zeke exhaled sharply. "You make it sound like we caused the wars. But the Fey and feybloods need to be controlled. They're too dangerous to just let them do whatever they want, especially when some of them would love nothing more than to see every arcana dead."

Part of me agreed with Zeke, the part that had been fed on by the Fey for most of my life. But the part that had been raised by my empathetic mother and generous father, the best version of me whom I realized I wanted to be around Dawn, won out.

"Maybe they wouldn't want to see us dead if we didn't treat them all like animals?"

"They are animals!" Zeke responded.

"Including your sister?" The words slipped out before running through my "stupid things not to say" filter.

Zeke's hands were suddenly around my throat, solid as an iron clamp and squeezing hard. The car rocked back and forth as Dawn swerved and shouted, "What the fuck?"

"Let go!" I gasped. "I'm sorry, okay?"

Zeke released me with a push that gave me minor whiplash. I rubbed my neck. Anger borrowed my mouth to speak, "*I* didn't call Vee an animal, Zeke, you did! And if you put your hands around my neck again, you'll get to feel your spirit being ripped from your body."

"You'd have a hard time doing that if you're already dead, fool."

"Jesus, you two," Dawn said. "I don't know what's going on, but you guys are taking this fantasy shit way too seriously."

"We're fine," I said, looking at Zeke, and took several deep breaths. This wasn't helping my case with Dawn. And Zeke's reaction aside, it had been a jerk move to antagonize him like that. I willed my anger to dissipate. "I'm sorry I said anything about Vee." Zeke shrugged and looked out the window. I glanced at Mort. "And thanks for the backup by the way, bro."

Mort raised his hands. "Don't drag me into your drama."

I turned back around and settled into my seat.

Dawn adjusted her rearview mirror and said, "So far, you still haven't told me anything that explains what's up with you and your family."

"Well, I was trying. You need to understand my world in order to understand what's wrong with it," I said.

"You'd be amazed at what I can understand," Dawn said. "So maybe skip the history lesson and get to the point? And then if I have any questions, like what a feyblood is, or which mushrooms you've been licking, I can just ask you."

"Fine. Remember Felicity? She was a witch. She didn't attempt suicide or get shipped off to some hospital; she was attacked with dark magic, or at least pretended to be. Either way, I was framed for it and exiled to the Other Realm for twenty-five years. I just got back a couple days ago, and someone tried to frame me again by really killing Felicity. Plus, I have a clan of witches seeking revenge for Felicity, and because sasquatches killed one of them and they blame me."

"Sasquatches?"

"Yes, sasquatches."

"I see. And Pete?"

"He was hit by a hex from that clan of witches."

"Right. So don't you have a ministry of magic or something you can go to for protection?"

I sighed. "We have governing bodies called Arcana Ruling Councils who are the nice folks that exiled me and now want to question us as suspects. So I need to figure out who's really behind all these attacks, assuming it's not the clan of witches, and to do that I need to talk to Katherine Verona's spirit. And to figure out how I can get to Magus Verona, I need to talk to a dead security guard who's in a protected crypt in Everett. And now you know everything."

Dawn drove in silence for several minutes. Finally, she said, "So, you're trying to get to this Verona person?"

"Yes."

"Well, shit, I have no other but a woman's reason, yet I always thought magic but a jest unseen, inscrutable, invisible, as a nose on a man's face, or a . . . something or other."

"Nice. So you still don't believe me."

"Not to sound like my old therapist, but I believe you believe." She shrugged. "I'm sure there's an explanation for all the magic stuff. There always is, like in that Sherlock Holmes movie. Some sick bastard put a chemical in Pete's shampoo that was set off when he began to sweat or something, and you think he was hexed. And maybe there really is this ARC thing, a bunch of dudes like the free-masons or Skull and Bones or whoever, who think their hocus pocus rituals are going to help them rule the world someday. All I know for certain is somebody hurt Petey, and if that someone believes the same crazy stuff you do, then maybe you're the best way to find the bastards, and make them pay."

"Mundies," Zeke muttered in the back.

Mort's phone rang. He checked the screen, then answered. "Hello? No, we're fine. What—really? You okay? All right. Okay. Thanks."

He hung up. "Mattie says Grayson left. There were two enforcers with Grayson, and they questioned everyone. They threatened to charge Mattie with obstruction, but they didn't arrest anyone."

"Enforcers?" Dawn asked.

"Arcana cops," I said, glancing at Zeke in his *Miami Vice* getup. "Zeke used to be one. Their outfits have changed though."

Dawn glanced in the rearview. "Now, that's a shame."

"Just table the label and drive," Zeke replied.

Dead Man's Party

Holy crap, traffic sucks.

It took almost three hours to reach Everett, between waiting for the Kingston ferry and then getting stuck in all the traffic headed north on I-5. The freeway was three times as wide as I remembered, but still clogged with cars.

When I complained about it, Dawn said, "Maybe you guys should have flown on brooms or something?"

"And mess up my hair?"

She laughed. "You always did worry too much about your hair."

"Well yeah, it's my best feature."

"I always thought your eyes were your best feature. They sparkle when you smile."

I may have actually blushed a bit. I cleared my throat. "Dawn, I wanted to tell you—" I glanced over my shoulder. Zeke and Mort were both watching me with too much interest. "Uh, I wanted to tell you how much I appreciate you looking out for Pete."

"Yeah, well, looking out for people seems to be my thing."

We reached Everett, one of the many little cities north of Seattle, just before 3 P.M. I didn't know much about it except it had a Boeing factory and the Museum of Flight. Like every other town or city we passed through, it had grown since the last time I'd seen it. Thankfully, Mort knew where we were going.

The Evergreen Cemetery sat on the edge of the city, on a little side street not far from the freeway. It had been around since the Civil War era, filled with actual stone and marble headstones, crosses, and statues worn and darkened by time and weather and sorrow. Dawn parked on the side of the road outside its gates, and we made our way across the rolling hills to the most prominent of the crypts, a large stone-gray ziggurat called the Rucker Tomb. I'd visited it many times as a child, climbing its stepped concrete sides and imagining myself exploring Mayan or Aztec ruins, while Father dealt with ARC business in the crypt below. It sat upon a raised concrete platform, and the front entrance was reached by stairs that passed between two man-size stone pylons. We stopped in front of the stairs.

"Please tell me you're not going to break into this thing," Dawn said.

"Not exactly," I replied. "Mort, you're up."

Mort turned his pinky ring around so that his persona gem was palm-side down, put his hand on the right pylon, and said, *"Aperire Ostium Per Mea Ius Ex Necromantiae."*

There was a moment's pause, then a voice came from within the stone, "Mortimer Gramaraye, you may enter."

The stone stairs receded from us with a low grinding sound, revealing a second set of stairs that led down rather than up.

Dawn touched the pylon. "Okay. I'll admit, that's some pretty cool Indiana Jones stuff right there. But nothing that requires magic to explain."

"Just wait," I said, and led the way down the stairs to a chilly stone passageway that smelled of Pine-Sol and earth, lit by hanging yellow bulbs. The walls were painted white, and half-columns lined the walls every few feet, with arches spanning the hall between columns.

We passed beneath several arches and reached the first sepulchral niche on our right, an alcove about eight feet tall, its base level with my knees. A man and woman stood smiling down at us. He wore a brown topcoat, vest, and ribbon tie, and had bushy sideburns that reminded me of Isaac Asimov. The woman wore a blue dress that gathered in at the waist then flared out in the rear. Each held a croquet mallet resting jauntily across one shoulder. In their left hands, the man held a small alchemist's crucible, and the woman a crystal ball symbolizing the prophecy branch of sorcery.

Dawn stared up at them for a second, then said, "Damn. Is this the part where I should start worrying you're going to drop me in hot wax?"

I laughed. "No. You're perfectly safe, I promise."

"But those are real dead people?"

"Yes."

"How come they don't look like mummies, or Courtney Love or something?"

"Magic," I said.

"Uh-huh, of course, magic." She didn't sound as confident in her denial this time.

Zeke sighed loudly. "Can we get this done, and save the tour for later?"

"You're right, sorry. Mort, lead on."

Mort took the lead. Side tunnels branched out to either side, with symbols and dates marked on the corner columns. The sepulcher alcoves were constant now on both sides of the hall, one after the other. The people entombed in Avalon Underhill had all worked for the ARC, or did something to earn a place here. We passed men and women of all ages, sometimes teenagers, and the rare child included through some family deal made with the ARC. They represented all five branches of magic: alchemy, wizardry, thaumaturgy, sorcery, and necromancy. And their clothing styles changed as we left the nineteenth century behind and began traveling through the twentieth-century sections. I paused by a man in a baby blue polyester suit. Note to self—go for a "timeless" look when I die.

The symbols and tools of the branches of magic evolved too, incorporating plastics and electricity, as well as refinements in the use of magic itself. It used to be, for example, a wizard had one, maybe two tattoos covering their entire body. But as the ingredients of the inks evolved, and the tools and spells became more efficient, the tattoos needed less space to do the same magic. Wizards could fit up to eight tattoos on an average body by the time of my exile. I could only imagine how many tattoos a young wiz sported today.

We passed the occasional live mourner being escorted by a necromancer, and a crypt warden making his rounds. We all bowed our heads, and both Mort and I touched our hands to our forehead in a gesture of respect that also served to display our blackstoned persona rings marking us as necromancers. Nobody stopped or challenged us.

Dawn acted like she was on a museum tour whenever no strangers were in sight. She stopped occasionally to read the silver plaques at the base of each alcove, then sprinted to catch up with us. "They remind me of stuffed pets," she said. "Why are they staring at us all creepy like that instead of being in a coffin?"

"I think the tradition started because people hoped necromancers or one of the other magical branches would find a cure for death," I said. "Sort of like those people who have their bodies frozen just in case we can cure and revive them someday."

"Is there? A cure for death?"

Her question made me think of Heather in biology class, hoping to create a true reanimation potion. And Grandfather had frequently grumbled about the unfair advantages of Fey immortality, first to me, and then to Grayson when I, being so wise in my teen years, decided his grumblings were boring. Heather and Grandfather were two of the most skilled and intelligent arcana I knew of, and even they had not been able to defeat death.

"No, there's no cure," I said. "At least, not one that doesn't require a constant flood of raw magic and serious Monkey Paw consequences. And trying to find one has become pretty much illegal."

"So why keep making these little die-o-ramas?"

"Just more fun, I guess."

"Seriously?"

"Well, which would you rather do? Plan a display for yourself, pick out an outfit and a pose and all that, or pick out a coffin?"

Zeke spoke up. "The ARC likes to keep them in a state

where the spirits can be questioned as easily as possible if we need to."

"And there's that." I sighed. "For some reason, Talking is less draining if the body is as close to its living state as possible and you have a sense of their personality, of who they were."

"We can talk to them?"

"Well, I can."

Dawn paused in front of a man dressed in a black Members Only jacket and extremely tight Jordache jeans.

"Hello! This guy looks just like Hugh Jackman. You're sure you can't hook a girl up, bring him back to life?"

"And you accused me of doing bad things with dead bodies?"

"Well, if you brought him back, he wouldn't be dead, now, would he? Maybe you could just animate him as, you know, a brainless hunk o' warm Wolverine goodness?"

"Uh, no. Trust me, both the cost and the results of raising the dead are pretty nasty."

"Well, damn. Way to crush a girl's dreams." We caught up with Zeke and Mort, and Dawn said, "If magic is real, so far it all seems dangerous and creepy. Where's the awe and the fun?"

I opened my mouth to argue, but stopped. What could I say? I'd asked the same question myself more than once.

"We're here," Mort said. "He should be down the hall on the left."

We turned down the side hall and began reading the name plates. We found the one we wanted fourth from the end. Devon Newman was short and sturdy looking, his gray suit stretched over an ample belly, the flattop buzz cut utterly failing to de-emphasize either of his large chins. He wore a Seahawks blazer rather than a dress shirt beneath his suit jacket. His right hand held a tiny paintbrush. This, I realized, explained what appeared to be a re-creation of a World War II battle around his feet, with tiny painted soldiers fighting over a miniature landscape, cotton smoke issuing from their guns and tanks; and on a raised plain a group of wizards battled feybloods with silver wire lightning and red plastic fire.

"Okay, Gramaraye," Zeke said. "Time for you to do your thing."

"Yeah. Lucky me." I closed my eyes and went through the mental exercises Grandfather had taught me, to clear my head of distracting thoughts, to bring my emotions to a neutral hum. I opened my eyes, looked into Devon's face and touched his hand.

The resonance of his spirit thrummed loud and clear.

"Devon, I summon you."

The connection was immediate. Devon wasn't warded against Talking. Few bodies in these general ARC crypts were, since it was cheaper and more efficient just to limit access to the crypt, and then ward the crypt itself against anyone outside of it from summoning the spirits of those inside.

I felt a pull, like some invisible part of me reaching out from my center to Devon's body, and then magic and life flowed out of me, draining away in a slow but steady trickle.

"Hello, Devon," I said.

There was a pause, and then Devon's voice replied, "Hello?" His mouth didn't move. "Shit. I'm dead, aren't I?"

"Yes, I'm afraid so."

It took extra energy to make his voice heard by the others, not just by me. But I needed Zeke to hear him. And I wanted Dawn to believe me. I glanced at her to see how she took it. She looked at me with a wide-eyed, uncertain expression, an expression tinged with a horror I recognized. "You're really talking to a ghost?" she whispered.

I nodded. This was not the time to explain the difference between a ghost and a spirit. I returned my focus to Devon. The faster we wrapped this up, the less of my life I'd lose.

"Devon, I've summoned you to—"

"Are you sure you're a real necromancer?"

"What? Yes. I'm Talking to you, aren't I?"

"Well, yeah, it's just, I've seen my fair share of summonings, and you don't seem to be doing it right, buddy. No offense, but I don't want to be accidentally unmade or nothing by a beginner, you know? Is your boss around, maybe?"

Mort snorted. I just sighed. On its own, necromancy really isn't all that showy or impressive to observe: no flashes of light or howling winds, no fire or lightning or transformations or even a bouncing table and flickering lights in most cases. It's really just a couple of folks talking, even if one of those folks is dead. So in order to ensure proper respect for their talents, early necromancers began to wear fancy robes, and added a dash of ritual and a lot of theatrics to the whole affair.

At the height of necromantic ritualization in the Middle Ages, a summoning could take up to three days, and involved elaborate costumes, lots of chanting, and occasionally a lovely assistant. Even as recently as last century, one ritual got so out of control that the ARC had to cover it up by claiming it was a rock concert by a group called KISS (Knights in Sorcery's Service), and then had to promptly create a real band by that name in order to make the story stick.

But I felt no desire to maintain those particular traditions right now.

"I *am* the boss," I said, shooting Mort a look that said not to argue the point. "We have some important questions for you, and not a lot of time for ritual."

"Well, no offense," the heavyset warden said, "but how about a little prid quo, uh, you know. Like, I answer your question, and you answer mine? Like, how's the 'hawks doing this season?"

Zeke blew out his mustache and stepped forward. "Tell him what I told you to say."

"Devon, I have an enforcer here with me. He wants you to know this is official enforcer business. They suspect someone might be planning to break into the EMP crypt, so to close any holes in the security they're asking each warden how someone might succeed."

"Oh, sure, ask me now when I can't even get a bonus or nothing. Do you know how many times I applied to be an enforcer? Or made suggestions about the security at the empie?"

"Well, they, uh, want me to tell you that's why you're being consulted, and they'll give a bonus to your inheritors."

"Fat lot of good that does me. And Linda already got her reward when I died. I'm sure she went around telling everyone at the funeral how she warned me about my weight, how she just knew it was going to kill me. But do you know what I had to go through just to sneak a couple burgers without her finding out? Talk about stealing past security! You'd think I was having an affair the way she—"

"Devon!" I said. "Enough! If you want to continue enjoying the benefits of an ARC crypt, and not be unmade, then I suggest you fulfill your obligations and start answering my questions. Now."

"Okay! Geez! What do you want to know, then, oh great one?"

"I told you, the enforcers want to know how someone might break into the crypt beneath the EMP."

"Fine. Well, if I was going to break in, here's what I'd do."

Zeke flipped open a small notebook and took notes while Devon outlined the security measures and how he'd bypass them. When Devon was done, he said, "Are we good?"

I looked at Zeke. He nodded.

"Yeah," I said. "We're good. Thanks, Devon. I dismi—"

"Wait! Can you get a message to my wife?"

"Uh, sure. What is it?"

"Tell her . . . I loved her, nagging and all."

Ahhh. True love. "If I see her, I will. I dismiss you."

I released the connection, and the hallway spun. I put out a hand to catch myself but missed the wall, and fell to the side. Dawn caught me.

"You okay?" she asked.

"Yeah. That didn't cost me much, really, but it's still a shock to the system."

"Cost you?"

"Life. It costs me life to Talk to the dead."

And it almost cost me lunch. My stomach tried to invade my throat, but fortunately my throat knocked it back down where it belonged.

"Let's get out of here," Zeke said. "We have some planning to do."

Mort led the way back to the stairs. I followed in a head-throbby daze.

"Finn?" Dawn said in a quiet voice. "Your mother, is she here someplace?"

"No. My mother's buried in our family mausoleum."

"But you could talk to her if you wanted?"

"No. She's warded."

And then I realized that I could in fact talk to her, for the same reason I could talk to Verona.

Dawn paused. "Could I talk to my dad?"

I sighed and gave her a sympathetic look. "It's usually not a good idea to Talk to someone you care about, unless there's an important reason."

"Because it would cost you some of your life."

"Yes, that. But there's dangers to you as well. As a rule, it's best to let the dead be dead." I put a hand on her arm. "And in my experience, they know how you felt, what you would say if you could."

We reached the stairs. Mort touched a fist-size square of silver on the wall, and after a few seconds the roof over the stairs receded, revealing a late-afternoon sky with a high chance of rain. If any mundies had been near, we would have heard a chime instead and been required to wait for them to leave before the way opened.

As we stepped out onto the lawn of the cemetery, Mort said, "You're going to owe me for this, bro. I don't mind lending a hand, but this—"

"A hand?" came a munchkin voice behind us. We all spun around. Out of the shrubbery atop the tomb's concrete platform stepped Priapus, the gnome leader. He had one eye bruised and swollen beneath its bushy white brow, and a scabbed-over cut ran along one bare arm, splitting the rose tattoo in half and impaling the flaming skull.

He glared from beneath his pointy blue hat, and raised a gleaming sickle. "One hand of a necromancer. I'll take that offer, deal breaker." A half-dozen more gnomes stepped out of the bushes and from behind tombstones all around us.

Dawn grabbed my arm. "Are those—?"

"Gnomes," I said. "Angry gnomes."

Just Like Heaven

I placed myself between Dawn and the gnomes on the tomb's concrete platform. The only thing worse than angry gnomes are angry gnomes at eye level.

"We don't want any trouble," I said. There were too many of them to fight or flee, at least without risking Dawn's life.

"We ain't here ta take requests," Priapus said. "We're here ta make good on the deal this one had with us." He waved his sickle at Mort again. "We acquired the Talker artifact as requested, and have suffered losses because of it. You now owe us the promised payment for the artifact, plus fair compensation for our losses from the sasquatch attack, plus compensation for the time and expense of waiting for ya to leave the protection of your home and to track ya here like."

Mort tucked his hands under his armpits. "I don't have anything to give you," he said. "Not here. If you'll just give me another day—"

"A day'll add further interest to your debt," Priapus said. "And we would need ta hold ya as guarantee against said payment thereof."

"What?" Mort said. "Can't you just take my word, as a necromancer?"

"Forget about it," the gnome said.

While the gnome and Mort were speaking, I edged closer to Zeke, and whispered from the side of my mouth, "Fight or flee?"

Zeke shrugged, his brows furrowed in a concerned and unhappy expression. "Not my problem."

Great. Zeke and his damn sense of right and wrong. Mort's

problem wasn't our problem, it was because he'd traded in illegal artifacts, and Zeke wouldn't soil his hands fixing that kind of trouble.

Mort sounded panicked as he said, "How am I supposed to pay you if you're holding me hostage?"

"Not hostage," the gnome leader said. "A guarantee of payment like. And these two'll get the payment for us." The gnome waved at me and Zeke.

Mort's eyes darted to mine. "But—what happens if they don't pay?"

"They'll pay," Priapus said. "They fought for ya against the 'squatches. If they'd do that, they'll pay ta save ya from our penalty for default."

"Finn?" Mort said, his tone desperate now. "You need me! You can't just abandon me."

The fact that he thought I would just abandon him to the gnomes made me want to just abandon him to the gnomes. Granted, it had already crossed my mind that abandoning him to feybloods might be karmic payback for abandoning me to the Fey. And I felt an instant twinge of annoyance that my brother's stupidity entangled me even further with the world of feybloods and magic I'd hoped to leave behind entirely. But besides the fact that I actually cared about him for some reason, he was right. We might need him to get into the EMP. I sighed. "What will all of this cost us?"

The gnome cocked his head to the side, and stroked his ZZ-Top beard for a second. "The debt, including one extra day of interest, requires no less than two hundred Toths of magic or artifacts of equivalent value thereof like."

"Two hundred?" I said and glared at Mort. I doubted we had half that. "We'll pay twenty-five, plus free preservation and dissipation rites for ten deceased."

"One hundred fifty Toths, since we can't be sure he won't weasel out and hide in your home again."

"Fifty, plus free preservation and dissipation rites for twelve deceased."

"One hundred Toths, rites for fifteen deceased, and ya retrieve for us one sock of natural fibers worn by a deadified wizard."

I blinked. "What—" I began, but stopped myself. Best not to ask what they needed a dead wizard's sock for. But it gave me an idea. "What if I offered you fifty Toths, and to place a gnome statue in the Inner Sanctum beneath the EMP in Seattle within, say, the next forty-eight hours?"

Priapus stroked his beard. "If ya fail to place the statue, the cost'll be the two hundred Toths, plus you must use your Talker skills for us however we require for one year."

I glanced at Mort. Damn it.

"Agreed, as long as it doesn't risk my health or cost me more than two years of life."

"Done!" said the gnome leader. "And witnessed."

"Witnessed," said the other gnomes like a munchkin chorus.

We shared little conversation in the car as Dawn drove us back to the Edmonds-Kingston ferry. In fact, Mort and Zeke both fell asleep in the back. On the ferry, Dawn and I quietly exited the car and made our way up to the top deck. The sky looked like rolling hills of gray, but several golden columns of sunlight cut through breaks in the clouds, highlighting the white peaks of the Olympic mountains, and creating glittering circles on the choppy blue-steel skin of the ocean. The wind's chill cut through our clothes, so we took shelter in a covered observation section.

"So," I said as Dawn reattached a ribbon that had blown free of her hair. "You've been hit with a lot today. You doing okay?"

"I don't know. I guess," Dawn said. "I mean, I always believed there was magic, and ghosts, at least on some level. But—" She shrugged. "It's not what I thought it would be."

I looked out across the water at the dark shoreline of the Olympic Peninsula. "So, is it something you could deal with? You know, on a daily basis?"

"Well, I kind of have to, don't I? I mean, I can't unlearn what I've learned."

"Actually, you can," I said. "We could make you forget everything that happened today."

She looked at me. "Please tell me you haven't done that before. Made me forget stuff?"

"No."

"Okay. Good. That would piss me off."

I smiled. "So now you really know where I've been the last twenty-five years, why I didn't call or write. It wasn't my choice," I said.

"I know. I get that."

"And what you said in the Belmont last night," I said. "I thought about it. And, well, if you're still interested after everything that's happened, after everything you've learned, I, uh— how would you feel if I kissed you right now?"

Dawn stared at me for two long, loud heartbeats. Then she said, "Why don't you try it and find out."

I stepped close to her, until I could feel the heat of her in the cool sea air. I slipped one hand around the back of her neck, leaned in, and kissed her.

In summoning a spirit, I always feel a moment of connection and then the flow of life energy from me. With that kiss, I thought maybe I knew what the spirit felt. I felt pulled into Dawn, into the feel of her, the smell of her, the presence of her. I felt summoned into the world of that kiss, felt energy poured into me through it. I consumed her kiss, pressed myself into her and pulled her into me.

The kiss ebbed and surged from deep to playfully light and back again, like the swell and crash of the waves against the ferry, though I soon lost all sense of the outside world, focused only on the warm world of Dawn's lips, the rhythm of her tongue.

The blare of the speaker announcing our approach to Kingston brought me back to the ferry, to the world of up and down, left and right, inside and out, the world where I existed separate from Dawn. We eased our way out of the kiss, blinked at each other for a second, and both grinned.

"Hey, sparkle eyes," Dawn said, her voice low and soft. "Now *you* know magic is real."

We held hands for the drive home from the ferry, exchanging ridiculously happy grins when we caught the other looking. That hour with Dawn finally felt like I'd come home.

Sadly, our actual homecoming meant that the moment had to end, and I had to start thinking again about dangers and plans. It was nearly 7 P.M. when Dawn's car bounced into her driveway, waking Zeke and Mort. Golden hour light cast long shadows from all the plants and piles of junk in Dawn's yard. We climbed out of the car and stretched, then moved as a group to the break in the hedge between our two properties.

"You want me to go see if the coast is clear?" Dawn asked.

"No," I said. "Enforcers aren't the only people looking for us and I don't want you in danger."

"I sure hope you're not going to act like you can keep this girl safe by locking me away. I can handle myself, you know."

Zeke snorted.

I gave him a quick "not helping" glare, and said, "I know you can handle yourself. Doesn't mean I'm going to send you into a trap though, especially since you don't have any magic."

Dawn crossed her arms. "Am I going to be hearing that a lot? How I don't have magic so I can't play in your reindeer games? Because that's gonna get old real quick."

"No. I just—"

Zeke cleared his throat and said, "Are we done here? We've got a lot to do tonight."

"Nothing stopping you from checking out the house," I said.

Zeke pulled out his baton but didn't extend it. "If I'm not back in a minute, get someplace safe." He touched the inside of his jacket, and his outfit went camouflage, then he disappeared through the break in the hedge.

I waited until he was gone, then said, "Dawn, look, I—"

"It's fine," Dawn said. "I get it. Bad things are after you, and I can't kick a witch's curse in the balls. I'm just telling you it's going to get old if this happens a lot, me getting left out or left behind."

"It won't. I promise." I pulled Dawn into my arms. "If Zeke says it's all clear, you can come in and be part of everything."

Zeke returned and generously spared a frown for Dawn and me before saying, "All clear, far's I can tell. Let's go."

We dashed across the yard, past Pete's cottage to the side door and into the house. I took Dawn's hand as we followed the sound of voices to the dining room. We found Mattie and Vee playing scrabble, while Sammy tapped intently on her phone and Father cleared the table of dishes.

Mattie looked up, her eyes going to Dawn's hand in mine, and back to our faces, and she beamed at Dawn. "Oh, that's so cool. Totally perfect. See?" she said, looking at Vee. "Anything's possible."

Dawn looked surprised. Vee blushed and avoided Zeke's questioning look.

"How's Pete?" I asked.

"Good," Vee said. "Healer came and went."

Mattie's face scrunched. "Ooo. Yeah. Um, Heather is with him now, said she might be able to help with the scarring."

"Heather's upstairs?" I said, and felt suddenly awkward. My hand started to slide from Dawn's.

Her grip tightened on mine, and she said, "I'd think carefully about the choices you make right now."

I squeezed her hand back. "Sorry. I'm not going anywhere."

"Except the EMP," Zeke said. "Maybe we could concentrate on that?"

Mort headed for the far exit. "Knock yourselves out. I've got to come up with two hundred Thoths worth of magic for when you fail." He left the room.

"I think I can help Pete," Heather said as she entered the room behind us. "I can make a potion that—oh." We turned to face her. She'd stopped by the door, her eyes on Dawn. "Hi." Her eyes flicked to our held hands, and her eyebrows twitched. "Like I said, I can make a . . . lotion—"

"It's okay," I said. "Dawn knows about our world."

Sammy stood up and left the room.

"Oh," Heather said. "I'm . . . surprised. Are you two engaged?"

"No," I said, uncomfortably aware of how sweaty my palm suddenly became in Dawn's hand. "But she's practically part of our family anyway, and she could have been hurt today because she didn't know the truth."

Dawn glanced between us. "So, Heather, you're a magic user like Finn, then? A witch?"

I winced. Heather gave a tight smile, then said, "I'm an alchemist. But speaking of witches, Finn, I assume you were out stopping the witches who so rudely interrupted our date yesterday? The same ones I assume attacked Petey?"

"You know what they say about assuming," Dawn muttered.

"Excuse me?" Heather said.

Mattie sprung up and said, "Hey! I know. Ms. Brown, why don't I take you back to the kitchen and see if we have whatever you need to make that potion?"

"Sure," Heather said and followed Mattie from the room. As she disappeared around the corner, I heard her say, "*Some*body's got a case of the mundies."

I looked at Dawn.

"What?" she said. "I know you like her, Finn, but there's something not right about her. And I'm not just saying that because she wants you."

"Heather's a friend. And she hasn't had an easy life, Dawn."

Dawn patted my cheek. "You're so cute. You don't even know how dangerous it is defending her right now, do you? But I know it's just because you have a big squishy heart, so I'll let you off this time with a warning."

Zeke blew out his mustache. "Enough with the jibba jabba! Can you please focus on the task at hand? We need to plan our break-in."

"Sorry," I said. "You're right. We can work out the broad strokes, but we'll need to gather the whole family for the details. I think we're going to need everyone for this."

"I'll get them," Vee said, and rushed from the room.

"Not Father!" I called after her. I didn't want to risk the enemy learning our plans through him somehow. I sat at the table, with Dawn next to me, and Zeke sat a few chairs down. "Okay, so, breaking into the EMP—"

Zeke and I went over his notes and discussed ideas until everyone had gathered around the table: me, Dawn, Sammy, Mort, Zeke, Vee, and even Heather. Mattie was assigned to keep Father in his room.

I stood up at the head of the table and said, "Thank you all for being here—"

"Oh look, Finn Fancy Necromancy Pants is thanking me for being in my *own home,*" Mort said.

I took a calming breath. "What I'm trying to say is, thank you all for coming together like this. I know things have been crazy since I've come back, and I'm sorry for that. I really am. I didn't want any of this, believe me. I have no idea why someone is trying to kill me, or send me back into exile. But I wanted to share with you what we do know, and what we plan to do about it."

"And you need our help," Heather said.

"Yes, I do. I—"

"The way you needed my help in the library yesterday?" She looked at Dawn.

I blushed, and avoided looking at either of them. "No. This is a little more serious than *research*." I cleared my throat. "Here's what I know. Twenty-five years ago, somebody used dark necromancy on Felicity, possibly with her help, and framed me for the attack, someone who might have been her lover, someone who could get past our house's protections, someone who had the power and influence to block her clan's immigration efforts. Then during my return from exile, somebody attacked the Fey. And Felicity . . . she came to warn me, but they killed her in the changeling's trailer, probably as another attempt to frame me."

"And I was attacked," Mort said.

"Yes. Someone is using feybloods to try to stop us from Talking to a spirit our family warded, to protect some powerful secret, I assume. And in every attack, it seems my enemy didn't want me harmed, only stopped, and framed."

"Someone who?" Sammy asked. "And why do they want you exiled so bad?"

"I don't know," I said. "But we hope to find out, by doing exactly what they're trying so hard to prevent. And that brings me to asking for your help. Because the only person of significance our family warded near the time of my exile is Katherine Verona. And she's under the EMP."

Mort shook his head. "Even I can't get you into there."

"I know," I said. "That's why we're going to break in."

"You're crazy," Mort said. "Even a wizard would be challenged to break into an ARC Sanctum, and you're no wizard. I heard what that warden told you. They have layers of security using all five magics."

Zeke stood up. "We got a plan to get past that. But it's gonna take all of you."

I glanced at Zeke. "Zeke and I have two plans, actually," I said. "Plan A is we break into the EMP, find out who's doing this to me, to us, and stop them."

"So plan A is suicide, got it," Mort said. "And plan B?"

"Zeke and I fake our own deaths and disappear."

"For how long?" Vee asked.

"Forever," I said. "You'd never see us again. It's the only way to be sure you're all safe." I glanced at Dawn. Would she come with me into hiding? She'd traveled the world with her last boyfriend. Was it fair even to ask her?

Sammy crossed her arms. "Except we'd have to hope that who-ever's doing this believes you're really dead and doesn't try to use one of us as bait to draw you out, right?"

"Yeah," Zeke said. "And our enemy'd get away with whatever they're doing."

Heather shifted in her seat. "I hate to be the one who says this, but . . . maybe you should turn yourselves in?"

"No," Vee said.

Heather leaned toward me. "Finn, you know I'm no fan of the ARC, but even I have to admit they've changed, have better spells and rules now then when you were exiled before. Surely they'll figure out the truth. I just don't want to see you hurt, and this all sounds way too dangerous, too big to deal with on your own."

"He's not on his own," Dawn said. "He's got his friends, and family."

Mort gave an irritated sigh. "None of the options look good for the family's reputation."

"Right," I said. "Obviously, there're risks whatever we choose to do. So which is it going to be?"

Smooth Criminal

➤ DAY 3 ➤

After a long night of planning, I spent my last day of freedom preparing for our final all-or-nothing gambit, and fitting in as much quality time with my family, and with Dawn, as I could, sharing memories and talking about plans for a future life I had little faith would happen.

The day passed too quickly, until Zeke, Sammy, and I sat in a corner of Pop, the restaurant inside the Experience Music Project building. The loud music, bright lights, and shiny decor made me feel like I was in a Jem and the Holograms music video, along with a hundred other people talking and eating and drinking. Sammy's computer screen lit her face, her brows scrunched in intense concentration as she hacked the lines of code I could see reflected in her black-rimmed glasses. Zeke wore a hat to hide his distinctive Mohawk, and his mustache had been waxed and pressed to his face until it looked more like a thin Vandyke from a distance. Zeke and I pretended to talk, but our real attention was on Vee at the bar nearby.

Vee wore a shimmery, slinky black dress that didn't look quite natural on her. Maybe I was just used to seeing her in jeans and a sweatshirt, or perhaps it was the way she sat hunched in on herself, obviously uncomfortable with the dress and the crowds. But the man beside her didn't seem to notice, given that the dress barely covered her private bits.

The man wore the security guard uniform and red wizard's persona ring of an EMP warden. Vee talked to him, laughing at what he said and occasionally flipping back her long blond hair in a stiff, rehearsed way like a bad actress. Zeke fidgeted constantly. I could tell he wanted to call the whole thing off and get Vee out of there.

The waiting was certainly nerve racking, leaving me little to do except to keep running over the plan, tripping upon everything that could go wrong.

"Plan A it is, then," Zeke said, surprise in his voice. He looked at his notepad and I glanced around the dining room at everyone sitting with determined looks on their faces. At least, I think it was determination. Those faces were a little blurry thanks to the tears that burned the edges of my eyes.

Not one of them voted for Plan B, for Zeke and me to run and hide. And nobody but Heather voted to go to the ARC. Not even Mort, though he had taken the longest to agree. I wanted to believe it was because he wanted to help us fight and not just because of the deal I'd made with Priapus, but I'd take his help either way.

"For Finn to do his Talking thing," Zeke said, "he's gonna have to actually reach Verona's body. And that ain't gonna be easy. The friggin' place was built from the ground up to keep out unwanted magics."

Seattle's Experience Music Project building was an interesting structure indeed. It sat in the shadow of the Space Needle and covered about half a city block, but there wasn't a right angle to be seen on its surface. It was all curves and odd angles, and actually looked like several weirdly shaped buildings made of rainbow-hued metal all welded together. Sammy said officially it was sup-posed to represent the fluidity and energy of music, maybe the visualization of a sound wave or even smashed instruments. But the true purpose of its shape was to help deflect any magical energy aimed at it or its contents, thus preventing attacks, scrying, or summoning of anyone or anything within. And that was just the visible structure. That didn't count the invisible layers of wards and traps that the ARC had added.

Inside, the museum held a series of large chambers filled with twists and turns, divided and subdivided into musical and pop cultural displays meant to induce ooos, ahhhs, meditative trances, and maybe the occasional seizure. It was an unsettling mix of pop cultural museum and music club, and, judging from the crowd at the bar in Pops, a singles watering hole.

I barely touched my appetizer as I watched Vee, too distracted to eat. And I wanted plenty of room for the pizza I'd ordered. I glanced at my Pac-Man watch: 6:47 P.M. The EMP closed at 7:00. Vee didn't have much more time.

"Now, there's three levels we gotta get through to reach Verona," Zeke said. "The first level is breaking in past normal mundy security, doors and alarms and cameras and such. Sammy, that's your job. For the second level, we need to have a warden's persona ring, and know the day's password." Zeke glanced at me, a miserable look on his face. We'd fought over this, but it really was the only way. "Vee, sis, we'll need you to go to the bar at the EMP before it closes and flirt with one of the wardens. We've been told a couple of them hang out there between shifts, hoping to pick up dates. You'll need to read the password from his memory, without that sucka knowing any better. Can you do that?"

"Yeah, but—" Vee glanced at Heather. "Maybe you can help me though? It . . . It's been a while since I flirted with a guy." She blushed scarlet.

"Oh sweetie, don't you worry about that," Heather said. "A man at a bar won't be interested in your words. Not with the dress I have in mind."

Vee touched the security guard's arm, leaning in and exposing even more cleavage. She said something, her left hand running up the side of his head and through his hair. The man's smile grew slowly wider at Vee's words.

Vee took the man's right hand—the hand with his persona ring—between both her own then, and brought it down between her thighs. Not so high up that they were breaking indecency laws, but enough that his fingers were brushing the hemline of her dress. The pair received amused, disapproving, or jealous glances from the people who noticed. Zeke growled.

Vee rubbed at the guard's hand for a minute as he talked to her with a creepy leer on his face.

Man, I owed Vee big-time.

Zeke started to rise, but I put a hand on his shoulder. Vee stood, and the guard joined her. She leaned in and said something, and he nodded and rushed off toward the front entrance. Vee nodded at us and headed in the opposite direction.

"Thank the gods," Sammy muttered, still clicking away at her laptop. "If I had to watch much more of that I was going to blow disgusto chunks."

I dropped money on the table, giving one last sad look toward the kitchen where my pizza must still be cooking, and Zeke, Sammy, and I followed after Vee. We all rendezvoused at the 5 Point Café several blocks away. The 5 Point was Sammy's recommendation, a small crowded place evenly divided between a dive bar and a greasy spoon diner. Vee already sat at the booth secured by Mort, a sweatshirt over her dress. But she sat straight, not huddled in on herself like normal. Zeke, Sammy, and I joined them.

"You okay?" I asked as we settled into the seats.

"Yeah," Vee said, sounding surprised at her own answer. "It was . . . fun, in a way. Especially sending him off to wait for me at another bar far, far away."

"Nice," Sammy said and grabbed a menu.

"Here." Vee held up a red persona ring. "Sarah did awesome. He shouldn't notice he's wearing a fake until he returns to work tomorrow. I got the password too."

Mort rubbed at his eyes. "So we're really doing this?"

"Afraid so," I replied.

We ordered food and chatted, killing a few hours until it was time for the actual break-in. They didn't have pizza, but the hash browns were damn well perfect.

"Once we get past the mundy security," Zeke said, looking around the dining room, "we'll need to get from the mundy museum down to the crypt. To find the door to the crypt, we gotta enter a code onto a command chair. But to reach the chair, we need the ring and password."

"And you know the code for the chair?" Sammy asked.

"Yeah. The dead warden told us."

"And if they've changed it since he died?" she asked.

Zeke cracked his knuckles. "Then we need to be prepared to defend ourselves while you figure the code out."

"Defend against what?" Mort asked.

"Bad things," I said, and looked at Heather. "We may need a pretty wide variety of protection potions. They have several defenses that use potions pumped in as gas, but they change frequently, so we're not certain what the effects will be."

Heather looked down at her hands as she squeezed them together. "Finn, I'm sorry, I can't help you. If you got caught, I—my son, I—I'm sorry."

Sammy rolled her eyes. "There's an easier way to protect against gas attacks than using more potions, believe me."

"Gas is the least of my concerns anyway," Zeke said.

"I've noticed," I replied.

Zeke glared at me, unamused.

Zeke, Mort, and I stood outside a side exit to the EMP, waiting in the chill night air. Zeke wore his enforcer outfit in full camo mode, with his duffel slung across his back. I wore Carhartt work pants and steel-toe boots bought in the city, and a leather biker jacket left behind by Dawn's ex. Not as good as the magical armor that Zeke had, but at least as good as +1 leather armor. If, you know, such a thing really existed.

Sammy's voice whispered in my ear through the device she'd lent me, a Bluebeard or something. "Alarm is down, cameras are on a loop, and the warden patrol just moved past you. You're good to go."

"Ten-four, good buddie," I said and nodded at Zeke.

Zeke used his skeleton key to open the door and his Casio watch to neutralize the threshold wards. We slipped inside. The lack of pulsing lights, pounding music, and noisy customers made the place feel a bit cold and cavernous, a dark structure of concrete, steel, and dead glass.

We moved past the ticket kiosk and headed down the second stairwell on the left, a long, narrow descent between concrete walls. Near the base, Zeke said, "Hold up." He dug through his duffel, and pulled out a glass potion bottle and some fishing line. He set up a booby trap with quick, efficient movements. "That should hold off any wardens for a bit if things go to hell."

We continued past the stairs into an antechamber, and to our left the wall lit up with row after row of etched hologram faces captured in glowing blue squares. The sign overhead read "Science Fiction Hall of Fame." I spotted Bradbury, Le Guin, Asimov, Butler, and more. One of the faces, H. G. Welles, looked up at us and said, "Your identity, sirs?"

"Warden Graham," I said, holding up my hand with the warden's persona ring. "Escorting guests."

Welles' gaze narrowed on the ring. He gave a nod. "Proceed, constable."

Past the antechamber was a tunnel of sorts, made of tubes of white light. There was room to skirt past the tunnel, but that would be a mistake. The tunnel was designed to strip away glamours and identify feybloods, and the door we needed would not open for us unless we passed through this first. I exchanged anxious glances with Zeke, then proceeded through. I felt the light tingle of magical energy, but nothing more. Zeke and Mort followed. So far, so good.

The science fiction museum itself appeared to be a maze of free-standing walls lined with props and displays. I spotted the command chair to our left and had a moment equivalent perhaps to when a believer spots a holy relic. Kirk's actual captain's chair from *Star Trek*. The rest of the museum fairly disappeared for me and I crossed to the chair. Encased behind protective Plexiglas, the chair sat thronelike upon a gray pedestal, with tribble dolls scattered around it like softball-size balls of fur. The chair itself was black leather, with wooden armrests, and silver control panels ran along each side covered in lights, switches, and buttons. A magnificent sight.

"We've reached the chair," I whispered.

"Try not to have a nerdgasm," Sammy's voice buzzed in my ear.

"Acknowledged, *Enterprise*," I replied. "Kirk out." Yeah, my sister knew me well.

Zeke waved at the chair, "Get ready, but don't start 'til I'm back. I'm gonna secure the perimeter."

He stalked off to set more booby traps on the other entrances.

"Sammy?" I whispered. "It's time to get Petey on the line."

"Will do," she replied.

"Thanks. You and Vee should head for the ferry now."

"I feel weird just taking off. We can wait a bit longer."

"We talked about this already. If something goes wrong, it won't help us if you get caught. And Zeke insisted Vee go home as soon as possible."

Mort gave me a nervous look. "Is there something wrong?"

"No," I said. "Everything's fine. Sammy and Vee are leaving is all."

"Fine," Sammy said. "On our way, Captain Bossypants. I'll be on the line if you need me."

"You're positive you can talk and drive at the same time?" I asked.

"You sure you can think and talk at the same time?" she asked.

"Not really," I replied. I wandered over to look at the nearby props while Sammy and Zeke were busy, but stayed within sight of the command chair—I didn't want to set off any traps. I saw the earpiece Uhura wore in *Star Trek,* some sunglasses from something called *Stargate SG-1,* and a whole ton of stuff from *Battlestar Galactica.* Apparently, there was a new series!

Gods, I hoped I didn't get exiled.

Zeke returned and plopped down his bag in front of the command chair. "Good to go, Gramaraye," he said.

"Pete's on," Sammy's voice buzzed.

"Hi, Finn," Pete said.

"Hi, Petey." I returned to the command chair. "Just hang on, I'll let you know if I need your help."

I turned the warden's persona ring around so the stone was palm-side down, then placed my hand against the Plexiglas. I could feel magic, dangerous magic, beneath my hand like a swarm of pissed-off hornets buzzing and beating against the Plexiglas. I swallowed and said, *"Aperire Ostium,* Meadowlark."

An archway opened in the Plexiglas, spreading out from my hand and granting access to the chair. The sense of dangerous magic dissipated.

"The daily password worked," I said. "Tell Vee thanks."

"Roger that, geek command," Sammy replied.

"Masks," Zeke said. He reached into his bag, and pulled out a gas mask—Sammy's simple solution to gaseous alchemical attacks. I pulled a similar mask from the satchel on my hip and slipped it over my head. It felt stifling, limited my peripheral vision, and smelled of pickles and farts, which I did my best not to wonder about since we'd purchased them second hand from an Army/Navy Surplus store.

I stepped up to the chair, and sat in it with reverent slowness. I ran my hands along the smooth wooden arms, then leaned forward and said in my best Shatnerian, "Sulu, set a course . . . for . . . Awesome, warp factor five." Nerdgasm achieved.

"Quit screwin' around, fool, and put in the code," Zeke whispered harshly.

Right. I leaned back and pulled the instructions from my pocket. On the right-hand console were five white buttons with round lights next to them. On the left-hand side, eight colored plastic switches, and nine lights of various shapes and bright colors that looked like costume jewelry.

I flipped four of the eight switches in the order described in the instructions, then held my breath and pressed the white button labeled "Jettison Pod." A single one of the jeweled lights flickered briefly.

Then nothing happened.

And more nothing happened.

I looked at the instructions, and at the switches again. Everything looked correct.

"Do you see a door anywhere?" I asked Zeke, my voice muffled by the mask. I stood to peer at the wall to our right where a door was supposed to have revealed itself.

The archway in the Plexiglas disappeared, replaced once again by a clear but solid wall, blocking my exit.

Pink gas poured out in a swirling cloud from the base of the chair, rapidly filling up the enclosed space.

"Crap," I said. "Pete, I think I'm going to need your help."

After the planning meeting in the dining room broke up, I spent several hours in my room, coding on my Commodore. It felt good, relaxing, like meditation. I could almost pretend everything that had happened—Felicity's attack, my exile, and all the craziness since my return—was all just a dream, a really bad dream.

Pete watched me, propped up in my bed and wrapped in bandages, chatting with me as I worked. He looked better, or at least not in so much pain, though I knew there would still be ugly scars under those bandages even with Heather's help.

"I'm still mad at you," he said at one point. "But I don't want to be. It doesn't feel good."

"It's okay. I understand. And I'm sorry, again. I love you, bro."

"Love you too." He took a bite of chocolate pudding. "And I love pudding. But I love you more."

I finished coding, entered the save command. I ran to the bathroom and then fixed some Mexican cocoa while the program saved amidst the loud buzzing and grinding of the floppy disk drive. When it was done, I moved my computer and monitor beside the bed, then booted the game back up. "I made you a game, Petey," I said.

What I'd created was a variation of a game we used to play together called Mastermind. In the original version, one person set up four pegs of various colors, hidden from the other player, and that other player had to guess the color and position of the pegs by process of elimination. Like in all puzzle games, Pete blew everyone else away when it came to Mastermind.

I'd created a version on the Commodore before exile, and tweaked it now based on the buttons on Kirk's chair. I'd set the game to randomly choose four switches to be "on," and the order in which they had to be flipped to win.

"Here," I said, "Watch me play."

I played a round. It took me eighteen tries to get it right.

"It's like Mastermind," Pete said.

"It's important you practice this, Petey. If something goes wrong, we'll need you to figure out this code—super fast."

I plopped back down in the chair as Pete said, "Okay. Try one, two, three, four."

As I reset the switches and began flipping one through four, Mort turned his ring around and pressed it against the outside of the Plexiglas, and said what I assume was the password, though the chamber cut off outside noise. The arch didn't appear for him, and the gas continued to pour out. It reached my waist now, and the skin of my legs began to tingle.

I hit the white button.

"Pete? Two lights flickered."

"Okay. Try five, six, seven, and eight."

Zeke's baton extended in his hand and burst into blue-white fire. He said something to Mort, who moved back, then Zeke struck at the Plexiglas. There was a bright yellow flash, and he was thrown back several feet to hit a wall—just as a flash of lightning speared through the spot where he'd been standing. I followed the path of the lightning to its source.

A dalek advanced on Zeke.

The robot from Doctor Who looked like a man-size salt shaker with gold bumps all over it and a single protruding appendage. This wasn't a real dalek, of course, at least not in the sense of being an actual robot tank with a genocidal alien slug inside. It was a prop donated to the museum, and animated through thaumaturgy and possibly a bit of science. That still made it dangerous, especially since I doubted Zeke had a sonic screwdriver in his arsenal.

The dalek pointed its appendage at Zeke, and lightning began to dance along its length, building up toward another discharge.

"Crap. Oh crap. Pete, we need to hurry." I flipped the switches and hit the white button. "Two lights flickered."

"Okay. Now try three, four, five, and six."

Zeke dove and rolled across the floor toward the robot as lightning arced over him. He came up and swung at the dalek. Another bright yellow flash as when Zeke struck the Plexiglas. He flew onto his back, and the baton spun across the floor.

The potion's gas had completely surrounded me now, making it increasingly difficult to see what was happening.

The dalek's arm lowered, pointing at Zeke again, the lightning building. I flipped switches as Zeke brought his knees up to his chest, then kicked out and up at the dalek.

The dalek teetered backward. The lightning swept in an arc up and across the ceiling as the robot tumbled over onto its back, revealing thaumaturgic symbols engraved all around its underside. It began rolling back and forth, trying to right itself using its appendage. Then the gas became too thick to see more.

I hit the white button.

The high-pitched wooshing sound of a vacuum filled the chamber, and the gas rapidly dissipated. The exit did not reappear, however, so I doubted the vacuum was because of anything I'd done. More likely, it was clearing the gas to allow wardens access to my dead body. Or to make way for something worse.

"Pete, two lights flickered and one lit up brightly this time."

Zeke stood over his bag holding a bottle, and he threw it at the dalek's base. Glass shattered and liquid splashed over the thaumaturgic symbols, melting them away. The dalek's thrashing slowed to a stop.

Something tickled my ankle. I looked down.

Tribbles surrounded me. Not just the few that had been on the floor to start. They had duplicated, multiplied, until now they were several layers thick and cresting the pedestal to cover my feet.

"Bat's breath!" What killed tribbles in the series? Bright light? Radiation?

Poisoned grain.

Great. And me without a shipment of poisoned quadrotriticale in my satchel. Thankfully, the fur balls didn't seem interested in devouring me. So that was good. As was the fact that it wouldn't hurt the least bit when they crushed me, since I'd already be smothered to death by that point.

I continued running through combinations with Pete as rapidly as I could flip switches and call out how many lights flickered or glowed. Four more tries, and the tribbles were up to my chest. I had to flip the switches by feel, and dig down to the lights to see the result when I pressed the button.

"Pete, I think we're close. Two glowing, two flickering."

A silver and crystal star floated into view outside my chamber, a softball-size core of fine crystal spikes with a dozen larger silver spikes jutting out in all directions. It took me a second to recognize it as a model of the spaceship that baby Superman rode to Earth.

There was a flash at its heart, and the lights in the room flickered. The Bluebeard thingy squealed in my ear.

Zeke jumped in front of Mort, holding his jacket open wide to provide as much protection as possible. The crystal spaceship exploded and spikes flew in all directions. I was temporarily blinded by golden flashes as several spikes struck the Plexiglas barrier. When I could see again, Zeke was down on one knee, clutching his right hand, which had a spike impaled through its center.

"Petey, what next?"

No response.

"Pete? Sammy?"

I pulled the mobile telephone out of my pocket and held it above the pile of tribbles, but the screen remained black no matter what button I pushed.

"Awesome." I reset the switches on the chair by feel. I could do this. Pete had gotten me most of the way there.

A small pile of tribbles tumbled down from behind, spilling over my arms. I flipped the switches again, changing the order from memory, then swept tribbles clear of the arm long enough to see the result.

Again, two solids, two flickers. Damn it!

I spotted movement. Something scrambled in the shadows low to the ground. Neither Zeke nor Mort appeared to notice.

"Zeke! Mort! Look out!" I shouted.

Another flicker of movement, leaving me with the impression of a fast-moving fleshy spider.

"Zeke!" I shouted so loud it felt like I'd torn my throat. He glanced up at me, frowning. I pointed behind him, sending tribbles flying with the motion.

Zeke glanced behind him.

The spidery creature leapt out of the darkness onto Zeke's face, a snakelike tail whipping around his neck. It was a freaking face hugger from *Alien*.

"You've got to be kidding me."

Another avalanche of tribbles settled over me, burying me up to my shoulders now. I had to tunnel my hand back down to the chair's console, wriggle and push with all my strength just to reach it through the tightly compacted fur balls. There was no way to see the lights now, but I knew which switches to flip. I just needed the right order.

And I needed it soon. Zeke stabbed at the face hugger using the spike embedded in his hand, but it had little effect. The creature wasn't made of real flesh and vital organs—thank the gods, since the last thing we needed was for Zeke to be splattered in acid blood. The thaumaturgic symbols were likely on the creature's belly, pressed tight to Zeke's face. To get it off his face, he would need to destroy the symbols. But to destroy the symbols, he needed to get it off his face.

The tribbles reached my chin now. I tilted my head back to give myself as much breathing time as possible. I reset the switches, and then flipped them in a new order, counting out their positions by feel, one by one.

Mort leaped forward and grabbed the face hugger, but he didn't appear to be pulling on it, just touching it.

The tribbles covered my mouth, filled my nostrils with the smell of dusty fake fur and tangy magic, making breathing difficult. I coughed, and on the inhale started to choke.

I hit the white button. A loud beeping sounded.

Panic scrabbled at the edges of my mind like the scratching and gnawing of a thousand tiny rats as the pressure built around my chest and head, and my lungs ached for air.

I thought of Dawn then. Dawn had the soul of a nomad artist, a bard. I could have just run away from all of this and taken her with me, gone far away and lived a life free—

Tribbles tumbled away from my face, and I sucked in a huge breath of air. The archway in the Plexiglas stood open and the tribbles spilled out, freeing my chest, my arms. The last button combination must have worked! I jumped up and half-stumbled half-waded out, pushing a small avalanche of fur before me as a blue steel door appeared in the concrete wall to the right.

Zeke and Mort stood over the face hugger, which lay unmoving on the floor. Zeke kicked it across the room.

"What happened to it?" I asked and spat out a remaining bit of fur.

"I dispelled the spirit animating it," Mort said.

"Dude," I said, surprised. "Good thinking. Really."

"Yeah. You did good, Gramaraye," Zeke said.

I swear, Mort actually blushed.

Zeke yanked the spike out of his hand, and sucked in a sharp breath. "You'd better get moving. I'll keep them fool wardens off your back long as I can."

I shook my head. "You'll be caught. Or worse."

"I'll be fine. But it's best if I don't have to worry about who's friend and who's foe. Make sure to close the door behind ya."

A screeching sound like a cat being given a bath in dog drool pierced the chamber, and a demon creature jumped out of the darkness onto Zeke's back. The thing looked like a naked Crypt Keeper whose head had been sliced off from the nose up.

Zeke grabbed at the creature, but it scrambled around on his back, swiping at his hand and clawing at his cheeks and neck.

An alien, the shiny black creepy-as-crap alien from the movie *Alien,* charged out of the darkness, hissing through its protruding silver teeth.

"Go!" Zeke shouted. His face flushed red, and veins stood out in his neck and forehead. He found the demon creature's bisected head by feel, dug his fingers into the creature's exposed rubber brains, and yanked the thing from his back. With a wild man's scream he swung it like a floppy club at the alien's head.

A clank sounded to our left as a cylon robot rounded the corner and raised a blaster rifle.

"Come on," I said, grabbing Mort and shoving him toward the door as Zeke's berzerker shout rang off the walls. "Go!"

Once we were on the other side of the door, I glanced back. Three wardens were closing in on Zeke, each holding glowing batons.

Zeke flung the torn-off head of the cylon at the nearest warden.

His gaze shot in my direction, but his eyes were wide, wild, and without recognition.

Mort grabbed my arm. "He said to close the door!"

"I know," I said. But that didn't make me feel any better as I pressed the warden's ring to the square silver plate beside the doorway, and the metal slab of the door slid closed between us and Zeke.

Two Tribes

I turned from the door and the muffled sounds of fighting in the science fiction museum, and led Mort down what felt like several floors of stairs to the Inner Sanctum.

The Inner Sanctum below the EMP looked like a Catholic cathedral turned into an attraction at Disneyland. Pillars and arches, frescoes and candelabra gave it a sense of ornate class and great age, though I suspected they were no more than fifty years old at most.

Between these touches of fanciness stood displays of the dead. Not simple sepulchral niches, but the kind of elaborate altar displays one might expect a rabid stalker to create in their basement out of loving devotion, worship, and the hope to one day bear the child (or possibly skin suit) of their object of obsession.

"Come on, we need to find Verona," I said.

We found Katherine Verona in between Ana Mendieta and Scatman Crothers and other arcana who had died in the eighties, wearing a wizard magus's formal red robes, her silver hair held up in a bun by two crossed wands. There were no war-related artifacts as I'd expected—no medals, war-era wands, silver-coated swords and bayonets, mana ration cards, or other items typically found surrounding a war hero. Instead, she sat in a comfortable and worn-looking armchair, surrounded by stacks of books on philosophy, ethics, history, and politics, as well as a collection of colorful knitted hats, slippers, gloves, and wine cozies in the shapes of Fey and feyblood creatures, including a Cthulhu-looking creature I suspected was a toilet roll cover.

I climbed the stairs onto the small stage to join her and pulled a crystal ball from my satchel, a grapefruit-size sphere that weighed twice what it should. I moved a stack of books, lay down at Verona's feet, and placed the crystal ball onto my stomach with my hands folded over it. The weight of the ball might help to anchor me to this world. And it would serve one other purpose.

I looked at Mort. "Remember. As soon as I stop breathing, you need to feed my body life energy, keep my brain from dying. And if you see any flickering in the crystal, you need to jolt me with as much life energy as you can. I'm, like, literally trusting you with my life here, brother."

This was the part of our plan that had me most worried. All Mort had to do was nothing, and I'd die. And Mort had always been really good at doing nothing.

"Hey, don't worry, man," Mort said. "I got your back."

I tried to read any deception in his tone or manner, but couldn't. And I didn't have much choice now, except to move forward or abandon the whole plan. I lay my head back and closed my eyes. After a brief meditation, I summoned myself.

Now, there is a very good reason young necromancers are told to never try to summon themselves, and it has nothing to do with growing hair on their palms. Rather, it pretty well rips your spirit from your body. It is a bit like running over your own head with a lawnmower: extremely difficult and rather unpleasant.

Everything went white, and I felt my spirit dissipating, my energy bleeding off.

My years being disembodied in the Other Realm proved extremely helpful now. It felt natural to control my spirit by will alone, to coalesce it into human shape and regain a sense of the world around me.

I floated above my own body. Mort leaned over me, one hand on my forehead, the other on my stomach just below the crystal ball. The ball rose and fell gently as my body continued to breathe.

Well, it looked like I wouldn't have to haunt Mort for the rest of his life, at least.

I willed myself over to Verona's body, and placed my hand inside her chest over her heart. Or at least I tried. I met resistance, like trying to push two powerful opposing magnets together. "Come out come out, wherever you are," I called. I spoke without a real mouth or lungs, so my voice was the vibration of the spirit energies in the room, my breath made of my will. Mort couldn't hear me. But I knew someone, or rather something, could. "I feel your presence, Anubis. By the bond of Gramaraye blood that bound you to this body, I call you forth. Reveal yourself."

The air by Verona's right side wavered, the shadows coalesced like black smoke hardening into Jell-O, until a semitransparent ebon figure stood beside Verona. It had the body of a male wrestler and the head of a dog with sharp ears. Its hand gripped my spiritual wrist firmly, preventing me from reaching into Verona's chest.

"You summon me, necromancer?"

"I wish your help to travel over and speak to this one whom you protect," I said with as much confidence and formality as I could.

Anubis looked down at my body. "Have that other necromancer allow you to die, and you may pass beyond the veil and speak to whomever you wish, without my aid."

"I wish you to guide me to this woman's spirit beyond, and then to return to my body and the world of the living," I clarified.

"Ah. That is another matter altogether, isn't it?" Anubis grinned a jackal's grin. "What you ask requires a bargain, a balancing. To bring back knowledge from the beyond to your world, you must give up something."

"I am prepared to offer you fifty Toths of magic," I said. "I have it there, in my satchel."

"Fah. I receive such nourishment with every binding. But few seek to travel beyond the veil with my aid. This is a rare opportunity for me to ask something greater than mana."

Why did that not fill me with awesome feelings?

"What's your price, then?"

"That gift which is most powerful in you, that has shaped who you are. Will you give this up to earn the answers you seek?"

My Talking gift. This creature wished to strip me of my ability.

And I could understand why. The Anubis had been at the beck and call of necromancers its entire life, and here was a chance to strip one of his most valued power.

"Do you swear that I shall be unharmed and unchanged in any other way?"

"What is harm?" said Anubis. "Is loss not harm of a kind? But I promise I shall take nothing from you except what is agreed, not life nor health nor any other part of you."

I knew the correct answer then, but I found myself pulled back and forth.

Being a Talker had only brought me the unwanted work of my grandfather's tutoring, the envy of Mort, the expectations of the family business, the promised future of trading my life to Talk to the dead. Talking had killed my mother, and as I'd learned these past days it was the reason that I'd been framed and exiled.

I should be happy to give it up.

But it had also shaped me, defined my life as Anubis said. The world wasn't as I'd left it. I no longer knew my place in it. I doubted that I could make games as I'd dreamed, Father had been driven mad and Mort barely kept the family business from going under. Without a Talker in the family, how long before the family home was taken over by more powerful necromancers, my family scattered to the winds?

My Talker gift might be the one thing to save my future, and the future of my family.

Yet, what future did I have unless I figured out the Legion's plans for me, and stopped them? And to do that, I needed to Talk to Verona.

"Wait, if I give you my Talking skill, how will I be able to Talk to Verona?"

Anubis laughed, a mirthless barking sound. "That is not a concern. And I shall not take my price until you have brought back answers from the spirit you seek. Agreed?"

I hesitated, then said, "Agreed."

"Then let us travel, necromancer."

Anubis held out his hand, and I took it. The Inner Sanctum blurred and disappeared.

A wooded coastline appeared far beneath my feet, the nighttime landscape lit by a full moon and the occasional flash of lightning or fire on the ground. The scene rushed up at me as though I were skydiving without a parachute. I could make out buildings now, houses and concrete bunkers squatting in the terracelike fields cut into the forested hillside, and more lining the coastline. Fort Worden, I realized, though not quite as I knew it. The Marine Science Center did not jut out into the water, the state park campgrounds and parking lots were absent. The concrete bunkers still held their car-size cannons.

And there floated a giant, rippling line of violet light just above the tide line—a breach between our world and the Other Realm invisible to mundane sight but blinding and hypnotically beautiful to the magically gifted. This must be the last Fey-Arcana War, the final battle when the Fey broke through here and along several other coastlines around the world—the last, desperate fight to keep them from turning us all into feybloods or changelings.

I landed in a stone circle high up on the hillside, the clearing around it enclosed by the forest on three sides, and a steep drop off on the fourth looking down the wooded slope to the beach far below. The stone circle was three times the size of the one where Mort had traded with the gnomes, and hummed now with power as a dozen thaumaturges and wizards worked together to charge the runes that covered every inch of blue stone.

Bright light flashed along the tree line, and a mixed group of arcana and allied feybloods fell back into the clearing as enemy feyblood advanced, bolstered in strength and ability by possessing Fey. The allied feyblood—dryads, satyrs, sasquatches, gryphons, leprechauns, and others who had long established a working relationship with humanity and connection with our world—fought against waer creatures, ghouls, trolls, lindworms, wendigos, unicorns, and other dark feyblood eager for the power and freedoms the Fey promised them.

Wizards wielded wands and rings, or fought with tattoos and swords. Alchemists lobbed gas grenades, or splashed healing potions on the wounded. Sorcerers cast illusions to frighten and confuse, or controlled the minds of the less intelligent enemy feyblood and turned them against their own. Thaumaturges crushed and broke the enemy lines with prepared boulders or tree trunks by moving a resonant pebble or branch across their palm. And necromancers darted forth to rip the spirit from enemy creatures, or snag the magic from both ally and enemy fallen in order to fuel the arcanas' spells and weapons.

The chill evening air reeked like spoiled steaks being burned over a dung fire as bodies were shredded, chopped, burned, boiled, petrified, and disintegrated. The only sounds louder than the explosions were the screams.

A call like Godzilla roaring into a jet engine rolled across the sky, and an emerald dragon the size of a big rig truck burst up over the tree line and swooped down to land in the clearing. A woman rode near its head, her wavy black hair dancing wildly around her face.

The dragon's claws dug furrows into the earth as it skidded to a stop a dozen feet away. I could feel the heat of the creature's internal fire as it hissed out a long breath that smelled of burnt cinnamon and, oddly enough, tacos.

The woman leaped off the beast's head. It was a jump that should have broken her legs and probably killed her, but the woman landed as though merely jumping off a chair, and crossed the distance to the stone circle where the Anubis and I waited. She wore what looked like gray coveralls with flared legs that ended at her shins, and she had the red sash of an Archwizard tied around her waist, flapping now in the sharp wind blowing up from the inlet.

She looked younger than when I knew her, her face lacking the lines of sorrow and pain I remembered, but still I recognized her. Katherine Verona.

"Interesting," she said, looking from me to the battle raging beyond the dragon. "Is this setting your doing or mine?"

"I don't know," I said. "I summoned you here—or rather, I sought you out—but I've never done this before. So, I guess it wasn't like this before I arrived?"

Verona raised her eyebrows. "You know what? I don't remember, actually."

I looked at Anubis.

"It is not part of our bargain that I explain the mysteries beyond the veil," he said.

I sighed and turned back to Verona. "I need to ask you some questions. My life and the lives of my family are in danger, and I need to understand why."

Verona's eyes narrowed. "You're Gavriel's grandson, the Talker."

"Yes."

"Then there is likely more at stake than your life, young man. Tell me, what has happened?"

I gave Verona my story, of Felicity's attack, my exile, and the attacks since I'd returned.

"Interesting," Verona said. "I always feared he would take it too far."

"What do you mean? Who took what too far?"

"Your grandfather, and the Arcanites who supported him. He was obsessed with finding a way to ensure a swift and total victory over the Fey, the feybloods, even the mundies in the next war, a way where we could dominate them all."

"Grandfather? But he died before any of this started." And he certainly wouldn't do anything to harm me, not knowingly.

Verona looked at the stone circle, then beyond, to the breach between worlds far below. "Our children pay the price of our sins and our follies," she said barely above a whisper. Then she shuddered, and seemed to realize anew where she was. She waved at the battle behind her. "Another war is inevitable, and the plots that men like your grandfather set in motion will continue to affect the course of history for generations to come."

"Everyone keeps talking about a war like it's inevitable. These Arcanites you mentioned, are they going to *start* the war?"

Verona shook her head. "That's the problem with youth today; you don't study our history enough. The Pax Arcana has brought peace, and given us rules for trade and more. But it did not change hearts, didn't eliminate all fear or greed, or any of the other things that lead to war. And most especially, it didn't eliminate the need or desire for the precious resource of magic."

"So . . . are these arcana groups preparing to fight the Fey to gain more magical energy? Or because the Fey are plotting to attack us?"

"Both, and neither. There are those on both sides who continue to desire peace. And there are those on both sides, individuals and groups, who believe that their own side could and should dominate the other. And there are many factions and plans and plots meant to achieve these goals, each believing their way is the one true path. Your grandfather was part of such a group who believed they had the best plan for victory. And you, I'm afraid, have become a victim of their plan."

"All right. So this group, these Arcanites, they had me exiled for fear that Grandfather told me something, or that I might know or learn something about their plan and expose them. I already guessed something like that. What I need to know is, who else is in this group; who's still determined to exile me? And what is it they're so afraid I might learn from you, that I might reveal?"

"All I can tell you with certainty is that your grandfather came to me seeking my support. He said he was close to perfecting some new power that would shift the balance of the entire war to come. And he said young men like you and James Grayson were the key to it all."

"Me? What new power?"

"I don't know. I chose not to join his little faction or share my knowledge, and he chose not to trust me with any details."

"But if you wanted to stop the war, maybe you should have joined him, at least long enough to discover his plans," I said.

Verona shook her head. "War is inevitable, but I don't feel I have the right to say whether it is good or bad, or to shape its outcome in any way."

"I don't mean any disrespect, Magus, but are you kidding? Look at this? How could this be good?"

I pointed at the battle still raging along the tree line, and Verona followed my gaze. A goblin leaped upon a necromancer who'd knelt to drain the magic from a gutted corpse. The glowing, ghostly form of a Fey spirit detached from the goblin and poured into the necromancer, who convulsed for a second, then rose haltingly to his feet, and turned to attack a woman next to him. She fell back, startled—and decapitated him with a silver sword. As his body and head fell to the ground bleeding out the dying Fey spirit, the woman stared at the place where he'd stood, a horrified look on her face. I wondered if he had been her brother, or husband, or just a friend.

"I know it's hard for you to understand," Verona said, watching the carnage. "Of course it seems like preventing war is the right thing. But when does the cost of stopping the Fey make us unworthy to survive the Fey?"

"What? You're right," I said. "I don't understand."

Verona sighed. "You know I helped build the foundations of the modern ARC system, yes? Well, it was supposed to represent law and order, and promote the good for all magicals. But they became like any government, where ritual replaces reason, where complacency and arrogance abound. The different factions have become so trapped in the goal of holding onto power that they've forgotten what that power was meant to be used for. They've become a kind of aristocracy serving their own interests. You see, good intentions often have unexpected and even terrible consequences, my boy, and I for one do not wish to see any more harm done from my choices. I was granted a strong wizardry gift, but that did not make me all knowing. It didn't give me the right to end thousands of lives, or the surety that the sacrifice was worth—" Her words choked to a halt, and a tear ran down her cheek as she turned away from me.

One of the thaumaturges energizing the stone circle around us stood, rubbing at his lower back, and stepped close to Verona. "The circle is ready, Magus," he whispered. "Did your daughter make it through the breach?"

"Your daughter?" I said, glancing down at the breach. "Your daughter Traveled into the Other Realm during the fighting?"

Without looking at me, Verona said, "Beatrice sent her spirit into the breach, into the body of a Fey who also wanted peace. The bond between our spirits allowed me to tap into the raw magical energy of the Other Realm through her, to draw enough energy to seal this breach. But the act . . . my spell caused Bea to overload with magic. Her Fey body—the energy—her death wiped out an entire Demesne. Thousands of Fey, and my daughter, died in an instant. And . . . I knew it would happen."

That was the secret weapon everyone had tried to get from Verona. But the weapon hadn't been a weapon at all. It had been her daughter.

"Oh, man. I . . . I'm sorry."

"So am I," she said softly.

Was this why the Legion—or Arcanites—really wanted me back in the Other Realm? To use me as a bomb? No, that didn't feel right. For one, why then hadn't they blown me up the first time I was there? For another, there was nobody living who had the kind of connection to me that Verona and her daughter had shared.

"Why tell me your secrets now?" I asked. "Aren't you worried I will tell someone else?"

Verona took a deep breath and exhaled sharply, her gaze sharpening again as she peered at me. "No. Even if you did, I suspect my secret is no longer secret anyway. And the Fey have certainly devised protections against such an . . . attack again. But more importantly, I think the world needs young men like you fighting to keep it sane, if not entirely safe."

"I thought you didn't want to get involved?"

"I don't. I'm not. Your grandfather, he thought he'd discovered the key to absolute victory, absolute power. Perhaps total arcana dominance would be worse for everyone in the long run than conflict and a new truce, a new balance. Perhaps not. Either way, I have not alone given you the means to destroy worlds, my boy, or even the sole means to see your grandfather's plans succeed or fail. I have only given you a piece of knowledge. What you do with it is up to you."

"It is time to go," Anubis said.

"Wait!" I said to him. "I still don't have the answers I need." I turned to Verona. "Please, there's got to be something more you can tell me, something you know? Felicity, our au pair. Was she part of this group, this plot? Is that why she testified against me? Is that why she was killed?"

"It's possible, but I don't know for certain. I'm sorry. I met her only the one time, a sweet girl."

Anubis grabbed my wrist. "It is clear she does not have any further answers for you. The time has come to leave."

"No!" I pulled against the Anubis' grip, but couldn't break free. "Please—Magus Verona, Felicity's clan said she had a lover. Do you know who that was?"

Verona cleared her throat. "That is a delicate matter."

"She's dead," I said. "And the answer could prevent more deaths."

"We are going," Anubis said. We lifted from the ground, and the moonlit battlefield began to fly away from us.

"Your grandfather was her lover," Verona shouted, her voice growing faint. "But after his death, I heard rumors of anoth—"

Darkness. Silence.

And then the blackness lifted as though someone slowly turned up the lights in a dark room. We were back in the Inner Sanctum, floating above my body at the feet of Verona's preserved body. The crystal ball rose and fell gently on my stomach, and Mort still held his hands on my forehead and sternum.

"And now," Anubis said. "Your payment."

"Wait," I said. "I didn't get the information I needed. I may still need to Talk to other spirits."

"You brought back knowledge from the other side, and the balance must be maintained. It is not part of our bargain that I wait for you to understand the knowledge you have received. And I never said I would take your Talker skill. You have a gift far greater than that."

I didn't like his wicked grin, or the gloating tone of his voice. "What gift?"

A memory rose up, enveloped me: my kiss with Dawn on the ferry.

"Love," Anubis said.

I could see the memory drifting away from me, drawn into the Anubis as a stream of multicolored smoke, and it melted from my mind like cotton candy in the mouth. Another memory rose, of Dawn and me picking strawberries together, and then that too was gone. The memories started to appear and be drawn away in an ever-quickening stream. I tried to grasp them, to hold on to them, even as I forgot what I tried to hold on to. Soon I struggled against the loss purely out of instinct. But it was like trying to hold on to water.

"Stop!" I shouted, but the Anubis ignored me. "Stop! Please!"

I tried to return to my body, like I had when escaping from the Other Realm, but the Anubis held on to me. This was my worst nightmare, to have my memories not just pawed through by the Fey, but actually taken, consumed, lost, along with the person they made of me.

In desperation, I sought out the crystal on my stomach, and turned my focus to it.

Come on. Flicker, damn it!

There. A flickering.

Mort gave a startled glance around the room, then took a deep breath, and closed his eyes.

In much the same way that summoning my own spirit had torn it free of my body, the surge of energy from Mort jammed my spirit and body back together with all the gentleness of a Terminator crushing a human skull.

I sucked in breath and shouted, "Stop!"

I sat up sharply, which had the unfortunate result of dropping the crystal ball onto my crotch. My shout turned into a groan of pain.

"Nice one," Mort said.

"Shut it, Mort." I eased the crystal ball away from the epicenter of the nauseating crotch quake.

"Why'd you shout 'stop'?" Mort asked.

I frowned. "I—I don't remember."

"Well, maybe you got a concussion there, dick for brains," Mort said.

"Hilarious. You're a regular Andrew Dice Clay," I said.

Mort helped me off the desk. "I sure hope you got the answers you wanted after all this," he said.

"Not exactly." I looked back at Verona sitting there, her face frozen in a sad and distant gaze. "She did tell me some important things, but I need to figure out what they mean." I slapped Mort's back. "By the way, thanks for keeping me alive, bro."

He shrugged. "Mattie would've been upset if you died."

"Uh-huh. Well, thanks anyway." Hopefully, this would be the start of rebuilding our friendship, and not just one more thing Mort held over me. Especially since I was about to repay his help. "We have one last bit of business."

I pulled a small gnome statue out of my satchel and placed it on the floor. A few seconds later, it tipped over to reveal a hole beneath it, and Priapus climbed out. He adjusted his blue hat as he looked around the room and grinned.

"As agreed," I said. "Passage past all the security."

"Pleasure doing business," Priapus said and whistled down into the hole. "Shop's open, boys!"

"Come on," I said to Mort. "Let's help Zeke and get the heck out of here, if we can."

We rushed back out the way we came, past the other bodies

and up the stairs to the science fiction museum. I glanced behind me as we sprinted up the stairs, unable to shake the feeling that I had forgotten something—like I'd left something important behind.

26

Don't You Forget About Me

Zeke sat in the center of the space before the captain's chair, a befuddled look on his face as if he'd fallen on his butt and didn't know what this gravity thing was all about. A circle of bodies—creatures from a dozen movies, and an equal number of men in security uniforms—surrounded him. A couple of the wardens moaned but didn't move.

"Give me a hand," I said to Mort as I hooked my arm under Zeke's armpit and lifted. Mort grabbed the other arm, and we hefted Zeke to his feet.

Zeke's head swiveled toward me, his eyes glazed. He opened his mouth as if to say something and drooled on his shoulder.

"Yeah, good to see you too." I leaned him against Mort for a second and grabbed up his bag, almost falling over at the unexpected weight of it.

"Let's get out of here before enforcers show up," I said, slinging Zeke's bag on one shoulder, and Zeke's arm across the other.

We made it out the side door and to our car without incident and caught the 10:50 P.M. ferry from Seattle to Bainbridge Island. Mort and I both tried calling Sammy, but our phones were still dead. Mort tried charging his with a cord from the car lighter, but it had no effect. Hopefully Sammy and Vee were home safe and all was well.

I left Zeke and Mort in the car and walked up to the top deck of the ferry alone, drawn by some desire. I watched Seattle receding from us as misty sea wind and the smell of the ferry's exhaust washed over me. The skyscrapers and Space Needle shone like Christmas against the night sky, their light reflected in the water along with the silver glimmer of the moon, and the neon colored streaks from the signs for Ivar's and Red Robin and the other water-front restaurants. The wind made me shiver but also made me feel very awake, my mind sharp.

A young man and woman sat out of the wind in the nearby covered area, cuddling and looking up at the moon. I felt a pang of loneliness, of loss for something I'd never really had. Maybe someday that would be me. Maybe me and Heather, if I could figure out what was up with her, why she thought we couldn't see each other.

But first I needed to get myself free of the mess left by Grandfather. I turned over everything I'd learned, working the clues like a Rubik's cube, trying to find the pattern, the answer.

Grandfather had been Felicity's lover. He'd not just supported the decision to bring her over from Austria, he probably suggested it in the first place. And he must have done so for a reason other than sex, given the difficulty and expense to bring her over. Maybe he'd even become her lover just to get what he wanted from her, although I found that hard to believe—and worse to imagine.

The Króls said Felicity had special skill with plants. And she'd taken care of our garden, presumably in honor of Mother, but maybe that too was part of Grandfather's plan. Could the secret power Grandfather discovered be some kind of potion? I'd have to go through the garden with Heather and see if the plants there gave us any clues. And if Felicity was a member of this Arcanite extremist group, it would explain why she would testify against me, and why they might have killed her to keep their secrets.

But that still left me with the question of why they were so determined to frame me at all.

I'd thought it was to keep me from Talking to Verona, but nothing she'd said seemed so devastating a secret it was worth all the effort and cost that the Legion—the Arcanites—had spent on me. Even if their plan was to send spirits into the Other Realm to nuke the Fey as Verona had done, surely the Fey were prepared to stop such an act now. And Verona seemed to imply the Arcanites had some other plan already in place with or without her secret weapon.

Gods, I wished I could just Talk to Grandfather. But even if I really had felt his spirit watching over me in the Other Realm and not just imagined it, he'd been warded by someone outside our family and was beyond my ability to Talk to at will.

Okay. Enough thinking on what I couldn't do.

Verona said that Grayson and I were key somehow to the new power Grandfather sought. Could that be it? It still made sense that this was all about my Talker gift somehow, since I couldn't think of anything else particularly special about me. Well, I could get all the way through Dragon's Lair on a single quarter, and I could rock the Star Blazers theme song on the recorder, but somehow I didn't think those were the types of gifts that a group bent on world domination would prize. And Grayson was a Talker as well. But I couldn't see how having me exiled helped them if they needed my gift somehow. And I couldn't see how my Talker gift tied in with plants or alchemy as any kind of ultimate weapon.

And . . . if Grayson was fine and active in the world, that either meant they didn't need him exiled like me—or that he was part of the Legion of Arcanites. Everything began to make sense. Grayson was Grandfather's student. And Verona started to say something about Felicity, maybe that she'd taken another lover? Grayson was a definite possibility. I could see how the Króls might consider him part of my family, or at least our household.

Well, I now had a better idea of why I was framed, and who likely did it, though I still didn't understand what exactly they needed me in exile for, or exactly how Grayson got past the house wards to possess Father, assuming Grayson was the culprit. He certainly wasn't in the house that night.

I'd talk it all through with everyone back at the house. Maybe they'd see something I missed. But either way, I'd contact Grayson and set up a meeting somewhere safe. If he wasn't part of the

Legion, maybe he could help us find out who was, especially now that I had a better idea of what to look for. And if he was part of the Legion, well, Zeke could help me set a trap.

The deck rumbled beneath my feet as the ferry slowed, signaling its approach to the Bainbridge ferry dock.

Mort parked in the lot of the hardware store and we took the back way to the house just in case anyone waited for us. Zeke was still pretty out of it, but at least he was able to walk after his two-hour nap so that Mort and I didn't have to carry him. I told him everything I'd learned from Katherine Verona, and my own theories. He grunted occasionally but didn't offer any additional thoughts or theories. I hoped he'd have more to offer when he recovered.

I sent Mort ahead to check the house for enforcers. My watch said it was a quarter after midnight. Technically, my three days were up. Would the enforcers wait until morning to grab me, give me one final night? I wasn't sure what eight hours might win me that three days had not, but there had to be something I could do, something I could use from all I'd learned to help prove my innocence, or gain more time from the ARC.

Actually, once they figured out who broke into the EMP, they would be hunting us in earnest, regardless of the three-day deadline. So either way, Zeke and I needed to find someplace new to hide awhile until we cleared our names.

I had an idea about that.

Mort came running back. "Finn, something's wrong! And I don't think it's enforcers."

"Help Zeke!" I burst into an all-out run, leaving Zeke to follow in a zombielike lurch with Mort's help. I skirted past the tangled garden, which seemed to writhe in the moonlight, and through the open back door. I noticed that the frame was splintered. But the buzz of the wards still washed over me as I crossed the threshold. How was that possible, unless someone let the enemy through the wards?

"Hello?" I shouted, checking each of the rooms as I passed. I reached the entry hall. Father sat on the stairs, his head in his hands, shaking back and forth.

"Father? What's wrong?"

Father looked up at me, but his eyes seemed fixed on some distant point behind me. "Interesting fact," he said, and then his mouth snapped shut as if trying to bite a fly as it buzzed past his teeth.

Goose bumps sprang up along my arms as pieces started falling into place.

"Finn!" a woman's voice called from above. "Upstairs!"

I hesitated, looking from Father to the top of the stairs. Mort and Zeke limped up the hall, panting.

"Finn?" the woman called again. "Hurry."

Crap. "Mort, keep an eye on Father." I ran up the stairs.

Pete lay on the floor. He looked as though he'd gotten into a fight with Freddy Kruger and an angry bear. His body was covered in groups of ragged slashes and bite marks, some small, some large. His pajamas and bandages were little more than shredded scraps pasted to him with blood. The entire hallway was covered in blood, the walls dented and slashed, the pictures fallen and trampled, and chunks of brown and gray fur lay scattered about. And someone I didn't recognize, a beautiful black woman with a lavender afro, sat with Pete's head in her lap, making soothing sounds. An empty potion bottle lay on the floor beside her. A healer?

"Is he—" The words choked in my throat. Pressure built in my chest and behind my eyes, demanding release. I made my way past the blood and broken glass to stand next to Pete, beside the healer. Would she call in the enforcers?

"He's going to live, I think," she said. "They didn't cover this in First Aid training. I don't really understand what happened."

Breath burst out of me in a mixed sob and sigh.

"Thank you. You're not a healer, then? How did you know my name?"

"What?" the woman said. "What the hell do you mean, how did I know your name?"

"I'm sorry," I said, raising my hands. "I didn't mean to offend you. I've been away for a while, so if you're a friend of the family's or something—"

"Friend of the family's?" the woman said, and her eyes brimmed with tears. "Oh man. I don't know what the hell is going on here, Finn, but you'd better get your shit together and fast or you're going to wish you could forget me."

Pete coughed. "Dawn, it's okay," he said, his eyes still closed. "Finn got hit with a forgetting spell or something. He'll get better. Right, Finn?"

I frowned. "Next door Dawn." That seemed familiar. Something I'd said to Joey once?

The woman, Dawn, closed her eyes and shook her head. "No. No, you don't have time to be worrying about me. Finn, you need to help Sammy and Mattie."

"What do you mean?" I said, looking around at all the blood again. Oh, gods. No. There was too much for it to all be Pete's. "Pete? What does she mean?"

"They were taken," Dawn said. "Vee and Heather too."

Pete coughed again. "I—I tried to stop them. There were too many. And Father wouldn't give me the gun."

"Waerwolves," Dawn said. "That's what Pete said, anyway."

Waer. Chosen so Vee couldn't infect them.

Infection. "No. Oh no." I looked down at Pete. "Oh man. Petey—" He'd been bitten by waerwolves.

"Finn!" Zeke shouted from downstairs, followed closely by Mort's panicked "Father! What—?"

The sharp crack of a gunshot reverberated through the house and set my ears ringing.

Father! I ran to the stairs.

Mort lay on the floor, hand pressed to his right thigh as blood oozed out between his fingers. Zeke grasped both of Father's wrists, and the two men wrestled against each other, pushing back and forth, turning in a slow circle. Father held the family revolver, straining to turn the barrel at Zeke's head.

"Father! Stop!" I shouted. But neither my father, nor the spirit possessing him, stopped.

Zeke still suffered the aftermath of his berserker rage. And Father had the strength and immunity to pain that comes with being possessed. This would not end well.

I considered jumping on Father's back, but given his strength I might only push him and Zeke apart long enough for him to shoot Zeke and me both. And Father couldn't be knocked out, not while being possessed.

Father fired the gun again. The bullet bounced off the shoulder of Zeke's protective jacket with a sharp yellow flash, the ricochet narrowly missing Zeke's head. Zeke was jerked to the side by the impact and lost his grip on Father's wrist. Father's free hand snapped to Zeke's neck, choking, and Zeke had to strain to pull it free.

"Finn!" Zeke said and coughed. "Banish whatever damn spirit's possessing him, or I'm going to have to hurt him!" He stumbled back as Father pushed hard against his hold.

"I can't!" I said. Forcing out a possessing ghost while it's controlled by another necromancer was risky enough for the possessed. But I knew now that the spirit possessing Father was my mother's ghost.

People who spend years of intimacy together often develop "sympathetic resonance," which meant Mother's ghost would be entangled with Father's spirit and it'd be difficult to clearly identify where one ended and the other began. I had to break the other necromancer's hold somehow.

How was Mother's ghost being controlled past the house wards? The question reminded me of my conversation with Sammy when I first saw Mother's ghost:

"How can mother's ghost be here? We diffused her energy properly."

"Apparently it has something to do with the garden," Sammy said. *"She put a lot of her energy into it."*

And Father's words:

"Branches and brains, make you do funny things."

Felicity had worked on Mother's garden. Felicity, a witch involved with the Arcanites. I jumped over the railing to the hallway, landed hard, and ran for the back door.

"Finn!" Zeke shouted. "Where the hell you going?" His breath came in gasps.

"To free Father!"

Another gunshot rang out.

I burst out of the back door into the cool night air and paused. The garden rustled. Something was in it, moving the branches and vines. Controlling Mother's ghost through the garden, controlling Father through Mother.

I didn't know what kind of twisted combination of witchcraft and necromancy was involved, but I had a pretty good idea of how to stop it. I ran to the garden shed, grabbed up a machete, and waded into the garden, hacking and slashing a path to its heart.

Another gunshot, and a shout of pain from Zeke.

Damn it! Damn it!

Thorns and vines grabbed at me, whether out of some supernatural will or just the normal tenacity of plants, I didn't know and didn't care. I shrugged off the bites and scratches and continued to slash. The air filled with the green smell of plant juices, and pulp and droplets splattered across my face and hands as I sought out the source of the rustling.

I broke free of the tangle into an enclosed clearing, and at its center stood a plant that looked like several rose trees entangled. Standing by the mass, its hands plunged deep within the branches, stood a small brown man with a branch growing out of the top of its head. A homunculus—a mandrake root given life through alchemy and dark necromancy. It hissed at me as I entered the clearing.

"Screw you too," I said and chopped at its head with all my strength.

The creature's scream cut short as its head and body split in half, splattering the dirt and weeds around it with dark fluid.

The garden's motions ceased. I stood for a minute panting, the night air chilling the sheen of moisture and plant bits that clung to me.

"Finn?" someone called. I looked back and saw Dawn silhouetted against the back door, leaning slumped against the door frame. "It's done," she said. "Your father collapsed."

I dropped the machete and followed Dawn back into the house. Mother's ghost greeted me as I entered. "Hello, kiddo. How was school?"

"Not now, Mother," I said, my voice thick as I fought back tears.

Zeke and Father both sat on the floor, Zeke leaning against the stair railing, Father against the wall opposite him. Zeke held the colt in one hand, his other pressed to his left ear. Father stared down at his hands and sobbed.

"You okay?" I asked Zeke as I moved to kneel beside my father.

"Yeah," Zeke said as though drunk. "Nothing a year of sleep won't cure."

"How about you?" I asked Mort.

"Hell no," he said. "I've been shot! I need a frickin' doctor."

Dawn knelt beside Mort. "I told you, it'll be okay. Just keep pressing."

I put my hand over my father's. "Father? Can you understand me?"

Father looked up at me. "My . . . desk." His hand twitched, waving in the direction of his room, then lurched out and grabbed my shirt, pulling me closer. The whole left side of his face began to spasm. "Ring around the rosies," he whispered. "The heart always knowsies—" Then his eyes rolled up into his head and he slumped into unconsciousness.

I pulled myself free of his grasp. The rhyme I didn't understand, but the first part was clear. I hurried back to Father's room and found a note on his desk, written in misshapen letters like when I tried to write with my left hand.

Finn,
Ezekiel must die by your hand and you take the blame for it, or
the girls die. You have until sunrise.

I read the words again.

And then I heard the wail of police sirens drawing closer. Someone must have reported the gunshots.

"Bat's breath."

27

Should I Stay or Should I Go?

Dawn rushed into the room. "Police!"

"I know. I hear them."

"You and Zeke need to get out of here. And I'll drive. I don't feel like getting shot for being suspiciously black at a crime scene."

"Go," Mort said. "I'll cover."

Dawn grabbed my arm. "I'll be next door. That-a-way," she said, and pointed, then ran out the back door.

"What are you going to do?" I asked Mort as I grabbed Zeke and flung his arm over my shoulder. Zeke still gripped the pistol in his other hand.

Mort shrugged. "I'll tell them some stupid meth head broke in thinking the mortuary might have drugs, and they shot up the place."

The sirens grew louder.

"Be careful," I said. "Enforcers'll be here soon, and they can read the truth."

"I know. Just don't tell me where you're going. And Finn?"

"Yeah?"

"If I die, I'm so going to haunt you for this."

"Right. Thanks."

I guided Zeke out the back door and into the night.

The sirens stopped in front of our house. The night was lit up with the red and blue flashes of the police lights as Dawn waved at me from a break in the hedge. I jumped as someone shouted from the front of the house, "Open up. Police." But nobody called for us to stop.

Dawn led us through a yard filled with piles of junk to a garage, and I helped Zeke into the backseat of an old station wagon.

"I need to lay down," Zeke said, his words slurred, and he slumped down across the seat.

"I need the keys," Dawn said. "Be right back."

I climbed into the passenger seat and looked over my shoulder. "Zeke, you with me enough to talk?"

"Wha—? Yeah. Jus' keep it down," he muttered, his eyes closed.

"Do you know this Dawn person?"

"Dawn's a mundy who grew up with your family," Zeke replied, his words slurred with exhaustion. "And you just decided last night to tell her all about magic, and started dating her. And if I were you, I wouldn't go breaking up with her until you figure this out, fool. You break her heart, she'll break your neck."

Zeke's words made my head spin. If they were true and I didn't remember Dawn, what else didn't I remember?

I didn't have time for self-reflection though.

"Zeke, the Legion left us a note. They want me to kill you and take the blame, or else the girls die. We have until sunrise."

Zeke's eyes snapped open. "How do we know we can trust them fools? Why didn't they just kill the girls and blame that on you? Not that I'm complainin', it just don't make sense."

"I'm guessing because they've already tried killing you and stopping me, but we keep managing to escape. So they're making us do it for them."

"Still, the ARC's lookin' for us now. This fool Legion of yours coulda just sat back and waited for us to get caught and blamed for the EMP, and the Hole and all the rest."

"I don't know, Zeke, okay? Maybe there's some kind of time limit we don't know about—I think they wanted me back in exile the day I returned. Maybe they're getting desperate. I just don't know."

Zeke grunted. "That's what worries me. I'd shoot myself in the head right now if I knew for certain it'd save Vee. But I'd rather shoot the bastards who took Vee. 'Cept, we don't where this Legion is or where they got the girls. And we don't know why the Legion's doing what they're doing, which means they could do anything. So question is, you got a better offer than a bullet in my head?"

"Honestly? I don't know," I said.

Dawn returned and climbed into the car. "Where to?" she asked, and started the car.

"Kingston." As Dawn pulled out of the driveway, I said, "Zeke, I think maybe, if I turn myself in and take the blame for everything, just accept exile, that will be enough. Maybe we can even get the enforcers to fake your death, put you in witness protection or whatever the ARC has like that."

Zeke grunted, his eyes closed. Was that agreement, or was it "fool" in tired speak?

Dawn looked at me, her face lit by the flashing police lights reflecting off the car's mirrors. "Oh, no you don't! I know I said I wished you'd never come back, but that isn't true. You can't just go disappearing again."

"I think you were right, actually," I said. "Everyone I care about has been hurt one way or another since I've been back. And I don't seem to have much of a life to return to anyway. Maybe the best thing, the easiest thing, is for me to just live out my life in exile, reliving memories of when I was happy, at least."

Dawn skidded the car to a stop on the side of the road. Thankfully, the police were out of sight.

"What—?" I said.

She leaned across and kissed me. Hard. And deep.

When she pulled away, I found myself following after her, not wanting the kiss to end. She pushed me back.

"Did that wake you up, Sleeping Beauty?" she asked.

"I—it didn't bring back any memories, if that's what you mean," I said. "But it felt . . . right. I liked it."

"Oh, I know that's true. There's no way you didn't like it. But maybe now you'll stop talking about how you don't have anything to return to?"

"Uh, yes," I said and thought of Zeke's warning. "Sorry."

"Mm-hmm. You'd better be." She shifted back into her seat and resumed driving. "Besides, there's no guarantee they'll let the girls go if you do what they want, right? So I'd come up with a better plan than surrender if you can."

"Well, if you have any ideas I'm all ears," I said. "But like Zeke said, we don't know who the Legion is, or where they are."

"There's Grayson," Zeke mumbled, eyes still closed. "You seemed to think that fool's one of them."

"Maybe." I turned the idea over for a minute. "No. That doesn't help us. If he's Legion, he'll just want you dead and me exiled, and if he knows we suspect him he might do something to the girls. If he's not Legion, I doubt he could help us in time, and he'd probably have us arrested while he figures it all out, which means the girls would die. Lose lose."

"Lose lose, my ass," Dawn said. "There's got to be something you can do, someone who can help. Don't tell me you've come this far just to give up?"

"You think I want to give up?" I said. "I'd love to fight. But in case you didn't notice, we've about run out of family and friends to help us. Zeke, you're one punch away from comatose, Petey's seriously injured, Mort's shot, and Sammy, Vee, Mattie, and Heather are all being held hostage. That leaves just me and you in fighting shape to mount a rescue, and we're not exactly fighters, or I'm not, anyway. And that's assuming we even knew where the girls were, which we don't."

"Can't we use that Kin Finder contraption to find them?" Zeke asked. "You could use my hair or whatever to find Vee."

"You'd have to be dead," I said. "Otherwise, if I tried to find the closest living body that your spirit energy resonates with, it would point right back to you."

"Fool machine. Well, what about that note they left you? Maybe there's some clue there you missed."

"It's not like the thing was a riddle. But you're welcome to check it out if you want." I dug in my pocket for the note, and felt the ring my father made for me still in the coin pocket.

Ring around the rosies. The heart always knowsies—

Why would Father say that? I'd thought his words gibberish before, but what he'd said about his plant, about branches and brains, had made a kind of sense once I understood it. It couldn't be a coincidence that he'd given me this ring, and then the rhyme.

I pulled out the ring, and held it up, examining it in the light of passing cars and streetlamps. It looked familiar, but I couldn't place it.

"What's that?" Zeke asked.

"Hang on."

What was it Father said when he gave it to me?

Not for the blood, but for the heart . . . Scribble scroble, nib to noble.

Blood. Scribble. Nib.

The Kin Finder 2000!

I felt like an idiot for not seeing it sooner. But what would this ring do differently?

Not for the blood, but for the heart . . . Scribble scroble, nib to noble.

"Dawn! Do you have a mobile phone with you?"

"Yeah, why?"

"I need to call Mort. I think we might be able to find the girls."

Zeke pushed himself up on his elbows. "If you find them, we should call in the enforcers."

"Some of them might be in the Legion."

"Well, I'd trust Reggie with my life, and he may know others he trusts. We have to tell someone. Vee's life's at risk, and like you said, we're pretty well outta friends and family."

"Yes, but—" And just like that, inspiration struck.

We were pretty well out of friends and family, true. But we had plenty of enemies.

◆

We set up camp in the last place the ARC, the Króls, or the Legion would look for us, hopefully—the Króls' house. And bonus, it was already warded to hide its occupants from the ARC. The wards were inactive when we arrived, but it didn't take much to seal up the physical hole from the grenade and patch the arcane holes in the house's protections. With luck, they would protect us from any scrying or curses from the Króls as well.

Zeke slept while I wrote a note by candlelight, and tucked it beneath the gnome statue in the front yard. Then I sat cross-legged in the living room with Dawn while we waited for Mort.

"Tell me about us," I said.

"This is weird," Dawn said. "But okay. We grew up together, but we weren't really close until this company wanted to tear down our homes and build condominiums in their place, and our parents didn't have the money to stop it."

"Really?"

How much memory had I lost?

"Oh yeah. But you had a plan to stop them. We followed this old treasure map to an abandoned restaurant where a family of criminals were hiding out. One of them was this freakish monster-looking dude named Sloth—"

"Oh, for cheese's sake—that's *The Goonies*!"

"Really? You sure?"

"Not funny. I really was worried for a second I'd lost, like, half my memory."

"You're right," Dawn said, all humor gone from her voice. "I don't think it's funny at all that you remember the freakin' *Goonies* but you don't remember me."

"I'm sorry. Really."

"We watched that movie like a hundred times together."

"I'm sorry!" I frowned. "I only remember seeing it a couple times with Petey. Until Mort started making him do the Truffle Shuffle."

"I don't give a rat's butt about Goonies! I want to know why you went and lost your memories of me? Why not your memories of, I don't know, *Gilligan's Island,* or even Heather?"

"It's not like I just gave them away," I said. "I think they were taken. And if it makes you feel any better, the creature that took them probably wanted whatever in me was most special, most powerful, not just any old memories."

Dawn frowned. "That shouldn't make a difference. But oddly enough, it does."

"So, uh, what now?" I asked.

Dawn picked at the carpet for a minute, then said, "You know, when you showed up after all those years away and I realized I still had feelings for you, I figured, what the hell, you probably needed some work, maybe a little counseling, but if the boy I grew up with was still in there somewhere you might just be worth it. Then, bam, it's ghosts and curses and waerwolves, and you with your stupid obsession over Heather. And you know what? I think I dealt with all that shit pretty damn well. So no way I'm going to go through all that and then give up. Shoot, if you'd been in a car accident and hit your head, you might've forgotten a whole hell of a lot more than just me. If Adam and Drew can go on fifty first dates, we can go on two, I guess."

"Adam and Drew?"

"That can be our next first date," Dawn said.

I wasn't sure how to feel about that. Dawn was making a pretty big assumption. Just because she wanted to keep dating, that didn't mean that I did. I still didn't really know her. And there was Heather. I remembered Heather wanted space for some reason, but that didn't change how I felt about her.

I also remembered Zeke's warning. Don't break up with Dawn until we figured out the whole memory thing. Probably good advice.

Mort arrived with a bandaged leg, the Kin Finder 2000, and, to my surprise, Petey.

"Who's with Father?" I asked.

"Marcus," Mort said. One of Father's old friends, and a good choice. I nodded and rushed them inside, carrying the bulky contraption. Pete looked horrible but not as horrible as I would have expected. His wounds were just pink puckered lines now, and the scars from the boiling curse were mostly faded. Pete himself walked a bit stiffly, using the sheathed, silver-coated sword from the library as a walking stick. He looked like he could collapse into sleep at any minute, but he was no longer on the doorstep of death. It was miraculous.

And terrible.

The healing potions may have saved his life and accelerated his normal healing, but this was something more. This was waer regeneration.

I hoped Pete couldn't read the worry on my face.

"Hey, Petey," I said. "It's good to see you, dude."

Pete looked at Zeke snoring on the couch, then at the floor, avoiding my eyes. "I'm sorry I didn't stop the waerwolves."

"Oh man, Petey, you did awesome. I'm just glad you're okay."

He choked back a sob. "Do you think they're going to hurt Sammy and Mattie? Or . . . Vee?"

"No, definitely not. We're going to save them, Petey, I promise." I put as much confidence in my tone as I could and patted the Kin Finder 2000. "This is going to lead us to them. Come on, help me set it up."

We set up the machine and fetched a pitcher of water, then I activated the machine with some hair from the control braid. The water boiled, the machine made its noises, and the pen on the mechanical arm drew a reference line on the paper below.

I rinsed out the pot, then carefully removed the ring at the tip of the mechanical arm and replaced it with the one Father made for me. It fit perfectly. I slid the pen into the new ring and inserted the tube from the machine into the end of the pen.

I placed a strand of my own hair into the pot and lit the candle beneath it, then laid my hand over the small crystal ball at the back of the machine and concentrated, thinking of Heather—of our many walks to her home, of our many talks on the pier, of our time together yesterday.

The water boiled, the steam passed through the machine with the normal series of *pings* and *clangs* and *sproings*. The noise woke Zeke.

"What time is it?" he asked, stretching.

"Maybe four hours until dawn," Mort said. "Here." He tossed Zeke two small bottles.

Zeke held them up, reading the labels. "Energy drinks?"

"Gut bombs. Mattie's friends love them. You'll crash like a bandicoot later, but it should give you what you need to get through the next few hours without your face hitting the floor."

Liquid dripped down into the pen.

The pen didn't move.

I closed my eyes, focused on how I'd felt as I made the mix tape for Heather. I peeked at the pen. Nothing.

I thought again about our lovemaking and of our kiss in the restaurant. More nothing.

Thinking of kissing made me think of Dawn's kiss in the car, the warmth and passion of it.

The pen twitched, making a line that was barely more than a dot on the page. In the direction of Dawn.

"Uh," I cleared my throat. "Okay. I think maybe Pete should try."

"Why not me?" Zeke said. "I'm assuming you fixed this fool contraption so it can work with the living?"

"Not exactly," I said. "It's still using a kind of spiritual resonance, I think, but it, well, I think it's supposed to locate your heart's true love."

"Really," Dawn said, her tone smug as she glanced at the small jot on the paper. "And you thought it would point to who? Heather?"

"Doesn't matter," I said, using the excuse of carefully removing the pot from the machine to avoid looking at her. "I was just testing it out. Hopefully it will work for Petey."

"Me?" Pete said, his tone pleasantly surprised.

"Him?" Zeke said, his tone unsurprisingly unpleasant.

"Yes, him!" I said to Zeke. "My brother, who has fought twice to protect your sister. My brother, who is the most honest, loving person I know. My brother, who may be our one chance of finding your sister and saving her. Do you have a problem with that?"

Zeke and Pete both looked at me with startled expressions, then looked at each other. Zeke's face flushed red, but he was either too exhausted or too embarrassed to explode. Breath hissed out of him like steam, and he deflated back into the couch.

"Whatever works," he said.

"Good." I rinsed out the pot. "Pete, can I have some of your hair, please?"

I set up the KF2K again, and this time had Pete put his hand on the crystal ball and think of Vee. The machine made its noises, the transformed water drip-drop-dripped into the pen.

The arm lowered. It drew a long straight line out from the center of the page, and rose back up.

Pete's grin lit up the room brighter than any candle.

"Good job, bro," I said. "Now let's figure out where the line leads."

Pete made quick work of it, flipping through the Thomas Guide and rapidly zeroing in on our target: the waters of the Strait of Juan de Fuca, not far off the shore of Fort Worden.

"Are they in a boat?" Zeke asked.

"I don't think so," I replied. "I think they're in the Marine Science Center. Or beneath it."

It made sense. The shifting nature of the ocean would help diffuse and confuse any scrying spells and mask any magic being performed beneath it. A perfect, Legiony place to hide.

Lucky for us, love was as deep as the ocean, wide as the sea, powerful as the tides, and all that sappy stuff.

A rattling knock on the downstairs slider door frames made me jump. Everyone else in the room did the same.

"That's for me," I whispered. "I think. Be ready to run for the car if not." I stood and crept down the stairs.

Priapus stood waiting outside the shattered glass door with arms crossed, his muscles bulging.

"It's okay," I called back up the stairs, then proceeded down to face the gnome over the line of salt and now-glowing line of wards we'd cobbled together on the floor.

"Ya wanna make a bargain?" the gnome asked. "Because I gotta tell ya, buddy, after the last few days it's gonna cost ya big-time."

"I got you into the EMP."

"Yeah. And every frickin' artifact in the room had security spells on 'em."

"I didn't think that was a problem for you guys."

"It ain't. But it takes time. And magic. And ta not have half the frickin' enforcers in the world bustin' inta the joint while we're doing it, see?"

"Sorry. It's not like I told them you were there, though. Did you at least get a dead wizard's sock like you wanted?"

"Don't worry 'bout what we got. If we hadn't gotten nothing of worth, buddy, you'd be a foot shorter about now. But like I said, you wanna make another deal with my family, it's gonna cost, *capiche*?"

"Actually," I said. "How'd you like to get a little revenge?"

28

Down Under

Zeke, Pete, and I waited in the Undertown Wine and Coffee bar, a café built in Port Townsend's underground world of Shanghai tunnels and funky basements. At 4 A.M., the place was filled with feybloods and arcana night owls enjoying coffee, tea, pig's blood, Danishes, and other delicacies mundane and magical before the place opened to the mundy morning crowd.

Reggie entered the café followed by his young sidekick Jo, wearing their black and white federal agent suits. They had their game faces on—nobody who looked in their eyes would waste their time with small talk, or bragging, or talking about last night's dream.

I felt for the gun in my jacket pocket.

"Zekiel," Reggie said as he stopped in front of Zeke, ignoring Pete and me. "About time you called me."

Zeke shrugged. "I just didn't want to bother you with my problems 'less I had to."

"And I didn't want to have to hunt you down like a criminal. But Gramaraye's time is up, and the ARC's looking for you now too. Situation's not good, man. What you said on the phone, about Vee being captured by whoever attacked your transfer, you're sure about this?"

"Deadly sure."

Reggie stared unmoving at Zeke for a second, then flipped the edge of Zeke's white jacket. "Looking good, old man."

"It still gets the job done," Zeke replied.

"Long as you're wearing it, I don't doubt it," Reggie said, and handed Zeke a small foil bag labeled PEANUT BRITTLE. "Brought this, by the way. Hope it meets your need."

"Thanks. Hopefully I won't need it. Look, Rege," Zeke said, his tone serious as he tucked the bag inside his jacket. "What we're about to do, it ain't official enforcer business. And it's gonna be dangerous. I don't want to see you guys lose your positions, or be exiled like I was."

Reggie put his hand on Zeke's shoulder. "We're not here as enforcers, Zekiel, otherwise you'd be arrested already. We're here as friends. How they treated you before, that was wrong. You just did what the ARC wouldn't. I'd have done the same, especially for little Vee, and now's my chance. So, give me the details. Who's the bad guy here?"

Zeke glanced at me. I stood up. "A group of arcana bent on starting another Fey-Arcana war kidnapped Vee and the others, and they want Zeke dead," I said. "And they may have sasquatch and waerwolf mercenaries with them."

Jo raised a single eyebrow. "Is this guy serious, Zeke?"

"He likes to make with the jokes, but this ain't one of them," Zeke said.

"Rogue feybloods are one thing. Rogue arcana—" Reggie shook his head. "I wish we could bring in the ARC on this one. Does this group of yours have a name?"

"Arcanites," I said.

Reggie grunted. "Nasty group. Works from the shadows. We hear rumors, but can't ever prove anything."

"So you guys in or what?" Zeke asked.

Reggie glanced at Jo and nodded. "Yeah, we're in, Zekiel. So what's the plan?"

"We go in, kill the bad guys, and save the girls," I said.

Reggie chuckled. "I like it. Simple. It's been a while since things were simple."

"I hope you're just joking," Jo said. "We need to capture these people, interrogate them. If—"

Reggie put a hand on her arm. "This isn't an arrest, Rook. This is old-school us versus them. If someone attacks you, put them down hard, or they might get back up and hit one of us from behind, got it?"

She gave a single sharp nod.

"Shall we get moving, then?" I motioned toward the door.

We left the café and moved to the far shadowy corner of the tunnel. I touched the wall and said, *"Aperire Ostium!"*

Reggie grabbed my arm. "Are you certain it's wise to use the tunnels? The feybloods have little love of our kind."

"We have safe passage," I assured him. "I made a deal with the local gnome family. It's the best way to get close to the Legion undetected."

"You ain't chicken, are ya?" Zeke asked.

"I've learned to be cautious," Reggie said. "Things aren't like in the old days, Zeke. And there's a lot of tension right now between us and the feybloods."

The doorway opened, and we marched single file into the dank and musty tunnel beyond.

We traveled through the tunnels, led by Pete, with Jo at his side "taking point." There were marker stones, but the gnomes and other feybloods who used the tunnels were known to switch or alter the markers at times to mislead intruders. Pete wasn't fooled for long, though. Even though we were underground, his uncanny sense of direction quickly warned him when we'd taken a wrong turn.

He also began sniffing at the air. And once, when he glanced back at me, I swear his eyes flashed yellow briefly.

I shivered. The worst thing that could happen was for Pete to have his first transformation in the middle of this mission. Bad enough that we had two enforcers with us, but Zeke hated waer creatures and disliked Pete regardless.

As we marched, I gave Reggie the basics of what had happened the last few days, though I left out the EMP and any other bits of possibly incriminating information. Then I joined Pete up front with Jo, sensing that Zeke and Reggie wanted to talk. The two men lagged behind.

After a minute, Reggie said, "I'm sorry I haven't been to see you yet, outside of work." He clearly meant his low voice for Zeke's ears only, but the tunnel's acoustics carried his words forward.

"Don't need to apologize," Zeke said. "You moved on, got a new partner. I've been gone a long time. I get it."

"Zekiel, that's not fair. I've been busy with work, and well, you've never exactly been easy to talk to, damn it. Especially about us."

"Well, this sure ain't the place to talk about it," Zeke said.

"You know, a lot has changed since you left. There are women enforcers in the field, obviously. And, well, there isn't the same pressure for us guy enforcers to be all, you know—"

"Rege, drop it. I mean it."

"Fine. But when this is all done, I expect to finish this talk."

The tunnels led us up a slow but steady incline, until we reached a dead end with footholds carved into the wall. A round door of stone rested in the ceiling above. Pete pushed up on the door, and it swung up and open. "We're here," he said.

We climbed one by one out of the grassy Fort Worden hillside beside Alexander's castle.

Alexander's castle wasn't so much a castle as a square brick tower with a cottage at its base. The tower had crenellated battlements like a castle, though, and I knew for a fact that brownies liked to perch atop it and fire their minuscule arrows at passersby, laughing as tourists slapped at nonexistent mosquitoes. It stood in a grassy field dotted with the occasional tree or bush, on a bluff overlooking the Strait of Juan de Fuca. Once we were all out of the tunnel we sprinted across the moonlit field to the tree line.

The dock and Marine Science Center were almost directly below us, beyond a narrow band of grass and rocky beach. "Our enemy is hiding beneath that building," I said.

Reggie grunted. "Crossing that dock unseen won't be easy even with our camouflage."

"That's why we wait here," I said.

"And what exactly are we waiting for?" Reggie asked. "An invitation?"

I took a deep breath. "The Króls. They hate us, but they have reason to hate the Legion even more. I requested a truce, and offered them the location of the ones responsible for killing their kin."

Jo spat into the predawn gray night. "You'd deal with blood witches? And you still expect us to believe you're not a dark necromancer?"

"I'm using my enemies against each other," I said.

Reggie rubbed at his bald head. "Assuming these Króls really are here, what exactly are they going to do?"

"I don't know. But whatever it is, I'm hoping it will create enough of a distraction that we can slip in and get to the girls quick and easy. And if not, the Króls should at least trip any alarms or traps before we do." All that role-playing experience had come in handy after all.

Movement. I squinted. Two figures slunk along the rocky shoreline to the edge of the pier. One looked back over his shoulder, scanning the park, the moon reflecting off pale skin.

The Króls. They'd received my message from the gnomes.

"They're here," I said.

The Króls stopped, and it looked as though one of them played a bone like a flute. After a minute, the ground darkened, and rippled. I squinted. What—?

"Rats," Jo said.

"What's wrong?" I asked.

"No, rats. The Króls have summoned a swarm of rats."

The image of the shiny, writhing mass was disturbing but not half as disturbing as seeing just how many rats were within range of the Króls' call.

The Króls sprinted across the dock, and the swarm of rats writhed around them, fanning out behind them in a train of seething darkness. The Króls entered the Marine Center building, and the rats disappeared after them like oil draining down a funnel.

"Let's go," Zeke said.

We hurried down a steep path to the park below, tree branches and berry vines snagging at us as we propelled ourselves down the slope. Pete bumped into me as everyone stopped and gathered at the bottom of the trail, then we sprinted across the open area to the dock. The concrete planks and soft lapping of water beneath us absorbed the sound of our footfalls, and we reached the building without incident. The door stood wide open.

"Wait here," Zeke whispered. He and the other enforcers slipped inside. After a few seconds, Zeke reappeared. "All clear."

We entered the main room of the Marine Science Center. Glass aquariums and imitation tide pools made of concrete and fake rock held starfish, octopuses, and other colorful sea creatures.

Zeke pulled back his sleeve and began tapping on his calculator watch. Jo put a hand on Zeke's wrist. "It's okay, old timer. There's an app for that."

She pulled out a mobile phone, plugged a tiny crystal into the end of it, tapped on the screen, and held it up. I could see that it showed the room on its tiny screen as if on a video monitor, but overlaid on the image were a series of colored lines and text.

"Looks like there's alarms and wards all over the place, but they've all been tripped already. And there's a door hidden . . . there." She pointed to a nearby tide pool.

She crossed to the tide pool, and tapped on the phone some more, then swiped her finger across it.

The tide pool wavered like a heat mirage. A glamour. The water and sea life inside it disappeared, replaced by a narrow stairwell leading down into darkness.

A roar of pain sounded from the darkness below.

Jo put away her phone. Reggie moved beside her. "Sounds like we'd better hurry or the Króls' distraction will be over." He leaped over the small wall and descended the stairs, drawing his two batons and snapping them out to full extension. Zeke hopped the wall and followed after, with Jo close behind.

A wolf howl echoed up from below. Pete growled.

"You okay?" I asked him, drawing the pistol from my jacket pocket.

In response he leaped after the enforcers.

"Okay, then," I muttered. "Ready or not, here we come." I moved to the wall and heard a scratch behind me. I spun around and raised the revolver, waited a minute in frozen silence, but saw nothing. Probably a seagull outside. I hopped over the low wall and descended the narrow stairs, the cold of the ocean seeping through the concrete walls that pressed in on either side.

The stairs dumped out into a featureless gray room, unremarkable except for a pair of ancient diving suits, the kind with the big round metal helmets. These particular suits, however, had metal claws extending from the gloved hands like talons, and lay on the floor, stabbing at their own bodies and twitching as if in pain.

The dark writhing shapes of rats pressed against the inside of the helmets' windows.

Moving on.

I hurried through the single door and emerged into a long hallway just in time to see Pete sprint through a door at the far end. Two more doors stood opposite each other at the center of the hall. The entire length of the hallway was littered with rat bodies, and bits of rat bodies, and lots of rat blood, interspersed with scorch marks and chunks of blasted wall.

I half-ran half-slid my way to the middle doorways. I spun in a full circle as I slid to a halt, and the Ratt song "Round and Round" began playing in my head.

Both doors were open and dented. I held the pistol in a tight grip and quickly bobbed my head around the edge of each doorway, checking the rooms. The room to the left looked like an office with officey furniture and officey lighting. The room to the right was a storage room with diving gear, a radio, office supplies, and a fine variety of rubber ducks. Both rooms were empty of people or feybloods, far as I could tell. The sound of clashing metal and angry shouts, growls, and grunts came from the doorway at the end of the hall.

I propelled myself through the slick carpet of rat remains for the far door.

"Finn?"

I spun around, almost losing my footing.

Heather stood behind me, holding herself as if cold, a frightened expression on her face.

"Heather! Where did you come from?"

"I . . . I was hiding. They were asking me questions, threatening me, and then . . . there were shouts from the hallway, and they left me locked in the room, but someone smashed open the door, and—it was terrible." She ran to me, grabbing me. "Please," she said into my chest. "Get me out of here."

"What about the others? Sammy and Mattie, and Vee? Where are they?"

"I don't know. They kept us separated. Please, Finn, take me out of here. I can't be here another second!"

"I—" There was a howl of pain that sounded like Pete. I grabbed Heather's shoulders, held her away so that I could look into her eyes. "Listen. The way is clear to the outside. Just climb the stairs back there and you'll be free. I need to help the others."

"No!" Heather grabbed me. "Don't leave me alone. Please, just take me out, and then you can come back."

I felt torn between the need to help Heather and the sound of battle coming from the doorway. Heather looked so fragile, I felt myself instinctively wanting to carry her away to someplace safe, to soothe her fear and tell her everything would be okay. To be her hero.

"I can't," I said to myself and to her, forcing her away from me. I guided her back to the door of the supply room. "I have to go. Stay here if you need to, and I'll come back for you, I promise."

I ran-slid to the doorway at the end of the hall and leaned against the wall, took a deep breath, and spun through the doorway with the gun held ready.

The door opened onto a catwalk above a chamber the size of a high school gym. There were no nerdy kids being pummeled mercilessly with rubber balls, but a battle every bit as brutal raged below.

To the left, Reggie and Jo were engaged in a Jedi battle with three enemy enforcers—two young men and a woman. The battle was hard to follow, they all moved so fast. Their glowing batons and suits threw off blinding flashes of blue and yellow sparks as blows landed and strikes were deflected. But I could tell our side was losing that battle—Jo held one arm to her side, and Reggie moved far too slow compared to the others. One of the enemy enforcers shouted, a tattoo flashing across his throat, and the force of his shout blasted Reggie back several feet, lacerating the top of his bald head as he ducked and covered with one arm.

To the right, Petey wielded his sword against three waerwolves. The beasts were fully transformed, each a wolf as large as a Saint Bernard, their brown and gray hackles up, their lips pulled back from vicious fangs. Pete whirled the blade side to side, Beastmaster style, so that it was a barely visible gleam, and fresh slashes oozed blood on his back, arms, and legs. The wolves moved around him, trying to flank him, but weren't leaping. The reason for their caution was evident in a fourth wolf who twitched on the ground, its back bent at a sharp and unnatural angle. Petey might not actually know how to use a sword, but he wasn't dueling swordsmen, he was chopping at wolves, and he possessed enough strength and speed to chop them in half.

Zeke had reached the far side of the room and attempted to climb the stairs to the catwalk opposite my own. The only exit I could see from the room led from that catwalk. But Zeke faced an enforcer who looked like he could bench press the Hulk, and the brute had the high ground, better equipment, better magic, and most importantly wasn't running on little more than caffeine and determination.

And between me and Zeke, in the center of the room, the Króls battled the two sasquatch mercenaries. Or rather, the two sasquatches clumsily battled each other, their claws ripping through each other's fur while the Króls each moved a doll covered in sasquatch hair. What remained of the rats swarmed around the Króls in a protective circle.

Grayson and the hostages were nowhere in sight.

I took all of this in during the few seconds my eyes needed to sweep across the chaotic battle of claws and fur, fiery batons and wizardry.

"Finn!" Heather shouted behind me, her voice panicked.

I spun around.

Heather held a wand pointed at me, and a burst of light like a photon torpedo fired from the wand right at my chest.

"I'm sorry," Heather said.

Take On Me

I'd like to say that the pain of betrayal was far worse than the pain of the wand blast, but they were pretty damn close.

One time, I licked a spoon that had been used to scoop ice cream until it was covered in a pale white frost, and my tongue stuck to the frozen metal. The icy feeling of the blast striking my chest felt exactly like pulling that spoon free, times a hundred and ten.

I screamed.

My butt cheeks twitched.

The spell from the wand crackled into the Pac-Man of energy that appeared out of my chest, then flowed out along my right arm, causing my arm to spasm. Frigid energy flew from my hand back at Heather a split second before the spasm jerked my finger on the trigger, and the ear-ringing blast of a gunshot echoed through the hallway.

Heather's eyes widened in shock as the wand blast hit her stomach. They narrowed in pain as the bullet followed close behind. She remained standing, the wand extended, her eyes clenched shut.

"Heather!" I stumbled toward her, shaking off the tingling edges of pain.

"I'm sorry, Finn," she said again, and opened eyes now brimming with tears. There was something odd about the way she spoke, as though she were a bad ventriloquist.

I tried to take the wand from her still outstretched arm, but it wouldn't budge. Not the wand, not her hand, not her arm. She stood frozen solid as a statue. She breathed in short pants, though, and her eyes worked frantically to look down, so at least her insides hadn't locked up. Contrary to popular myth, it is rather hard to survive being completely frozen, what with your heart and lungs stopping and all.

The bullet hung frozen as well, half buried into the flesh of her stomach. I lifted her shirt. The ripple from the bullet's impact was visible, as if molded into her skin.

That had to hurt.

"Why the hell did you try to freeze me?" I asked.

Tears ran down her stiff cheeks. "I did it for Orion."

"Orion? Does Grayson have him too? Where are the girls?"

"You don't understand. It's not just Grayson," she said. So Grayson really was behind this. "There are others, powerful arcana. And Grayson is— I can't betray him. Orion would hate me, I would lose him completely."

"Wait, you're saying Orion is in Grayson's little Arcanite cult? I hate to question your parenting choices here, but maybe you need to set a good example for your kid. Like no killing old friends or their family?"

Her eyes looked past me, to the doorway. "Grayson promised you wouldn't be hurt. Or Mattie. In fact, he ordered me to keep you out of the fight."

The fight. Shit.

"Don't die, I'll be back."

I rushed back to the catwalk and took in the status of the battle as I sped down the stairs to the main floor.

The Króls seemed to be doing well, with the sasquatch siblings now bloodied and swaying unsteadily. Unfortunately, the Króls were the only ones on Team Finn that I didn't give a crap about.

Reggie was on one knee, and Jo fought desperately to keep the other enforcers off him. She disarmed one of the enemy enforcers, but he shouted something even as the baton spun from his hand. A tattoo no larger than a fist flashed briefly across his throat, and his entire body became wreathed in blue-white fire like the batons. He threw a flying spin kick at Jo, and Jo was knocked back, smoke rising from the burned side of her head.

Zeke had been driven back down to the bottom of the stairs and was completely on the defense now, protecting his head with his baton and his arms as the brute enforcer rained a vicious stream of blows down on him.

The wolves surrounded Pete, and one leaped from the side, its teeth clamping onto Pete's sword arm. Pete howled in pain, grabbed the wolf by the scruff of the neck with his free hand, and swung it in a vicious overhead arc down into the wolf who leapt from the other side, driving them both into the floor. The top one yelped in pain; the bottom one's cry was choked off by the blood bursting from its jaws.

The third wolf tackled Pete from the front, its teeth snapping for his neck.

The choice was easy. I knelt in the shadow of the stairs and took aim at the wolf on top of Pete. Praying they didn't swap places, I fired twice.

The wolf jerked and cried as a dark burst of red blossomed on its shoulder. Pete threw the beast off him. I tried to get another clear shot as Pete regained his feet, but the two surviving waerwolves limped to the far side of him. It would be too risky to shoot from this angle, especially with my lousy aim.

I turned to the enforcers. Reggie had regained his feet, but Jo knelt on her hands and knees, and the flaming enforcer kicked her in the gut, lifting her off the floor in a burst of blue-white fire. Jo hit the floor hard and shouted something, her hands pressed to the floor. The concrete flowed up over her, covering her. The fiery enforcer's next kick to Jo's side sent up a cloud of concrete dust.

Zeke tripped on the bottom step, and fell back. The brute enforcer raised his baton.

Shit! I fired at the brute enforcer's head. The bullet ricocheted off the metal stairway a foot to his right, but it distracted him long enough for Zeke to recover and swing at the brute's kneecap. The blow bounced off in a flash of light but forced the man to retreat a step. A half step. And then he resumed his assault on Zeke.

The gun was not cutting it. Or rather my aim was not. And I

would have to get close to the brute to summon his spirit. First things first. I dug the Króls gnome statue out of my satchel and stuck it on the floor.

The statue tipped over, revealing a hole beneath it. Priapus's head poked out just far enough for him to survey the scene. Then he leaped out, twin sickles ready.

"So you wasn't lyin'," he said, eyes fixed on the Króls and the sasquatches. He whistled. More gnomes began jumping out of the hole, fanning out behind Priapus. "Tonight, we collect wergild, boys!" he said as they gathered.

I fired at one of the waerwolves as it stalked out to the side of Pete, but I missed. Damn it!

"Priapus, I need your help with these other enemies."

"Do we look like friggin' heroes to ya?" the gnome asked.

"You can keep the enemy's equipment. And you can take the waerwolf carcasses—fur, teeth, musk glands, the works, without ARC penalty. That alone should bring you a small fortune. Deal?"

Priapus licked his lips and glanced between his dozen gnomes and the enforcers. "We don't get involved in the affairs of wizards," he said. "I'm sure you can figure why." He looked at the waerwolves. "The fur folk, however, them we can fight. But if things go badly, we vamoose, no breach of contract, got it?"

"Fine. Agreed."

"And witnessed," the other gnomes chorused.

I pointed out friend from foe to the gnomes just to be safe, and then ran around the edge of the room, circling behind the enforcer battle to approach the stairs on the far side.

Surprised and angry cries from the waerwolves drew my attention. Seaweed entangled the beasts, springing up from the concrete floor in a thickening mass. Pete lunged in with his sword, stabbing at them.

Seaweed sprang up around the sasquatches and the Króls as well, and the rat swarm rushed at the gnomes, who formed a wedge with Priapus in the front, sickles held at the ready.

I reached the stairs and snuck beneath them as best as I could, keeping my eyes on the brutal enforcer's legs as he descended the last few steps. With luck, he wouldn't know what hit—

"Gus, behind you!" one of the other enforcers shouted.

Damn spoilsport!

Gus the brute shouted and charged Zeke, pushing him back from the stairs. So much for the old ankle grab. I left the shelter of the stairs and snuck up best as I could behind Gus. I couldn't sense his spirit with all the chaos and magic around us, but if I could just touch his head, I could summon—

Gus heel-kicked my stomach back through my spine. At least, that's how it felt as I lifted off the floor on a rocket of pain, and then fell flat onto the cold concrete. I moaned, and somewhere the thought that I should move before I got my skull stomped on wrestled with the voice going "Ow! Ow! OW!" in my head.

I grabbed the gun from the floor and inched my way backward, seeking the shelter of the stairwell, knowing I would be too slow.

And then Pete stood above me, swinging his sword at Gus.

I managed to sit up and survey the scene.

Pete and Zeke had Gus on the defensive now, attacking him from both sides.

The flaming enforcer lay sprawled on the floor dead or unconscious, and Reggie and Jo pressed the remaining two enforcers back into a corner.

Harry had torn free of the seaweed and knelt beside the limp body of his sister, his head bowed. As I watched, he stood and ran in a loping gait for the stairs leading up to the exit, his mouth open wide, a low keening noise trailing from him.

The gnomes sliced and diced the rats and advanced now on the Króls. As the sasquatch fled, the gnomes began to turn in pursuit, but Giselle shouted a string of words that sounded like Klingon with a German accent. Red-black lines pulsed along her throat and arms, and darkness rippled through the air before her like mud stirred up in a fast-moving stream. Priapus shouted a command and the other gnomes knelt and overlapped sickles. The wave struck the point of their wedge and split along it. As the split curse hit the edges of the rat pile, the rats melted away and their bones collapsed to sludge in seconds, like the bad guys at the end of *Raiders of the Lost Ark*.

The gnomes advanced on the Króls again.

We might actually win this thing, I thought.

My hair lifted on my head and arms, and I smelled ozone. Lightning flashed from the catwalk above me, striking Jo in the back. Her arms flung out to her side and she jerked like a rag doll being shaken, then fell to the ground, her head flopping over. Her eyes stared at me. Dead.

"Nooo!" Reggie shouted.

One of the enemy enforcers kicked Reggie in the gut.

I scrambled away from the stairwell, turned, and raised my pistol to aim at the source of the lightning.

Another lightning arc, and the Króls were flung in opposite directions. As my sight recovered from the flash, I saw a young man of no more than twenty above me with his hand outstretched. He had blond hair and a trim beard—the man who attacked the Fey during my transfer! His scowl reminded me exactly of Heather's father.

Great.

"Orion!" I shouted. "Stop! We can talk!"

Orion's scowl focused on me.

Dumb move, Finn. I should have at least tried to shoot him in the leg or something. But if I missed I'd lose any chance of talking this out, or worse, I'd have to tell Heather how I accidentally killed her son by shooting him in the crotch. Not a guilt, or an image, I wanted to live with for the rest of my life.

Which at the moment I estimated to be about thirty seconds.

"Finn," Orion said. "Leave now, or the girls die."

I noticed he didn't mention that anyone but me should leave, and nobody stopped fighting. Well, except the gnomes. The last of them dropped down into their gnome hole. I noticed the waerwolf carcasses were gone as well. Amazing. Two things I never try to figure out—how time travel works, and the spatial laws of gnome product transportation.

"I have a better idea," I said. "How about we all leave, and discuss this over sundaes down at Elevated? I mean, come on, Orion, this is crazy! Me and your mom, we used to be best friends."

Orion laughed, the glowing tattoo on his throat dancing. "Oh, man, you don't have a clue, do you? All I ever heard from Father was how smart you were, how talented. He was so worried you'd figure it out before we could kill that relic of an enforcer and—"

His brows furrowed as his eyes shifted to the battle between Zeke, Petey, and Gus. He whispered something. Lightning danced on his hand.

"Pete, Zeke, look out!"

Zeke's gaze flicked upward.

Giant Gus moved in to strike him.

Pete bellowed and charged low into Gus, lifting him off his feet and sending him flying into Zeke.

I fired at Orion. The bullet struck the catwalk and Orion flinched.

Lightning lanced down and struck Gus in the back as he crashed on top of Zeke. Both men hit the floor hard.

"Gus!" Orion shouted. "No! Shit! You bastards!"

Was he sounding a bit breathless? He couldn't have enough magic for many more strikes like that. Zeke moaned and heaved Gus's limp body to the side. Pete offered a hand up.

Orion slapped the railing. "Why won't you just freaking die!"

Movement behind me. I turned, raising the pistol. Reggie limped up to me. His eyes were red and radiated fury as he looked up at Orion. I glanced past him. The other two enforcers were on the ground, one of them bent at an extremely unhealthy angle.

I took careful aim at Orion. I only had one bullet left before I had to reload.

"We're coming up there, and taking the girls home," I said. "Your mother could use your help, so I suggest you do the same. There's no need—"

"The first person to come up those stairs gets barbecued," Orion said. Without taking his eyes off us, he leaned back and shouted over his shoulder, "Send out the beast-blood." He glared at me. "If you shoot me, your sister and niece die. If you don't leave right now, they die. If you don't take responsibility for these deaths," he waved at Zeke, Pete, and Reggie, who were still very much alive, "the girls die."

"Zeke!" Vee's voice rang out in the chamber, and someone shoved her at the rail next to Orion, her hands bound behind her.

"Vee!" Petey called.

"And as proof that we're not bluffing—" Orion began.

Zeke's face went red, his eyes bulged. He tilted back his head and roared.

He didn't have the energy reserves to go berserk. It would kill him even if Orion didn't!

"Zeke! You can't—"

Zeke charged up the stairs, a berserker yell ringing off the walls. Orion raised his hand, lightning dancing along his fingers.

I shot. The bullet bounced off Orion's chest with a bright flash, knocking him back a step. His robes were enchanted like enforcer armor.

Damn it! That was cheating.

Petey started after Zeke. I grabbed him. "Wait! If Vee falls—"

He looked up and sheathed his sword. "I'll catch her," he said.

Orion raised one hand again, the other rubbing his chest. I frantically opened the gun chamber, dumped out the empty shells, and scrambled in my pocket for bullets.

Vee head-butted Orion from the side. But whether because of the angle, or because her hands were tied behind her back, it appeared to have little effect other than throwing both of them off balance.

Orion recovered and unleashed lightning point blank as Zeke bound over the top of the stairs. Zeke's arms flailed, his steps became the erratic dance of a drunkard, his lips pulled back from his clenched teeth, and his mustache began to smoke.

"Zeke!" Vee screamed. "Zekiel!"

Zeke flung something smoking at Vee. She flinched, then a glow surrounded her, and she disappeared. No, not disappeared. I saw a squirrel's bushy tail over the edge of the catwalk. Then Zeke plowed into Orion, and they both fell to the metal walkway hard enough to make it jump.

Squirrel-Vee tumbled from the walkway and into Pete's cupped hands.

I snapped the gun closed, just two bullets in the chamber, and ran up the stairs. Pete and the others followed close behind.

Zeke lurched up into a sitting position, straddling Orion, and began to beat at him with blistered, blackened hands.

"Zeke, stop!" I said. "Vee's safe! You did it."

The punches slowed to a halt, and Zeke fell over onto his back with a groan, next to the pile of Vee's clothes.

There were wisps of smoke rising from his eyes.

"Vee?" he said through cracked lips.

Pete set Vee down, and she scampered over to Zeke's head. There was a shimmer, and Vee sat on her knees beside him, naked, with one arm over her privates and the other across her chest.

"I'm here," she said, her voice breaking. "Hang on, big brother. You're going to be okay."

Pete grabbed her clothes from the catwalk and draped them over her, blushing bright red. Bits of peanut brittle tumbled onto the walkway.

"I think I might've overdone it a bit," Zeke said, his voice hoarse and low.

"Yeah," Vee said. "You look a bit overdone. But not much worse than the time Father took us to the beach and you got that sunburn."

Zeke laughed, but it turned into a cough.

Reggie wiped at his eyes. "You always were a fool, Zekiel. The bravest fool of us all. Don't you go and leave again."

Vee looked at me. "Please, do something."

"I—" I bowed my head. There was nothing I could do. Not now. My power wasn't much use on the living.

Zeke's hand grasped at the air until Vee grabbed it. "You got plenty of folks here who'll look out for you," he said. Another fit of coughing wracked him. When it passed, he whispered, "Pete?"

"Yeah?" Pete pushed his way past me and Reggie.

"You ain't a total fool, I guess. Get Vee outta here alive. Swear it."

Pete put one hand over his heart. "I swear it, Zeke."

A smile split Zeke's lips. "Good. I love it when a plan comes together."

A faint breath rattled out of him. And then he was still.

"No!" Vee said and buried her face on his chest. "No." Her body shook as she cried.

Orion groaned and stirred.

"Oh good," Reggie said and pushed away from the support of the walkway rails. "I want to kill this little bastard myself." He stalked toward Orion.

A scream echoed out into the cavernous chamber from the nearby doorway. Sammy! I jerked to my feet and rushed to the door, pistol raised. The door led to another hallway. At the far end of the hall, Sammy writhed on the floor as if she lay on a bed of hot coals. Grayson's voice called from out of sight, "I'm tearing her spirit from her body, slowly. If you don't wish me to continue, then I'd like Finn to please join me."

Karma Chameleon

Sammy's screams came from the center of her being. They tore at my heart like serrated claws.

"Reggie!" I said as the bloodied enforcer limped over to Orion. "Don't!"

"He didn't say nothing about this punk being alive," Reggie said, putting his boot on Orion's throat.

"Grayson!" I shouted. "We have Orion. Let's talk a trade!"

Sammy's cries eased into quiet sobs. Grayson shouted back, "Bring Orion to me or the girls die."

"Screw that," Reggie said. "He'll kill her anyway. We don't negotiate with assholes."

"Please!" I said to him. "You're an enforcer. Don't forget what that means!"

Reggie pressed down on Orion's throat. Orion began to thrash and gasp and push against Reggie's foot. "Not so easy to summon lightning when you can't speak, huh boy?" Reggie said, grinding his foot a bit. Then he pulled his foot back and kicked Orion across the jaw.

Reggie raised his foot again but hesitated as Sammy's scream escalated into throat-tearing howls. His boot stomped down on the catwalk. "Go ahead. Take the punk. But he's a dead man walking."

"Grayson!" I shouted. "Stop! I'm coming back. With Orion."

"I should go with you," Pete said.

I shook my head. "You have to keep Vee safe, Petey. Get her out of here as soon as I'm through that door."

Reggie put a hand on my shoulder. "We'll be right behind you if you need us." He slipped something cold into my hand. I glanced down. Zeke's collapsed baton, with pieces of burned skin still clinging to it.

"Thank you." I tucked the baton up beneath my sleeve, then helped Orion to his feet. He sucked air in sharp, painful-sounding gasps, like a small dog about to vomit. He cried out in pain as I lifted on his arm. I lifted harder. Sammy's screams stopped and turned to gasping sobs as I helped Orion shuffle through the doorway.

The thick metal door clanged shut behind me, causing me to jump, and the wheel lock turned. Reggie struck the round window with his baton and was thrown back against the catwalk railing with a flash of yellow light.

"They're not getting in," Grayson said. He stood now at the end of the hall, near Sammy's head.

"Help," Orion choked out, pushing me to the side.

Anger flashed across Grayson's face at the sight of Orion, and his eyes glittered as they returned to me. "You've caused me serious problems," he said. "Not all of them your fault, nor entirely unexpected, but I must admit I'm glad to be done with it."

"We're not finished yet," I said. "Not until everyone gets out of here alive."

"A little late for that, don't you think?" he asked.

"Screw you." My fingers dug into Orion's arm and he screamed in pain.

"Do you really want to push me?" Grayson said, and he extended his hand over Sammy's head.

I shoved Orion away from me, toward Grayson, then raised my gun. "Take him and let us all go."

"I think not." Grayson touched the wall. "In fact, I'd say your friends have about, oh, fifteen minutes to live."

I heard a muted roar behind me. I spun and looked through the window. Water cascaded into the room from above, and the far door swung closed.

Anger surged up in me, volcanic and powerful. I stuffed the gun in my pocket and grabbed the wheel on the door, straining to turn it until my arms, my back, my neck muscles all burned.

The wheel didn't budge.

I turned back and drew the gun from my pocket.

"Kill me and they all die," Grayson said.

"You bastard!" My voice trembled with the anger and frustration coursing through me. "Is this the war you wanted? Killing innocent arcana and enforcers? For Merlin's sake, you practically grew up with Pete and Sammy! How could you kill them?"

"I don't want war, Finn. A war is inevitable. I merely intend to win it for the good of all arcana, including your family. Now, come, we have much to discuss. We may as well do so in comfort, away from the distracting noise of your companions."

"Are you crazy? I'm not going to have tea time with you while you drown my friends and family!"

"No, of course not. But come, and I'll offer you a way to save them." He lifted Sammy to her feet and guided her around the corner. "Come, Finn! We have some time, but that's no reason to waste it. Especially when there is so little of it to waste. Bring Orion, won't you?"

Damn it. I grabbed Orion's arm and half-carried, half-dragged him after Grayson.

The hall opened up into what looked like a living room from the 1970s, with a green shag carpet, orange sofa, a number of brown leather lounge chairs, and a bar along one wall. Grayson shoved Sammy through a door in the far wall, closed it, and flipped a deadbolt, then turned to me with a smile.

"Do you like the accommodations? The ARC occasionally uses this place to hold trade negotiations with some of the ocean feybloods. The rest of the time, I find it a safe, quiet place to think."

"What do you want, Grayson?" I plopped Orion on the couch. He moaned and shifted into a less painful position, then promptly passed out.

"Oh, we have much to talk about, I think." Grayson sat in one of the brown chairs.

I crossed my arms, the revolver resting in the crook of my elbow. "Why don't we skip to whatever this offer of yours is?"

"I don't think so. Once the offer's made, I doubt very much you'll desire to sit around talking with me. And I wish very much to talk with you now that the need for masks is gone. So we shall have our chat and deal with unpleasant offers after, yes?" He waved at the chair across from him.

I remained standing and cocked the pistol.

Grayson sighed. "As you wish. I have to say, that was quite the move, blowing up Felicity's body. I expected you to hide it, or just run, but an explosion? You've got a touch of your father's flare for the crazy." He chuckled.

"Yeah. I'm the crazy one. So what's your offer? What do you want in exchange for not murdering innocent people?"

"Come now, surely that's not the question you really want to ask me? The one that's burning inside of you?"

"Right now? Yeah, it pretty much is."

"Well, it's not time for that question." He nodded at a clock on the wall. "We have at least ten minutes before the water reaches the catwalk and it's sink or swim time for your companions. Until then, why don't we play a game of twenty questions. You used to like that game, I believe."

"How about we don't and you just tell me what you want?"

"What I want is for you to understand the choice you must make."

"So just tell me whatever it is you think I need to understand, and I'll make the choice."

Grayson slapped the chair arm and shouted, "Enough! You can do as I ask, or you can let your friends die. I will not debate this matter further."

I looked at the clock. Another minute ticking away. "Fine. What am I supposed to be guessing with my twenty questions?"

"Why."

"Because I need to start somewhere. I can't just ask if it's bigger than a breadbox."

"No, I mean you must figure out why."

"Why what?"

"Figure it out."

"Aaughh!" I shouted at the ceiling. This was insane! "Look, I understand all about your little cult and its holy crusade, okay? Magus Verona told me. You're seeking some super power to win the war and rule the world, cue evil laugh. Great. I get it. But if you're going to try to convince me you're doing the right thing, forget it. You can't kill my friends and family and expect me to drink your Kool-Aid."

"The needs of the many outweigh the needs of the few, Finn. I know you're familiar with this concept. If we let the Fey or feybloods conquer us and take control of all magic, how many of your friends and family do you imagine would survive? Surely you don't want that?"

"What do you care what I want? Why the recruitment effort? Are you really that desperate for approval?"

Grayson sighed through his nose. "You haven't changed at all."

"Sure I have. I've got these killer abs now thanks to the changeling. Wanna see?"

"I'd hoped you of all people would appreciate what I've done, and appreciate your own role in it. As much as Orion has served me well, you were the closest to a son I ever had."

"Okay, now you're just being a freak," I said.

Grayson slapped the chair arm again. "You will show me respect!" he shouted.

Realization crept over me then like a frozen blanket of human skin.

"No. You—no. How? What have you done?"

A satisfied smile oozed across his face. "So you finally figured it out."

"Immortality," I said. "You always said it was their biggest advantage. Grandfather."

Grayson—Grandfather—gave a single nod of acknowledgment. "They have that advantage still. This," he waved at himself, "is far from a perfect solution. There are very few who could achieve it, and fewer still willing to do all it requires. But it is a start, and it allows me to continue seeking a true solution."

I paced the room. The seconds ticked by, the waters rose in the other room.

"That's why you erased my memory about Talking to warded spirits. You didn't want me talking to Verona because you were afraid she knew, that she might tell me."

"Ah, so that's why you broke into the EMP." He chuckled. "Actually, I hadn't even considered Katie. I blocked your memory for fear you would summon your mother's true spirit."

"You're kidding me." What had Father said when I begged him to tell me who attacked Felicity? *Go ask your mother. She knows everything about everything . . .*

I felt like an idiot.

And an asshole. I'd found some answers with Verona, yes. But maybe, if Zeke had not been depleted from that break-in, he would have survived going berserk on Orion. And I would remember Dawn.

Orion groaned in his sleep, and more pieces fell into place.

"You're Orion's father."

"Yes."

"So you—" I felt sick. My grandfather had slept with Heather. He'd done so as Grayson, but that didn't make me feel any better. "Why Heather?"

"She came to me, actually, when I was my old self. I'd gone to her parents, made them an offer for their help in seeking an alchemical solution to death. But they were too far gone, using their own potions. The next day, Heather came to me and offered her services in exchange for a solution to her own problems." He grinned. "Her services as an alchemist, that is. The other came later, after my rebirth. Sad, I suppose, that she came to me hoping to escape her parent's fate, and yet now she makes mana drugs for me. But for a while, I could almost see why you chased after her."

I gritted my teeth against the huge Fuck You that struggled to escape. Instead, I said, "And Felicity?" It had been difficult to believe he'd been Felicity's lover. Now I knew he'd continued to be after his death, as Grayson. "You used her to create and control Mother's ghost and possess Father through the garden. But why?"

"Actually, that was a happy accident. I was experimenting with many different solutions to the problem of death, in every branch of magic and combinations of them. I thought Felicity's ability to manipulate the connection between plants and spirit held promise, that it might be combined with necromancy somehow. Imagine anchoring your life energy to a tree that lives hundreds of years. But it proved to be a dead end."

"So you had her frame me. And then you killed her."

"As I said, she proved to be a dead end. Yet, she almost proved useful still in the end. I made sure word of your return reached her, knowing her guilt would bring her out of hiding to warn you about me, to ask your forgiveness. And when our attack on the Other Realm failed to trap you there, she made the perfect backup plan. Well, until you blew her up. What a waste."

I shook my head. "You really are a heartless bastard."

"Wars are not won by the soft hearted."

"Sounds like an excuse to be an asshole and not apologize for it."

"Watch it, Finn. I will only tolerate so much disrespect. Especially after I've treated you so well."

"Yeah, why *is* that? Why are you so determined to send me back into exile? Why were your lackeys told not to harm me? It's not to make a bomb of me, is it?"

"And now we get to the why," Grandfather said.

And even as he said it, I knew the answer. All those times I'd felt his presence in the Other Realm had not been my imagination, or a friendly visit, or an attempt to blow me up. But it had given him something, just as Verona's daughter had given her the power to seal the breach. "You need me there. Somehow, your immortality depends on me being in the Other Realm."

"Depends? No. But the cost of maintaining it without your

help is—well, let's just say I must drain a lot of bodies to get the same amount of magic I can tap through our bond while you're in exile."

"Our *bond*?" Gods. How much of me truly was my grandfather? His teachings, his influence—

"Yes, our bond—our blood, our Talker gift, our spiritual resonance—they allow me to . . . tunnel past the barrier between our realms as long as you are there."

I began pacing, my irritation mounting. "You do nothing but use people! Me, Felicity—Grayson. How did he feel about you taking his body?"

"James believed in the cause. And a soldier knows they may have to lay down their life for their cause."

"But he wasn't a soldier. You practically raised him. He was like a grandson to you!"

"Actually, James too was my son. A bastard, but mine. And until a child reaches adulthood, they are little more than parrots, repeating back what they've been told to believe by adults, by their friends, by television. Every parent seeks to mold their children in their image, views their children as their immortality. I just took a more literal approach."

I bit back my response and turned away sharply, hiding the horror and disgust on my face.

This was the point in the movie where the idiot says go to hell and gets shot, or tells the bad guy he's going to tell the press everything and steps into the elevator with the trap door. I eyed the clock. I had to play this smart, be the clever hero, not the idiot idealist. I'd criticized Verona's choice of not playing along with Grandfather enough to at least learn his plans. I'd be a fool to make the same mistake.

But Grandfather was insane. He'd killed his own son! How could I hope to reason with him? How could I expect him to spare anyone that wasn't important to his cause?

I couldn't. Not unless it gained him something. Not unless it gained him me.

"Okay," I said, taking a calming breath, and turned back to face him. "Okay. I get that you want to protect arcana from the Fey and feybloods. After twenty-five years of them feeding off me, believe me, I get it. But all I've seen you do is use feybloods to kill arcana."

"And you used the Króls to fight my feybloods, or did they just happen to arrive by coincidence?"

"That's not the same."

"Of course it is. If I need to risk someone on a menial job, why risk my own soldiers before the war? Why not risk my enemy's soldiers?"

"Huh." I uncocked the gun, lowered it to my side. "I guess I can see that. And you really believe this war is coming soon?"

"You spent years in the Other Realm, Finn. You know how inhuman those beings are. Do you really think they're not plotting against us? Do you really think the changelings are anything but scouts for their coming attack? And the ARC lets them continue with that ridiculous 'exchange program'! While I'm trying to perfect immortality, I guarantee the Fey are seeking ways to use magic as we do, or new ways to defend against it."

Actually, I knew that was true, didn't I? What else could my protective Pac-Man tattoo be?

Grandfather must have seen the flicker of doubt on my face, because he leaned forward, pushed his point. "Here's my offer, Finn. Join our cause, the cause of protecting your family and friends, of protecting all arcana from the growing Fey threat. Do so, and I shall spare the lives of these girls, and everyone in the water room."

This was it. We were getting down to it, the moment of truth.

"If you need me in exile, what good will joining you do?"

"I'm afraid I can't tell you that, unless you agree to join me."

I paced for several heartbeats. "If you're really willing to let everyone live, then I guess I have no real reason to oppose you. What you said about the Fey . . . you're right. I can't deny what I've seen. And more than anything, you're my grandfather. It's hard to remember that when you look so different, but I owe you my loyalty, and my trust, don't I? So . . . yes, I'll join you. I just wish you'd come openly to me in the first place."

Grandfather smiled as I spoke. "Good. I hope you'll understand if I ask for a little proof, however."

Damn. "Like what?"

"Kill Samantha."

"Sammy? How could you ask that? She's my sister! Your granddaughter."

"Therefore a fitting proof of conviction for both of us. And an acceptable loss. She's little more than a mundy, Finn, worse even, since her body rejects magic, rejects the very thing that makes us special. And clearly, she won't be continuing the family line with her habits."

"Surely there's got to be some way to prove myself without having to kill my own sister!"

"I'm surprised, Finn. She never seemed to care much about anything, not you, not our family, not even life as far as I could tell. And if you kill her with your gift, the resonance will prove your guilt beyond any doubt. It will guarantee your exile for life."

"We don't need that. Can't you just arrange my exile, especially with the ARC already after me? Between Felicity, the EMP—"

"Your destruction of Felicity's body made tracing her death to you problematic. Breaking into the EMP isn't worthy of exile. And while there are many on the ARC who support me in secret, I don't have the open influence to simply send whomever I like into the Other Realm."

"But—"

"Come now, surely you can see the need for this. One mundy out of billions, to save all arcana. One rather unpleasant sister to save your loving brother and niece, and all those friends who fought for you."

I felt Zeke's baton, hard and cold against my wrist. I wanted so badly to let it drop into my hand and swing it at Grayson's head. Swing it at my grandfather. But he controlled the exits and the water. And he had decades of experience over me as a necromancer.

He could rip my soul from me in the time it took me to extend the baton and swing.

Zeke might have been able to strike, with his berserker speed. But I wasn't Zeke.

I realized what I had to do. It wasn't what I wanted. But it was the only real choice I had. The only way I could save my brother, the only way I could keep my word to Zeke and save his sister. He'd shown me how far he would go to save her, to protect us all. I had to trust in that example.

"All right. I'll do it. Stop the water, please."

"Very well." Grandfather stood, crossed to the corner of the hallway, and placed one hand over a square metal plate on the wall. "The water has stopped. Do as I ask, and I'll drain it. Betray me, and you'll have just enough time to hear the water start again before you die."

"I understand."

I crossed to the locked door and did my best to clear my mind. The problem was, all those little meditation tricks I knew to put myself in a state of readiness, I'd learned those from Grandfather. So using them reminded me of him, which sort of ruined the whole point of trying to meditate.

And then there was the whole killing Sammy or everyone dies thing to mess with my cool.

I opened the door. Sammy sat on the floor, rocking gently back and forth in Mattie's arms. Welts covered her skin, and her eyes looked puffy, swollen as she cried: an allergic reaction to the magic Grandfather had used against her. Mattie gave me a frightened look as the door swung open, then her eyes widened in recognition.

"Uncle Finn!" She burst into tears. "I knew you'd come. Is Dad with you?"

"Everything's going to be okay, Mattie," I said. "I need Sammy for a minute. Sammy, can you come out here, please?"

"Is that bastard dead?" Sammy asked in a weak voice.

"No. But I need your help."

Mattie stood. "I don't think she—"

"It's okay," Sammy said. She struggled to her feet with Mattie's help and walked with ginger steps to the door. She glanced past me to where Grandfather stood, then looked me in the eye. "I'm trusting you."

"I know," I said, trying to keep my voice from betraying me. I took her arm and led her out into the room. I glanced back at Mattie. "Don't worry. It'll all be over soon."

"Wait!" Mattie said, stepping toward me. I closed the door in her face.

"Don't waste time, Finn," Grandfather said. "It's best if you do it quickly, like ripping off a bandage."

"Finn?" Sammy asked.

"I'm sorry, Sammy. It'll be quick, I promise."

She looked from me to Grandfather. Tears welled in her eyes. "You bastards can take your Talking and ram it up your ass."

She kicked me in the balls.

You know that feeling you get when you've eaten way too many jalapeños or other spicy food followed by ice cream, and you have a sudden, painful, sweat-inducing pressure low down to get it out of you by the path of least resistance?

And have you ever had the explosive, tear-inducing pain of being hit in the nose?

Combine the two, and that's how I felt. Except in my balls.

Sammy made a break for the hallway. Grayson didn't bother to chase after her or stop her, he just stepped well back from kicking range as she passed and said, "There's nowhere to go." To me he said, "That is why you don't waste time apologizing, Finn. Just do what must be done."

"Yes, sir." I limped after Sammy, into the hallway. She pounded at the door while Vee tried shouting something from the other side. I looked back. Grandfather watched us from the end of the hall with arms crossed.

"Sammy," I said. "There's nowhere to go. You said you trust me. Trust this—if you don't let me do this, everyone is going to die— you, Mattie, everyone." I took a deep breath and raised my hands.

She pressed her back against the door, her eyes confused and terri-fied. "Don't be ashamed if you scream," I said, and flicked my eyes to the side, doing the eyeball equivalent of nodding over my shoul-der at Grandfather. "It's expected."

I raised my hands as if feeling the air between us, and began my summoning. The low chant wasn't necessary, of course. But it helped me to concentrate. And it let both Sammy and Grandfa-ther know that I'd begun.

I gave Sammy a quick, emphatic frown and flicked my eyes to the side again.

Her eyes widened in understanding, and she fell to the ground screaming.

Zeke's baton felt cold against my skin, his blood and flakes of skin resonated against my arm. I focused on that and summoned his spirit.

"Hello?" Zeke's voice was hollow, distant, and only I could hear it.

"Good," Grandfather said. "I can feel her spirit energy. Now tear it free."

"I'm sorry," I said, leaning toward Sammy, and toward Zeke's growing presence. "You're dead. But at least you died to save Vee and the others."

Grandfather sighed. "I told you, don't apologize, Finn. If you really want to end her pain, finish her."

"I'm . . . dead?" Zeke said.

"Yes," I said, looking back at Grandfather. "But this isn't easy for me. I may need your help this one last time."

"School's over, Finn," Grandfather said. "You must do this alone. Do it now, and this will all be over."

"Vee, is she safe?"

"I . . . doubt it," I said. "You're possessed, Grandfather, of far greater strength than me. And you possess complete control. I get that you're the only one who can open the doors and set Vee and Pete and everyone free. I'm no fool to oppose your will. But that doesn't make this easy."

"Got it," Zeke said.

"Wait. The resonance—" Grandfather said, anger seeping into his tone. His hand slapped the wall, and I heard the roar of the water resume in the chamber, a roar that sounded much louder than last time. "You've killed your friends! And yourself." He raised his hands.

I summoned Grandfather's spirit.

"Fool!" Grandfather shouted. I expected him to easily slap my attempt down. He was my grandfather, the man who'd taught me everything I knew of necromancy, a master with a lifetime of experience over me. And energy already poured from me to sustain Zeke's summoning. But maybe all those years in exile, where even a simple movement was an act of will, had strengthened me more than I realized. Because when he pushed against my will, I held on. I could feel myself rapidly losing ground, but I held on.

More importantly, as long as he fought me, he wouldn't be able to fight Zeke.

Grandfather's resistance evaporated as suddenly as a trap door released beneath my feet.

"Quickly," Zeke's voice echoed out of Grayson's mouth. "I . . . can't hold on for long."

Grayson/Grandfather's hand jerked up as if yanked on a cord and slapped against the wall. Then it jerked away again, and I could tell Zeke was fighting to maintain control.

The door behind me hissed open. But the water didn't stop. A low wave rushed in, washing over Sammy, splashing across my boots. Sammy gave a startled shout and scrambled to her feet. She looked from me to Grandfather uncertainly. Beyond the door, Pete called out, "Finn!" He started to enter the hall.

"Pete, no!" I said. "Help Sammy and Vee. Get everyone out."

"Finn!" Zeke's voice shouted. "I can't hold this fool much longer! He—!" Zeke screamed, and Grandfather fell to his knees.

I snapped Zeke's baton into full extension and charged. "Zeke!"

Grandfather rose unsteadily to his feet, panting. His hand reached for the wall. "You will regret—"

I struck him across the skull. His head snapped to the side and he fell to the ground. A thin wave lapped against him, but he didn't move.

"Mattie!" I crossed the room and yanked open the closet door. "Mattie, come on, we have to go. Hurry."

"But—"

"No buts! Just go!"

Mattie ran. I went to the hall and watched. Pete stood just beyond the door, dripping water.

"Get her out of here," I shouted. "I'm right behind you."

Pete nodded and helped Mattie into the water. Together they swam out of sight. I returned to the room and shoved Orion off the sofa onto the floor, into the inch of water that now covered the carpet.

"Wha—!" He jerked awake, sputtered, and cried out in pain as his movements aggravated his injuries. I raised the baton, ready to strike.

"Orion, this place is filling with water. You've only got a few minutes to get yourself and your father out, unless you know how to stop the flooding."

"I'm going to kill you," he said and pushed himself unsteadily to his feet.

"Better men have tried," I said and nodded toward Grandfather. "Your father, for one. You might want to get moving if you're going to save him."

Orion's eyes widened as he looked at Grandfather's prone body. He looked down at the water now lapping around his ankles.

He fled down the hallway in a quick, limping gait.

"Great." Not that I could blame him, I supposed. But that left me to save Grandfather.

I really didn't want to save him. But I couldn't just leave him to drown.

Well, I could, but it would probably haunt me, and I'd relived enough bad memories for a lifetime.

I grabbed him under his arms and dragged him down the hall. The frigid water was up to my knees, which made it harder to walk but easier to drag Grandfather to the catwalk stairs. I took several deep breaths and then descended the stairs backward until I was swimming, holding Grandfather's head above water.

The freezing water sucked away my breath. The weight of Grayson's body dragged at me, made it hard to kick my legs freely. And I couldn't swim in a straight line. The water cascading down made that impossible. I had to swim around the perimeter of the room. I watched the water rising as I went, watched the exit doorway slowly disappear.

Water completely covered the doorway when I finally reached it. I dove, and tried to drag Grandfather with me.

He jerked and began to thrash, making the world a confusion of up, down, or sideways, of darkness, bubbles, concrete, and steel. I hit my head on the door frame, and air burst out of my lungs. I lost my hold on Grandfather and kicked hard, trying to propel myself free of his thrashing. My foot hit something soft and yielding, and I was through the door into water littered with rats and rat parts.

I swam up and managed to suck in a gasping lungful of air before water and something slimy splashed over my face and I nearly choked again. Water enveloped my fingers pressed to the ceiling. There was no more air to breathe. My feet found the wall beside the door, and I pushed off, swam down the hall for the room with the killer diving suits and the exit. I felt nauseated, dizzy, my hands and feet numb, my boots made of lead. I realized as I swam that I couldn't see Heather anywhere in the shifting green of the water, but I didn't have the time or energy to search for her. I fought the urge to cough away my air and pushed it out instead in small bursts, hoping to delay the need to breathe back in as long as possible. Everything began to feel surreal.

The strain on my lungs became an ache, and then agony. The world began to go dark, and I couldn't tell if it was my mind or the lights in the hall that dimmed. I saw the doorway, scrambled at its edges with numb fingers. Spots danced on the edges of my vision.

A memory of lips soft and warm and melting flickered across my mind like a firefly.

I sucked in water.

I drowned.

Epilogue

Consciousness slammed into me like a punk rock tyrannosaurus. I coughed out water, and air rushed into my lungs, harsh as sand.

My chest felt bruised, sharp spikes of pain lanced through my sides whenever I moved, and my muscles ached. All of them. But my head ached the worst, both inside and out. It felt abused and not quite right, as though my brain had been featured as the bad girl in a David Lynch movie.

I was alive.

Yay?

I coughed some more and blinked. I lay on the icy floor of the Marine Science Center, with the fake rock wall of an indoor tide pool near my head. Dawn's face came into focus, leaning over me, her tears falling warm on my cheek.

"Finn! Damn you! Don't ever scare me like that again." She wiped at her face.

More people pressed in around me. Pete, Vee, Sammy, Mort, Mattie, even Father.

But not Zeke.

I cried then for Zeke's sacrifice, and for the love of the people around me as they all made sounds of happiness and concern and thanks—or at least lukewarm relief in the case of Mort.

"Everything's going to be okay, Uncle Finn," Mattie said.

"How'd I get here?" I rasped. "How long was I out?"

Sammy replied, "You were dead for a minute or so."

"Dead?" I asked.

Flashes of memory. The desperate gasping of drowning, each

attempt to draw in breath only bringing in more water, more darkness.

"Pete dove in and saved you," Vee said.

Pete blushed. "I just pulled you out. Dawn saved you with a kiss."

"CPR," Dawn corrected. "Here, drink up." Dawn held a metal bottle to my mouth and coaxed something sweet down my throat— our last healing potion. Warmth spread out from my chest, dissolving the worst aches, followed by several unpleasant and sharp pops in my chest and ribs that took my breath away. When I sucked in my next breath, it felt more like a dull burning than blazing agony. Weariness crashed into me anew. I yawned long and hard.

"What about Orion?" I asked when I could speak again. "And Heather, and Grand—Grayson?" For some reason, I just wasn't ready to share the truth about Grandfather. It's almost as though my being framed for murder and then fighting for my life for three days had made me a bit paranoid or something.

"I didn't find nobody but you down there," Petey said.

"Orion's graciously decided to confess," Reggie said, appearing between Vee and Sammy. He wiped his hands across his pants. Was that blood covering them? "That should pretty well clear you and Zeke. In fact, Zeke might receive a hero's internment rights for helping to prevent a war. I'm sure we'll need to ask you more questions though, once you've recovered."

"And Heather?"

Dawn's face became a neutral mask. Pete shook his head. "We didn't see her anywhere. Do you think she's . . . dead?"

"I don't know," I said. "I think she got out, but . . . she was injured."

Reggie grunted. "If she's out there, we'll find her. And the Króls as well, especially if you share with us how you found them the first time."

"Happy to," I said and tried to stand, but dizziness and gravity teamed up on me and I fell back on my butt.

"Easy, lover boy," Dawn said. "Your friend there called for some kind of healer. Just rest 'til they get here."

"Yeah," Mattie said. "Take a moment and enjoy the yayness. We're all free, and safe, and together. We won!"

Not all of us, I thought, and met Vee's eyes.

"Indeed," Mort said. "I guess this means you'll be sticking around for a while. You'll have to really figure out what you're going to do with yourself now."

Dawn looked away.

"First," I said, "I want to figure out what exactly I've forgotten."

Vee cleared her throat. "I'll do what I can to help."

"Thanks. And I want to help Father." I smiled up at him.

"Oh, good," Father said. "Do you think one of these fishes grants wishes?" He wandered off toward one of the aquariums, and Mattie went after him.

I glanced at Mort. "And I have an idea about what I want to do for work. Or at least, as a side job to our family business." Mort crossed his arms, his expression saying he expected the worst. I looked between Pete and Vee, standing shoulder to shoulder. "Father's modification to the Kin Finder put the idea in my head, but Pete, Vee, you're the ones who really inspired me."

"Us?" Pete said, beaming.

"Yep, you. I've decided I'm going to help arcana and feybloods find their true love."

"Wait," Mort said. "You want to start an arcana *dating* service? In a necrotorium?"

"Makes sense to me," Sammy said drily.

"We have a reputation!" Mort said.

I sighed. "I'm not asking you to join me, Mort."

"Well," Sammy said, "you came into a den of evil evilness to save me; I suppose I could at least build you a website or something. With hearts and lovey crap on it." She wrinkled her nose. "But I thought you wanted to get free of magic and the family business, and make games?"

I shrugged. "I just wanted to control my own life. And I can do that with my magic, just not using it the way everyone else wanted me to."

Lady preserve me, a voice whispered in my head. *If he'd stayed dead I'd at least be free of this nonsense.*

"What the—" Oh gods. Was Grandfather's spirit taking me over? I didn't sense any will opposing mine.

Wait, you can hear me? the voice asked, surprise and excitement so strong it screamed like feedback in my head.

"Yes!" I said. "And stop turning it up to eleven! Who are you? What do you want?"

Sammy frowned. "Finn? Who are you talking to?"

It's about bloody time. I guess your dying had some use after all.

Mort snorted. "Maybe that blow to his head knocked a screw loose."

I shook my head. Nothing rattled. "I don't have a screw loose. I have a voice in my head. And before you ask, no, it isn't telling me to redrum anyone. Yet." I concentrated on the voice. *I asked, who are you?*

You, sir, are talking to Alynon Infedriel, knight of the Silver Court. Your changeling.

I closed my eyes.

"Ah, bat's breath."